ROOT OF THE TUDOR ROSE

Mari Griffith

Published by Accent Press Ltd 2015

ISBN 9781783753291

Copyright © **Mari Griffith** 2015

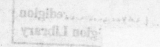

for Jonah

... who always said I could

TABLE 1 ROYAL HOUSES OF FRANCE AND ENGLAND

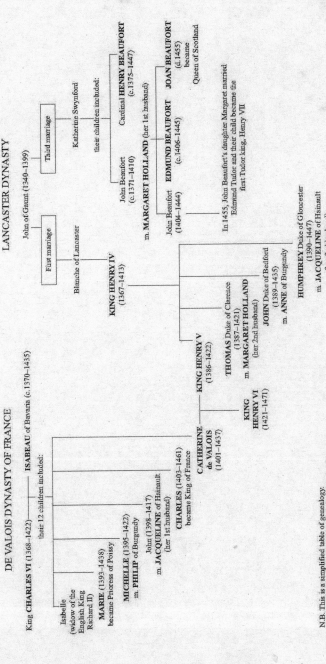

DE VALOIS DYNASTY OF FRANCE

LANCASTER DYNASTY

King CHARLES VI (1368–1422) ——— ISABEAU of Bavaria (c.1370–1435)

their 12 children included:

Isabelle
(widow of the
English King
Richard II)

MARIE (1393–1438)
became Prioress of Poissy

MICHELLE (1395–1422)
m. PHILIP of Burgundy

CHARLES (1403–1461)
became King of France

CATHERINE
de VALOIS
(1401–1437)

John (1398–1417)
m. JACQUELINE of Hainault
(her 1st husband)

KING HENRY V
(1386–1422)

KING
HENRY VI
(1421–1471)

John of Gaunt (1340–1399)

First marriage

Blanche of Lancaster

KING HENRY IV
(1367–1413)

THOMAS Duke of Clarence
(1387–1421)
m. MARGARET HOLLAND
(her 2nd husband)

JOHN Duke of Bedford
(1389–1435)
m. ANNE of Burgundy

HUMPHREY Duke of Gloucester
(1390–1447)
m. JACQUELINE of Hainault
(her 2nd husband)

Third marriage

Katherine Swynford

their children included:

John Beaufort
(c.1371–1410)
m. MARGARET HOLLAND (her 1st husband)

Cardinal HENRY BEAUFORT
(c.1375–1447)

EDMUND BEAUFORT
(c.1406–1445)

JOAN BEAUFORT
(d.1455)
became
Queen of Scotland

John Beaufort
(1404–1444)

In 1455, John Beaufort's daughter Margaret married
Edmund Tudor and their child became the
first Tudor king, Henry VII

N.B. This is a simplified table of genealogy.
Characters who appear in the story are show in **bold type**

TABLE 2 ANCIENT WELSH ROYAL HOUSES

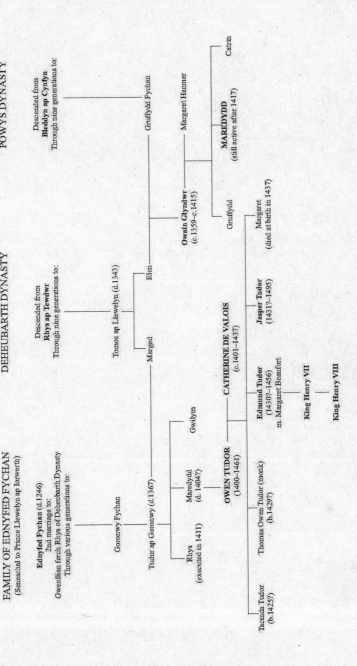

FAMILY OF EDNYFED FYCHAN
(Seneschal to Prince Llewelyn ap Iorwerth)

Ednyfed Fychan (d.1246)
2nd marriage to:
Gwenllian ferch Rhys of Deheubarth Dynasty
Through various generations to:

Goronwy Fychan

Tudur ap Goronwy (d.1367)

Rhys (executed in 1411)

Maredydd (d. 1404?)

Gwilym

OWEN TUDOR (1400–1461)

Tacinda Tudor (b.1425?)

Thomas Owen Tudor (monk) (b.1429?)

DEHEUBARTH DYNASTY

Descended from
Rhys ap Tewdwr
Through nine generations to:

Tomos ap Llewelyn (d.1343)

Marged

Elen

CATHERINE DE VALOIS (c.1401–1437)

Edmund Tudor (1430?–1456)
m. Margaret Beaufort

King Henry VII

King Henry VIII

Jasper Tudor (1431?–1495)

Margaret (died at birth in 1437)

POWYS DYNASTY

Descended from
Bleddyn ap Cynfyn
Through nine generations to:

Gruffydd Fychan

Owain Glyndwr (c.1359–c.1415)

Margaret Hanmer

Gruffydd

MAREDYDD (still active after 1417)

Catrin

Part One

Henry

'... a heart of gold,
A lad of life, an imp of fame:
Of parents good, of fist most valiant:
I kiss his dirty shoe, and from my heart-string
I love the lovely bully ...'

William Shakespeare, *King Henry the Fifth*
Act IV, Scene 1

Chapter One

France, September 1418

Leaning heavily on her stick, Sister Supplice shivered as she hobbled along the cold flagstones of the passageway to the dormitory, the flame from her candle guttering in a sudden draught. She dreaded the coming winter: the convent at Poissy was a chill unforgiving place when the weather turned bad and the old nun knew that her painful joints would be almost unbearable by December. Of course, she was grateful that her Father in Heaven had kept a roof over her head and food on her trencher in exchange for her obedience, which was more than could be said for her father on earth. The Marquis had been only too pleased that his plain, unmarriageable plum pudding of a daughter had resigned herself to taking the veil: not that she'd been given any choice in the matter.

Now, she pushed all those old resentments to the back of her mind because the only important thing was that the grey light of dawn heralded the day she had dreaded for so long. She had always known it would have to come and now it was here. Pushing open the door of the narrow cell where Catherine slept, she looked down at the girl's face, untroubled in a dreamless sleep. If only this last moment of innocence could be preserved for all time.

Sister Supplice felt as fiercely protective towards Catherine now as she had always felt, ever since she first set eyes on her. It must have been fifteen years ago, she realised with surprise, that two piteously thin, fair-haired little girls had been brought without ceremony to the convent, bewildered and hungry, their eyes brimming with tears. The Princess Marie de Valois, ten years old, was holding the hand of her three-year-old sister,

Catherine, and once the men of the royal guard had delivered them into the safe keeping of the nuns, they were left almost entirely alone, attended by only one servant, a slovenly woman with a dirty face and several missing teeth.

'They're stinking!' Sister Marie-Thérèse had hissed, wrinkling her nose in disgust. 'They're absolutely filthy and their heads are jumping with lice. I don't think they've been given clean clothes since May Day!'

'Please try to contain your disapproval, Sister,' Mother Superior had admonished her. 'The convent is hardly in a position to turn down a request from the King to care for two of his children.'

'But the King is …'

'Yes, thank you, Sister, we are all aware of the King's malady.'

The nuns knew as well as anyone that the King was quite, quite mad, poor soul, but that was the Lord's will and it was not their place to judge His Highness. So there had been nothing for it but to look after the King's daughters as best they could. At least they were to be paid quite reasonably for doing so, which was just as well since they were expected to be responsible for both the welfare and the education of the royal princesses.

Sister Consolata, who loved nothing better than a juicy secret, blamed the Queen. 'They say she's taken the King's brother into her confidence. And into her bed!' she whispered to Sister Supplice, elbowing her in the ribs.

Mother Superior silenced them with a frown. 'That will be all, Sisters. Indulgence in tittle-tattle is unbecoming in a bride of Christ. It is my sincere hope that the King's faith in the convent of Poissy is not misplaced and I trust you will treat His Highness's daughters with dignity and Christian charity while they remain in our charge.'

The nuns had been genuinely aghast at the children's plight and when they weren't preoccupied with their daily tasks and devotions, they seized every opportunity to gossip. In horrified whispers, they told each other that the little princesses had been sent to the convent for their own safety. It was well known, they said, that Queen Isabeau was no better than she should be, what

4

with her poor, mad husband locked up in St Pol. Why, she wouldn't even pay for servants to look after him! Squandered the money, probably, on gowns and fripperies. Disgusting! Then there was the King's cousin, the Duke of Burgundy, 'John the Fearless' as people called him. In the nuns' opinion, he was just as bad as the rest of the family, squabbling with the Queen over the guardianship of the royal children while the poor king was under lock and key.

Worst of all, they'd heard that the Queen's own brother had tried to abduct them, just a few weeks before the two youngest girls had arrived at the convent. No wonder they were dirty, neglected, and frightened. Sister Supplice remembered that they smelled like little animals and that once they had been stripped and washed, Mother Superior had ordered that their flea-infested clothes be burned.

Since then, however agonising the pain in her knees, Sister Supplice had always knelt during Lauds and prayed fervently that this would not be the day when the dreaded royal warrant would arrive and Catherine would be snatched away from her, to be taken back to court, where her future would be decided. If only they would send for Marie instead, she thought uncharitably; after all she was the older of the two, the more marriageable. But Marie had taken easily to convent life; she was already a postulant and would soon be starting her novitiate. There would be no question of Marie returning to court.

On the other hand Catherine, though outwardly pious enough, had shown no interest at all in taking the veil. She had learned to read and write and showed an aptitude for languages, becoming quite fluent in Latin and even managing to learn a few words of English. Her neat stitches in the altar cloth she was helping to make were testament to her skills as a needlewoman and she chanted the responses to the litany in a pleasant, tuneful voice. There was nothing more the nuns could teach her.

Still soundly asleep, the girl turned on her side and muttered something. Sister Supplice touched her shoulder.

'What is it, my little one? Another nightmare?'

She worried when Catherine cried in her sleep as she sometimes did, waking up distressed, without ever being able to describe what she had been dreaming, sobbing about lots of people shouting and horses going too fast. And, the oddest thing of all, she always said she had the sweet taste of marchpane in her mouth.

Gently, Sister Supplice shook her shoulder. How could young girls possibly sleep so heavily? Perhaps it was because they were growing so fast at this age. It worried her that the shapeless grey woollen convent dress Catherine wore each day could no longer disguise the fact that she had become a young woman; attractive, even beautiful. But great beauty, to Sister Supplice's way of thinking, was as much of a disadvantage to a woman as great ugliness. People would rarely look beyond either to see what lay beneath.

What worried the old nun most of all was the rumour she'd heard last week from Sister Madeleine, who kept the postern gate and dealt with the tradesmen. She'd said a pedlar had told her that the Queen was trying to bring about a marriage between her daughter, Catherine, and the English King Henry V.

The selfish, dissolute woman! It was nothing short of a sacrifice to offer the little one's hand in marriage to the great arrogant brute of a foreigner whose avowed intention was to conquer the whole of France. Sister Supplice crossed herself at the thought of Agincourt, the bloodiest of battles. The very name struck loathing, terror, and shame into French hearts.

'Catherine, wake up,' she whispered, more urgently now, shaking her harder. 'Oh, come, you must wake. It is very important.'

Catherine turned again, yawned and stretched her arms, then sat upright with a jolt, her eyes wide open.

'Have they have sent for me, Sister?'

'Yes, child, it is what we have been expecting.' Sister Supplice's throat tightened. 'You must get up and make yourself ready to leave for the castle at Meulan. The warrant from Her Highness the Queen arrived late last night with twenty men of the royal guard sent to escort you, but Reverend Mother wouldn't allow their captain to see you.' She had thoroughly approved of Mother Superior's indignant refusal to comply with the man's peremptory demands. Her Royal Highness the Princess Catherine had retired for the night, he was told, and that was that. He would have to wait until morning to see her and, no, the convent could not possibly accommodate twenty men, not without prior warning. They would have to make their own arrangements. There were plenty of barns to provide shelter and there was a perfectly good inn less than a mile away.

Sister Supplice hadn't slept at all. She spent the night on her knees, ignoring the pain, praying for something, anything that would mean Catherine having to remain in Poissy. Life without her was unimaginable.

But Catherine was already on her feet, dragging her coffer out from under her bed and starting to gather together her few belongings.

'You don't have to go, Catherine!' Sister Supplice sat heavily on the edge of the narrow bed, anxiously twisting her fingers in the skirts of her habit. 'You can refuse to leave. Wouldn't you like to stay here and become a postulant like Marie? If you take the veil you will always be safe. The Lord watches over His handmaidens.'

Catherine paused for a moment and gave Sister Supplice a fond smile and an almost imperceptible shake of her head. Then she continued her packing.

'Think, Catherine! Think! If you go to court, you might have to marry King Henry and go to live in England! My dear, you're young, you don't understand what will be expected of you. The indignity of it! If you are made to marry the King, you will be forced to share his bed and … and … submit to him. And he is a brute. A beast! Everybody says so. He … he probably has a tail!'

Startled, Catherine hesitated before wrapping her Book of Hours carefully in her spare shift and putting it in the coffer. Live in England? Marry King Henry? No, surely not! A marriage would be arranged for her, of course, that was only to be expected, but not with the King of England, not after the way he had inflicted such devastation and suffering on France and her people. Impulsively, she bent and kissed the old nun's

7

cheek.

'Oh, Sister Supplice, my dear father the King would never dream of making me do such a thing. So please, don't worry. No, really, you mustn't. But I will have to leave very soon. The Queen commands my presence. I am duty bound to obey.'

Catherine was relieved that there could be no argument with that. She had begun to feel more and more like a prisoner in the convent over the last few months, prey to a strange feeling of restlessness. She had tried talking to Marie about how she felt but her sister didn't understand what she meant. For Marie, a woman's greatest privilege was to serve God. Catherine's ambitions were a great deal less lofty and less well-defined but she did know that she wanted to be outside the convent walls, where she might enjoy music other than plainsong, where she might meet other young people of her own age, where she might even learn to dance. She had no idea how all this would come about but it would certainly not happen within the confines of the convent at Poissy.

Within the hour the captain of the guard, a sullen-looking man dressed in the livery of King Charles VI of France, had his men assembled in the quadrangle, adjusting their saddles and making ready for the journey. Horses tossed their heads and snorted, harnesses jingling, clouds of their warm breath white on the cold air of early morning. In the north cloister, Catherine was taking her leave of the nuns who had been her family for so long when Mother Superior came to a sudden decision. Striding out into the quadrangle, she began to berate the captain. Why had a chaperone not been sent to accompany the Princess Catherine? Surely she was not expected to travel with an entirely male escort party!

Catherine held her breath in a moment of pure panic. What if Mother Superior refused to let her go? She would be as trapped as a hen in a coop. She watched as the captain produced the royal warrant yet again, waving it imperiously under Mother Superior's nose, jabbing his finger at it to make his point. Illiterate, he could not read Queen Isabeau's signature, though he swaggered with the authority vested in him by the royal seal.

Mother Superior knew when she was beaten. Her shoulders

slumped, she walked back to the cloister and made Catherine give her solemn word that, during the course of the journey, she would remember everything she had been taught about seemly behaviour. On tenterhooks to get away, Catherine would have promised anything.

Then she caught a glimpse of Marie in her postulant's robe, standing next to Sister Supplice, her fist bunched up hard against her mouth in an effort to control her feelings. Her sister's anxious face made Catherine suddenly aware that this parting could be for a very long time.

'God go with you,' Marie whispered, embracing her, 'and kiss dear *Papa* for me. Oh, and kiss *Maman*, too, of course.' Catherine bit her lip to control its trembling while Sister Supplice wept like a mother bereaved.

As the journey began, mounted on a sturdy, docile little palfrey and with her heart very full, Catherine turned and looked back over her shoulder. A lone, bent figure stood at the convent gate, leaning on a stick and waving farewell.

Their route to Meulan took them north-west along the banks of the Seine and the pleasure of riding beside the sparkling waters of the river did much to lift Catherine's spirits. Freed from the constraints of convent behaviour, she occasionally leaned over in the saddle and stretched out her hand to pick some late berries from the hedgerows, savouring their sweetness as they burst in her mouth, relishing the liberty of being able to do so without fear of being chastised or corrected. The captain of the guard addressed her deferentially as 'Your Highness' and she straightened up and held her head erect as she remembered that, of course, he was a servant. He was riding alongside to defend her, not to tell her how to behave.

At mid-morning, the captain chose a sunny spot on the river bank where they could stop and rest. Slaking their thirst with small beer, they made a modest meal of the bread and cheese which the nuns had packed into their saddle bags. The horses, tethered in the shade of the willow trees at the water's edge, cropped the sweet, damp grass and swished their tails at the flies. After finishing her meal, Catherine made a decorous excuse and retreated behind a thicket of young hawthorn to relieve herself. Mother Superior would have approved of her seemly behaviour, she thought wryly, smoothing down her skirt before rejoining her protective entourage.

There was no one to meet the travellers or bid them welcome to Meulan at journey's end in the afternoon. The captain of the guard escorted Catherine into the great hall of the castle, its high stone walls hung with dusty tapestries. Smoke drifted up from a great pile of applewood logs in the hearth where a young boy was trying to get a fire going with a pair of leather bellows nearly as big as himself. From the minstrels' gallery came the sound of a rebec as a musician repeated a rhythmic phrase over and over again in an effort to master it. Since there appeared to be nowhere to sit, Catherine hung back and stood near the door as servants scurried in and out, carrying benches and setting up trestle tables. The captain stopped a passing footman, commandeered a bench for Catherine, and had it placed against the wall. Then he sent the man off to inform the Queen that her daughter had arrived. Catherine eased herself gingerly down onto the seat, the muscles in her buttocks and her back stiff and painful after the long, unaccustomed ride from Poissy. Fascinated, she watched the controlled activity going on around her.

'What do you know of this, Captain?' she asked.

He shrugged. 'It seems that a banquet is being prepared, Your Highness, and my guess is that it will have something to do with the English King.'

'King Henry?'

'Aye, he spends much of his time in France these days. No doubt he's come to pick over our bones.'

'He's not expected to come here tonight, is he?'

'No, my Lady, probably not, or we'd have heard about it in the guard room. But he does spend a deal too much time hereabouts. Him or his damned lackeys.'

He spat out the words and Catherine, taken slightly aback, felt a worm of apprehension begin to gnaw at her stomach. Why *had* she been brought here? The Queen would hardly have summoned her to court for the pleasure of her company. After all, she had done without that pleasure for fifteen years, apart from a few fleeting visits to the convent. Catherine remembered the upheaval those rare royal visits would cause, with Mother Superior seeming to relinquish all her authority as she fawned over the Queen. The nuns would be tripping over each other in their excitement, even Sister Supplice, who was usually so calm except when anyone mentioned the English invaders. And now the captain, too, was clearly agitated by the mention of the enemy.

'Did you fight at Agincourt, Captain?'

'I did, Your Highness, and lost three good fingers to an English hatchet on the battlefield.' He pulled the leather mitten off his mutilated left hand and Catherine recoiled at the sight of it. 'Still, I got out alive which is more than most men did. Six thousand French dead and many more maimed, nobles and commoners alike.'

'Was it really as bad as everyone says?'

'Oh, yes, and a good deal worse. It was as if the gates of Hell itself had opened, men and animals drowning in pools of blood and filth, screaming in pain.' He warmed to his subject. 'And King Henry takes no prisoners: the poor bastards were herded up in the mud and killed where they stood. He is a brute, a beast, the very spawn of the Devil. Begging your pardon, Your Highness,' he added. He had gone too far but, by God's bones, he'd been honest.

Catherine's eyes were wide with dismay at the captain's account of the battle and she felt real revulsion at the sight of his hand.

'Excuse me, Your Highness.'

She turned at the sound of a voice, glad of an interruption. A dark-haired young woman of about her own age was curtseying deeply to her.

'Yes, what is it?'

The young woman straightened up. 'The Queen wishes to see you immediately, my Lady. I am to take you to her.'

Catherine had been summoned to her mother's presence. She took a deep breath and squared her shoulders.

'Very well, er … what is your name?'

'Guillemote, my Lady. I am to be your personal maid.'

A personal maid! How different her life was about to become. She rose from the bench and inclined her head in dignified dismissal of the captain. Then she followed the girl called Guillemote towards a heavy oak door behind the dais at the far end of the great hall. A liveried footman held open the door and a small brown dog scampered around them, yapping noisily as they crossed the threshold.

'Catherine! There you are, child! Why are you so late arriving? Did that nincompoop of a captain lose his way?'

Catherine was caught up in the whirlwind which was her mother, Her Highness Queen Isabeau of France. She had forgotten how things happened around the Queen, how servants rushed hither and thither to do her bidding, how she barked commands and demanded immediate obedience. She was wearing a tall, conical headdress of intricate design which made her appear to tower above everyone around her, and her high forehead and plucked eyebrows gave her a look of haughty superiority.

'Come,' the Queen fussed, slapping at the dust on Catherine's cloak, 'we must clean you up before our visitor arrives.' She seized Catherine's arm and began propelling her towards the stone staircase which led to the upper floor.

'Visitor?' Alarmed, Catherine tried to pull back. 'Is King Henry coming here tonight?'

'King Henry? Good heavens, child, no. What on earth made you think that?'

'But the captain of the guard said …'

The Queen tightened her grip on Catherine's arm. 'Don't listen to servants' idle tittle-tattle, Catherine, they never get anything right. No, the King is not expected but his special envoy is. Sir Robert Waterton. Come along. We need to impress him.'

Still Catherine hung back. 'But why? Why, my Lady?'

'Because it is our business to make the English realise that France and the French are not just here for the taking. We must put a price on ourselves.'

Catherine felt a sense of relief. What her mother had said

made perfect sense. 'Oh, I see. Yes, of course, I understand. The King of England is a monster, isn't he? Everyone says so. The captain said he killed all his prisoners at Agincourt in cold blood. And … and … Sister Supplice says he probably has a tail!'

'Oh, for pity's sake! Don't be so naïve, Catherine. And take no notice of the insane prattling of nuns. A tail? What nonsense! As it happens, I have met King Henry and he is very charming.' Queen Isabeau, who had been carrying another small, yapping dog under her arm, threw the poor creature to the floor and turned to look critically at her daughter.

'Look at you!' she said, 'covered in dust and smelling like a horse. Come, we have work to do.'

Queen Isabeau was as imperious as ever. It would have been pleasant, Catherine reflected as she climbed the spiral staircase behind her mother, to have been greeted with affection, perhaps even kissed. She was sure her father would have kissed her.

'How is my dear Papa?' she asked. 'Will I see him tonight?'

'No,' the Queen paused on the stair for a moment and turned to look down at her daughter, her forehead creased in a frown. 'Your father will not be joining us. He is not well. And for his own safety, I have ordered that he be kept at St Pol until this latest bout of illness passes. He has servants there to look after him.'

'So his old malady still troubles him?'

'Grievously,' said the Queen. 'When I saw him last month, he kept saying he was made of glass.'

'Glass?'

'Yes, glass. He insisted on having iron rods sewn into his clothes to protect him and he wouldn't let anyone near him, for fear they'd break him.'

'Not even you, Maman?'

'Least of all me,' said the Queen, tightening her grip on the handrail before turning to climb the last few stairs to the upper solar.

Catherine had few clear memories of her early childhood before she and Marie were sent to the convent at Poissy but she retained a strong impression of her father as a big, affectionate bear of a man. She remembered laughter, warmth, and security within the safe circle of his arms while she sat on his knee and he told her stories, taught her nursery rhymes, and played little games which involved much counting of her fingers and toes. But other memories always intruded: memories of being awakened at night and clinging in terror to her sister, their hearts hammering with fear, pulling the bedclothes up over their ears to muffle the sounds of wailing and shouting from the King's room and the running footsteps of servants in the corridor outside. In her later years in the convent, her sleep sometimes disturbed by a hooting owl or a snoring nun, she had thought about those far-off, frightening nights in the nursery at St Pol and realised that her dear father lived more and more in his own dark world of madness. It saddened her to think of him so sorely troubled.

There was a discreet knock at the door.

'Ah, Guillemote, there you are,' said the Queen, as it opened. 'Now, go and heat up some water to wash the Princess Catherine's hair. And make sure you use good soap of Marseilles. Then rinse it in a solution of lemon juice to lighten it, braid it when it's dry, then dress her in one of my gowns. The new red one, I think, with that lovely fair hair. No, wait! Not the red, it will make her look too brazen. The green is more subtle. Yes, the green might well complement the colour of those eyes. And no, on second thoughts, don't braid her hair. There's no need to, she is not married: not yet. Besides, it has an attractive wave to it. We can take advantage of that. Get on with it, girl! We haven't got all night.'

Bobbing a hasty curtsey, Guillemote hurried away to do her bidding while the Queen pushed her daughter down on to a chair in front of a small dressing table and turned her towards a looking-glass, propped up by its handle in a holder. Meeting Catherine's startled gaze was the oval face of a fair-haired young woman with large, blue-grey eyes, fringed with dark lashes. High cheekbones counterbalanced a slightly elongated nose and the pale, translucent skin was flushed with embarrassment. For the first time in her life, she was seeing the reflection of herself as an adult. Bending forward, she examined

14

the mirror image more closely and heartily disliked what she saw.

'My nose is very big,' she said, pushing the mirror away.

The Queen turned her daughter's head from side to side, studying her from every angle. 'Hmmm. Yes, you are inclined to have the Valois nose, I'm afraid, and there's not much we can do about that. But it's a long nose, not a big one. Elegant. Aristocratic. And at least there's no mistaking your blood line; the whole royal family on your father's side has the Valois nose.' Isabeau continued her minute inspection of her daughter's face. 'Your skin is good, quite flawless, and you're lucky you have my eyes. Let me see your teeth.' Catherine winced as the Queen prised open her mouth; she might have been assessing the age of a sheep. 'Ah, good! You still have all your teeth so your breath will be sweet and a little tincture of myrrh will sweeten it even further. That's excellent.'

'Isn't this sinful, Maman?'

'Sinful? Why should it be sinful?'

'Well, the mirror. We had no mirrors at Poissy …'

The Queen snorted her derision. 'God's knees, child! Mirrors are not sinful, though nuns will have you believe that if you look into one you'll see the devil's backside. No, it is not sinful to make the most of every advantage you have in this life. Surely those old hens taught you the Gospel according to St Matthew?'

'Yes, yes, of course.' Catherine was shocked at her mother's blasphemy.

'Then remember the parable of the talents, Catherine. "To him that hath shall be given." So let's see what talents you have. Well, your hair is pretty enough but it will certainly benefit from a good wash. Did you ever comb it in that convent? It doesn't look like it. And this dress! Dear God! It's no wonder that women who wear clothes like this end up as virgins.'

'They're nuns, Maman.'

Queen Isabeau grimaced. 'Exactly,' she said. 'And to think that your sister Marie has chosen to become one. Poor misguided child! Thank God I still have you.'

The tuneful little musical phrase went round and round in Catherine's head. She'd first heard the rebec player practising it to perfection in the great hall during the afternoon and, joined now by the shawm and the rhythm of the tambour, it had proved the most popular dance of the evening. Catherine watched from the royal dais as some thirty men and women wove colourful patterns around the big room to the rhythms of popular dance tunes which she was hearing for the first time. She was enchanted by the music and elated at the changes which the expert ministrations of her mother and the maid, Guillemote, had wrought in her own appearance. Her gleaming hair tumbled to her shoulders under a delicate veil held in place by a circlet of gold. She had been laced into her mother's gown of green watered silk and loved the way it shimmered in the candlelight when she moved. Fifteen years of convent-bred inhibitions were beginning to drop away from Catherine like a discarded cloak.

Of course, she had not danced at all; that was certainly not something she had been taught by the nuns and her mother's restraining hand on her left arm ensured that she was not tempted to exhibit her lack of dancing skills in front of the English King's envoy. Sitting to her right on the royal dais, Sir Robert Waterton, too, seemed keen to touch Catherine's arm at any excuse. A square-jawed man with a slight cast in his eye, he leaned towards her conspiratorially, his foetid breath hot in her ear.

'You are even more beautiful than the miniature portrait which my sovereign lord, King Henry, has of you,' he whispered. 'He gazes upon it often and says he thinks you must be very lovely.'

'King Henry has a portrait of me?' Catherine's eyes opened wide in disbelief.

'Yes, of course he has,' said Queen Isabeau. 'I sent him that miniature I commissioned last year. The artist came to the convent. Surely you remember?'

Catherine did remember but had assumed that the portrait was for her parents. Apparently not. And now that she thought about it, no portrait had been painted of her sister Marie, though that hadn't struck her as particularly odd at the time. She began listening to the conversation on either side of her in mounting concern.

'Of course, Catherine's beauty is the envy of every maiden in France,' Queen Isabeau was pointing out. 'She takes after me.' That was certainly true. Catherine had, indeed, inherited her mother's high forehead and fine cheekbones. Thankfully, she had not inherited her mother's imperious attitude and fiery temper. 'In fact,' the Queen went on, 'it is generally accepted that she is the most comely princess in the whole of Europe. Her hand in marriage would be a great prize for any man.'

'Indeed, my Lady,' Sir Robert replied. 'There can be few men on God's earth who could resist your daughter's charms. Of course, I am not acquainted with *all* the princesses in Europe but I have met several of them. The Princess Catherine is certainly a great deal lovelier than the Princess Marie of Anjou, whom I met some time ago.'

'And what was so displeasing about her? You must admit that her bloodline is impeccable.'

'Indeed, yes. But there was nothing much to be gained from it. Besides, she was too dark, too swarthy-looking.'

Queen Isabeau nodded. 'And have you met the Countess Jacqueline of Holland, my Lord?'

'Oh, indeed. She is one of the more attractive ones. There was once some suggestion that she might make a suitable wife for the King's younger brother, the Duke of Bedford.'

'Ah, but she was already betrothed to my son, John. They would still be married if he had lived. God rest his soul,' Isabeau said, crossing herself briefly. 'But yes, you're right, she is quite attractive. Of course, she is our kinswoman,' she said, to prove her point.

Sir Robert Waterton leered again at Catherine. 'Sadly, the beauty of the bride is not the only thing to be taken into consideration in negotiating a royal marriage. There is the matter of the marriage settlement. His Highness King Henry would not agree to any dowry which does not include Normandy and Aquitaine. And eight hundred thousand crowns,' he added, as an afterthought.

Catherine's cheeks blazed. She was being bartered. Her

mother and this deeply unpleasant man were haggling over her bride price like farmers at market, both hoping to turn a profit on the mating of a highly prized animal. And the chosen stud was to be the Beast of Agincourt.

Sister Supplice had been right after all.

That first night at Meulan, Catherine's bedchamber seemed awash with weeping. Hot tears of betrayal and bewilderment coursed down her cheeks and shuddering sobs shook her whole body. Queen Isabeau, turning with an impatient swish of her skirts before sweeping out of the room, had told her to pull herself together and be grateful that she had the prospect of a glittering future as Queen of England.

Full of compassion, Guillemote made her mistress a posset of hot milk laced with wine and spices and sat beside her while she drank it, holding a cloth under her trembling chin, stroking her shoulder and making little crooning, soothing sounds to comfort her in her obvious distress.

To her new maid Catherine seemed very young, yet they were probably around the same age. But surely, Guillemote thought, a princess must know how things are done: for all her convent upbringing, the concept of an advantageous marriage arranged by her parents can't have been anything new to her. Still, being forced to marry the Beast of Agincourt was asking a great deal of her, the poor thing.

Guillemote, born and brought up in the service of the Valois family, was well aware of the Queen's dynastic scheming for all her children. But now, still with her arm around the sobbing Catherine, she saw the pain and confusion these tactical transactions could cause; she also knew that they did not always work out for the best. Many years ago, Catherine's oldest sister, the Princess Isabelle, had returned home to France, a widow at the age of eleven after an unconsummated marriage to the English King Richard II. Then, nine years ago, the Princess Michelle had been married to her cousin Philip of Burgundy but these days, having failed to produce an heir to the Burgundian title, she wore a face that could curdle milk.

The Valois sons were two sickly boys and both dead before

the age of twenty. This meant that the next in line to the throne of France was now Catherine's younger brother Charles, a sly fifteen-year-old with a bulbous nose and pustular skin, the Queen's last child and the runt of her litter. Guillemote had loathed the *Dauphin* Charles ever since the day, six months ago, when he pushed her roughly against a wall outside the palace kitchens, fastened his slobbering mouth over hers, pulled up her skirts, and tried to shove his hand between her legs. After a desperate struggle, she had managed to fight him off but the sound of his crowing, high-pitched laughter still rang in her ears.

One day, Charles would become king of France. Recalling her revulsion at the sensation of his tongue probing her mouth, Guillemote thought him entirely unsuited for the highest office in the land – but she was only a servant so how could she possibly judge? That sort of thing was for others to decide. All she could do was try to bring some comfort to her poor young mistress.

Chapter Two

France, May 1419

It felt chilly on the river despite the spring sunshine and Catherine pulled her woollen cloak closer about her shoulders. The sumptuous barge which her mother had insisted upon hiring for this important occasion was making slow, stately progress north-west from Paris along the River Oise. Queen Isabeau was determined to create an impression at the meeting which had finally been arranged between the French and English kings with their advisers. They were to meet at Pontoise at three o'clock, to discuss the terms of a possible treaty which, if agreed upon, would include a marriage between the French Princess Catherine de Valois and the English King Henry V. Over the last few months, the reluctant prospective bride had finally been persuaded of the desirability of the union and had been made very aware that she represented the last hope of a royal marriage as the foundation of a strong alliance between the two countries. It had been drummed into her that the alliance would be of great benefit to France: but she was still filled with trepidation at the thought of what was to come.

On the river bank, an unnecessarily large contingent of men-at-arms rode alongside the barge as it continued majestically on its way. On board, His Royal Highness King Charles VI of France, his crown slightly askew, lay slumped against opulent cushions of crimson velvet. He was snoring open-mouthed after two glasses of the excellent red wine which had been a gift from his cousin, John the Fearless, the Duke of Burgundy, who accompanied them. Sitting between her parents, Catherine watched as the barge rounded a bend in the River Oise and the landing stage came into view. She felt a twinge of nervousness

21

and wondered yet again what the afternoon held in store for her. Her mother had spoken highly of King Henry and described him in glowing terms; but she found it difficult to imagine him.

'What does King Henry look like, my Lady? Did you think him handsome when you met him?'

'I have told you, Catherine, more than once. He is a fine-looking man, a man's man, a warrior king. I'll wager he can make a woman feel like a woman in every sense of the word …' She threw a scornful look at her husband and added, 'which is more than can be said for some.'

Queen Isabeau was clearly nervous about the meeting. Now and then she would get up from her seat to pace up and down the deck, from prow to stern and then back again. She was at her most elegant today, her forehead smooth and high with finely plucked eyebrows emphasising the shape of her large, blue-grey eyes. A delicate veil in the palest shade of lilac drifted down from the tip of her pointed headdress and heavily jewelled sleeves protruded from slits in the seams of her purple, ermine-lined cloak. A small lap dog with ridiculously short legs and a sharp, shrill bark did its best to keep up with her pacing but succeeded only in waking the King.

'Dear God!' he squealed, 'keep that animal away from me!'

Catherine put an arm around his shoulders, soothing him. 'Hush, Papa. It is only Maman's little dog, Cherie. She won't harm you.'

'Where are we? Where are we going? What are we doing in the middle of this river? We'll drown! We'll surely drown! Who will save us?' The King of France was rocking to and fro like a child.

'We are going, my Lord,' Queen Isabeau silenced him, 'to meet King Henry of England with a view to negotiating a marriage contract between him and our daughter Catherine. She will become Queen of England as soon as a reasonable dowry can be arranged.'

'Two hundred thousand crowns!' quavered the King, jabbing the air with his forefinger. 'That's what I said last time and I'm not going to offer any more than that. Two hundred thousand crowns. He's very lucky to have her! Two hundred

22

thousand. That's my last offer …'

'Oh, do be quiet, Charles,' said Queen Isabeau irritably as she sat down next to him, 'you're not at a cattle market. Besides, he is demanding eight hundred thousand. God only knows where we will find such a sum of money.'

'It is unreasonably high,' agreed the Duke of Burgundy, 'but it will be interesting to see whether, having met the Princess Catherine, King Henry will lower his price.'

The Queen stood up again, suddenly tense, her fists clenched at her sides. 'I can't go on with this. Not under these circumstances.'

'What, Maman? What do you mean?'

'I really don't think that your father can contribute anything at all to this dialogue. He'll loll around in a chair, babbling and farting like a big baby. His behaviour is hardly likely to impress the King of England!'

She clapped her hands loudly. 'Take him away,' she said through clenched teeth as two of the King's body servants moved swiftly into position on either side of him. They took most of his weight between them and manoeuvred him towards the rear of the barge. Docile as a lamb, he smiled affably at them both. 'And make damned sure,' added the Queen, 'that nobody sees him!'

Catherine watched as her father was taken away. She had spent a great deal of time with him in the eight months since they had both returned to court, she from the convent at Poissy and he from his enforced confinement in St Pol. His behaviour often swung between elation and depression but, on the days when he was at his best, she took great delight in his company; she fretted about him on the days when he was locked in his room.

On his good days, they would walk in the palace garden together, talking at length. The King would confide in her his hopes for the future and for the marriage which would unite France and England, bringing an end to decades of battle and bloodshed between the two countries. Partly out of affection for her father, Catherine had slowly begun to accept the idea of marriage to the King of England.

23

This was not one of her father's good days and she knew that her mother was right in not allowing him to attend the meeting. In fact, he seemed particularly bad today, querulous and nervous, inclined to shy away from everyone, holding his arms over his head as though to protect himself. In his youth, her father had been known as 'Charles the Well-Beloved'. Now they called him 'Charles the Mad'.

The barge was pulled into line with the landing stage and, standing behind her mother as they both waited to be helped ashore, Catherine felt the steadying hand of her uncle, John the Fearless, under her elbow. The moment had come; she was about to meet the man her parents wanted her to marry. Would he be a brute, as Sister Supplice had warned her? A bully? Or would he be charming and difficult to resist, as her mother had described him? She would soon find out.

Meticulous preparations had been made for the meeting. Two pavilions had been erected in a field near the landing stage, matching exactly in size and design, one for the French delegation and one for the English. Guards were stationed along the deep ditch which surrounded three sides of the enclosure and the fourth side, equally well guarded, was bounded by the River Oise. The pavilions were linked by a covered walkway to a marquee in the very centre of the compound, the neutral territory where negotiations would take place. The blue and gold royal flag of France, fluttering slightly in the breeze off the water, was being raised high above the nearest pavilion as Queen Isabeau approached it on the arm of the Duke of Burgundy. Catherine followed, a few steps behind.

Once inside, Guillemote helped Catherine remove her heavy cloak to reveal a loose, sleeveless mantle over a close-fitting gown of pale green, buttoned up modestly to her throat. Her hair was neatly braided under an arched crown and she looked both virginal and regal.

Queen Isabeau peered into her daughter's face, scrutinising her appearance, then pinched her cheeks in an attempt to bring some colour to them.

'You're a bit pale,' she said, pushing a stray curl back into place under the crown, 'but we've done well with you. And it was certainly worth spending the extra money on that gown. The colour is so lovely, the pale grey-green of young sage leaves: it complements your eyes beautifully. We must remember how flattering it is. You look for all the world like a queen, Catherine.' She paused. '*Queen Catherine*! How easily the title trips off the tongue!'

'My Lady,' said Catherine, 'you are sure, aren't you, that this marriage is really the best thing for France?'

The Queen gripped her daughter's wrist. 'Oh, for heaven's sake, Catherine, how many times must I tell you? It is the *only* thing for France,' she said in an urgent whisper, 'the only thing that will bring about some measure of peace. Henry wants Normandy and Aquitaine and he is not going to give up easily. He's ruthless. What land we don't relinquish, he will take by force, as he took Rouen. That siege lasted so long, the wretched townsfolk were reduced to eating rats to stay alive.'

'Ugh! He doesn't sound very pleasant.'

'Believe me, Catherine, strong kingship has nothing to do with being *pleasant*! But at least he's tolerably handsome. You can't have everything. And France will have a strong ruler in Henry, even if he *is* a foreigner. Your poor father hasn't been much of a figurehead for his people. No, I believe that Henry will be good for France.'

At the sound of a bugle-call outside the pavilion, the Queen jumped anxiously to her feet. 'What's that?' she demanded. 'Are they here yet? How many are there? Dear God, I wish I wasn't so damned nervous about this meeting!'

The Duke of Burgundy peered past the guard. 'It's … yes, my Lady, it's the English. King Henry has arrived.'

'Is he alone?' demanded the Queen. 'How many men-at-arms does he have with him? Are his brothers there?'

'How should I know? But he's certainly got plenty of men-at-arms. At least, oh … five hundred, I'd say, at a rough guess.'

'One or two of his brothers are sure to be with him,' said the Queen, 'they say all three of them are very supportive: the Duke of Clarence, the Duke of Bedford and the Duke of er … of er … Gloucestershire.' She hesitated over the name, then mispronounced it.

'Then perhaps Catherine can work her magic on the Dukes,' said John the Fearless, smiling at his niece. 'Perhaps she can persuade them to convince their brother to drop his unreasonable demands for money.'

Averting her gaze as King Henry approached, Catherine noticed for the first time that the buckle on her left shoe was crooked. Keeping her head bent, she listened avidly to what was going on around her. Above the muted buzz of voices from the assembled crowd of French and English dignitaries, she heard the English King greet her mother.

'Queen Isabeau! Such a pleasure to see you again and I am sad to hear that His Highness the King is indisposed.' The low voice continued in fluent, impeccable French with a slight accent. 'But, my dear lady, I cannot tell you how delighted I am that the Princess Catherine is here with you. And if it please you, Ma'am, I should like to be presented to your daughter. That is if she truly *is* your daughter.'

'What can you mean, Your Grace?' The Queen seemed startled.

'I mean that she could be a heavenly creature who has strayed here from the Elysian Fields, the paradise where heroes are granted everything they ever wished for. Can it be that my wishes are granted, even before I reach Paradise? Can it be that the Princess Catherine is as beautiful as her portrait?'

Blushing furiously, Catherine kept her eyes firmly fixed on her crooked shoe buckle. She heard the relief in her mother's nervous laugh. The Queen, back on the familiar ground of courtly compliments, had recovered her composure. She could play this game with the best of them.

'Come, Sire, I assure you she *is* my daughter. She has my eyes, or so they say.'

'Then she is indeed blessed with beauty,' said King Henry, bending to kiss Isabeau's hand. She still seemed flustered, not at all herself.

'Come, Catherine,' she said. 'Raise your head, child. King Henry would look on your face.'

Catherine raised her head and looked into the face of the

26

man who would rule her destiny and the first thing she noticed about him was his long neck. She realised that she had never asked her mother how old Henry was and she was surprised to see plentiful strands of grey in his brown hair. He must be quite old, she thought, at least thirty. Perhaps even older than that! Then she noticed the scar on his right cheek, white and puckered, running parallel with his aquiline nose and stopping just short of his eye. It was the one thing which marked him out as a warrior. Otherwise, for some strange reason, his face reminded her of a priest she had once known in her convent days at Poissy, lean but somehow gentle, with understanding in the mild brown eyes. Despite what the captain of the guard had said, the King didn't *look* like the spawn of the Devil. In fact, Catherine rather liked the look of him.

The two parties faced each other across the negotiating table. Henry, sitting almost directly opposite Catherine, seemed reluctant to take his eyes off her. She looked down at her lap whenever she caught his glance, feeling confused, aware that she was blushing again.

Then the negotiations began in earnest. Objections were raised to every suggestion from the French and, though he agreed that Catherine was in many ways very suitable to be Queen of England, Henry was adamant that he had every right to expect a handsome dowry from her parents, though that was only one of many points at issue. Back and forth, back and forth went the arguments. Catherine's attention wandered as the voices droned on and she tried to stay alert in the warmth of the tent by identifying members of the King's entourage. They had all been presented to her but she was confused by their unfamiliar English names. There appeared to be several dukes and earls present. She had heard the names of Exeter, Warwick, and Huntingdon, though she wasn't at all sure which was which. And her mother had been right in guessing that some of the King's younger brothers would be with him. She had been introduced to the Duke of Bedford, a tall man with a round face, slightly pointed nose, and twinkling eyes. The one with the longer, more handsome face who was now sitting on the other side of the King was his youngest brother Humphrey, the Duke of Gloucester. As he had bent to kiss her hand in greeting, she had been surprised to hear how his title was pronounced, as though it had only two syllables instead of three. She had also felt rather disconcerted by the way he stared at her when he straightened up again, seeming reluctant to let go her hand.

Henry was, without doubt, the most charismatic of the three English royal brothers. She stole a glance at him while he was pressing home an argument. The eyes which she had thought mild and priestly at first, now burned with concentration as he met argument with counter-argument. She felt frustrated at having to sit there listening to the political bickering which was going on all around her, particularly since she didn't understand most of it. Her sole interest was the King. How could she possibly know how he would be as a husband if she was only able to listen to him arguing? She wanted to get to the man, the real man who had made the charming assumption that she had strayed into his life from the Elysian Fields, the heroes' paradise. She quite liked the idea of a hero as a husband, though she would never have admitted as much.

She laid her hand on her mother's jewelled sleeve. 'My Lady,' she said, with half-closed eyes, 'my Lady, I feel faint.'

'Do you, Catherine?' The Queen gave her a shrewd look. 'Yes, I see. It *is* rather warm in here. Perhaps you had better leave the room for a little while.'

Catherine pushed back her chair, rose, and began to make her way out of the negotiating tent with the attentive Guillemote close behind her. King Henry raised his head at the disturbance. 'Is the Princess Catherine unwell?' he asked.

'She feels a little faint, my Lord,' said Queen Isabeau. 'It is *very* warm in here.'

'Then please, she must make use of the amenities which have been placed at my disposal. They are next to the river and very cool. She must sit there and rest awhile. In fact,' said the King, pushing back his own chair, 'I shall make it my responsibility to ensure that she is comfortable.'

This was more like it, thought Catherine, straightening her back as the King came towards her. She curtseyed and smiled at

28

him as he took her hand and drew her arm through his, steering her away towards the English pavilion. John the Fearless made as though to follow them but Queen Isabeau grasped his arm.

'Let them go. Catherine doesn't need a chaperone. She is not stupid. She will come to no harm.'

Muttering under his breath and rubbing his elbow where Isabeau's fingers had gripped it like a vice, John resumed his seat and watched as the Princess Catherine left the negotiating tent with the King of England.

'Come, my Lady, would you like some refreshment?' Henry asked, smiling as he pulled out a chair for her to sit at a small table in his private quarter of the English pavilion. They were alone, save for the presence of two guards. 'Sweetmeats, perhaps? A little marchpane? A goblet of wine?'

'Thank you, Your Highness, but no,' said Catherine, smoothing down the skirt of the sage green gown. She didn't trust herself to relax; she hated the sickly-sweet taste of marchpane and wine would surely go straight to her head. The King took the other chair and held out his hand across the table towards her, palm upward.

'Give me your hand, Catherine.' It was not a command, nor yet a plea. Catherine hesitated, then put her small hand in his: big and calloused, it was a soldier's hand but warm and dry to the touch.

'That feels good, Catherine. Your hand is so very small and soft. My hand wants to curl around it and look after it. Do you think you would like that? Do you like me just a little, perhaps, though I'm a soldier with a soldier's ways, rough and ready?'

'Your Highness ... Sire, I ... so many questions. I ... I cannot answer them all.'

She felt his hand closing around hers. 'Catherine, I have gazed for many an hour at the miniature painting I have of you and tried to imagine how it would feel to touch the real princess. Now I know and the sensation pleases me greatly. I would find it very easy to cherish you and to rule over France and England, justly and wisely, to the greater glory of God.'

Though she had been the one to contrive this meeting,

Catherine felt a little dizzy with the speed at which events were proceeding. 'But, Your Highness,' she protested, 'it will take me a great deal of time to learn the English tongue. I know only a few words, which I learned at the convent from Sister Supplice.'

The King laughed and his grip on her hand relaxed a little. 'It's not so difficult. But I'll wager that Sister whatever-her-name-was didn't teach you the kind of words I want to hear you say, Catherine!'

'My Lord!' This time Catherine succeeded in snatching her hand away from his.

'I'm sorry, Catherine. I jest. But, I assure you, you really must not worry about the English language. French is still the language of the English court, as it has been these many years, though I would wish that English was more widely spoken. I do my best to encourage it. Perhaps, as you begin to learn the English tongue, you will inspire others to do the same.'

Catherine was not at all sure about that. She was only too pleased not to have to worry about learning to speak English. 'Do you speak any other languages, my Lord?' she asked, making conversation.

'Oh, indeed. As it happens, I have more than a little Welsh. I was born in the town of Monmouth, you see, and spent much of my childhood there. My nurse made sure I had quite a repertoire of Welsh nursery rhymes.'

He laughed and, smiling, reached for her hand again, holding it upright this time. Then he began to recite, pointing first to her thumb then to her fingers one by one.

'Modryb y fawd,
Bys yr uwd,
Pen y cogwr,
Dic y Peipar,
Joli cwt bach'

Catherine recognised one word in the jumble of unintelligible ones.

'Ah, *jolie*!' she said, laughing. 'We have this word in French.'

Henry smiled at her, still holding her hand. 'It's not so

30

difficult. They are just babies' names for their fingers. This is Auntie Thumb, and here's your porridge finger, the one you use to get at the last scrap of oats in your porringer.' He held up her index finger and, teasing, made as though to lick it. Laughing again, she tried to pull away as he went on. 'The long one in the middle is the trickster, then here's Dic the Piper, and the little tail. You would find it easy to teach that to your children.' He paused and gave her a quizzical look before going on. 'To our children, perhaps?'

Catherine lowered her eyes, embarrassed, and his smile faded abruptly.

'But then,' he said letting go her hand, 'why should you teach our children any of that nonsense? There are plenty of children's rhymes in French and in English, come to that. Welsh will benefit them nothing. Damned country. My principality, my burden. So near to England and yet so very different.'

'Indeed, my Lord? How so?'

Henry sighed. 'In many, many ways,' he replied. 'Some years ago when I was younger, I was often in Wales for months at a time, campaigning long and hard against the rebel armies of Owain Glyndŵr, who called himself Prince of Wales, though he had no right to. That was my title, before I became king. The heir to the English throne is always known as the Prince of Wales; it's a long-established tradition. Anyway, that was when I *really* picked up the language. And this scar,' he added, fingering his right cheek. 'I have a Welsh archer to thank for this disfigurement.'

'Oh no, my Lord, it is barely noticeable!' Catherine was pleased to take refuge in the sweet inaccuracies of courtly conversation. Queen Isabeau, she thought, would be proud of her.

'Perhaps not. But, come, Catherine, you haven't answered my question.'

'My Lord, you have asked me so many!' She was trying to keep a light tone in her voice, just as her mother would have wanted her to.

'Only one question is important, Catherine. And that is –

31

could you learn to love me, do you think?'

Faced with that one question, Catherine had to reply. And she found the reply unexpectedly easy. 'Yes, Your Grace,' she said, measuring her words with care. 'Yes, I think I could.'

'Thank you, Catherine.' Henry reached for her hand again, raised it to his lips, and kissed it. 'Thank you. Now that I know your heart, I feel I can continue to press my suit for you and to negotiate for the French lands which are rightfully mine. The prize is magnificent and well worth fighting for. And I am a fighter, a soldier, first and last.'

It was a grim-faced Queen Isabeau who led the way back to the barge, after the talks had broken up with no resolution. She was already working out her tactics for the next meeting with Henry.

'Tell me, Catherine,' she said, 'exactly what did you and the King talk about?'

'Nursery rhymes, Maman.'

'Nursery rhymes?'

Catherine allowed herself a secret smile. 'Yes, my Lady. And then he asked me if I could find it in my heart to love him.'

'Oh, he did, did he? And what did you say in reply, child?'

'I said I thought I could, my Lady.'

'Good,' said the Queen with a self-satisfied smirk. 'That will give us something to work on.'

Chapter Three

Montereau, France, September 1419

John the Fearless pulled on his boots and stood up to adjust his belt. He was getting too old for this business of negotiation; his fiftieth birthday was on the horizon and he had long been of the opinion that life would be a lot easier if only the Burgundy branch of the House of Valois ruled France, rather than the Orléans branch, the mad ones.

He tugged at his tunic to make sure it lay straight under his belt. No use turning up at Montereau looking like a country bumpkin, not for a meeting with that little bastard Charles, anyway. At least the sixteen-year-old had grown an inch or two and seemed to have fewer pimples than he'd had a year ago, but the more he grew up, the more he began to look like his uncle, his father's brother, the late Duke of Orléans. It might have been a family resemblance, of course, but John well knew what a slut Isabeau could be and he was quite certain that the rumours about an affair with her brother-in-law had been true.

Of course, that kind of behaviour would have been tolerated, even admired, in a man but never in a woman. Not that this would worry Isabeau, who had a very clever head on her shoulders and scant morals when it came to getting what she wanted. She would have made a good ruler, he thought, though she was a really dreadful mother. When she was younger, she had children every year or so with little more apparent effort than shelling peas, but she couldn't be bothered to look after any of them. And yet she managed to produce several sons in her years of child-bearing.

His own wife had done just the opposite. Margaret had given birth to six daughters and only one son among the seven children who lived. But young Philip was a healthy lad and had shown promise from childhood. Now, at the age of twenty-three, he was a man in his prime and a son to be proud of. There had been wisdom in arranging a marriage between Philip and the King's older daughter, Michelle, cementing a relationship between two quarrelsome branches of the ruling House of Valois. With luck, perhaps the pair would soon manage to produce a son and then the Burgundian accession to the throne of France would be as good as assured. The Dauphin was the only obstacle to the Duke's ambition and it shouldn't be difficult to discredit that pimply little weasel in some way. John the Fearless had nothing but contempt for his nephew.

A valet brushed a few flecks of dust off the Duke's shoulders then helped him buckle a scabbard onto his belt. With great care, John slid his sword into it, checking that he could reach the handle easily. The scabbard seemed a trifle long but that didn't matter: he wasn't planning a sword-fight. This was just another diplomatic meeting designed to bring about a reconciliation between the dissenting factions of the royal House of Valois. And, if he was to be on time, he had better set off. He opened the door and went out to join the group of advisers who awaited him.

The Dauphin Charles had stolen from his mother, Queen Isabeau, a long-handled Nuremberg mirror in an ornate ivory frame. He had no conscience at all about this, even though the mirror was very valuable. Now he took it from its hiding place at the back of a cupboard and propped it up on a table near the window, where the light was good. He picked up a comb and ran it through his lank hair then, moving his head from side to side, studied his profile, proud that he really had got the 'Orléans nose', as his mother always said he had. He bent closer to the mirror and squeezed the yellow pus from an angry-looking red spot in the crease of his nostril.

He was not looking forward to this meeting with his father's cousin, John the Fearless. Fearless? Not according to what he'd heard. The Duke of Burgundy hadn't even fought at Agincourt. John the Shameless was more like it, thought Charles, though

John-the-Entirely-Without-Scruples would have suited him even better. It was well known that he had ordered the murder of Charles's own uncle, the Duke of Orléans, in the most vile way, by having the poor man stabbed mercilessly and his hands chopped off. Unable to defend himself, he was left screaming in agony, helpless, and bleeding to death in the street. That infamous incident had caused a public outcry and Queen Isabeau had absented herself from court for several weeks, distraught with grief at the cold-blooded murder of her husband's brother. But John the Fearless had never been called to account for the crime. In fact, he had been granted an official pardon by his cousin the King and that was an end to it, even though it was common knowledge that the King was mad.

Twelve years had passed since then and, by now, it was far too late to do anything about it so they might as well try to patch things up. For Charles, one of the most distressing aspects of the whole situation was that John the Fearless appeared to favour the English. He couldn't understand that, any more than he could understand why his mother was so keen to see his sister Catherine married to the English King. The whole situation was a stinking, sorry mess.

Checking his appearance once more, Charles brushed a cloud of dandruff off his shoulders before carefully returning the stolen mirror to its hiding place at the back of the cupboard.

The two parties were to meet on the bridge over the River Seine at Montereau, in order to attempt to reach a truce. There was a pressing need to discuss ways of tackling the problem of the overbearing English presence in France. English soldiers were living off the land, stealing the chickens, screwing the women, guzzling the wine. It had to stop but it never would as long as France was divided, with the two warring factions of the royal family refusing to agree about anything.

At the stroke of five o'clock, Charles approached the bridge, flanked on either side by a group of close advisers and guards. John the Fearless, with his men, stepped on to the bridge from the other side. They advanced at a snail's pace towards the fenced-in area at the apex of the bridge.

The Duke and the Dauphin entered the restricted zone with

their men at exactly the same time and it was sealed off behind them. Each was as tense as a taut bowstring. As convention demanded, John the Fearless went down on one knee before the Dauphin, the son of the King. Attempting to rise again, he cursed the long scabbard on his belt which had become entangled in his boot, restricting him. With his hand on the hilt of his sword, he attempted to free the scabbard. It was a movement open to misinterpretation.

The polished blade of a hatchet flashed in the late afternoon sun and Charles stepped back as his uncle fell forward, a surprised look on his face and blood oozing from a deep gash in his skull. There was a moment of absolute, stunned silence which seemed to last to infinity; then complete uproar. Suddenly, the air was filled with oaths and screams and flailing knives as bodies thudded to the creaking wooden slats of the bridge.

Death came, swift and vicious, to several men in Montereau that late summer afternoon, before the chaos subsided into an icy horror. As Charles stared, transfixed, at the dead body of John the Fearless slumped at his feet, the angelus bell began to toll its triple measure. The sonorous rhythm found a persistent echo inside Charles's brain. 'John the Lifeless,' tolled the bell, 'John the Lifeless.'

Queen Isabeau tore up the third draft of yet another letter to King Henry then, reaching for her quill, she dipped it into the ink horn and began again:

The Castle at Troyes,
September 11th 1419

Your most esteemed Highness,

I find myself becoming daily more concerned that the business between us is still without resolution ...

She got no further. The door burst open and, startled, she knocked over the ink horn, ruining the fourth draft of the letter.

'What is the meaning of this? How dare you enter this room

unannounced!'

'Your Highness, I'm sorry. I'm so sorry …' Panting hard, her steward dropped to his knee, sending her little lap dog scurrying for cover beneath the escritoire. 'I have news, Your Highness, grave news concerning the Dauphin.'

'Charles? My son? What kind of grave news? He's not … surely he's not …' Isabeau crossed herself.

'No, my Lady, he is not dead. Pray do not distress yourself. He is not dead. He lives. He yet lives, despite the fact …' the man hesitated.

'Yes, yes. What is it, man? Spit it out! Despite what fact?'

'The Duke of Burgundy, Ma'am. The Duke of Burgundy is dead. Killed on the bridge at Montereau at the hour of the angelus yesterday. Murdered.'

'Murdered!' the Queen was aghast. 'The Duke of Burgundy? Murdered? Not by Charles, surely!'

The man hesitated. 'I don't know, Ma'am. The messenger who brought the news was gabbling in his excitement and, to be honest, he couldn't tell me exactly what had happened but he was quite certain that John the Fearless was dead. Murdered, he said. Murdered. He was quite certain of that.'

Queen Isabeau slumped back into her chair. '*Mon Dieu!* This is terrible,' she said in a hoarse whisper. 'Go! Go and find out everything you can. I need to know exactly what happened. I want to know my son's part in all this. I must know. Every detail. And I want the truth! Go, I tell you, this minute! And be sure to bring the Dauphin back with you when you return. Tell him I wish to speak to him as a matter of the utmost urgency.'

The steward got shakily to his feet and bowed to the Queen before leaving the room. Isabeau leaned forward and put her head in her hands. It was some time before she raised it again.

When she did, she went in search of Catherine and found her with Guillemote, both working on one of Catherine's gowns. Guillemote was mending a tear in the hem and Catherine was embroidering a garland of tiny flowers on the bodice.

'Leave that, Catherine,' Isabeau ordered, 'and come with me.' The Queen turned on her heel and left the room. Alarmed by the tone of command in her mother's voice, Catherine jabbed her needle through the fabric and pushed the garment to one side. Guillemote caught it as it fell to the floor.

'What is it, Maman?' Catherine pulled the door closed behind her. Isabeau looked around to make sure they couldn't be overheard.

'It's Charles. I always knew that one day he would do something stupid enough to get us all into trouble. He has been involved in some sort of brawl.'

'Is he all right?'

'Oh, Charles is perfectly well, apparently. Which is more than can be said for John the Fearless, poor soul.' She crossed herself. 'He's dead.'

'Dead? My uncle of Burgundy?' Catherine's hand flew to her mouth. 'He's dead?'

'So it seems. Murdered, they say. I knew that he and Charles were to meet at Montereau, it's been arranged for some time. But it seems the situation got out of hand.'

Catherine looked stunned. 'What happened?'

'I don't know, Catherine, I really don't know. My only fear is ...' Isabeau hesitated. 'I can only pray that Charles had no part in this murder. But he can be such a stupid boy: between the two of us, I wouldn't be at all surprised.'

'I can't believe that ... that my uncle is dead.' Deeply shocked, Catherine was pushing her clenched fist hard against her mouth, trying to stop her lips trembling.

'Apparently it's true. Of course, we'll know more very soon. Bad news has a habit of travelling fast.'

'What will happen? What will happen to the family? Aunt Margaret? The girls? Anne and little Agnès will be beside themselves with grief. Michelle, too. And what of cousin Philip?' Catherine was beginning to appreciate the seriousness of the situation.

'Philip will inherit his father's title,' said Isabeau abruptly, 'of course. And as for Michelle, well, your sister is now the new Duchess of Burgundy. Get used to it, my dear, there's going to be a new Duke of Burgundy at our negotiations with King Henry from now on.'

'But Philip is young, he hasn't the experience ...'

'No, he hasn't. But we might be able to turn that to our advantage,' Isabeau was plotting already. 'Leave me now, Catherine. I have much to do. Go back to Guillemote and your sewing. There's no point in upsetting yourself. Who knows, some good might come of all this, though you might not think so at the moment.'

Isabeau went straight back to her escritoire and began another letter. John the Fearless was dead and she could lose no time in extending her deepest sympathy to the new duke and duchess in their loss. She was even more anxious, though she did not say so, to ensure that the young duke would be prepared to continue the association with the English which his father had favoured. The fragile alliance must not be threatened by the events of the previous day. She needed young Philip of Burgundy's support for her plans.

There was one more letter which Queen Isabeau wanted to write but, having thought about it, she decided against committing herself to paper. She didn't want anyone to have proof of what she was about to do. Instead, she summoned one of her closest advisers, the Bishop of Arras, to a meeting in her private chamber and asked him to make an excuse to request an audience with King Henry. She urged him to point out to the English King in a subtle way that not only had the Dauphin Charles disgraced himself at Montereau but that there were, in any case, serious doubts about his right to the throne, doubts which could be verified if need be. Then, of course, if King Charles should happen to die – and he was, after all, gravely ill – there would be nothing to prevent Henry from claiming the throne of France for himself, especially if he was married to Catherine. But if the large dowry he was demanding could not be found, then Catherine could not become his wife. So, in the circumstances, would he not like to reconsider his demands?

The Bishop nodded doubtfully. He had tremendous respect for Isabeau's political acumen but was less sure of his own gifts as an actor.

Henry, a tactical soldier, was bemused by the turn of events. It was quite obvious to him that the murder of John the Fearless had entirely changed the political landscape. John's son Philip, the new Duke of Burgundy, was inexperienced, as was his faintly unpleasant cousin the Dauphin Charles, and neither young man was mature enough to present a serious challenge to what Henry wanted.

And what Henry wanted was the throne of France when old King Charles died. He wanted Catherine, too, so much more now that he had met her. He wanted her the way any man wants a beautiful woman. He wanted her in his bed, whether or not she brought the throne of France to their union. The thought that he could now have them both was irresistible.

It was time to make his move.

Queen Isabeau had spent a considerable amount of money on dancing lessons for Catherine who, having worked hard with her dancing master for several months, was now confident of her new skills. Her favourite dance, and quite the merriest in her repertoire, was the *saltarello,* the latest fashionable dance from Italy, and she revelled in the ease and fluidity with which she was now able to perform all the little kicks and jumps required of the dancers. She felt well-equipped to deal with the Christmas festivities at Troyes where the French court, their religious devotions completed, would be spending the rest of their time in music, dancing, and feasting.

Guillemote had tossed a handful of pine cones onto the crackling logs in the small fireplace in Catherine's bedchamber, and their fragrance mingled with the delicious smells of spit-roasting goose and wild boar which wafted up from the palace kitchens. Sitting at her little oak dressing table, Catherine could hear occasional snatches of music or a shriek of laughter from another room and was thrilled at the prospect of the festivities to come. She had decided on a crimson gown for the dancing and Guillemote, having finished dressing her mistress's hair, was now beginning to lace up the back of the bodice.

The excited barking of a small dog in the corridor outside the room heralded the arrival of the Queen and, a moment later, the door burst open to admit her. She was brandishing a piece of paper above her head as her yapping lap dog pranced around in excited circles in front of her then stood on its hind legs, pawing at her skirts. Pausing only to send the little creature skittering across the floor with the toe of her shoe, Isabeau pushed poor Guillemote impatiently out of her way and made a beeline for her daughter.

'Catherine! Catherine! Such good news!' she screeched, flinging her arms around her daughter's neck from behind and nearly upending her chair.

'What, my Lady? What is it?' Catherine attempted to stand, her unlaced gown falling from her shoulders. Isabeau took a step back and waved the piece of paper in her hand, a ribbon and seal dangling from it.

'Catherine, look! Look! It's from Rouen, where King Henry and Philip of Burgundy have been holding discussions. It is a copy of an agreement made between them yesterday and sent to us for our information. It will be formally issued today under the great seal of the King.'

'Let me see, Maman ...' Catherine reached out her hand, her gown falling off her shoulder again.

'Oh no, child,' Isabeau held the letter in an embrace against herself. 'Oh no! This is too important. I've waited too long for this. I'll read it to you.' With reverence, she held the piece of paper in both hands while she took a deep breath and began to read.

Catherine had succeeded in getting to her feet and Guillemote, who had been cowering against the wall since the Queen had shoved her to one side, began to make another attempt to lace up the crimson gown while her young mistress stood, anxiously clenching and unclenching her fists at her sides. Queen Isabeau, in a voice cracking with emotion and excitement, began to enumerate the proposed terms of the treaty designed to bring about a general truce between England and France. It was dated the twenty-fourth of December 1419.

Catherine listened intently. There were several points made in the agreement about the division of land between England and France; Normandy and Aquitaine were both to be handed back to the English crown and there were formal endorsements of some concessions made by Philip of Burgundy earlier in the month. Both the King and the new Duke agreed that, after the debacle at Montereau, the Dauphin's opinion should not be sought on any matter.

'Charles won't be pleased at that,' Catherine said. 'He is the Dauphin. He will inherit Papa's title.'

'Dauphin or not, his opinion doesn't count for anything,' said Isabeau, dismissing Catherine's comment with a wave of her hand. She began to read again. There was a clause in the agreement which secured the interests of Philip's wife, Michelle. Isabeau gave a whooping cheer at that, having heard that Michelle had become deeply melancholy after the death of her father-in-law, convinced that he had died at the hand of her own brother. Then Isabeau paused for a long moment and looked at Catherine.

'Now, Catherine, do you want the good news? The *really* good news?' She was quivering with excitement.

'Yes, yes, Maman. Don't tease me!'

Isabeau took a deep breath. 'Catherine, Henry wants to marry you. And ...' Isabeau didn't take her eyes off her daughter.

'Yes, Maman? What else?'

'He has dropped his demand for a dowry!'

'What? Completely?'

'Absolutely and entirely!' Isabeau let the letter fall to the table and held out her arms to her daughter. The pair hugged each other, not knowing whether to laugh or cry and doing both at the same time, tears running down their faces.

Saucer-eyed, Guillemote watched the two of them, the Queen of France and the future Queen of England, embracing and jigging around the room like a pair of over-excited children. How things were going to change from now on, she thought. She would have to go to England with her mistress and live among English people. And everyone *knew* that Englishmen had tails!

Guillemote crossed herself fervently.

Chapter Four

Troyes, France, May 1420

Catherine had to fight the urge to sneeze as motes of thick building dust danced in the shaft of coloured light streaming in through a magnificent stained glass window in the great Cathedral of St Peter and St Paul. At least, she assumed the window to be magnificent since her view of it was rather obscured by a tower of wooden scaffolding supporting a stonemason's work platform. Today the mallets and chisels lay unused and silent while a peal of bells rang out the message that the business in hand was the ceremonial signing of the Treaty of Troyes, followed by the betrothal of His Royal Highness King Henry V of England to Her Royal Highness the Princess Catherine de Valois of France.

Her one abiding memory of that May morning was the look of triumph on her mother's face as a fanfare greeted her entrance into the cathedral on the arm of her son-in-law Philip of Burgundy. At exactly the same time, King Henry made his entrance with his brother Thomas, the Duke of Clarence, from the opposite door. The four, with their attendants and advisers, met at the crossing which intersected the nave and the transepts, before moving in procession towards the high altar, on which lay the final draft of the Treaty of Troyes. The document already bore the signature of King Charles VI of France who, suffering another bout of his old malady, was not present. Now came the turn of the King of England, then the Queen of France, to sign the document, witnessed by several members of the French and English aristocracy. Under the terms of the Treaty, it was agreed that Henry would become ruler of both countries on the eventual death of the King of France.

Then Archbishop Henri de Savoisy summoned Catherine up to the high altar to take her place at the side of her future husband. Peace was declared between their two countries, God's blessing was invoked, and the formal betrothal took place.

Things moved quickly now. For Henry, the most urgent task was to send a message to his brother, Humphrey of Gloucester, who was performing the duties of Regent in England. He wished to inform Gloucester of recent developments and to issue his instructions. An official proclamation was to be made at St Paul's Cross in London, of the peace between England and France and of the King's impending marriage. He ended with an instruction to the Duke and the Council to destroy his seals and to strike new ones, bearing the inscription: *Henry by the grace of God King of England, and Regent of the Crown of France, and Lord of Ireland.*

Guillemote had been staying up until well into the night, working by candlelight alongside two of the royal seamstresses, helping to stitch Catherine's trousseau. The wedding gown was the most beautiful thing Guillemote had ever seen and she stored it with great care in the garderobe, as near as possible to the latrine chute where the bad smells would protect it from the unwelcome attention of moths. Though she was almost afraid to touch it, it did need a very minor last-minute alteration. She worked first in trepidation and then with reverence on the sumptuous cloth of gold.

Her painstaking devotion to her mistress was rewarded by the sight of her on a fine morning in early June: Catherine looked magnificent in her bridal finery. It was such a shame, Guillemote thought, that because of the ongoing building work, the great cathedral at Troyes was deemed unsafe for such an important wedding ceremony. The smaller church of St Jean-au-Marché was to be used instead.

A large, excited crowd had gathered in the market square to catch a glimpse of the wedding guests as they arrived. When the last guest had been ushered into the church, Catherine took her place between her mother and Philip of Burgundy, under a canopy of red silk held aloft by four men of the royal guard.

Her sister Michelle, looking whey-faced and thin, stood passively behind her husband.

Guillemote had to swallow hard to control her emotions as she hovered on the periphery of the wedding party, watching to make sure that no last-minute adjustment was necessary. Earlier that morning, she had washed Catherine's long fair hair in her favourite soap of Marseilles and rinsed it several times in an infusion of rosemary leaves, polishing it between two lengths of silk as it dried, until it shone. Now, unbraided as befitted a bride and held in place by a little headdress of twisted gold, it cascaded in burnished waves to Catherine's trim waist.

Everything about her was golden; she shimmered with beauty. Her creamy skin seemed to reflect the rich gold of her gown and even her shoes were decorated with little gold buckles. Guillemote had fussed with the long train of the gown, making sure it was correctly folded and supported by Catherine's attendants. She couldn't bear to think of it dragging in the dirt and whatever else might be on the ground. Nothing must be allowed to spoil Catherine's appearance.

Inside the church, the call of a single bugle-horn warned the waiting soldier-king that his bride approached and when Catherine made her entrance on the arm of Philip of Burgundy, Henry was spellbound at the sight of her. He felt an enormous sense of pleasure and of triumph that she came to him not only as his bride but as the living symbol of the unification of France and England. He was about to achieve the pinnacle of his military ambition and to possess the object of his desire at one and the same time.

Archbishop de Savoisy began the marriage ceremony by taking Catherine's right hand and placing it in Henry's. Henry squeezed her thumb and gave her a secret smile.

Trinity Sunday, the second of June 1420, was the day when the English and French royal families had the opportunity of getting to know each other, united at last under the terms of the Treaty of Troyes and by the day's royal wedding.

As far as Henry was concerned, it was very much Catherine's day and he was fully prepared to indulge her. At the

45

reception which preceded the wedding feast, he stood back for a moment and watched the elegance with which she moved among the wedding guests, smiling and laughing with her family. He delighted in her girlishness as she shared a secret with two of her cousins, their heads bent close as they whispered together. Duke Philip's sister, Anne of Burgundy, was the youngest and the most inclined to giggle at whatever little confidence was being exchanged. The Countess Jacqueline of Hainault, who had travelled from Holland to attend the wedding, was taller than the other two and not unlike Catherine in looks, though her features were heavier and less well-defined. There was no doubt in Henry's mind that Catherine was by far the most beautiful of the three cousins. Catherine's sister Michelle, the new Duchess of Burgundy, watched them impassively as she stood to one side with her husband, the Duke. Henry grimaced when he noticed that Philip was draped from head to toe in black, in mourning for John the Fearless.

The bridegroom's family was less well represented and King Henry felt a deep regret that his uncle, Bishop Henry Beaufort, was not among the guests. Beaufort was his father's half-brother and a man he had always liked and admired until a grave misunderstanding had arisen between them, and the Bishop had made his resentment plain by not attending his nephew's wedding. Yet, despite their disagreement, Henry found himself hoping that his uncle would like his new wife. Then he smiled to himself. How could anyone not like her!

He took great pleasure in seeing the way his brothers looked at Catherine. Thomas, Duke of Clarence, with his wife at his side, was necessarily circumspect. The rich and autocratic Duchess Margaret was a year older than her husband and had the air of a woman who was not to be trifled with. Margaret had been married before and it was a source of great sadness to her that she had no children from her second marriage. But she was a devout woman and prayed that the Lord would grant her fervent wish for a second family.

Humphrey of Gloucester was not present but John of Bedford, enchanted by his new sister-in-law, was following her around the room like a big puppy, taking every opportunity to offer her sweetmeats or to re-fill her goblet, his round face aglow, his rather beaky nose twitching with pleasure. Henry gloated as he watched. This beautiful creature was his bride, entirely his and his brothers' tongues could hang down to their knees for all Henry cared because nothing could take her away from him. No one else would ever have Catherine, not now, not ever. No one but Henry.

The King of England and his new queen sat close together throughout the wedding feast, at the centre of the long table on a raised dais at the end of the room. Over their heads was a canopy of red silk, richly embroidered with the coats of arms of both families, with their symbols entwined. French royal traditions had prevailed throughout the wedding day and at the end of the evening, the feasting and dancing over, Henry stood and held out his hand to Catherine, smiling his encouragement as he caught the sudden expression of uncertainty on her face. Then, as she rose from her seat at the table, so too did several other people, including Queen Isabeau, the Duke and Duchess of Burgundy, the Countess Jacqueline of Holland, and Archbishop Henri de Savoisy.

'Why so many people?' demanded Henry, frowning. 'Is this really necessary?'

'It is a family tradition, my Lord,' said Queen Isabeau, 'and it is quite a short ceremony so I would be grateful if you would indulge my wishes.' She leaned towards him, gave him a very knowing look and dropped her voice. 'I promise that it will not keep you long from the joys of the marriage bed.' Henry smiled at her words. He understood his new mother-in-law only too well. He knew that had she been twenty years younger, she would have been pleased to share those joys with him; she didn't have to tell him so.

Following the Queen's example, yet more people rose from the table and accompanied the bridal couple to their bedchamber where they all clustered in a semi-circle around the foot of the bed, their heads bowed. Then the Archbishop was handed a silver bowl. Dipping his fingers into it, he began to sprinkle holy water.

'Bless, oh Lord, this marriage bed,' he intoned, 'that it shall

47

be as fruitful as the garden of Eden, so that the husbandman who plants his seed and the goodwife who receives and nurtures it shall, through your divine mercy, be delivered of strong sons to be brought up in the true faith. Amen.'

'Amen.' The French nobles and their wives crossed themselves with great solemnity.

'Amen,' said Henry, trying to keep a straight face. He had every intention of planting his seed at the first possible opportunity and, without actually pushing anyone, he almost shooed them out of the room. Queen Isabeau, the Duchess of Burgundy, and the Countess Jacqueline of Holland accompanied Catherine to her dressing room, where Guillemote was waiting to help her take off her wedding finery.

Relishing the prospect of having his new bride entirely to himself, Henry abruptly dismissed the valet who had helped him shrug off his heavy, ornate doublet. Alone at last, he pulled on a *robe de chambre* and sat down to wait for Catherine.

She came to him attired in a simple white nightgown, hesitating in the doorway of the bedchamber. Relishing the sight of her, Henry rose from his chair, took her hand, and pulled her gently into the room, closing the door behind her.

'My Lord,' she whispered, her eyes downcast, blushing in the candlelight.

'Henry,' he corrected her, smiling. 'We are man and wife now, Catherine, safe from prying eyes in our own bedchamber. Man and wife. You must no longer think of me only as your king. I am also your husband.'

'Henry,' she said quietly. 'My husband.'

With her hand still in his, he led her towards the bed where the covers had been turned back. Bending, he put his finger under her chin, raising her face to his. 'Catherine,' he choked, suddenly overwhelmed. He buried his face in her shoulder, the faint scent of lavender in the soft hair at the nape of her neck rousing him to a passion he hoped he could control. He knew he mustn't frighten her or take her too roughly, he must remember that she was not a strumpet from the stews at Southwark. Catherine was young, not yet nineteen years old, an innocent from a nunnery. But he found his passion difficult to manage.

His hands slid down her spine and pressed her body against his own. Then the two, their arms entwined, fell as one onto the goose-feather mattress. Panting now, and between urgent kisses, Henry had begun to tug at the fastenings of Catherine's nightgown when there was a loud rhythmic knock at the door.

'Who the hell …?'

Catherine drew away from him, clutching her nightgown to her breasts. 'That will be the soup,' she said, by way of explanation.

'Soup!' he bellowed. 'God's wounds! Who ordered bloody soup?'

'It's … er … it's the custom,' she said as the door opened and a long procession of the French wedding guests came into the bedchamber. Some were carrying bowls of soup and bread on trays and others had flasks of red wine, all of which they set down on a table near the bed, with spoons, goblets, and napkins for the bridal couple. Then they inspected the bed for signs that it had been used for its matrimonial purpose and though it was hardly rumpled as yet, they seemed quite satisfied that it soon would be.

Henry watched, flabbergasted, his passion subsiding as quickly as it had been aroused. Having delivered their ceremonial meal, the guests processed through the room, nodding, smiling and wishing the bride and groom every blessing on their marriage. Then they were gone.

Henry fell backwards onto the bed, almost helpless with laughter.

'Dear God, are there any more pantomimes to be endured?'

Catherine, sitting on the bed beside him, was smiling. 'No, Henry. I think they realised that you would soon be fulfilling your intentions, even though we hadn't … well, you know … we hadn't …' she hesitated. 'Well, anyway, there should be no more pantomimes.'

'You promise?'

'I promise. But …' Catherine hesitated again.

'But what?'

She looked at her new husband uncertainly, her eyes large and luminous in the candlelight. 'Well, now I have to prove something to myself,' she said.

'Prove what, sweetheart?' asked Henry, pushing a tendril of hair away from her face and trying to pull her down towards him. God, he thought, swelling again, how he wanted her.

Catherine held back from him, a small frown creasing her forehead. 'Well, Guillemote says ...'

'What does Guillemote say, my love?' Henry was reaching up to nibble at her earlobe now, his eyes half closed, not really listening.

'Guillemote says that all Englishmen have tails.'

Henry stopped nibbling. 'What?' He hoisted himself up onto his elbow and looked at her, astounded. 'Englishmen have tails! She really thinks that?'

'Yes, she does. Many French people do. Now, I suppose, I will find out for myself.'

Henry rolled over onto his back, guffawing with laughter. Then he paused and looked up at Catherine who was watching him with a small, hesitant smile on her face.

'Oh, my love,' he said, pulling her down towards him so that her head was on his shoulder. 'Come, give me your hand.' With infinite tenderness, he reached for her hand and guided it downwards on to the flat of his stomach.

'Englishmen do have tails, you know,' he whispered against her hair, smiling in the half-light, 'but not on their backsides.'

'What!' Catherine's eyes widened in alarm and she tried to draw back from him but her hand was imprisoned in his.

'This is mine,' he said, 'but it's at the front, not at the back. And this Englishman's tail is wagging very hard indeed.'

Henry spent the next two days doting on his new wife and tutoring her gently in the ways of love. Catherine made the joyous discovery that, though she had not really known what to expect once the door of the bedchamber was closed, she was able to respond to her new husband's ardour with pleasure and with a surprising appetite for more.

Two new harps had been ordered from John Bore, the London harp-maker, one for Henry and one for Catherine as a wedding gift. Henry played his instrument with considerable skill and sang in a warm baritone voice. They were delighted to realise that her voice blended pleasingly with his and they discovered the joy of singing together. She could have stayed in their bedchamber forever, making music, making love.

But it couldn't last. The following day, a ceremonial mid-day feast was held in the great hall of the castle at Troyes. Some of Henry's own military musicians, the pipe and tabor players, had joined the musicians of the Valois court, making quite a large ensemble in the minstrels' gallery. They were already playing popular airs and gigues as the guests arrived. King Charles was still confined to bed so Queen Isabeau and her daughter Michelle were escorted to the royal dais at the end of the room by Philip of Burgundy. A fanfare on the bugle-horn from the minstrels' gallery and a scatter of applause greeted the entrance of the bridal couple as they made their way through the room and took their places once again at the centre of the high table under the same red silken baldaquin. Archbishop Henri de Savoisy said a short grace and, after much scraping of chairs and benches, some eighty guests sat down to await their meal.

They were not disappointed. No sooner had the assembled company settled themselves at the tables than the food began to arrive, born aloft on trays by troops of servants. The royal chef had excelled himself. Course after delicious course was served and the table on the royal dais was graced with three dressed swans, their wired necks elegantly bent and decorated with garlands. Alongside each bird was a bowl of rich *chaudron* sauce.

'This makes a change from battlefield fare!' said Henry to his new mother-in-law. 'Do you always eat as well as this?'

'The Valois court is renowned for it,' said Queen Isabeau, 'so there are always plenty of guests at our table.'

'I'm not surprised. What's the secret?'

'Tradition, mainly. A tradition established by my father-in-law's master cook Guillaume Taillevant. Our present chef was one of his students and he himself now has several apprentices working with him in the kitchens.'

'Mmmm,' said Henry, licking his fingers before dipping them in a small bowl of water infused with rosemary and orange peel. He wiped them on his sleeve then turned to Catherine. 'I hope you won't be disappointed in our English food, my sweet. Maybe we should persuade one of the apprentice chefs from the palace kitchens to come back to England with us.'

'But there's more to life than food,' she said, giving Henry a conspiratorial smile as she squeezed his hand under the table. It was quite clear what she was thinking. 'How soon shall we set out for England, my Lord?'

'Not for a little time yet,' said Henry. 'I have things I must attend to here in France. And the longer I leave them, the more urgent they become.'

They had been so engrossed in each other that the Duke of Clarence had to tap his brother's shoulder to attract his attention.

'Some of the younger English knights are keen to spend tomorrow in the tiltyard, jousting for the favours of the ladies of the French court,' he said as Henry craned his neck to hear him above the din. 'I told them I thought we should ask your permission before arranging anything. What do you think? Shall we give the young bloods their heads?'

The Duke was forced to step back rapidly. Henry had leapt to his feet and was banging the table with the handle of his knife. There was sudden silence in the great hall and all eyes turned to the royal dais. The bridegroom, who had smiled adoringly at his new wife for the last two days, now looked thunderous. He breathed deeply and waited until he had everyone's attention.

'My lords,' he roared, his voice reaching every corner of the room, 'I understand that there are those among you who have a mind to spend the morrow in jousting.' There was a general murmur of agreement and one or two people clapped their hands until Henry banged the table again.

'I will not permit it. We have all enjoyed a time of great celebration over the last weeks, a celebration of my marriage to the Princess Catherine and of the peace which has been agreed with the people of France, the peace which now entitles us, in due course, to return home to England.'

At this, a great cheer went up. Henry smiled as he waited until he had everyone's attention again, then he went on. 'But that peace is still uncertain and I am not naïve enough to assume that neither the treaty nor my marriage will meet with everyone's approval. There are those here in France who believe that this union with England should be resisted at all costs. We must root out those pockets of resistance and bring them to heel. So there will be no *playing* at fighting in the castle tiltyard tomorrow. I will not run the risk of injury to any one of you, so let us not squander our energies by *pretending* to fight.'

Several people muttered their disappointment. Henry paused and looked around the great hall then he spoke again, his voice lower now, more threatening. 'Once again, my Lords, I implore you – nay, I command you – to stiffen the sinews because tomorrow, by the grace of God and with the blessed intercession of St Crispin and St John of Bridlington, I intend to begin preparations for the siege of Sens. You will hold yourselves in readiness for that.'

There was a shocked silence then everyone babbled at once before breaking into spontaneous applause. Puzzled, Catherine turned anxiously to Henry as he resumed his seat beside her.

'But, my Lord, it is so pleasant here at court. Why must you return to battle so soon? '

'Because your fellow countrymen must learn who is now the ruler of this country.'

'My father is the King.'

'Yes, of course he is,' Henry was quick to agree, 'but while he still suffers from his malady, I intend to guard his interests and Sens must be brought into line with Paris where the citizens acknowledge that they now have an English overlord. It's time for the people of Sens to do the same and stop this bickering and bloodshed.'

Catherine sighed and put down her knife. Raising her goblet, she took a sip of wine.

'So, my Lord,' she said, 'when will we travel to England? When will I see my new country? When will I taste English food?'

Startled, Henry looked hard at her but she appeared simply

to want an answer to her question. 'In due time, Catherine, in due time,' he said. He didn't want to introduce her to pease pudding and brawn too early in their relationship.

The first six months of marriage to Henry had altered Catherine's outlook on life quite considerably. No longer the little convent girl, she was fast becoming a sophisticated young woman, growing in confidence and always beautifully dressed. The Duchess of Clarence had taken her in hand and spent hours with her every day, grooming her for her future role as Queen of England, explaining what kind of behaviour would be expected of her as King Henry's wife, and giving her intensive lessons in the English language. She was anxious to impress upon her young sister-in-law that the King was determined to see English become the common language of the court and that, as Queen, she should set an example.

With great patience, Margaret explained how things were done in England and explained which noble Englishmen were responsible for various aspects of governance. But she also took pleasure in helping Catherine choose patterns and fabrics for new gowns and would sit for hours watching the patient Guillemote as she devised new ways of dressing Catherine's hair. Being considerably older than the young queen and very much more experienced, Margaret proved a patient tutor.

And Catherine proved herself a willing pupil in all aspects of her intensive education. Her dancing lessons continued as well as her harp lessons and she had always loved singing. So during that autumn, on the rare occasions when Henry could find time to be with her, she would delight and entrance him by singing, to her own accompaniment, the songs she had learned from the precious song-book which had been another wedding gift from Henry.

He, on the other hand, had been preoccupied with subduing the French and bringing them to heel. Sens had fallen to the English without much trouble. Then, in December, the Dauphin Charles had been summoned to attend a meeting where he was required to answer charges relating to the death of John the Fearless at Montereau. He did not appear. As a result, a sentence of banishment was passed and a declaration made that the Dauphin was incapable of succeeding to the throne of France.

Henry's future as King of England and of France was assured. Now, he turned his attention to the movement of his troops. It was high time the fighting men of England went home.

Catherine had heard people talk of the sea but she had never seen it herself. As they arrived in Calais, she caught her breath in surprise at the vast expanse of grey water which looked as though it reached to infinity and she felt quite weak-kneed at the prospect of travelling on it in a ship, even with her husband at her side.

Henry was as excited as a small boy when the bosun piped them aboard the *Grace Dieu*. The huge vessel was almost brand new and towered over every other ship in the French port.

'Welcome,' said Henry, giving Catherine his hand to help her onto the deck, scrubbed spotless in their honour. 'Welcome, my dearest lady, as you step onto English territory for the first time.'

'*Grace Dieu*, it is an English ship, my Lord?'

'Oh, indeed. The pride of the fleet of the Cinque Ports. Perhaps I should have insisted she be called *God's Grace*. After all, she's English through and through, built from good English oak, the best there is. Ah, Captain Payne! The *Grace Dieu* does you proud, sir.'

Captain William Payne bowed low. 'Thank you, Your Highness, and you're very welcome aboard. Welcome, my Lady. Yes, she is an excellent ship. The whole crew takes a great pride in her.'

'She could put paid to any challenge from a French vessel!'

'It is very unlikely that we will be challenged, Sire. The French now openly acknowledge our supremacy in the channel.'

'Aye, perhaps we are the victims of our own success, Captain. Now that we are more at peace with France, this ship won't be needed for battle. I'm glad of that. It means that we have achieved what we set out to do.'

'Indeed, Sire, and the whole of England rejoices in your success. I know that there will be many people waiting to welcome you home.'

Henry smiled. 'And do you expect a calm sea and a following wind for our voyage today, Captain?'

'Yes, Your Grace. She'll cut a fine feather between here and Dover, you see if she doesn't.' Catherine remembered that curious expression and mentally added it to her burgeoning English vocabulary.

On the first of February, under full sail and at the head of a convoy of troop ships, the *Grace Dieu* moved out into the channel with elegance and speed, her bow wave feathering out to either side of her, gulls swooping and calling noisily in her wake. Blinking against sudden tears at the sight of the rapidly receding French coastline, Catherine turned her face resolutely towards England and her future.

In the biting cold wind, and finding it difficult to keep her footing on deck once the ship had reached the open sea, Catherine was pleased to be shown to a seat in the comparative warmth and comfort of the Captain's accommodation on the quarterdeck. But within the hour, she was feeling very sick indeed. She hadn't realised that a ship, even one as magnificent as the *Grace Dieu*, could buck like a horse as she fought her way through the waves. With her stomach churning painfully, Catherine felt certain that she would disgrace herself by vomiting in front of everyone. Seeing her face drained of colour, Captain Payne, with a sympathetic smile, produced a small phial containing a decoction of chervil which he claimed would put paid to her sea sickness. He also advised that she should move to a position where she could keep the horizon in view at all times. Between them, with Guillemote hovering anxiously in their wake, the Captain and the King helped Catherine make her way to a sheltered seat on deck.

Eventually, her nausea abated a little and Catherine closed her eyes. When she opened them again, Henry was no longer at her side but leaning on the ship's rail, gazing into the distance where majestic, ghostly white cliffs were just visible, rising sheer out of the sea.

'Dover,' said Henry, 'the gateway to England. God, it's good to be going home!'

Once past the mud bank at the mouth of the port, Captain Payne barked the order to heave the great ship across the wind and the little town of Dover came into view, nestling between the towering white cliffs, boats bobbing at anchor in the sheltered harbour, the grey castle keep on the hill above the town rising like a finger pointing towards heaven. Leaving all other thoughts aside, Catherine hoped fervently that England would be dry and warm.

On an ebb tide, the draught of the *Grace Dieu* prevented her from going any further inshore so Captain Payne gave the order to drop anchor a little way out and small boats were deployed to take the royal party ashore. Catherine could see crowds of people on the beach and on the headland, waving and shouting in welcome. Above the din of pipes and drums, she heard great shouts of 'God Save the King! Long live the King! God save England and St George! God save Harry!'

'Harry? They call you Harry in England?'

Turning to her husband as he looked towards the crowded foreshore, she saw an expression on his face that she had never seen there before; it was pure, unalloyed joy, as though Henry was looking at the greatest love of his life.

Nodding, he spoke quietly then, almost as though he was talking to himself. 'Yes, they do call me Harry, especially when they're pleased with me!'

Standing up suddenly in the small boat, he let out a great roar and raised both arms above his head, waving to the crowds on the shore. Mad with excitement, they waved back and, as the boat approached, several of them began wading fully clothed into the sea. Waist-deep in the freezing water, they reached out and grabbed the prow of the boat and began tugging it towards the shore with great rhythmic shouts of 'Wel-come! Wel-come!'. When they had beached it, willing hands helped the King and his new queen from the boat and on to dry land.

Catherine stumbled. It was an odd sensation being able to stand on firm ground after the incessant motion of the *Grace Dieu*. Guards were clearing a path, holding back the crowds of people who were pressing in from all sides, calling to the King, vying with each other for his attention and chattering excitedly in a foreign language. Henry turned and reached out to Catherine with both hands, steadying her.

'Welcome, my little landlubber,' he smiled. 'Welcome to England. We're safely home.'

Chapter Five

London, February 1421

The journey from Dover to the palace at Eltham was a revelation for Catherine. No sooner had the long procession of courtiers, servants, and guards left the port than she became aware that, every now and then, groups of people would appear as though from nowhere and run alongside the royal procession, waving excitedly with cries of 'God save the King!' and 'God save Harry of England!'. The eager, noisy welcome they received at every village and hamlet they passed through made her realise that Henry was a popular king, much loved by his people, and she had been delighted to hear shouts of 'God save the Queen!' when they saw her at his side. She waved back at them excitedly, despite the disapproval of the Duchess of Clarence who thought Catherine should be a little more restrained and dignified. Margaret had elected to return to England with the royal couple so as to continue the education of her young sister-in-law, while her husband Thomas stayed in France to oversee his brother's interests there.

Uppermost in Catherine's mind was her coronation. It had been arranged for Sunday, the twenty-third of February in Westminster Abbey and she was full of questions about what she could expect.

'Leave it all to Humphrey and to Dick,' said her husband as they took breakfast together in their private solar at Eltham. 'You concentrate on looking your prettiest for the people who will, no doubt, flock to see you, my love. Apart from that, you just need to repeat your vows. Don't bother to learn them. They'll be in Latin, not English, so you're unlikely to make mistakes.'

'Dick? Who is Dick?'

'Whittington. Richard Whittington. He has just stepped down as London's Lord Mayor for the third time. Unprecedented. You'll like him, he's very generous. He's forever saving fallen women and the like. Richest man in London.'

'Really?'

'Oh yes, he's a mercer and a good one. Top of his trade. It means he can lend us money when we need it for troops and supplies. His terms are good, too.'

Catherine looked puzzled. 'He lends you money? But you are the King!'

'My dear love, the crown is constantly in need of money. You should know that. Your father's court is one of the poorest in Europe. Wars don't come cheap, which is why I need people like Dick Whittington. My uncle, Henry Beaufort, is another source of finance, but then he, too, can easily afford his magnanimity. He gave us fourteen thousand pounds before the last French campaign.'

Catherine still disliked being reminded that her husband had been responsible for the deaths of so many of her fellow countrymen. She changed the subject.

'When will I meet him? Your uncle?'

Henry hesitated. 'I don't know. I have sent a messenger to invite him to your coronation but have had no reply as yet. Still, my brother and Whittington will attend you so you'll be in good hands.'

'I wish you were going to be with me, too.'

'Etiquette forbids it, my love. I've already been crowned. So it would make no sense. Besides, it's you the people will want to see. Humphrey will be my representative at the ceremony, and Dick will represent the people. Dick deserves favour. He has always been generous and God knows what I would have done without him in the past. If it wasn't for him and his apparently bottomless coffers, victory in France would have been twice as hard to achieve.'

There was that reminder again. Catherine made a light-hearted reply. 'And perhaps we wouldn't be married,' she said.

'And perhaps we wouldn't be married,' Henry agreed, dropping a kiss on top of her head as he rose from the table. 'So we have even more cause to be grateful. Anyway, I've sent for him and for Archbishop Chichele. Humphrey, too, of course. He's organising the whole thing. Those three will tell you all you need to know about the ceremony. Humphrey has arranged a meeting here at Eltham to advise you, so that you will know exactly what to expect.'

Richard Whittington was the first to arrive. He was really quite an old man, his hair and his neat beard were white but he stood straight-backed and walked well and there was a look of great honesty about him. He bent low over Catherine's hand when she offered it to him to be kissed.

'Your Highness,' he said. 'It is the greatest honour to be asked to advise you in the matter of your coronation.'

Catherine inclined her head and murmured a reply just as the Archbishop of Canterbury, Henry Chichele, was shown into the room, closely followed by Humphrey of Gloucester, carrying a ledger and a sheaf of documents. Gloucester took immediate charge of proceedings, calling for chairs to be arranged around a table, with a clerk sitting at a desk nearby to note what had been agreed.

Catherine watched all three men as discussions began. Richard Whittington and Archbishop Chichele both seemed very pleasant in an elderly, avuncular way, smiling as they told her about the arrangements which had already been made. She warmed particularly to Henry Chichele. His was a powerful face with slightly protruding eyes of a piercing blue which wore an expression of determination tinged with curiosity. She had first met him two years ago when, having been with Henry at the siege of Rouen, he had stayed on in France for the meeting in Poissy. It took her a moment to place him in her memory of that day, having met so many English noblemen at the same time. She remembered the babble of English voices which had been so difficult to understand. She understood them very much better now and felt a great deal more confident these days, now that she was married to Henry and about to be crowned his queen.

'So I'm afraid there is no avoiding that problem, my Lady,' Gloucester's voice cut across her reverie.

She tried not to look startled. '*Pardon*?'

Humphrey gave her an irritated look. 'My Lady, since your coronation is arranged for the third Sunday in Lent, certain restrictions must be observed and this will clearly affect the type of food which can be served at the banquet following the ceremony. We would like to know whether you have any preferences for dishes which do not contain meat.'

'We must not gainsay the teachings of the Holy Mother Church,' Henry Chichele agreed. 'The eating of meat cannot be allowed.'

'How many courses do we expect to be served?' asked Humphrey.

'At least five,' said Richard Whittington. 'So someone will have to be very inventive with fish!'

Humphrey looked up, annoyed at the disturbance as the door suddenly burst open to admit the King, closely followed by a tall man in the dark robes of a bishop. Catherine rose from her seat in surprise. She had thought Henry to be in Westminster. He hadn't been expected here at Eltham.

'My love,' he said without preamble, grabbing her hand. 'This is going to be such a wonderful coronation. I would like you to meet my dear kinsman, Bishop Henry Beaufort, my Lancaster uncle on my father's side. He was in London after all, when I had thought him away and about his business in Winchester.'

'And his cup runneth over,' said Henry Beaufort, smiling at Catherine as he bent to kiss her hand. 'My dear lady, I am enchanted. Everything I have heard about your beauty is evidently true.'

'I told you, Uncle, didn't I?' Henry was excited. 'Is Catherine not the most exquisite creature?'

'Yes, yes, indeed. And well is she named. My late mother was named Katherine and she, too, was a renowned beauty in her day.'

'Then history is repeating itself,' said Henry. He turned to

62

his brother. 'Humphrey, are things going well?'

'Everything is in place,' said Gloucester. 'Whittington has made some very interesting suggestions about how London will stage a memorable welcome for the Queen, and the Archbishop is pleased with my arrangements for the Abbey church, are you not, your Grace?'

'Yes, my Lord Duke, and now I have your assurance that the rules governing Lent will not be broken, I am perfectly happy with everything,' said Henry Chichele. 'There will be no meat served at the meal to celebrate the coronation. But that is now more a matter for the Westminster palace cook than for me. We men of the church should concern ourselves more with the spiritual aspects of the occasion, rather than the secular ones. Don't you agree, Bishop?'

He turned to Henry Beaufort, who chuckled in agreement. 'Yes, I dare say so. But a meal consisting entirely of fish is surely unlikely to stimulate the appetite.'

'That's exactly what I said!' agreed Whittington. 'How many ways are there of dressing up a poor fish! Could he be served as pudding with a sweet custard sauce?'

Catherine grimaced and amid the laughter, the King held up his hand for silence. 'Ah,' he said in a conspiratorial voice, 'but we have a trick up our sleeves. We have brought a chef with us from the royal kitchens of France. If anyone can rise to the challenge, Anton will.'

Guillemote found England a very confusing place but it was unthinkable that she should desert Catherine. Like Anton, the chef, she had grown up in the service of the Valois family and they had both been brought to England to serve Catherine. Neither of them questioned the decision.

So here she was in a foreign land where people spoke in a foreign tongue and confused her even further by having foreign names. And now she worked with three English women, all of whom had been newly recruited to Catherine's service by the Duchess Margaret and all of whom had exactly the same name: Joanna. They, too, had found it confusing but had solved the problem with much merriment by using each other's surnames,

Troutbeck, Courcy, and Belknap. The three Joannas. Catherine and Guillemote promptly nicknamed them *Les Trois Jo-jo*.

Now, in the Palace of Westminster on the morning of February the twenty-third, Catherine stood in her dressing room. She was clad only in her shift, a kerchief tied over her neatly braided hair. The Duchess Margaret watched intently, scrutinising every detail as the women dressed the young queen for her coronation. Catherine held up her arms obediently as Troutbeck and Courcy, one either side of her, lowered a magnificent gown of white embroidered silk over her head. Guillemote busied herself with adjusting the tapes in the lining of the garment which would lift Catherine's small breasts and present a pleasing outline under the bodice. Troutbeck turned her attention to attaching the ornate sleeves to the bodice of the gown while Courcy addressed herself to the problem of getting the sixteen small, fashionable buttons at the back of the bodice to line up correctly with their corresponding button loops. Then Guillemote untied the flimsy kerchief which covered Catherine's hair and stood back to look at her mistress with a critical eye.

'How do I look?' Catherine's voice sounded small.

'Pale, my Lady,' answered Guillemote. 'You always do when you're wearing white. Try pinching your cheeks.'

'That's no good,' said Belknap. 'It won't last. If we use a little brazilwood, the colour will remain in Her Majesty's cheeks throughout the day.'

'She must not look like a painted doll,' said the Duchess Margaret in some alarm.

'Don't worry, my Lady, she won't. I'll only use a little of this.' Joanna Belknap picked up a small pot of brazilwood chips which had been soaking in rosewater. 'There's no need to use very much of it. Besides,' she added, 'it's very expensive. It comes all the way from the Orient.' Barely moistening a cloth with the pink liquid, she applied it lightly to Catherine's cheeks, while Guillemote held up a hand mirror for Catherine to watch her progress.

'For pity's sake, don't drop any on the gown!' said the Duchess, who had never come across the precious cosmetic aid.

'It will stain it!'

'Don't worry, Your Grace, I'm being very careful.'

'Oh, that's a lot better,' said Troutbeck, peering closely at Catherine as Belknap stood back to admire her handiwork. 'You look very beautiful, my Lady.'

'Yes, my dear, you do. You look very beautiful,' the Duchess agreed. 'I'm sure the King will approve.'

'Thanks to you, all of you,' said Catherine, smoothing down her skirts. 'Now, where is my cloak? It must surely be almost time to leave for the abbey.'

It was. Henry awaited her and she felt a curious mixture of elation and nervousness when she saw the pride in his eyes as he accompanied her to the door of the Palace. He bent to kiss her before the hasp was lifted.

'This is your day,' he whispered, 'so God be with you, sweetheart. I will be awaiting your return tonight.'

Then the heavy door opened, letting in a rush of cold air. The crowd of people who had gathered outside shouted and waved at their first glimpse of Catherine. Smiling broadly, Henry took her by the hand and escorted her to where Richard Whittington was standing with Archbishop Chichele and the Duke of Gloucester. With due ceremony, the King kissed the hand of his queen and presented her to the representative of his people. Whittington greeted her with a smile and bowed low. Then he held out his left arm to escort her and she placed her right hand on it, straightening her back as she did so. She heard a barked order and a drum roll before the bugle-horns sounded a fanfare. Then she and Richard Whittington, walking behind the Duke and the Archbishop, moved off slowly under a silken canopy held aloft by the Wardens of the Cinque Ports in all their regalia, on the short procession from the Palace to the Abbey.

Smells were what Catherine always remembered. The holy oil with which she was anointed by Archbishop Chichele smelled musky and old, while the Archbishop's robes were perfumed with the incense he had burned in countless celebrations of the mass, not quite disguising the odour of sweat as he stood in front of her, holding her crown aloft in both hands before placing it on her head. Despite the weight of it, she held her head erect, and when the ceremony was over she rose with dignity from her throne and followed the Archbishop as he led the coronation procession out of the Abbey. The great west door was thrown open and the newly crowned Queen of England emerged into the cold, damp February air as the Edward Bell in the tower started to chime a deep, sonorous note. It was a signal for the huge throng of people crowding around the Abbey steps to start cheering and it seemed that they could go on cheering all day and all night without tiring. Standing under the silken baldaquin, which did little to keep off the mizzling rain, she smiled for them and waved at them, delighted by their approval and the warmth of their welcome.

The great crowd of people, their enthusiasm undiminished by the weather, seemed reluctant to let her go but the royal procession eventually moved off towards the Palace of Westminster for the coronation feast. Inside the Palace, the great and the good jostled to be near their new Sovereign Lady and the presence of so many nobles was causing some anxiety for the Duke of Gloucester. He hovered anxiously as everyone took their places according to rank, lest arguments should arise about who had the right to sit closest to the royal dais and who must sit below the salt.

When the babble of voices subsided and everyone was seated, a steward made a sign to the Master of the King's Music and two bugle horns played an exultant fanfare. The guests rose to their feet and began applauding as Humphrey of Gloucester escorted the Queen towards the high table. He appeared to be limping slightly so Catherine gave him a sympathetic smile as he helped her to negotiate the step up to the dais. She stood for a moment at her place between the royal guest, King James of Scotland and Bishop Henry Beaufort, the smile never leaving her face while the guests continued to applaud her. Then, as Humphrey of Gloucester took his own place next to King James, Bishop Beaufort held up his hand for silence and said grace.

It had taken the utmost skill to turn the Lenten fish into a meal worth eating but Anton had excelled himself. The guests were presented with eels, sea bream, conger, sole, chub, barbell with roach, fried smelt, crayfish, and baked lamprey. Hawthorn leaves, red haws and dates with mottled cream garnished dishes of carp, turbot, tench, perch with gudgeon, crab-fish, prawns, fresh sturgeon with whelks, and roasted porpoise. The subtleties decorating the high table represented Catherine's own emblems and symbols, which delighted her.

Too excited to do much more than push her food around her platter, the young Queen became aware that her immediate neighbour, too, seemed to have lost his appetite. James of Scotland toyed with his food and looked longingly down the body of the hall to where a group of young noblewomen sat together. Henry Beaufort watched him with some amusement.

'Don't worry, my boy, she still loves you!' he said and laughed.

'Does she, Sire? How do you know?'

'Because she told me so,' Beaufort replied, his eyes twinkling.

Catherine was curious. 'Who loves you?' she asked, craning her neck to see who the King of Scotland was looking at.

'My young niece, Joan,' said Henry Beaufort, 'my late brother's daughter. A charming girl and a credit to the family. Nothing would please me better than to see her married to His Highness. I would be prepared to perform the ceremony personally. I might even be prepared to pay for the wedding!'

'So many girls are called Joan,' Catherine said, 'or Joanna. It is very confusing. Which one is she, my Lord? Show me.'

James pointed out a cool beauty in a blue gown, who raised her fair head at that precise moment and caught his glance. She gave him a radiant smile and a little wave of acknowledgement. He waved back.

'Why don't you ask her to marry you?' Catherine asked.

James looked morose. 'I already have and she is willing to be my bride,' he said.

'Then what is stopping you?'

'The King, my Lady.'

'My husband? Why so?'

'Because I am not here in England as his guest, your Highness. I am to all intents and purposes a political prisoner and he will not grant his permission for our marriage.'

'A prisoner?' Catherine was very surprised at this. James was certainly not treated like a prisoner. In fact, Henry seemed very fond of him.

'I was seized and abducted when I was a child, my Lady, many years ago, before your husband came to the throne, and I have been at the English court ever since. But it has suited the King's purpose to keep me here. He demands a very high ransom from my people for my return – though I confess that I have no wish to return to Scotland without Joan as my queen.'

'But Joan is my husband's kinswoman, the Duchess Margaret's daughter.' Catherine frowned as she tried to understand the problem.

'She is indeed,' agreed Bishop Beaufort on the other side of her. 'She was the last of the children born to the Lady Margaret when she was married to my late brother John.' The Bishop crossed himself before continuing. 'Then, after his death, Margaret became the Duchess of Clarence when she married the King's brother Thomas. So, my Lady, young Joan is your niece by marriage.'

'Yes, of course,' she said with another exaggerated frown of concentration, at which her companions smiled. 'And the King refuses to allow you to marry my niece, eh? Well, we'll see about that!' Then her frown melted into the sunniest of smiles. 'I'm sure I can help.' She was confident of being able to swing Henry's opinion and she genuinely did want everyone to be as happy as she was that day.

She chose her moment carefully, waiting until she and Henry were lying in their canopied bed with the heavy curtains drawn around it for warmth in the draughty room. They had made love, not with passion but with the certainty of satisfaction which is the particular prerogative of the happily married. Now they lay side by side, Catherine's head in the crook of Henry's arm, their legs still entwined, their skin still damp from Henry's pleasure. She decided to test her strength.

'Henry?'

'Yes, my love.'

'Are you happy?'

'Mmmm. Of course. Why do you ask?'

'Because I would like everybody in the world to be as happy as we are.'

'Oh, yes? Now is that everybody, my sweet, or do you have anyone particular in mind?'

'Joan,' said Catherine. 'She is very lovely and so unhappy.'

'Joan who? Belknap?'

'No.'

'Courcy?'

'No.'

'Not the old trout?'

Catherine gave a little squeal of laughter. 'Oh, Henry! How can you call her that! Poor Troutbeck! No, not Joanna. Joan. Joan Beaufort, your uncle Henry Beaufort's niece. Margaret's daughter. Your kinswoman. My kinswoman, too, by marriage. I am concerned for her.'

Henry raised himself on his elbow and looked at her in the dim light. 'Ah, but she wants to marry James of Scotland,' he said, 'and I have expressly forbidden it.'

'But why, Henry? They are both very much in love and they could be as happy as we are.'

'Because, well, because … because there was a time when he refused to bear arms under my banner. Insolent young puppy. Needs to be taught a lesson.'

'But he has a great deal of respect for you, Henry. He said so only this afternoon.'

Henry was quiet for a moment. 'Did he really?'

'Yes, he did. Talk to him tomorrow. For my sake. You could make him the happiest man in Christendom.'

'Next to me.'

'Next to you, of course.'

Henry paused then, after a moment, he said: 'Very well, you sweet witch, you have beguiled me yet again. As long as James has come to his senses, I don't really mind him marrying. I'm not against the marriage in principle but he's still very young. It won't hurt them to wait a year or so. Anyway, I will discuss it with him tomorrow since you have asked me so prettily. In the meantime …'

Henry reached for her again and didn't see her little smile of triumph as she slid her body obligingly under his.

Chapter Six

Leicester, Easter 1421

March had turned very cold, just when Catherine thought that spring was coming at last. No sooner were the catkins dancing on the hazel trees to gladden the heart than winter delivered one last stab in the back, riming the reed beds with hoar frost, freezing the cart tracks on muddy roads, and making life well-nigh impossible for travellers. Still, Henry had sent for her and she was glad to go to him, even though it meant an arduous journey from London to Leicester.

It had upset her that he'd wanted to leave Westminster within a few days of her coronation. Why? She didn't understand. Was he in any way displeased with her? Perhaps he was, because he was clearly irritated by having to explain to her that he now needed to make contact with his subjects again as a matter of urgency. He had been away in France too long. The people would forget what he looked like unless he went out to meet them and how else would he persuade them to finance his army?

Catherine had tried to argue that there were plenty of people in London who saw him very regularly but Henry had countered her argument by pointing out that, though it was crowded, London was quite a small place. The real money lay with the big landowners outside London. Those were the people he wanted to talk to. Those were the people whose money he wanted, the people who would send their tenants to swell the ranks of his army.

So he left with a small retinue headed by his confessor, Bishop William Alnwick, a man who had served him well throughout his time in France, a man on whom Henry relied for spiritual guidance and Christian fellowship. Alnwick rode behind the King as they left Westminster heading west towards the town of Bristol. From there they would strike northwards through the Welsh marches, first to Hereford and then on to Shrewsbury.

Catherine felt surprisingly lonely without him. She would like to have a companion of her own age and social status. There was Margaret, of course, but she was old. Nevertheless, Margaret stayed close by Catherine's side and nothing would dissuade her from visiting Leicester and spending Easter there, particularly while her husband Thomas was still in France, looking after his brother's interests. So the women travelled together in some style though Catherine did wonder why Margaret thought they needed a retinue of over a hundred people, including knights, baggage handlers, four choristers, and ten priests as well as Anton, the royal chef.

As the royal party rode through the magnificent Turret Gate of Leicester Castle on the eve of Palm Sunday, Catherine was overjoyed to find Henry waiting for them. Royal protocol precluded an emotional reunion in public but she had no doubt of his pleasure at seeing her again. At every turn she saw him gazing at her with hunger in his eyes and he lost no opportunity of touching her hand, of whispering an endearment or squeezing her thumb as the secret sign of their physical need for each other.

So it came as no surprise that he strode through her dressing-room and into the bedchamber just as Guillemote and Les Trois Jo-jo were unpacking her boxes and coffers and helping her change out of her travel clothes.

'Out!' he ordered them, clapping his hands loudly and with a broad grin on his face. 'Go, get out of here at once. I can no longer endure the parting from my wife, no, not for one moment longer. Out!'

He chased them out of the room and they went, squealing with laughter, still clutching combs and mirrors, dropping shoes in their hurry, leaving their mistress clutching her shift to her breasts, her hair un-braided and falling over her shoulders. Henry turned the key in the lock behind them, then leaned back

72

heavily against the door.

'Catherine, it's only been a few weeks … but …' He looked at her dumbly for a moment, his smile fading, shaking his head in wonder, his need for her draining the colour from his face. She held out her arms to him and he moved towards her.

He buried his head in her shoulder. 'I have dreamed of this moment, Catherine. I have lived it, re-lived it.' With his face against her neck, the dear familiar scent of lavender almost overwhelmed him.

'Don't talk, Henry, please. Just let me feel you close to me. Close to me, Henry. Please, Henry, please …' She pulled him towards the bed.

It was with great urgency that he took her and, though she arched her back and responded to him with a desire that matched his own, he wondered afterwards whether he had been just a little brutal, hurting her perhaps.

'Catherine, I'm sorry. I have never felt so great a need. Did I hurt you?' He was lying on his back still panting slightly, his forearm on his forehead, his passion spent. 'My sweet love, please forgive me. Soldiers can be rough brutes.'

Lying naked beside him, Catherine breathed a dramatic sigh and smiled an age-old female smile as she looked up at the pattern in the fabric of the canopy above them.

'My Lord,' she said solemnly, 'I hope you don't expect me to *walk* in tomorrow's Palm Sunday procession!'

The royal family spent much of Holy Week on their knees in full religious observance of Easter in the little stone church of St Mary-de-Castro.

At Henry's side, Catherine watched the consecration of the holy oils and the commemoration of the Blessed Eucharist and by Easter Sunday she permitted herself the sacrilegious thought that, surely, God was at last satisfied with her devotions. She had said '*Attende Domine*' so many times that she felt sure she had persuaded the Almighty to attend to her most fervent prayer and grant that, before too long, she should conceive a child, a male heir to the throne of England.

All too soon Guillemote and Les Trois Jo-jo were packing

her clothes yet again because Henry, who always found it difficult to relax, was impatient to move on. The court was to be based next at York while the King and his Queen, with a smaller retinue, made pilgrimages to Beverley and Bridlington. Henry's father had placed him under the patronage of St John of Bridlington when he was a young boy and it pleased him greatly that the date of St John's day of translation, the twenty-fifth of October, was also St Crispin's Day, the very day on which he had won his most celebrated battle at Agincourt six years previously. Though he would vehemently deny that he was at all superstitious, Henry felt he owed a great deal to St Crispin and to the intercession of St John. He was always keen to go to Bridlington.

What Catherine looked forward to most was a few days' rest since, never the best of travellers, she had found the jerky movement of the royal coach had given her a feeling very akin to sea sickness and she was very tired. She awoke in York the following morning to the sound of Henry's squire coming into their bedchamber to rouse his master. She had been sleeping deeply. Henry dropped a kiss on her forehead and followed the squire into his dressing room. Sitting up and swinging her legs over the side of the great bed, Catherine reached for the little bell she kept by the bedside which would bring Guillemote to her at any time and for any reason. When Guillemote arrived moments later, she heard her mistress in the garderobe, being very violently sick.

'Dear God, Guillemote,' she said in a weak voice. Guillemote held her forehead as she leaned forward and retched again. 'I have never felt so ill.'

Guillemote's mind was racing. The oldest of thirteen children, she had often observed that when her own mother vomited before breakfast, there'd be yet another baby later in the year. But she didn't want to raise Catherine's hopes, not just yet.

'Can it be that you have eaten some English food which has upset you, my Lady? Or I wonder if it could perhaps be the effects of the long journey?'

'I wish I knew. But until I feel a great deal better, I won't be making any more journeys, not for a few days, anyway.'

'Come, my Lady. Let me help you back to your bed.' Guillemote was fussing with cloths and rosewater, trying to clean Catherine's mouth. 'I'll fetch the Lady Margaret. She'll know what to do.'

'Yes,' Catherine agreed, climbing back into the great bed and pulling the covers up under her chin. 'Margaret will know what to do.'

Coming back into the bedchamber, Henry was alarmed to see her looking so pale. He took the maid to one side. 'What is it, Guillemote?' he asked.

'I don't rightly know, Your Highness. She seems calm enough now but she has been quite ill.'

'Then I won't leave for Beverley until tomorrow. There's no pressing need.' Henry turned back to the bed and stroked a tendril of damp hair away from Catherine's forehead. 'Don't worry, my sweet, I'll tell Alnwick to send a messenger to Beverley and Bridlington to inform them of the delay. But perhaps we should consult a leech-doctor. I'll have one sent for.'

The Duchess of Clarence found Catherine sitting up in bed, propped up on pillows with her knees drawn up to her chin, drinking a hot posset which Guillemote had made for her.

'So, Catherine, my dear. Might it be that you are with child?' Margaret greeted her, getting straight to the point.

'With child, my Lady?' Catherine looked stunned. 'But surely …'

'Well, you have been very sick this morning, Henry tells me; he's even asked Bishop Alnwick to send for a leech doctor.'

'Yes, but …'

'I have every hope that a leech doctor will not be needed, though it will do no harm to bleed you a little, I suppose. Now remind me, when was it that you and Henry were together in Leicester? How many weeks ago?'

'But that was during Holy Week!'

'And what has that got to do with it?'

'Well …'

'Are you telling me that meat was not the only thing that

75

was denied to Henry during Holy Week? Surely you don't expect me to believe that you denied him his pleasure, too?'

'No,' said Catherine in a small voice, her eyes wide.

A broad smile on her face, Margaret looked at her young sister-in-law with affection. She seemed so small in the great bed, vulnerable, little more than a child herself. 'Babies can be conceived in Holy Week, Catherine, just like any other time of year. Whatever makes you think they can't be? They are our Saviour's greatest gift to any woman, especially a queen.'

Catherine shook her head in disbelief. Queen Isabeau had been right. She had spent far too long in the company of nuns.

Henry was overjoyed. Margaret had gone to find him, to tell him that Catherine had some very special news for him, news which she really should tell him herself. He knew, of course, that there was only one situation which was important enough to make Margaret say that.

'She's not …? Margaret, are you saying that she might be …?' He couldn't bring himself to use the word.

'I'm saying nothing,' Margaret beamed, 'even though it would give me the greatest pleasure to be the bearer of good news.'

Henry almost ran out of the room, so anxious was he to get to Catherine. He burst into their bedchamber to find Guillemote helping her into a loose robe.

'Catherine! Margaret says that … you might be … you could be …'

'Yes, my Lord,' she smiled. 'It does seem reasonable to suppose that I am with child.'

Henry covered the distance between them like a hound, half-leaping to envelop her in a huge embrace. Guillemote instinctively raised her arm to restrain him.

'Oh, Your Highness! Be careful! You mustn't be too rough with her.'

'Of course, of course. I'm sorry. Oh, Catherine, you cannot possibly know how happy this has made me!' He seized both her hands and covered them with kisses.

Catherine, feeling better, was of a mind to tease him. 'I

think, perhaps, that you are now the happiest man in England?'

'No, Catherine.'

'No, my Lord?'

'No. I am the happiest man in the world!' He seized her hands again then frowned suddenly. 'It will be a boy, won't it?'

They spent the evening as a family, over a modest meal in the private solar, Catherine, Henry, and Margaret, waited upon by Guillemote and entertained by only two of Henry's musicians whom Margaret ignored completely as she prattled on about the prospect of a Christmas baby. All the signs and portents were good, she said excitedly, pointing out that the child had probably been conceived in Leicester Castle, the seat of the Dukes of Lancaster. He would be a fine young man and a great king, continuing the traditions of his father, his grandfather, and his great-grandfather, the wise and powerful John of Gaunt. Henry listened, beaming indulgently.

Catherine sat back in her chair, her hands resting lightly on her belly. With a fixed smile on her face, she watched Henry beaming with pleasure and listened to Margaret's exited chatter as though from a great distance, while her own mind was filled with trepidation. The hopes and fears of the entire English royal family were vested in that small scrap of humanity which was growing in her womb and her overwhelming feeling was that there would be testing times ahead. Despite the sophistication of her life in royal circles, she couldn't quite shake off her convent upbringing. A phrase from the Book of Genesis niggled at the back of her mind: '*In sorrow thou shalt bring forth children.*' Though she would never have admitted to her anxiety in front of Margaret and Henry, she did wonder how much giving birth to a baby would hurt.

They retired early to bed and Henry held her gently in his arms as though she was something very precious indeed. Feigning sleep, with her head on his shoulder, she prayed silently that her baby would be a boy so that she could give Henry the one thing he desperately wanted; an heir to his throne. Though she would have to endure the curse of Eve in order to do it, this would be the culmination of everything that

77

she and her mother had worked for.

The King was awake before cockcrow, slipping his arm gently from under her head in case he should wake her. He intended to make a very early start this morning. Now it seemed likely that Catherine was pregnant, he wasn't going to take any risks with her health. Needs must make this pilgrimage without her but he was more anxious than ever for the blessings of St John and St Crispin. They would, he was certain, grant that Catherine was carrying a male child.

Before setting out, Henry had asked Sir Walter Hungerford to remain with Catherine and Margaret in York, confiding in him that there was now an added reason why the Queen needed his protection. He had every faith in Hungerford, a mature man in his middle forties. Devoted to King Henry, as he had been to his father before him, Hungerford was a royal councillor and had been steward of the King's household for several years. Sir Walter smiled and said he would be both honoured and delighted to be responsible for the safety of the Queen and the Duchess of Clarence.

Now Margaret really came into her own as Catherine's adviser. She was a good deal younger than Catherine's own mother but still an experienced older woman. Queen Isabeau had never concerned herself with any aspect of Catherine's education, either religious or secular, with the result that her daughter was remarkably ignorant about the workings of her own body. The nuns at Poissy had confined themselves to teaching her the catechism and how to turn her mind to pious thoughts. Beyond telling her it was the will of God that all women must endure the loss of blood each month and explaining the practicalities of dealing with that, they had studiously ignored every other aspect of the female body. Of course, Catherine was well aware of how the child had been conceived but she had no idea of how her pregnancy would affect her or what changes she could expect as it progressed.

So she plied Margaret with eager questions which Margaret did her best to answer, excited at the prospect of Catherine bearing Henry the baby which would become heir to the throne of England and, in time, the throne of France.

Despite the misery of her morning sickness, the time passed quickly enough for Catherine while Henry was away and it didn't seem long before a swift horseman in the King's livery brought the message that the royal party would return from their pilgrimage the following day. Catherine decided that there would be a special feast to celebrate Henry's safe return and it was not the only thing they had to celebrate. She had no doubt that rumours were flying around the court already. After all, they had talked quite freely over supper in front of two of Henry's musicians, the worst of gossips, but no official announcement about Catherine's pregnancy had been made, so this seemed to her a very appropriate occasion on which to make it.

She and Margaret summoned the royal chef from the kitchen to discuss what food might be served. Tomorrow would be Thursday, a flesh-day, so meat was permitted and Anton favoured venison. True, it had come almost to the end of its season but he knew of a carcass which had been correctly hung for twenty-one days and the haunch and the shoulder would both be delicious cooked slowly in red wine and served with a juniper sauce. Chicken, too, he thought. It was a pity that grapes were out of season since he liked to serve his roasted chicken stuffed with grapes. Still, it was the best time of year for lamb, now at its youngest and sweetest, so they would certainly spit-roast two or three depending on their size but, for this special occasion – and here Anton grinned broadly because he'd heard the gossip and already knew the reason for the celebration – he would be very happy to serve dressed peacock.

'But you must not carry it to the table, my Lady,' he warned, wagging his finger dramatically, 'the way the English ladies do. *Mais non!* It will weigh too much. It is much too 'eavy for you now that you are, er, *enceinte*!'

'Oh, Anton!' Catherine laughed, pretending to be scandalised. 'You must not say that to anyone else. It is still a secret!'

'No secrets from Anton,' he said, tapping the side of his nose conspiratorially. 'Anton, 'e knows everything! I myself will bring the peacock to the table.' He mimed the way he would present the peacock, bowing extravagantly to them both. 'It will be beautiful, the most beautiful peacock you 'ave ever seen! His 'Ighness the King will marvel at the size and the colours of the tail feathers and it will taste –' here he paused to kiss the tips of his fingers in a Gallic gesture, 'mmm … divine!'

They couldn't but approve Anton's suggested menu and, leaving them laughing at his antics, the chef went back to exercise his tyranny in the kitchen.

Henry and his small retinue had reached Wicstun, where they were to spend the last night of their pilgrimage before undertaking the final twenty miles of their journey back to York the next day. Henry retired early, soon after nightfall, so as to make best use of the morning light to get the journey under way. He wanted to reach York as soon as he could, if only to take Catherine in his arms again; Catherine, his queen, who carried the heir to his throne within her womb. He had prayed earnestly to St John of Bridlington that she should bear him a son. He knew the saint would not let him down.

The slightest sound in the night always had Henry reaching for his sword, on the defensive in an instant, and it seemed to him that he had only been asleep for a matter of minutes when there was a scuffling sound outside his door accompanied by muffled whispers. He leapt up.

'What's going on?' he demanded, wrenching open the door. 'What's all the noise?'

Outside, his guards were restraining a messenger wearing royal livery. The man's clothes were dishevelled and his boots were caked with mud.

'Beg pardon, Your Highness,' muttered a guard. 'Can't be too careful.'

'Of course, of course. What is it?'

'This man says he's got a message for you, Sire, from the Duke of Gloucester. Says he's got to give it to you personally. Says it can't wait 'til morning. Messenger reckons he's been riding for near ten days to get here, what with havin' to find out where you were and everything.'

'Where have you ridden from?' the King demanded as the messenger delved into a large leather scrip which was strapped around his neck and under his arm. Henry snatched the message from him.

'From Windsor, Your Grace, an' I been ridin' since the first day of April. I came quick as I could. I must have wore out about eight 'orses, I reckon …'

'Alright, man, alright. Go now, go to the kitchen. One of the guards will show you where it is. Get something to eat and a night's rest. I'll see you're well paid in the morning for your trouble. Guard, go to it. Leave two men outside my door and bring more candles.'

Henry kicked the door closed as he tore at the royal seal on the letter. He felt a sudden throb of fear. With trembling hands he tried and failed to read the message in the dim glimmer of a rush lamp burning in a wall sconce near the fireplace.

The guard returned with two lighted wax candles which he placed on Henry's table. Bowing, he backed out of the room. Now Henry spread the letter on the table and arranged the candles so that he could read it.

A moment later, the guards outside his door heard a dreadful sound. It was neither a cry nor a shout. It could have been the yowling of a dog fox with its paw in a trap or the anguish of a soul in agony. It chilled their very bones to hear it. They looked uncertainly at one another.

'Best fetch Bishop Alnwick,' said one. 'Sounds like he's had bad news.'

William Alnwick found Henry slumped over his table, motionless, his head on his arms.

'My Lord, what is it? The guard said it was bad news …'

Henry shuddered. 'Thomas,' his voice was muffled against his sleeve. 'My brother … Thomas …'

'The Duke of Clarence?'

Henry raised his head and stared ashen-faced at Alnwick. 'Dead,' he said. 'The Duke of Clarence, yes. My brother, Thomas, yes. Dead. Dead since before Easter. And I never knew! Dead all the time I was in Leicester, dead all the time I was in Beverley, in Bridlington. I could at least have prayed for

81

him if I had known. Dead all that time … and I never knew!'

'How could you know? He's in France.'

'Was in France,' Henry corrected him in a dull voice. 'Was in France. Keeping the peace, looking after my interests. I should have known that the French wouldn't honour the truce. You can't trust them, I should have realised that. I should have brought Thomas home. He'd still be … oh, God, he'd still be …'

'What happened, my Lord?'

Henry held out the letter and, in silence, Bishop Alnwick read the brief message. It begged to inform His Highness that his brother Thomas, Duke of Clarence, had been killed in battle on the twenty-second day of March, having bravely sought out and attacked a Franco-Scottish force at Baujé in Anjou. The English force had been heavily outnumbered and the battle was lost. The message ended with a request that Her Grace, the Duchess of Clarence, should be informed of her husband's death.

'How am I to tell her?' Henry whispered. 'What can I say?'

Bishop Alnwick paused for a long moment. 'Perhaps I should tell her,' he said. 'It will not be easy but I'll do what I can.' He crossed himself slowly. 'The Duchess is a deeply pious woman. She will understand that it is God's will.'

Anton was supervising the roasting of lambs. The kitchen at York was not laid out to his liking but he was so genuinely delighted at the good fortune of his royal mistress that he would put up with a few inconveniences, just to help her celebrate the announcement of her pregnancy in style.

He himself was dressing the peacock, stepping back every now and then to judge the effect of his artistry. He needed to adjust … those two tail feathers just … so! He stepped back again, onto the foot of someone standing just behind him.

'*Quel crétin*! Get out of my way, you stupid …' Anton stopped and turned around. 'Oh, Sir Walter! I'm so sorry. I thought you were one of the scullions, they are always getting under my feet …' His voice trailed off as he saw the look on the face of Sir Walter Hungerford. 'What 'as 'appened?'

'Something dreadful. Dreadful. The King has not returned. He has ridden on to Pontefract. But Bishop Alnwick has returned and has brought the gravest news. I come to tell you that there will be no celebration today, no feasting. The King's brother, the Duke of Clarence, has been killed in battle in Anjou.'

'*Mon Dieu!*'

'Bishop Alnwick is with the Lady Margaret now. At the moment, food is the last thing the royal ladies want to think about, though the rest of the household has to eat, of course, so not everything will be wasted. Perhaps you could use up the lambs at least. I'm sorry. I know you've been to a great deal of trouble.'

Sir Walter turned and left the kitchen. Anton crossed himself and sighed. Then he looked around him at the huge quantity of food which had already been prepared and was ready to be served; breads, salads, vegetables, sauces and purées, fruits in spiced wine, jellies, flans, and cheeses. The long trestle tables pushed against two walls of the room groaned with the weight of it.

Anton opened the kitchen door. There was the usual raggedy gaggle of beggars outside, waiting for the used trenchers and whatever food was left over from the table. Anton stood to one side to let them in to the kitchen.

'*Entrez, mes amis,*' he invited them. 'Tonight, you shall eat like kings.'

Chapter Seven

Windsor Castle, England, Summer 1421

These were bleak days for the King, bleak and despairing. He spent hours closeted with his advisers, discussing at length the best tactics for retaliation. Then when his advisers had left he would sit with his two remaining brothers, John and Humphrey, until well into the night, plotting retribution. His main worry was getting together sufficient money to raise an army. The royal coffers were all but empty and Parliament had refused to impose yet more taxes, forcing Henry to spend weeks begging and borrowing from anyone who would lend to him, promising to pay back with interest as soon as he had France obediently under English rule.

Neither John of Bedford nor Humphrey of Gloucester was in any position to lend money but they had always been supportive. Henry watched them now, as they sat opposite him with ledgers, scraps of parchment, and ink horns spread out before them on the table, frowning in the candlelight as they discussed how an army of sufficient size might be raised. They hadn't changed very much since they were small boys, he reflected. They might have been back in the school room, John with his round, earnest face and handsome Humphrey, absently pulling at a lock of his russet-brown hair and looking on while John crossed out yet another column of figures. But there was one person missing; Thomas should have been there, too.

Henry was not a man who readily admitted to feelings of affection but, as the first-born, he had always been fiercely protective of his younger siblings, raising his fists to fight their childish battles, hiding their little misdemeanours from their parents. In later years, on the battlefield at Agincourt, he had saved Humphrey's life, defending his badly wounded brother by standing astride him as he lay helpless on the ground and protecting him until he could be dragged away to safety. Humphrey had survived, with nothing more to show for his injured leg than an occasional limp. But Thomas was dead and there was nothing Henry could have done to save him. In his private moments, he was almost deranged with grief. He wanted to kill whoever had delivered the mortal wound. He wanted that more than anything. The King had never been a man to turn the other cheek. An eye for an eye and a tooth for a tooth was his belief.

Henry wanted revenge.

'You know,' said John with a frown of concentration, his quill pen poised in mid-air, 'if we add Uncle Henry Beaufort's monies to what we have here, there should be sufficient to pull together a decent number of men and horses and equipment.'

'And keep them in France for as long as it takes to quell the French?' asked Humphrey. 'How much has he given?'

'Seventeen thousand, six hundred and sixty-six pounds, three shillings, and fourpence,' said Henry promptly. 'And it was readily offered. I'll have to pay him back, of course.'

'And with interest,' John added. 'It's true he's a man of God but he's certainly familiar with Mammon.'

'I don't much care how he regards his wealth,' said Henry, 'as long as he's prepared to lend it to us when we need it. And I'll worry about paying him back when I've brought those French bastards to heel.'

'Then our problems are solved,' said Humphrey. 'We go to France.'

'In the meantime,' John said, gathering his writing materials together, 'we go to bed. Come, it's late and the candle burns low.'

'There's little to tempt me to bed,' said Humphrey. 'Henry has the most beautiful woman at court to grace his pillow, even if she is with child. But my bed's a cold and lonely place. So, I'll have another goblet of wine.'

'I thought your bed was being warmed by that young, er ... what was her name?' John started saying but Henry cut across him.

'Ah! I knew there was something I had to tell you both. Talking of beautiful women ... I'd almost forgotten. I have received a message from Calais to request permission for the Countess Jacqueline of Holland to visit England. It seems she has run away from her husband.'

Humphrey raised his eyebrows. 'John of Brabant? I'm not surprised, if what I've heard is true. Looks like a rat.'

'Rotten teeth, too,' said Henry. 'They say his breath stinks!'

'How very unpleasant,' said John, curling his lip in distain, 'particularly since she seems such a charming woman, if a little too vivacious for my taste. But I confess to having been quite taken with her at your wedding to Catherine.'

'So, tell me, Henry,' said Humphrey, 'have you invited the Countess to come to court?'

'Indeed I have. She's Catherine's kinswoman, of course, so she'll be company for her while I'm in France.'

Humphrey drained his goblet. 'Do they know each other well?' he asked, reaching for the decanter.

'Oh, yes, I think so. And of course, when she was a lot younger, the Countess Jacqueline was married for some years to Catherine's brother, John. Before he died, that is.'

'Yes, I'd forgotten that,' said John. 'And has she any money to add to your army funds?'

'I imagine not. Not if she's run away from her husband. No doubt she'll be destitute, near enough. So I have arranged a small payment for her each month while she remains here as Catherine's companion. She arrives from Calais sometime next week. Would one of you be prepared to meet her at Dover?'

'I think I should be the one to do that,' said Humphrey. 'If nothing else, I should do it officially in my capacity as Warden of the Cinque Ports. I shall travel to Dover at the end of the week with a deputation to welcome her.' He poured himself a generous measure of wine. 'So, let's drink to the prospect of another attractive woman at court. I've used up all the available ones under the age of forty!' He raised his glass to his brothers with a lewd laugh.

Now that there was to be an heir to his throne, there were some things that must be done before the King left for France. Henry would leave nothing to chance. He singled out the sour-faced Elizabeth Ryman, one of the older ladies of the court, and asked her to be wholly responsible for the physical welfare of his unborn child from the moment of birth. She would be given a small band of dedicated nurses to assist her and the gift of a sizeable manorial estate in recognition of her services to the Crown.

Catherine was mortified by this decision and, a few nights later, found the courage to confront her husband as they prepared for bed. She had learned that, if she wanted a favour of any kind, the bedchamber was the place to ask it.

'My Lord,' she began pleasantly enough, 'there is really no need for Mistress Ryman to concern herself with the baby, you know. That will be my duty. Indeed, that will be my pleasure. So, Henry, for my sake, please tell Mistress Ryman that her services will not be needed.'

Henry regarded her with a flinty expression on his face. 'Catherine, I will not have my judgement questioned. This is my wish and my decision stands. Mistress Ryman will assume her duties the moment my son is born. Oh, and Catherine, you will arrange to be in Westminster for the birth.'

'In Westminster? By why, my Lord? I am very happy here in Windsor and …'

'It is my particular wish, Catherine. My son will be born in the Palace of Westminster and he will immediately be placed in the care of Mistress Elizabeth Ryman. He will be the heir to the throne of England and his wellbeing is of paramount importance. It is imperative that he is given constant attention of the highest standard. My Lady, you will see to it that my wishes are observed.'

She bit her lip and said nothing as he turned aside to sleep but she lay awake in the darkness for a long time, trying very hard not to feel hurt. It was bad enough that her husband was planning to invade her native country yet again, to kill her countrymen, without the fact that she had the bleak prospect of remaining in England alone. She had no real friends here, apart from Margaret, and Margaret could sometimes be quite distant since her husband's death. Sleep evaded Catherine, nor did she particularly want to sleep. She'd had a vivid, frightening dream recently and could only pray that her childhood nightmares would not start plaguing her again.

As she awaited the birth of her baby, Catherine was surrounded by people who were preoccupied with their own concerns. Henry was entirely engrossed in planning the invasion of France and Margaret spent most of her time kneeling at the *prie-dieu* in her private solar, praying for the eternal rest of her dead husband, not wanting to talk to anyone.

So Catherine sewed and embroidered or practised playing her harp but did none of these things with much enthusiasm. Or else she would pick up a book, having become particularly fond of the tales of Geoffrey Chaucer, now that her command of English had improved so much. She was totally absorbed in *The Parliament of Fowls* when she felt the baby kick in her belly for the first time. Excited but alarmed she dropped the book and rushed to find Margaret.

Rising from her prie-dieu and kissing her rosary, the Duchess embraced her sister-in-law. Then she stepped back and regarded her with sad, lack-lustre eyes. 'The Lord giveth and the Lord taketh away,' was all she said, crossing herself.

Catherine found herself spending more and more time with Guillemote. As old friends, they spoke French comfortably together and Guillemote, having lived through so many of her mother's pregnancies, was surprisingly informative about the process of having babies. She managed to allay some of Catherine's fears about the pain she could expect to endure but still, in her heart of hearts, Catherine felt very apprehensive. Women died in childbirth. It was a fact.

The King was so busy that it was several days before he remembered to tell Catherine that her cousin, the Countess Jacqueline, was expected at court. Catherine was overjoyed at the news but, despite her excited questioning, Henry could tell her little beyond the fact that his brother Humphrey had elected to meet Jacqueline at Dover and, no, he had no idea about what arrangements had been made for the visit or how long she would be staying. Nevertheless, Catherine hugged herself with delight. Here, at last, was the friend she had despaired of finding in England. The prospect of having Jacqueline at court meant that life promised to take on a new and thoroughly enjoyable dimension. There would be so much to catch up on, so much to talk about, that she could hardly wait for her cousin to arrive. They hadn't seen each other since the wedding at Troyes and they hadn't had a chance to talk very much even then. Catherine hadn't met Jacqueline's new husband either, though she had been concerned to hear that the Duke of Brabant was a thoroughly unpleasant man.

She would love to have travelled to meet her high-spirited cousin but, though she was no longer troubled by morning sickness, her pregnancy made her disinclined to leave the comfort of Windsor. Travel made her queasy at the best of times, now she avoided it at all costs. She was pleased to think that Jacqueline would be escorted safely to Windsor, even though her escort would be Humphrey of Gloucester. Try as she might, Catherine couldn't quite bring herself to trust her husband's brother.

A few days later, the horses of Jacqueline's escort party clattered over the drawbridge and into the outer ward of the castle. No sooner had the Countess been helped to dismount than the two women were embracing each other with great excitement. Humphrey of Gloucester stood to one side, an indulgent look on his handsome face.

'Jacqueline, you haven't changed a bit!' said Catherine with a broad smile, holding her cousin's hands in both her own as she took in every detail of her appearance. Jacqueline smiled back. She had the Valois nose and the same fair colouring as the rest of the family, but she had the merriest pair of blue eyes and, from under an elaborate horned headdress, they regarded Catherine with great affection.

'No, my dear, of course I haven't changed!' said Jacqueline, 'except that I'm a great deal happier now than I have been for a very long time. It's good to see you, Catherine, and I'm so pleased to be here in Windsor with you.'

'I trust that His Grace the Duke looked after you well during the journey?'

'Humphrey? Oh, yes! Yes, he was *most* attentive.' Jacqueline turned to Humphrey of Gloucester who met her look with a quizzical lift of his eyebrows. Catherine immediately sensed a frisson between them, an impulse of energy, a secret. Oh, surely, Jacqueline had not fallen under the spell of the handsome Humphrey during the course of the short journey from Dover! Surely not!

There was little opportunity to discuss the matter during the next few days for Windsor Castle had been turned upside down. Advisers, money-lenders, and military men were in constant attendance on the King, making last-minute arrangements for the expedition to France. Elsewhere, sounds of loud clanging and hammering accompanied the extensive new building work which was being undertaken. Repairs were also being made to the existing fabric of the building and it was all in anticipation of the birth of the heir to the throne. Catherine sometimes felt quite remote from all this activity, as though none of it had anything to do with her or with the child she carried in her womb but every time she tried to snatch an hour with Jacqueline, she always failed to find somewhere quiet enough for the two of them to talk. Either that, or she was told that the Countess was in consultation with His Grace, the Duke of Gloucester.

Then one morning, early in June, Henry was taking his leave of her in the privacy of their bedchamber. He held her close and stroked her hair while she clung to him.

'God be with you, my sweet love,' he said, 'and with our baby son. By the grace of God and with the help of St Crispin and St John of Bridlington, I will return from France and be in Westminster in good time for his birth.'

'God speed, my Lord, and a safe journey,' Catherine responded as he embraced her. She would miss him, she was sure of that, but nothing like as much as she would have done without Jacqueline's company to look forward to.

She was glad, too, that John of Bedford was to govern the country in his brother's absence and was to oversee the building work at Windsor. She was fond of John and had always felt safe and secure in his company. He stood with her and Jacqueline now as those members of the court who were to remain at Windsor gathered in the outer ward to bid farewell to the King and his companions-at-arms. Climbing the mounting block, Henry waited as one of his knights came towards him, leading the huge black war horse which was to carry him into battle. Once the King was in the saddle, James of Scotland guided his own horse into place behind him, followed by Humphrey of Gloucester and the Earls of March and of Warwick. A bugle call signalled the letting down of the drawbridge and the King of England and his companions rode out to join the army of four thousand men who were about to undertake the long journey south to Dover and thence to France.

Catherine waved farewell as dutifully as any wife but in truth she could hardly wait to talk to her cousin, now that Humphrey of Gloucester had left Windsor with the King and could no longer monopolise her.

'Jacqueline, you are a married woman!' Catherine blurted out, as soon as they were alone. 'And yet you seem very close to the King's brother.'

'True, I am married. Indeed, I have been twice married. But that means nothing. Catherine, despite having had two husbands, I might as well have remained unmarried. Well, until now.'

'What do you mean? Have you …? With Humphrey? Not already, surely?' Catherine's questions hung in the air.

'Yes, I have. And yes, we did! Catherine, I make no apology for it. Humphrey is all I ever dreamed of. He's handsome, charming, cultured, clever. A real man.'

Jacqueline executed a little pirouette from sheer joy, not noticing the look of disbelief on Catherine's face.

'But what of your husband?'

'Husband? Brabant? He is no husband to me, Catherine. He hates women. He would rather share his bed with a pretty boy than with me. He disgusts me!'

'So you never …?'

'I repulsed him. And he repulsed me. Our marriage was doomed from the start. He preferred the company of his lewd, debauched friends. That and drinking. He was almost always drunk. Sometimes too drunk to stand but never too drunk to hit me.'

Catherine was aghast. 'Hit you? But, Jacqueline! That's terrible! Terrible! You must have been so unhappy. But what about John? You were happy with John, weren't you?' She crossed herself. 'Surely, before he was taken from us, you and he …'

'Ah, sweet John,' Jacqueline smiled. 'He was my playmate. I loved him very much but we were only children. Catherine, I was only three years old when we were betrothed and he came to live in Holland. Of course, he was your brother but he was like a brother to me, too.' She paused and sighed heavily. 'Poor little John. Ours could have been a good marriage if only we'd been a little older and he'd been a little stronger. And if John had lived, of course, he would eventually have inherited your father's throne and I would have been Queen of France. And now you will be, when Henry becomes king.' Smiling, she held out her hand to Catherine. 'I'm glad. At least we're keeping it in the family!'

Catherine squeezed her cousin's hand in return. 'Yes, I hadn't thought of it in that way. But that doesn't solve your problem, Jacqueline.'

The two women delighted in each other's company. They spent nearly all their time together, gossiping and giggling and looking forward to the day when the baby would be born. Jacqueline made no bones about being envious of Catherine's pregnancy and Catherine would smile, sometimes a little smugly. Nothing seemed to be required of her, other than to entertain Jacqueline, to distract poor Margaret from her grief, to concentrate on the coming baby, and, at Henry's insistence, to make sure the child was born in the Palace of Westminster.

She really hadn't understood that, particularly since Windsor was undergoing such extensive renovation in preparation for the royal birth. There was surely a good reason for it but, though she asked him several times before he left for France, Henry had always remained tight-lipped and was clearly irritated by her demands for an explanation. Eventually he told her why.

'There is a prophecy,' he'd said with a dismissive shrug. 'I don't know where it originated but it foretells that I, Henry of Monmouth, will small time reign and much get; but Henry of Windsor shall long reign and lose all. But as God wills, so be it.'

'But, Henry, that's all …'

'Yes, I know. It's probably nonsense but I don't want to tempt providence.'

Well, to Catherine, the answer was very simple. 'Then we must not call our son Henry,' she said. 'John would be a good name, a strong name. John of Windsor. What do you think, my Lord? Or even Louis. He will reign over France one day, so perhaps we should give him a French name as well as an English one.'

Henry frowned. 'My son will be named Henry and that's an end to it. My father was the fourth king to bear that name, I am the fifth, and my son will be Henry the Sixth. There is no question about that. And he will be born in Westminster. You will see to that, Catherine. It is my particular wish.' That had been his last word on the subject.

Catherine would really rather have the baby in Windsor, it was such a comfortable royal palace, much less formal than Westminster and much more of a home. However Henry had insisted on it and would brook no argument. She would have to move to Westminster towards the end of November for her month of lying-in prior to the birth, though the prospect of travelling there didn't please her. Still, she remembered that her husband had been born in Monmouth and she should be grateful that there appeared to be no element of tradition in that. She certainly wouldn't want to go all the way to Monmouth to have her baby: she wasn't even sure where it was.

Margaret, a fount of religious knowledge, gave her another reason why the Palace of Westminster was favoured for royal confinements. It was, she said, because the Benedictine monks of Westminster Abbey had a relic in their possession, a girdle which had once belonged to the Virgin Mother of Christ, she who had brought forth her son without pain. The monks revered

94

it greatly and kept the ancient, fragile piece of plaited fabric in a long box made of fragrant sandalwood, lined with silk and exquisitely inlaid with pearls to represent the Virgin's tears. It never left the Abbey except when it was loaned out for a royal birth at the Palace and even then it was very closely guarded. That made perfect sense to Catherine. Of course, the monks would be very reluctant to travel the distance from Westminster to Windsor with anything so valuable, running the risk of attack by footpads or highwaymen. Margaret had finally convinced her that she could relax as she approached the impending birth, unafraid of the curse of Eve and confident in the knowledge that the holy relic tied around her belly would enable her to bring her child into the world with no pain.

And she prayed that she too, like Maria Immaculata, would bring forth a son.

As Catherine's pregnancy progressed, she and Jacqueline began work on a layette for the baby, sewing companionably during the afternoons and talking of this and that, more often than not of the difficult situation in which Jacqueline found herself. She told Catherine how she had been tricked into her desperately unhappy marriage to the Duke of Brabant.

'I should never have allowed myself to be taken in like that. And do you know who was behind it all, Catherine? Our dear uncle, John the Fearless. He must have known that I would never have children with Brabant so he made sure that if my so-called husband and I should both die, then everything goes to your brother-in-law, Michelle's husband, our cousin Philip of Burgundy.

'Cousin Philip? But surely, he wouldn't be such a snake!'

'Oh yes he would. And he is. He stands to inherit all the royal lands in Holland. They were all mine but became Brabant's, of course, when I married him.'

'Then he's not going to give them up easily, Jacqueline.'

'No, of course he isn't. That's why I'm so desperate for an annulment. But Humphrey will advise me what to do. When he gets back from France, he plans to come to Holland and fight for me. He will go to Parliament to request money to raise an

95

army.'

Catherine knew how hard Henry had tried to get Parliament to pay for the army he had taken to France, but without success. She felt certain that if Parliament had refused the King, then the Duke of Gloucester could go and whistle for funding for his hare-brained scheme, but Jacqueline seemed to like the romantic idea that her handsome lover was coming to her rescue. Catherine didn't want to disabuse her of that dream, not when she saw the radiant expression on her cousin's face.

'So tell me, Jacq,' she said one afternoon, pulling a length of thread twice through a stitch in a tiny garment to secure it, before biting it off with small white teeth, 'do you think the Pope will grant an annulment of your marriage?'

'Well, one of them will, either Pope Martin in Rome or Pope Benedict in Avignon.'

'But, Jacq, Benedict is not the pope. He is the antipope! Henry always says so. If Benedict granted you an annulment, it wouldn't be worth the parchment it's written on. Henry would certainly never accept it. He only acknowledges Pope Martin in Rome. And he's right. Martin is the true Pope.'

'When you're as desperate for an annulment as I am, Catherine, you'll do anything. Applications have been made to both of them but they've both been dithering for months. And they've both been told the truth, that the marriage was never truly consummated.'

'Will they demand proof of that?'

Jacqueline gave a wry smile. 'Too late, Catherine. I might have been a virgin when I went to Humphrey's bed but, believe me, I'm certainly not a virgin now.'

It had been a remarkably mild autumn and, on the threshold of winter, there were leaves still clinging to the trees. Catherine, feeling heavy and bloated in the late stages of pregnancy, had lost all sense of time and was quite startled when Joanna Troutbeck asked her which clothes she wanted packed for the month of her lying-in at Westminster.

'Surely, we don't have to worry about that already, do we, Troutbeck?'

'Yes, my Lady, we do. I think the sooner the better. It's already December so, even now, you won't have the full month of your lying-in if the child is to be born at Christmas.'

'But I'm so comfortable here at Windsor.'

'But remember, Catherine my dear,' said the Lady Margaret, 'that the King particularly wants his son born at Westminster, so we really should be going there within the next day or two.'

'It's easy for Henry to make the rules, he doesn't have to have the baby,' Catherine sulked, 'nor does he have to make the journey to Westminster. I'm not looking forward to that.'

She had never felt more disinclined to travel, making every excuse to dally and dawdle in the comfort of Windsor, claiming a headache the next day and an upset stomach the day after that. Guillemote was most concerned for her; she had seen her mother grow sluggish like this as the time for the birth drew near. But she didn't want to alarm Catherine.

'It's this dreadful English food,' she said, putting the blame where she always did. '*Mon Dieu*! I don't know how you eat it while you're pregnant! It is sickening. I will ask Anton if he has a little of his special calf's foot jelly for you. You'll enjoy that and it will settle your stomach before you have to make the journey.'

'Yes, yes, Guillemote. Thank you. You're very kind.' Catherine moved her hand back and forth over her distended belly, as though to rub away the dull ache she'd been feeling for some hours.

Guillemote was in the kitchen consulting Anton when the first real wave of pain hit Catherine like the kick of a mule. Her knees buckled under her and when Guillemote returned, she found her mistress crouching down with her head bent, moaning quietly. A damp stain was spreading across the floor.

'Oh, my Lady, the baby wants to come! I thought so.' Guillemote set down the little pot of calf's foot jelly on the table and began fussing over Catherine. 'I knew we should have made the journey to Westminster weeks ago. This baby wants to be born now, not at Christmas, and here in Windsor, not at Westminster and there's nothing we can do about it! Come, my Lady, let me help you to bed, then I will fetch the midwife and the Lady Margaret.' But the Lady Margaret had already arrived, having heard the first scream of pain.

'Guillemote,' Catherine begged, 'please fetch the girdle of Our Lady! I must have it, I must wear it while my baby is being born, otherwise the pain will be too much ...'

'But, my Lady, the girdle is in Westminster.'

'Don't worry, Catherine,' the Lady Margaret soothed her. 'Don't worry about Our Lady's girdle. I have here something equally good, possibly a great deal better.'

'What is it?' moaned Catherine, wincing as another dragging contraction assailed her.

'The Silver Jewel,' said Margaret, 'the most precious relic of all. I arranged to have it sent over from France as soon as I knew that you were having Henry's baby.'

'The Silver Jewel?' Catherine turned dark questioning eyes towards her.

Margaret crossed herself before taking a highly ornate silver casket from a coffer which she was carrying and opening it with great reverence. She took out a small piece of what looked like old leather. 'It is Our Lord's foreskin. Here, take it in your hand. Don't be afraid. It is renowned for its mysterious power to help women in labour. You won't need Our Lady's girdle as well.'

His Royal Highness Henry of Windsor pushed his small, sticky head into the world on the sixth day of December 1421, his indignant, newborn wailing almost drowned in a babble of joyful welcome from Queen Catherine's ladies.

'A boy!' they called excitedly to each other, 'Oh, God be praised, it's a boy!'

'A boy!' said Margaret with tears in her eyes as she watched the midwife cleaning the child before handing him to his mother. She returned the holy relic to its silver casket, crossing herself fervently. It had done its work. It had given Catherine a relatively easy birth and she had produced a boy. A boy! Thanks be to God! Margaret crossed herself again and muttered a few words of gratitude to her Maker.

'A boy!' said Catherine in wonder. Her ladies were helping

her to sit up in bed, propping her up on pillows as the midwife placed the baby in her waiting arms. She looked down at the little wrinkled pink face, the eyes tightly closed and knew a moment of the purest imaginable love. 'My son!' Her pain almost forgotten, she touched the baby's face and traced the line of his mouth gently with her little finger, smiling as he instinctively tried to suck it.

'A boy!' said Jacqueline, aware of a curiously strong emotion. 'The heir to the throne of England!' Though she would have denied it strenuously, jealousy had her heart in its cold grip.

'The heir to the thrones of England *and* France,' Catherine reminded her gently. 'He looks very small to have all that responsibility, don't you think?'

'He looks … he looks beautiful.' The words caught in Jacqueline's throat.

'Jacq,' said Catherine quietly.

'What is it?'

'Jacq, will you be his godmother?'

'I? But, I … yes, of course, Catherine, I should be very, very honoured. And I know that Humphrey will be pleased.'

In London, the bells rang out from every bell tower and *Te Deums* were sung in every church. Flags were flying and the taverns were full of noisy, elated citizens celebrating the birth of young Prince Henry, the heir to the throne.

In Windsor, all was quiet as Catherine slept, exhausted after the effort of giving birth. The baby had been taken away from her and handed to a wet nurse to be fed, his mother's own full breasts denied him.

In France, nearly three weeks later, a royal messenger spurred his sweating horse on towards the English encampment outside the besieged town of Meaux. It wasn't far to go now; the animal could give him another two miles at full gallop.

The King was with the Dukes of Exeter and Warwick and his chamberlain, Lord Fitzhugh, the four in deep discussion about how best to bring about an end to the siege. What food they had was rapidly dwindling, there were enemy marksmen lurking just beyond their lines, there was no sign that the French would surrender and the incessant rain meant they hadn't had a decent, dry night's sleep in weeks. Hunger and exhaustion were beginning to take their toll of the English troops and dysentery was rife.

The messenger, still in his rain-soaked woollen cape and mud-spattered boots, was ushered into the royal presence and, on hearing the news that Catherine had given birth to a son, Henry gulped emotionally, not trusting himself to speak. He crossed himself then dropped to his knees where he stood, giving fervent thanks to God, to St John of Bridlington, and to St Crispin for granting him his dearest wish. His lips moved silently in a long prayer of thanksgiving while his companions stood with bowed heads. Then he got briskly to his feet.

'Forgive me,' he said, his eyes bright with tears but grinning from ear to ear, 'but this is such good news. The best Christmas gift a man ever had. A son! My son, Henry.' He turned and beckoned the messenger to come forward. 'Tell me, my good man, do my son's looks favour his mother or me?'

'I have not had the privilege of seeing the child, Your Highness,' said the messenger 'but I imagine he is a handsome babe, whoever he looks like!'

'Quite so, quite so!' Henry laughed, clapping the man on the back. 'A diplomatic answer, if ever I heard one! My son, Henry! I expect his arrival caused a real rumpus at the Palace of Westminster!'

The messenger was silent for a moment, confused. Then he spoke in a low voice. 'The child was born at Windsor, Sire,' he said. 'Windsor, not Westminster.'

'Windsor? *Windsor*! But I expressly commanded that the court should remove to the Palace of Westminster for the birth. Why was my wish ignored?' Henry's face was flushed a dark red.

'I ... I don't know, Sire,' said the messenger, cowed by the King's unexpected outburst, 'I'm not certain but I believe ... well, my wife said ... and I expect she's right, women are usually right about such things ... and she was one of the midwives so she should know ...'

'Yes, man, what did your wife say? Spit it out!'

'Well, my wife said that it was Her Majesty's intention to lie-in at Westminster for the birth. She was quite sure of that. And the baby was expected at Christmas. But my wife said she was sure that the babe could not endure to wait in his mother's belly for all that time. He was impatient to come out and get on with the business of following in his father's footsteps.'

Henry paused for a moment, then let out a great hoot of laughter. 'Yes, my man, I expect your wife is right. And your diplomacy is second to none. Here, take this for your pains. And give my compliments to your wife; a wise woman indeed! I'm delighted ... delighted ... with the news you have brought me.'

Pressing a purse full of coins on the messenger, Henry all but pushed the man out of the door. Then he sat down heavily, put his elbows on the table, and his head in his hands.

'My Lord, you seem upset.' Lord Fitzhugh was full of concern.

'Mmm?' Henry looked up at him and sighed. 'Well, yes, just for a moment. You see, there was an old prophecy ... nonsense really, I suppose ... that I, born in Monmouth would achieve much but not live long and that my son, born in Windsor, would live for many years but lose everything I had fought for. That's really why I wanted him to be born in Westminster, or anywhere but Windsor, to deny that prophecy. But, as I say, it's probably all nonsense.'

'You shouldn't listen to soothsayers, my Lord,' said Warwick, 'they're nothing but trouble. You're a man in your prime and will live for many years to come and lead England on to greater and greater glory.'

'And I,' said Exeter, 'am already planning how we will celebrate your fortieth birthday, Sire, five years hence, when you are king of both England and France!'

'Possibly,' said Henry, 'possibly. Given that my father-in-law is dead by then.' Then he threw an arm around the shoulders of both dukes, smiling broadly. 'But you're right of course, all of you. I shouldn't listen to soothsayers. No one but the Almighty can possibly know what the future holds. But, thanks be to God, the future of the English throne is secure, now that I have a son. So, come, let us go and tell our commanders to convey the good news to the troops, God knows they're demoralised enough after all this rain. Then we'll call for wine, the very best wine of France, so that we can wet the head of the little one who is destined, one day, not only to become King of England but also King of France. And let us redouble our efforts to subdue this quarrelsome country for the sake of my son's inheritance!'

Chapter Eight

France, May 1422

With a fair wind astern, the *Trinity Royal* was in full sail and bound for France. Below decks, a large contingent of royal servants, guards, and domestic staff lolled about, telling jokes, amusing each other with guessing games and indulging their enthusiasm for the new craze of playing cards to pass the time. On the top deck, John of Bedford, knowing that his sister-in-law was a poor traveller, offered her marchpane and sips from a beaker of wine. Catherine wanted neither and refused both. She was determined to defeat the distress of *mal de mer* by using the old sailor's trick she'd been taught by the captain of the *Grace Dieu*. Huddled in her miniver-lined cloak, she stood a little apart from her ladies and other members of the royal party, scanning the horizon for a glimpse of the French coast, recalling all the things which had happened to her since she last crossed the channel. She tried very hard not to worry about her baby son.

It was strange, she reflected, how a baby took over your life. She had never known such overwhelming love as she felt for that one small human being who had not yet even learned to call her Mother. Perhaps she should teach him to call her *Maman*, she mused, he was half French after all.

She knew she'd miss him dreadfully while she was in France but she was torn between leaving the baby and seeing Henry. Still, when they both returned to England, the baby would be old enough for his father to take a real interest in him. Perhaps he would even be old enough to recite that little finger-naming rhyme, the one Henry had shown her the very first time they met, all that long time ago at Pontoise. All she could remember was that the little finger was '*jolie*' something. '*Jolie cwt bach*', was it? She wasn't sure. Still, '*jolie*' was a description that certainly suited the baby. He was so beautiful that sometimes she would want to kiss him all over, on top of his soft, downy head, behind his ears, on the smooth skin inside his chubby elbows, on his plump little rump, behind his knees, on the soles of his little feet, just to enjoy the delighted way he wriggled and laughed, enjoying it just as much as she was.

That was usually when Elizabeth Ryman made an excuse to take him away from her.

Of course, the baby had no lack of doting women around him, making soft cooing noises over his crib and encouraging him to grip their fingers with his little hand. Foremost among them was the Countess Jacqueline, who had formed a deep and lasting affection for the child from the moment she had stood at the christening font, holding him in her arms ready to hand him to Archbishop Henry Chichele for his baptism. On either side of her stood his two other godparents, his uncle John of Bedford and his great-uncle, Bishop Henry Beaufort. Catherine, having not yet been churched after the birth, was absent from the christening ceremony.

So when it came to leaving the baby behind in Windsor while she journeyed to visit her husband, Catherine had no doubt at all that she had left him in good hands. Jacqueline had given her every assurance. She would look after the baby, she promised, even if it meant elbowing the frightful Ryman woman out of the way. Catherine need have no fears about that!

Henry, free of his military duties after the eventual surrender of Meaux, met Catherine at the Château de Vincennes, a short distance from Paris. Their sumptuous private accommodation was on the second floor of the huge, square *donjon* which towered above the rest of the château. Here they had everything they needed and, soon after they arrived, Guillemote had served them with a simple meal and a jug of wine then left them alone to spend their first evening together exactly as they wished. Apple wood burned in the grate for, though the sun was high and warming during the day, the nights were chilly. But

Catherine, alone with her husband at last, didn't intend that Henry would remain chilled for long.

He looked pale and had lost a considerable amount of weight. She fussed over him, feeding him small mouthfuls of food with a spoon, much as she might have fed his baby son, and he let himself be pampered, smiling wanly. She babbled about the baby and how he had nearly said 'Maman' a few days before she left Windsor. He was only six months old, of course, and couldn't be expected to say very much at all, but it was plain to see that he was a very intelligent baby and she was quite sure that if Henry had been at home, his little son would be calling him 'Papa' by now.

Henry smiled and put a gentle finger on her lips. 'Hush, Catherine,' he said kindly. 'Tell me about my clever son tomorrow. I am tired to my very bones, sweetheart, and I need to sleep. I wouldn't do justice to a woman tonight. Not even you.'

'But, Henry …'

'Tomorrow, my sweet. You can't possibly know how the prospect of a warm, dry, comfortable bed can beguile a soldier after months of damp and wretched discomfort. We endured incessant rain and very little food before Meaux surrendered. I lost many of my men to dysentery because of it. The flux. A horrible, stinking disease. And, believe me, it is no respecter of kings.'

'Is that what troubles you, my Lord?'

'It is, but at least I have a few days of warmth and rest to look forward to, and decent food to give my bowels something to grip. Anton is sure to know what is best for that.' He turned towards her, suddenly anxious. 'He has come over from England with you, hasn't he?'

'Yes, yes, he has,' said Catherine. 'I made sure of that. I knew you would appreciate his cooking after months of soldiers' victuals.'

'Then I'll eat whatever he suggests,' said Henry, pulling back the covers on the bed and climbing into it. 'But let me sleep tonight, my sweet love, please. It's all I really need. Blessed, blessed sleep.'

Well, there was nothing for it, thought Catherine, but to accept the situation with good grace. She curled up against Henry's broad back and closed her eyes, willing herself to sleep.

She woke with beads of sweat on her forehead, her heart hammering. The room was as black as pitch and it took her a moment to realise where she was. She reached out a hand and felt the warmth of the mattress where Henry had been lying. She'd been dreaming again but it was not a pleasant dream. There were horses, several horses, going too fast, and there were men shouting. Children too, screaming in terror. She lay on her back, staring wide-eyed into nothingness until her heart resumed its normal beat. Then she heard the sound which must have awakened her, the piercingly beautiful and haunting sound of a blackbird singing in the darkness outside the window. But there was another sound too, ugly and disturbing. Catherine turned onto her side, pulled the bedclothes up over her shoulder for warmth, and listened to her husband groaning in the garderobe.

She slid out of their warm bed early the next morning, taking the little bedside bell out into the corridor to summon Guillemote so that it wouldn't wake Henry. Guillemote came running, barefoot at her mistress' command.

'The King is ill, Guillemote,' Catherine whispered. 'He was up several times in the night.'

'What ails him, Ma'am?'

'The flux.'

Guillemote's eyes widened in alarm and she crossed herself swiftly. 'The flux! Then we must pray for him, my Lady.'

'Yes, yes, of course, but he seems to think that all he needs is some solid food to settle his stomach. Would you ask Anton's advice, please? He probably knows what's best.'

'Certainly, Ma'am.'

Guillemote dropped the slippers she'd been carrying, pushed her feet into them, and bustled away towards the kitchen. Catherine returned to the bedchamber where Henry was still fast asleep. She looked down at him for a long moment then

106

knelt at the side of the bed, studying his face. It was very drawn and there were more lines around his eyes than she remembered, more grey in his hair and in the stubble on his chin. His skin had taken on a translucent quality and the scar tissue below his right eye stood out lividly, knotted and tight. She wanted to reach out and touch it, make it whole again, make him better; but she was afraid of waking him. He needed all the rest he could get. Still kneeling, she crossed herself, closed her eyes and prayed for him.

Later that morning, Anton climbed the spiral stairs of the donjon and was shown into the royal solar. He was confident that he had the answer to the King's problem.

'Hare,' he said, emphasising the aspirate.

'Hair?'

'*Oui*. Hare.' Anton, anxious that the King should understand his meaning, held up two fingers at either side of his head in imitation of a hare's long ears. 'Jugged hare, Your 'Ighness. And Anton will make a delicious sauce with 'is insides and mix 'is gall with pepper. And your pain – it will go. Phut!' He clicked his fingers.

'You can rid me of the pain, Anton?' The King's face brightened.

'I will try, Sire,' said the little Frenchman, bowing low again, 'with some help from *Monsieur Lièvre*, the clever Mr Hare.'

'Then get to your kitchen, man, and work miracles for me,' Henry said, smiling as he lay back on his pillows. He remained in bed that day and for the rest of the week, letting Catherine pamper him and eating as much of Anton's delicious jugged hare as he could force down his gullet.

While her husband remained confined to his sickbed at the Château de Vincennes, Catherine took the opportunity to visit her parents at St Pol and was shocked by the sight of Queen Isabeau, who had finally begun to look her age. She was now fifty-two years old and had grown very fat. Her skin had yellowed and all that remained of the once-handsome Queen's beauty was her remarkable eyes.

The King, her father, cried when he saw Catherine at his

bedside but had no idea who she was. He spent most of his time in his bedchamber and his wife craved companionship and gossip.

Absently stroking the small white dog on her ample lap, Isabeau was greedy for information about her grandson and Catherine was only too pleased to boast to her mother about the baby, how handsome he was and how clever. She recounted the stories of her coronation, too, and her mother was much amused to hear of the miracles which Anton had wrought with the fish.

For her part, Catherine was keen to hear news of her siblings. The Dauphin Charles, Isabeau told her, had retreated to Bourges with his tail between his legs at around the time of the Treaty of Troyes. He had been there ever since.

'And I hear he's about to be married,' she added.

'Really? To whom?'

'To Marie of Anjou,' said Isabeau. 'No doubt her mother forced them into it. She's fearfully determined and she seems to have taken him over completely since he left here and fled south. I know her of old. Dreadful woman!'

Catherine suppressed a smile at the thought that there was another royal mother as domineering as her own. 'And how is my dear sister Marie?' she asked.

'She is so highly thought of at that convent in Poissy,' Isabeau said contemptuously, 'that she will no doubt end her days there as Mother Superior.'

Catherine remembered how pleased Marie had been to be accepted as a postulant. 'I'm sure that will make her very happy,' she said.

'Michelle, on the other hand, is hardly likely to be a mother at all, superior or otherwise. She has still not presented her husband with the son and heir he expects of her.'

'There's still plenty of time for that,' said Catherine from the lofty standpoint of a woman who had recently produced a healthy male child with little difficulty.

'I don't think so,' said Isabeau. 'Frankly, I don't think it will ever happen. She's getting old now and losing her looks. She's twenty-seven. Philip goes to her bed, of course, in the hope of getting a son, a legitimate one, that is. From what I hear, he's busy fathering brats from Dijon to Flanders but he still hasn't managed one with Michelle.'

'But she is not without hope of a child, is she?'

'Who knows? But she's such a sour-puss nowadays that I'm not surprised he goes elsewhere for his bed sports. And she's been like that for the last three years, ever since John the Fearless was murdered. For some reason, she seems to want to take the blame for it, as though it really was her own brother that killed him. She wears a face as long as a fiddle so it's no wonder Philip is behaving like a tom-cat. Who can blame him? She's brought it on herself.'

Barely a month later, Catherine remembered what her mother had said when news reached the Château de Vincennes that Michelle had died. At first, Catherine refused to believe what she'd heard. Michelle? Dead? Surely not. But, if so, why? And how? Henry, feeling better but not yet inclined to travel, urged her to return to St Pol with a small escort party, so that she could learn more about what had happened to her sister and comfort her parents in their distress.

The messenger who had first brought the news from Ghent was summoned to appear before both Isabeau and Catherine to give an exact account of what had happened but he seemed unable to tell them anything of any significance except that Michelle had appeared to be well and healthy until a day or two before her death. No, she had not had an accident and, as far as he knew, neither had she died from any complications arising from a possible pregnancy. There was no report of any sickness in Ghent and no one else seemed to be involved. She had just – and here the messenger shrugged – well, she had just died. He couldn't tell them any more except that the funeral had been well-attended. She had, after all, been a popular duchess.

Isabeau was stroking her lap dog's head so hard that the whites of its bulbous eyes were showing. She dismissed the messenger with an imperious wave of her hand. 'Poison, do you think, Catherine?' she asked when they were alone. She wore a grim expression on her face.

'Surely not, Maman!' Catherine was tearful and shocked by

the suggestion. 'Who would benefit from poisoning her?'

'You never know,' said Isabeau darkly. 'These days, you never know. And it's always notoriously difficult to prove.'

'Then we must heed the words of Saint Augustine, my Lady. *"Nothing is more certain than death and nothing less so than the hour of its coming"*.'

The Queen cast her eyes to the ceiling, surprised that her daughter could still find solace in some of the more trite platitudes of the saints. Then she shook her head, her mouth a bitter downturned line as she pushed the small dog off her lap. It scurried for cover under her chair, away from the painful pressure of her stroking.

Philip of Burgundy seemed not to mourn his wife at all. Within an indecently short time after her death, he sent a messenger to Henry with a request for help in relieving the town of Cosne-sur-Loire.

Catherine was sitting with Henry in their solar at the Château de Vincennes when the message arrived.

'My Lord, you mustn't even think of it!' she objected. 'You're just beginning to get back on your feet and now you're proposing to go rushing off again, helping Philip with some stupid little siege that doesn't concern you.'

'Everything that happens in France concerns me, Catherine,' said Henry, 'and as it happens, the Dauphin himself is the cause of this particular problem. He has established his centre at Cosne, so it is hardly what you call a stupid little siege.'

'That doesn't make me personally responsible for it! Charles may be my brother but he makes his own decisions. I don't want you to fight him, Henry! I don't want you to fight Charles!' Catherine was on her feet now, her voice rising, her fists clenched and her eyes bright with tears, trying to make him listen to her, fearing that he would become very ill indeed if he went back into the field of battle too soon. She had so recently lost her sister that she couldn't bear the thought that she might lose her husband as well. And if she didn't lose her husband, then she would very probably lose her brother. Hysteria threatened to overwhelm her.

'That's enough, Catherine,' Henry silenced her sternly. 'This is not a matter of what you want or don't want. I'm going to Philip's aid and there's an end to it.' Catherine subsided, sobbing, into a chair.

But she was right. It was far too early for Henry to venture back into the fray. He had always been a man who drove himself too far too often but, this time, his sheer determination to confront the Dauphin was not enough to see him through. He set out from the Château de Vincennes on horseback but soon became too weak to ride. He never reached Cosne.

The physicians in attendance on the King were seriously worried about him. They set up a temporary field hospital and tried all the herbal remedies they knew, to no avail. No amount of bleeding seemed to make any difference whatsoever and they dared not try to purge him. The best idea seemed to be to take the King back to the Château de Vincennes and a messenger was sent on ahead to make sure that the Château would be ready to receive him. Another messenger was dispatched in haste to summon John of Bedford to attend his brother at the Château.

Catherine spent many anxious hours watching from a casement window high up in the donjon until she eventually saw a group of soldiers approaching the Château flanked by men of the royal guard and with the royal standard fluttering above a horse-drawn litter. She ran down the long spiral staircase and met the group at the door, trying not to get in the way as the King's stretcher was being man-handled into a room on the ground floor. As his body servants began to remove his stinking clothes, she tried to get Henry to speak to her.

He turned his face away from her and his voice was barely audible. 'Catherine, grant me my dignity, please. This bloody flux is no sight for the eyes of a gentlewoman. Go. Leave me. I will send for you when I am clean.'

Catherine hovered nervously outside the makeshift sickroom as priests, doctors, scribes, and servants came and went. The urgent sound of footsteps running in corridors awakened a sudden dim memory for her and she felt real fear.

When he arrived, John of Bedford greeted her briefly before being ushered straight into the King's room. Sinking heavily onto the chair at the bedside, he was deeply troubled to see how emaciated and hollow-eyed his brother had become in such a short time. 'Well, Henry,' he said as jovially as he could, forcing a broad smile, 'what would you like to discuss? Are you sure you're feeling up to it or would you rather leave things until you're feeling a little better?'

'I'm dying, John,' said Henry through parched lips, 'let's not pretend otherwise.' He raised his hand feebly to quell his brother's loving denial. 'Comfort my poor wife when I am gone. I cannot leave her much, the jewellery must be sold to pay off debts but she is provided for. Come, have you brought a scribe with you? Good. There are things I need to arrange and I must tell you what they are.'

With what little energy he could muster, the King dictated a codicil to the will which had been drawn up before he sailed for France and before the birth of his son. The fact that there was now a male heir to the throne made the corrections imperative.

'He must be known as the Prince of Wales,' Henry insisted between laboured breaths, 'he is the eldest son of the sovereign. It is my particular wish.' The scribe made a note of the fact. Slowly and painfully but with deliberation, Henry went on to dictate his wishes for his son's education and upbringing. His brother Humphrey of Gloucester was to be made responsible for the baby, guarding and protecting him in all things. The Prince's household was to be run by Henry's trusted friend Sir Walter Hungerford. John of Bedford was to oversee English interests in France.

During the ensuing days, Catherine spent hours lingering near sickroom, fanning her face in the oppressive heat, waiting to be summoned to her husband's bedside. He had not yet asked for her but she wanted to be near at hand when he did.

Then, on the last day of August, she rose abruptly from her seat as a priest, clutching a rosary, emerged from the King's room followed by John of Bedford, his eyes red-rimmed and swollen. He didn't need to tell her what she already knew in her heart.

'He's dead?'

John nodded mutely.

'And he never sent for me,' she said in a dull voice.

The early days of September passed in a dim, grey muddle. Not that Catherine cared very much. She had been shocked by the sudden death of her sister then, with her husband's death so soon afterwards, she had simply let other people take over her life. She did what she was told to do, she ate when food was put in front of her, and she tried to sleep when she went to bed but that was the hardest thing. The bed felt vast and lonely and that was when she missed Henry most of all, missed curling up against his broad back. She remembered how, in winter, she would warm her icy feet on the backs of his legs until he squealed in laughing protest before turning towards her, taking her in his arms, and warming her thoroughly. She smiled at those memories but her throat ached with longing for him and tears were never far away.

She tried to take an interest in arrangements for the funeral. John of Bedford had explained to her that, really, Henry must be taken home to England for his burial. His people would want to pay homage to him in his own country. It was unthinkable that he should be buried in France.

'But, surely, that won't be possible, it … it will take too long to convey him back to England!' She couldn't bring herself to say that the journey would take many weeks and that, in this heat, her husband's corpse would surely soon begin to rot. John understood her hesitation and explained to her as kindly as he could that Henry's organs had already been removed and given a Christian burial in a French graveyard. By now his body had been embalmed in aromatic herbs and balsam, wrapped in lengths of silk, and placed in a wooden coffin which had then been sealed inside another made of lead. It would safely make the journey to England, no matter how long it took.

In the second week of September, Catherine stood outside the door of the donjon, watching as the funeral cortège assembled for its slow, solemn journey across France. Several princes, lords, and knights of the royal household and four hundred men-at-arms would accompany Henry's coffin on its long journey home to England. Suddenly she gasped, gripping

John's arm. 'Henry!' she cried. 'It's Henry. Look, John, look!' She pointed to a figure lying on top of the coffin, dressed in Henry's robes, wearing a crown and holding an orb and sceptre.

John caught her as her knees gave way and her body slumped, cursing himself for not having warned her of what she would see. It was an effigy, a manikin made of boiled leather, but from a distance it might have been her husband, back from the dead. Shaking uncontrollably, she covered her face with her hands, blotting out the image, as John put his arm around her shoulders to comfort her.

Catherine joined the funeral cortège later in the month, escorted by John of Bedford. By the second week of October, having made frequent stops for masses to be said for the dead king in churches and cathedrals all along the route, the long, bleak procession of mourners reached Calais and waited for suitable ships to convey them across the English channel.

It was in Calais that she received the news which, if she'd been honest with herself, she had been half-expecting for years. Nevertheless, it was news which nearly pushed her over the edge of reason. In a message sent with great haste from Paris she learned that, on October the twenty-first, her father, King Charles VI, had finally succumbed to his torment. Now her world really had come to an end, she had nothing to live for. There was too much death. Her sister, Michelle, had been taken from her too suddenly and, though they had seen little of each other as children and had never been very close, Catherine still felt a great sadness at her death. And now the only two men who had ever loved her were both dead. She had no husband, no father. Nothing.

She no longer even had the comforting presence of John of Bedford since, on hearing of the death of the French king, he had decided that he must stay on in France to represent England at the funeral and make certain that, in any public declaration of succession to the French throne, the French people would be left in no doubt that Catherine's son, King Henry VI was now their sovereign. They must not expect to see the Dauphin Charles on the throne of France.

Death and decay seemed to be everywhere that October. The

beauty of autumn leaves, turning red and yellow, falling to the ground in great colourful drifts to reveal the skeletal shapes of trees, was just another aspect of death for Catherine. In desolation, her world seemed to close in on her and her troubled mind painted pictures of anguish and grief as she slept. The horses returned to haunt her and the screaming children came again in the night.

She almost forgot the reason why she had, until now, always looked forward so much to this time of the year; but Guillemote had not forgotten. So when she came into the royal bedchamber to wake her mistress on the morning of October the twenty-seventh, she brought with her a small posy of autumn flowers, Michaelmas daisies, hawkbit, and a few late roses, to place on Catherine's bedside table.

'Happy birthday, Your Highness,' she greeted her.

Catherine opened her eyes. 'Happy birthday, Guillemote? I hardly think so.' She blinked back sudden tears. 'I'm twenty-one years old today and already my life is over.'

Guillemote was thoughtful. 'My Lady,' she said, 'I believe I have been in your service long enough to presume to correct you occasionally, without fear of punishment.'

'That is most impertinent of you, Guillemote,' Catherine said, with a wry smile of affection for her friend.

'Forgive me, Your Highness,' Guillemote continued, 'but I have been thinking. Bad things often come in threes and you have suffered three most distressing bereavements in just over three months. You can no longer be the three things you have been in the past. You can no longer be a sister to Michelle and you cannot be a wife to your husband nor yet a daughter to your father. So, on this birthday you must look forward to being a mother to your son. He is still a little baby and he is already a king but he will not be ready for kingship for many, many years. Until he is, he will need all your help and all your devotion. Today, on this birthday, the direction of your life must change.'

Catherine felt herself losing control, her lower lip trembling. 'Guillemote,' she said, 'dear Guillemote. Your thorough lack of respect is very refreshing.'

It was then that the tears came, floods and torrents of tears, seeming to wash through her shuddering frame, sluicing away all the sorrow, all the bitterness and all the frustration of the months gone by. At first, Guillemote tried to comfort her but, wisely, she decided to let her mistress weep for all that she had lost in such a very short time.

Catherine remembered Guillemot's words as she stood alone on the deck of the *Trinity Royal*, her eyes firmly fixed on the horizon. She was within sight of England and, as she watched the white cliffs rising steeply out of the water, she knew that the reception she was about to face would be very different from the last time. Her gaze came to rest on the closely guarded catafalque which supported Henry's coffin with its hideous boiled leather effigy of the King. Then she remembered that other homecoming, less than two short years ago when the people of Dover, in a frenzy of enthusiasm, had waded waist-deep into the freezing water to welcome them both, the living Monarch and his Lady, waving and shouting their greetings, jostling each other to get near the boat.

'*Long live the King*!' That tumultuous welcoming shout still seemed to echo in her memory as she looked at the people who now waited in dark, silent groups on the foreshore, watching as the heavy lead coffin was lowered on ropes and pulleys from the *Trinity Royal* and manoeuvred carefully onto the wooden jetty in the harbour mouth. Henry was back on English soil and the only sound that welcomed him was carried on the wind from the tower of the little church of St Mary-in-Castro, where a single bell tolled the death knell for the departed king.

Catherine was still the Queen of England and there was still a King Henry. But Catherine was now the Dowager Queen and her son was king of both England and France. He was barely ten months old.

Part Two

Owen

Maent yn dweud fy mod yn caru,
Lle nad wyf, mi allaf dyngu.
Yn lle 'rwyf yn caru mwyaf
Y mae lleiaf sôn amdanaf.

People say I have a lover,
Who she is they can't discover.
Though she holds my heart in tether
No one links our names together.

'Maent yn dwedyd' ('They Say') – an old Welsh folk song.

117

Chapter Nine

Windsor Castle, November 1422

'*Diawl*!' Owain cursed loudly as he knocked over the ink horn.

'Clumsy devil!' Maredydd jumped up from his seat. 'Thank God there wasn't much ink in it, it's hardly spilled at all. Here, let me help you to clear it up. You're going to have to do better than this if you want to impress old Hungerford.'

The two were alone in a small room behind the great library of Windsor Castle, entirely illegally. To be fair to Maredydd, he was doing a favour for his young kinsman, who had newly arrived at Windsor from the far north of Wales having used up what little money he had on the long journey south. He was desperately in need of employment and Maredydd knew that one of the household clerks, thanks to his unsavoury habit of frequenting the cheaper whorehouses of Southwark, had recently died of the pox. There was a vacancy.

Before his mishap with the ink horn, Owain had been leafing through columns of figures in a parchment ledger. Now he straightened up, rubbing his back. 'The light is going,' he said. 'I can barely see what I'm doing. But I think I've got the hang of it.'

'Not my line of business,' said Maredydd. 'We gentlemen-at-arms don't concern ourselves with such things. Anyway, you shouldn't appear to know too much about the accounting systems, otherwise Hungerford will want to know how you came by the knowledge. And we're not supposed to be here.'

'Let's go into the town, then,' said Owain. 'I've worked up a rare thirst squinting at those books.'

'Let's find something to eat first. We'll see if we can scrounge something from that pompous little Frenchie in the kitchen.'

This was a quiet time of day for the kitchen staff, the debris from the midday dinner had been cleared away and the scullions had finished their cleaning and scouring. With order restored to his realm, Anton was standing at a table in his private room at the back of the main kitchen, next to the larder. This was the inner sanctum where he stored his most expensive ingredients: sugar, sweet galingale, and grains of paradise. Here the kitchen accounts were kept and it was here, under lock and key in a small coffer on a high shelf, that he kept his precious copy of *Le Viander*, a collection of recipes written by the great Valois family chef Taillevant and given to him as a gift on completion of his apprenticeship in the Valois kitchen. With pestle and mortar in hand, he was grinding valuable imported sugar and spices for a *poudre-douce* when Maredydd knocked at the half-open door.

'*Entrez*!', he trilled and looked up. 'Ah! The 'andsome Welsh gentleman-at-arms! And why are you not at the funeral?'

'Someone has to look after the shop. Windsor can't be left unattended while everyone else is weeping and wailing at Westminster. They've left twenty of us to guard the place but I've just come off duty.'

'And now you are going into the town, perhaps, to drink your English ale?'

'In the absence of Welsh ale, my friend, English ale will have to do. But first we need some food, if there's any going. Can't drink on an empty stomach.'

'We?' Anton looked past Maredydd to where Owain was waiting outside the door. He put down the pestle and mortar and stepped out into the kitchen. 'Ah, *oui!*' he said, his eyes widening appreciatively. 'And who is this?'

'My young kinsman, Owain. He is hoping to find work here at Windsor very soon.'

'So am I!' said Anton.

'So are you what?'

'So am I 'oping 'e will find work 'ere at Windsor very soon.'

'Back off, you French fop-doodle,' Maredydd threatened

120

him. 'My cousin is no gentleman of the back door. Leave him alone!'

'*Mared, paid*!' Owain said quietly. '*Gâd iddo fo.*'

'What language does he speak? Is this Welsh?'

'Yes. And he doesn't want to talk to you in that or any other language. Look, just give us a hunk of bread and cheese each and we'll piss off, out of your kitchen, then you can get back to prettifying your poxy peacocks, or whatever it is you do in here.'

'All right, all right.' Anton closed his eyes and held up his hands in a gesture of submission. 'No offence meant.'

'None taken,' muttered Owain.

'The goat's cheese is good,' Anton said grudgingly. 'You must 'elp yourselves, *mes amis.*'

Sitting on a bench outside the kitchen, Owain sank his teeth into a chunk of crumbly white cheese, only half-listening to Maredydd as he fumed about the Frenchman's overt behaviour. Owain, an undeniably handsome man, had learned to ignore such reactions in other people. Growing up, there had been times when he had cursed his looks, the deep brown of his eyes, and the way his dark hair curled over his forehead. Even when he was a very small boy, his nurse had once found him in front of his mother's mirror, trying to pull out his long, black eyelashes because he thought they made him look like a girl.

He recounted the story later that evening when he and Maredydd were sitting in front of a peat fire in the tavern at the sign of The Swan, with their elbows on the table, each cradling in his hands a pewter tankard of the alewife's finest ale.

'It hurt like hell,' said Owain. 'Do you remember Megan?'

'Megan? No, why should I?'

'No, of course, you'd have been away with your father's army when I was that age. Well anyway, Megan was my nurse and she said my eyelashes would just grow back but they'd be twice as long and there'd be twice as many of them. That stopped me!'

'Can't change what God has ordained. You were the one who got the looks in the family.' Maredydd looked up as two other gentlemen-at-arms approached the table. 'Hey, Will! How are you?'

'Hey, Mared! Who's your friend?'

'He's my kid cousin.'

'First cousins, eh?'

'Er, no, not quite. His father was my father's cousin so I suppose he's my second cousin, really.'

'He's family, anyway. Another Welshman, then. What's yer name, mate?'

'Owain ap Maredydd ap Tudur ap Goronwy Fychan,' said Owain.

There was a startled silence. 'What? That's not a bloody name. It's a disease of the throat!'

'No, no, it's my name,' Owain explained earnestly. 'It tells you who I am. "Ap" just means "son of". You know, like the Scots have "Mac". So I'm Owain, son of Maredydd. He was the son of Tudur …'

'… and Tudur was the son of Goronwy Fychan.' Maredydd finished for him. 'I explained all this to you years ago, Will, when you were bleating on about *my* name. We're proud of our lineage where we come from.'

'Sounds like it. This is Harry, by the way, he's new around here, too. Will and Harry. Good old English names. Keep it simple, I say. Now, where's that ale? Before I die of thirst!'

They went about the business of buying their ale, chivvying and teasing the alewife's daughter as she filled their tankards from an earthenware jug. Owain turned to Maredydd and spoke to him in Welsh.

'Why do they find my name so amusing?'

'It's ignorance. You'll get used to it. They mean no harm but they see us as foreigners. I've given up trying to tell them that we were here first, that we are the ones who speak the old language of Britain. They won't have it. They don't want to understand. They see us in the same light as the French or the Spanish, any foreigner, anyone who isn't English.'

'That's a pity. Theirs is such an ugly language.'

'Don't tell them that,' Maredydd warned. 'The best thing is just to fall in with them and try not to be too different. You'll get on much better that way.'

Will came back to the table with a tankard in his hand and sat down next to Owain. 'Listen, mate, I can't be doing with that name of yours. What did you say it was, again?'

Owain took a deep breath and smiled. 'It's Owain,' he said as Harry took a seat opposite them.

'That's a stupid name, for a start,' said Will. 'Owain. O-wine. "Wine! Oh, Wine!"' he mimicked in a high falsetto voice. 'Oh, I must have wine!'

Harry laughed at his friend's joke. 'Stick to beer, mate,' he said. 'It's simpler.'

'Look, Will,' Maredydd said, trying not to lose his temper, 'call him Owen. It's near enough. He'll answer to it, don't worry.'

'Owen what, though?

'Ap Maredydd,' said Maredydd.

'That's your name,' said Will. 'Can't call him that. It's too confusing.'

'Ap Tudur, then.'

'What about the last bit, you know, where it sounds as if you're going to spit or be sick or something?' Will made some disgusting coughing, spitting noises in his throat and Harry, a willing audience, guffawed again.

'Look,' said Maredydd, getting dangerously irritated, 'we'll keep it simple. Just call him Owen.'

'All right, Owen,' said Will. 'And what was the other name again?'

'Tudur,' said Owain, giving the name its correct Welsh pronunciation.

'Teed … er? T … t … tudduh? How did you say it again?'

'*Tudor* will do,' Maredydd said. 'It was his grandfather's name. He can be Owen Tudor. Even you should be able to remember that name, surely.'

'Owen Tudor?' Raising his eyebrows, Will looked at Harry. 'Not very memorable. What do you think, Harry?'

Harry shrugged. 'I don't suppose it'll go down in history,' he said. 'But what's in a name? Call a whore "my Lady" and she'll still lift her skirts.'

Will yelled with laughter, slapping his thigh. 'So do plenty of fine ladies, I can tell you! Well, welcome to Windsor, Owen Tudor. How do you like your new name, eh? Let me baptise you with this heavenly liquid!' Dipping his fingers into his tankard, he flicked a few drops of ale in Owen's face.

Despite the number of people crowded into the abbey church at Westminster, it was cold. Sitting with Jacqueline between Humphrey of Gloucester and John of Bedford, Catherine felt too cold to shiver. Her feet were numb and, glancing down the row of royal mourners, she could see that Margaret was rubbing the backs of her hands in an effort to warm them. Next to her sat James of Scotland, with Margaret's daughter Joan, and her youngest son Edmund Beaufort. Behind them sat other noble lords, friends of the dead king, members of his entourage, and some of those who had fought alongside him. The abbey church was packed with people.

Henry's coffin, draped in black velvet and cloth of gold, was drawn right into the nave as far as the choir screen by four great destriers, each fully caparisoned and led by a knight in armour. The huge black war horses were positioned in line in front of the high altar, pawing the ground and snorting, nervous in a strange environment, wary of the flickering candles. On a command, the knights raised their hands to their helmets and removed them. Symbolically, they then stripped off their weapons and their breastplates, handing each item to their armourers. Turning to the horses they took the protective chanfrons off their heads, then removed every other item of equestrian armour until the great beasts stood before the altar, their bare flanks gleaming dark in the candlelight, calm by now and as quiet as the animals in the stable at Bethlehem. Now the final requiem mass could begin and Henry's body would be committed for burial. The warrior King had been ceremonially divested of the armour which he had required in this world. He would have no further need of it. There were no wars in heaven.

Sir Walter Hungerford was expected to arrive at any moment and Owen was told to take a seat and wait for him in the castle library. He marvelled at the windows of white glass which flooded the big room with light and he was amazed at the number of books it contained, probably at least forty, maybe more. *The Expedition of Godfrey of Boulogne* was here, alongside *The Chronicles of Jerusalem* as well as the complete works of St Gregory and a beautifully bound copy of *The Canterbury Tales* by Geoffrey Chaucer.

Owen jumped to his feet as the door opened suddenly to admit four sombrely dressed men with two clerks following close behind them. Caught with a copy of *Le Roman de la Rose* in his hand, he looked around furtively for somewhere to put it as the clerks started arranging benches and chairs. With his back to the table, Owen managed to put the book down without being noticed but he wanted the ground to swallow him up.

'Ah,' said Sir Walter Hungerford, 'are you the person who is waiting to see me about the clerk's job?'

'I am, my Lord.'

'Then I'm sorry, young man, but I'm afraid I won't be able to see you today. It's not convenient. I have a meeting now with the late King's brothers and His Grace, Bishop Beaufort. You'll have to come back tomorrow.'

'What time would you like to see me, Sire?'

'What? Oh … let's say ten of the clock, shall we?'

'Certainly, Sire.'

Owen had begun to move towards the door when Humphrey of Gloucester spotted *Le Roman de la Rose* on the table. 'Wait!' he said quickly, 'have you been looking at the late King's books? Fingering them?'

'Er … yes, my Lord, I'm sorry,' Owen confessed. 'But my hands are clean and I've been very careful with them. They aren't harmed in any way.'

Sir Walter seemed unconcerned. 'So you can read, can you?' he asked.

'I can, Sire, yes. I can both read and write.'

'Good, good. Very well, I'll talk to you tomorrow. What was your name again?'

'Owain ap … er, Owen Tudor, Sir Walter.'

'Owen Tudor? You don't sound too sure! Is that a Welsh name?'

'Yes, Sir Walter. Yes, it is. It's an English version of my name.' Owen was backing slowly away. 'If you will excuse me, then, I will return tomorrow. Good day to you, my Lords.' He left the room as quickly as he could and a clerk closed the door behind him.

Humphrey of Gloucester reached out and picked up *Le Roman de la Rose* from the table where Owen had put it. 'I hope that Welsh lout hasn't marked this with his dirty thumbprints,' he said. 'It's a beautiful book.'

'I don't suppose he has,' said John of Bedford, 'he seemed a decent enough fellow.' He was anxious to begin the meeting. 'Now, my Lords, we have met to discuss how best to run this household for our young nephew, the King, so we must make a start. Sir Walter? Where would you like to begin?'

Walter Hungerford looked up from a sheaf of documents in front of him. 'Well, I suggest that we keep Elizabeth Ryman on in her general capacity. The King is in good hands there. I understand that his wet nurse is no longer needed and has been dismissed. She has been replaced by a sensible young woman called Joan Astley. Mistress Ryman tells me that she's been very highly recommended but she's costing us twenty pounds a year. That's a considerable sum. Hopefully she'll be worth the money.'

'He's been weaned then,' observed Henry Beaufort. 'So he's going to need a governess soon.'

'Oh, surely not,' protested John. 'He's just a baby. Probably just needs his mother to keep an eye on him.'

'No,' said Humphrey sharply, a little too sharply. The other men around the table looked up. 'I don't think that's a good idea. Look,' he lowered his voice, 'we need to be a little careful here, a little circumspect. I don't think we should encourage his mother to spend too much time with him.'

'Why ever not?' John asked.

Humphrey shrugged. 'She's French,' he said, 'so, of course, she can't be trusted. She might try to influence him too much. Besides, she'd only speak French to him and he needs English as his first language. You know how strongly Henry felt about that.'

'You have a point, I suppose,' said Henry Beaufort, 'though I'm not sure that I agree with you.'

Sir Walter, sensing a political argument in the making, tried to steer the conversation around to practicalities. 'I understand that one of the things which most concerned the late King in making his will was that debts had to be repaid as a matter of urgency and it seems to me that it would be sensible to monitor our costs more closely. Now, we're short of a clerk so I propose taking on another one, someone who's had a reasonable education. He won't need much in the way of payment, maybe twelve or thirteen pounds a year. I think I have just the young man for the job.'

'Not that lout who was here a few minutes ago?'

'Hmm? Yes, as it happens. I will interview him formally, of course, but I think he'll do nicely. He has a cousin who already works here – one of the senior gentlemen-at-arms. Seems a good man. He recommended that kinsman of his.'

'But ... but he's Welsh!' Humphrey objected. 'And you certainly can't trust *them*!'

'Oh, you can't tar them all with the same brush,' said Henry Beaufort. 'I think my nephew the King was actually rather fond of the Welsh, once he'd managed to subdue them. You know, people like Davy Gam. D'you remember him, Humphrey? Dead now, of course. Looked like a cross-eyed goat but he was very loyal. Henry knighted him on the battlefield. And the Welsh did give Henry excellent service at Agincourt. You, of all people, should know that.'

'Yes, perhaps so,' Humphrey agreed grudgingly. 'They're not bad bowmen.'

'They're excellent bowmen,' said John, 'especially the men of Gwent and Glamorgan. It's the wood they use, you know –'

'My Lords,' Sir Walter interrupted, 'I would be grateful if you would simply agree to the appointment of another member of clerical staff. It may not be for very long, just until we get things properly organised.'

'Well, you'll need to talk to the man, Sir Walter,' said Humphrey. 'What was his name again? He didn't seem very sure!' He laughed.

Sir Walter Hungerford chuckled. 'Didn't he say it was Tudor? Owen Tudor? Something like that. Now, gentlemen, where were we?'

It wasn't quite dark in the nursery and Elizabeth Ryman sat in the firelight, a bowl of frumenty on the table in front of her, trying to feed it into the unwilling mouth of the King of France and of England. Grizzling, the baby kept trying to push her hand away. 'Mistress Astley!' she called. 'Joan, come and see what you can do with him. I don't know what's the matter. He's very bad-tempered.' She got up from her seat by the fire as Joan Astley came in to the room. Joan was a round-faced, matronly young woman of generous proportions who adored babies and seemed to be able to do anything with them.

'I expect he's teething, Ma'am,' she said as Elizabeth Ryman handed the child over to her.

Joan knew exactly what the problem was, having explored the King's painful gums with her finger only this afternoon. Tincture of white willow bark was the answer. She swore by it.

'Hello, my little kinglet,' she whispered, smiling and taking the vacant seat by the fire. She positioned the baby comfortably in the crook of her arm. 'Who's got nasty old toothache, then? Eh? Let Joanie make it better for you.' She took a small glass phial from her apron pocket and shook it before removing the stopper. Dipping her finger into the liquid, she rubbed it gently on the baby's painful gums, soothing the hurt, lulling him to sleep.

This was how Catherine saw him for the first time in over six months. Having returned to Windsor with Jacqueline after Henry's funeral, she went immediately in search of her baby son, without even stopping to remove her heavy, rain-sodden woollen cloak.

'I must see him, Jacq,' she said. 'You have no idea how I have longed for this moment. Has he changed very much?'

'Oh, yes,' said Jacqueline, 'he has. He's a big boy now and quite heavy. Strong, too. Well, he's nearly a year old.' Then she stopped, her hand on the handle of the nursery door and a broad grin on her face. 'Ready?'

Catherine hesitated, then darted into the room as soon as the door was open. She couldn't wait to feel her baby's arms around her neck, to see his toothless smile. Surprised, Joan Astley struggled to get to her feet without waking her small charge. Seeing the newcomer with the Countess of Hainault, she assumed her to be the Queen but she couldn't quite manage a curtsey while she was holding the baby.

'Don't worry, please don't worry,' said Catherine. 'Just give him to me! Let me hold him.'

'Careful, my Lady,' said Joan, handing the baby over to his mother. 'He's teething.'

'Oh, I don't care. I just want to hold him.'

The baby opened his eyes and, seeing a stranger, screamed. Catherine held him tightly to her, thoughtlessly pressing his small face against the damp, scratchy fabric of her cloak, tears squeezing beneath her closed eyelids. She had tried so hard not to lose control at Henry's funeral, clinging to the thought of this moment as her reward for maintaining her dignity. But her baby had screamed at the sight of her. It was difficult to bear. 'Please don't cry,' she begged him. 'Please, please don't cry. Maman is home now, back with you again. Things will be different now.'

'Shall I, Your Highness?' Joan Astley stood, holding out her arms for the baby, who was bawling loudly. 'Don't upset yourself, please. And the King is upset, too. It's a difficult time. Let me take him from you. I can calm him.'

Jacqueline was all concern. 'You mustn't worry, Catherine,' she said, 'he'll soon get used to you again.'

Catherine was rooted to the spot with misery. 'Yes, you're right. It was too much to expect that he would know me after all this time. And I didn't want to upset him. I'm sorry. I should have thought.'

The baby – her baby, struggling and crying in his nurse's arms – was a beautiful child with soft, creamy-white skin and brown eyes. Henry, she thought; he has his father's eyes. Light, straw-coloured hair lay like threads of silk across his head. She gazed at the child in wonderment as Joan tried to pacify him. Eventually his frightened tears subsided and he blinked up at the three women's faces above him, his nurse, his mother, and

129

his godmother.

'Has he stopped crying at last?' Elizabeth Ryman asked as she came bustling back into the nursery. Seeing Catherine, she immediately dropped a deep curtsey. 'Oh, Your Highness! I'm sorry, I didn't know you had returned from Westminster. I should have been here to greet you.'

She rose and turned to Joan Astley. 'Let Her Highness have the baby, Joan,' she ordered. Joan hesitated and glanced at Catherine who shook her head.

'Let me take him, Joan,' said Jacqueline, holding out her arms to little Henry. 'He knows me.'

The child went to her without a murmur, nestling against her shoulder, his thumb in his mouth. Jacqueline looked over his head at Catherine.

'I'm sorry, Catherine,' she said.

Closing her eyes and not trusting herself to speak, Catherine nodded. She felt she had reached the lowest ebb in her life.

'I'm sorry you've had to come back a second time.' Sir Walter strode into the castle library shortly after ten o'clock the following morning with a ledger under his arm. 'Do sit down.' He motioned Owen to sit on a bench as he set the ledger on the table in front of him.

'Thank you, Sir Walter.'

'Now, young man, your cousin … er, Meredith, is it?'

'Maredydd, Sire. Maredydd ap Owain.'

'Yes, well, that,' said Sir Walter. 'He tells me that you have mastered reading skills and that you can recite your times tables up to twelve. Is that so?'

'Indeed, Sire.'

'Nine twelves are … what?' Sir Walter shot at him.

'Er … one hundred and eight,' said Owen after only a moment's hesitation.

'Good, good. Languages?'

'Welsh, Sire, my native tongue. And English, of course. I have sufficient Latin to serve its purpose in church. Oh, and a little French.'

'Really? And where did you receive this fine education of

130

yours? Did you study with monks? At Westminster, perhaps?'

'No, Sire, I was taught at home in Wales. But, yes, I did study with monks, with the Dominican Friars at Bangor. That is where I learned to read and write and they also gave me lessons in arithmetic. One of the itinerant bards taught me to play the *crwth* and I picked up the strict metres from him, too.'

'Picked up the what?'

'The strict metres, Sir Walter, the rules which govern the composition of poetry in Welsh. The bards will always teach them to anyone who is keen to learn.'

Sir Walter's eyebrows shot up. 'Really? How very interesting. Well, you won't be needing those in the English court. We don't go in much for poetry, not these days, not since Chaucer died, God rest his soul. But, apart from that, my boy, I think you will suit our purpose very well. Now, let me show you this ledger and explain what I'd like you to do.'

Sir Walter was a patient tutor. He took Owen through the columns of the ledger, showing him how he would like to see the figures presented and how he wanted to have certain domestic expenditures tracked in order to see where money was being spent unnecessarily.

'I think there are significant savings to be made. Do you agree?'

'I think you may be right, Sir Walter. If I can keep an eye on where the money goes over the next six or eight weeks, I'll have a much better idea.'

'Good,' said Sir Walter, closing the ledger, 'then I'd like you to start here next Monday morning. Be at your workplace immediately after morning mass. The seneschal of the Castle is Sir William Gifford and you will be answerable to him in all things. Including punctuality!'

'Of course; thank you, Sire.'

As Sir Walter was getting up to leave he turned back with another question. 'Tell me,' he said, 'what made you want to leave Wales and come to work in London?'

Owen hesitated. There was no point in telling Sir Walter how everything changed after the family had become resigned to the death of Maredydd's father, whose memory he hero-worshipped. Neither was there any purpose to be served by telling him about his scheming kinsman Gwilym ap Gruffydd who had gained control of the family lands in Anglesey. There had been a girl, too; but Rhiannon was betrothed elsewhere. He might as well move on.

'Perhaps,' he answered slowly, 'perhaps a sense of adventure. I suppose I wanted to emulate my kinsman, Maredydd. He's older than I am. And he was invited to enter His Majesty's service after the pardon.'

'Pardon? What pardon?'

'Oh, I'm sorry, Sir Walter, I thought you knew. He is Maredydd ap Owain, the son of Owain Glyndŵr. Ours is an old and honourable family.'

'So *that's* who you are, the pair of you! Kin to Glendower, the self-styled Prince of Wales! I thought there was something about you both.'

'Will that make a difference to my appointment, Sir Walter?'

Sir Walter shrugged. 'Well, I can't really see why it should. But it's difficult to forget the insurrection and the Welsh wars. Glendower and his followers were very persistent and very, very cunning.'

'They were fighting for Welsh freedom, Sire. It was an important cause.'

Sir Walter shrugged again, more eloquently this time. 'Not everyone would agree with you. Frankly, I was rather surprised that the King seemed to favour a policy of conciliation towards the Welsh, after all the trouble they gave him, and his father before him. And Glendower, the so-called freedom fighter, never even had the good grace to acknowledge the pardon he was offered after the revolt had been quelled.'

Owen was becoming increasingly irritated that Sir Walter couldn't be bothered to pronounce Glyndŵr's name correctly. But he really needed this job so he swallowed his pride and answered politely.

'In the family, Sir Walter, we believe that he was dead by then but we can't prove that. Anyway, there was a second pardon offered and Maredydd accepted that on his father's behalf. That's when he was invited to enter the service of the King. He served with His Highness in Normandy.'

Sir Walter sighed. 'And now you, too, are entering the service of the King. But a new king, King Henry VI. He'll need all the help we can give him, poor little mite.'

Owen smiled. It seemed such a strange thing to call the monarch. But then, that's really all he was; a poor little mite, a small baby who was forced to rely on the integrity and genuine concern of those who had the care of him.

'I'll do my best to serve him, Sir Walter,' he said. 'As long as you're sure that my background isn't going to make any difference to my position as a clerk in his household.'

'No. Not unless you want it to. Your cousin has already proved his loyalty to the House of Lancaster and you're likely to do the same, I suspect. So it makes no difference to my decision. Good luck, my boy.'

Sir Walter turned on his heel and left the room.

Chapter Ten

England, November 1422

John of Bedford had been trying to find Catherine. No one seemed to have seen her and he'd almost given up when he spotted Guillemote. He thought he recognised the little French woman with the bright, intelligent brown eyes.

'Ah,' he said, 'you're ... er ... you're the Queen's tiring woman, aren't you?'

'I am Guillemote, my Lord Duke, Her Majesty's personal maid.'

'Ah, yes. Then be so good as to tell me where she is. I wish to speak to her.'

'I believe, my Lord, that she is with the Countess Jacqueline. If you would care to follow me, please, I will ask if she will see you.'

The Duke found himself admiring what went before him. Guillemote had a pleasing figure with a trim waist and there was a look of organised determination about her. She was probably an excellent personal maid, he thought. She'd no doubt make some man a half-decent wife, too. Frenchwomen of her type were not always particularly pretty but he had found them to be diligent, intelligent, loyal, and, more often than not, possessed of a surprising sense of humour. Just the sort of wife he would have liked, he thought, the sort you knew wouldn't stray or embarrass you in any way. Not that he'd ever had any choice in the matter. There had apparently been a suggestion many years ago that he should be married to the Countess Jacqueline but it had come to nothing. In retrospect he was rather relieved about that since she was a bit boisterous for his taste. In temperament, she was far better suited to his brother Humphrey and they did appear to be quite entranced with each other. He himself had no prospect of marriage. John often felt quite lonely.

Guillemote stopped outside Jacqueline's door and knocked it discreetly. 'Just wait a moment, please Your Grace, I'll see if Her Highness is here.'

John crossed the corridor to sit on a windowsill in the embrasure opposite Jacqueline's room. He didn't have long to wait. Catherine emerged, alone, and gave him a watery smile.

'John,' she said, 'Guillemote says you are anxious to see me. I hope you haven't been waiting long.'

'No, not at all.' John smiled warmly at her and got to his feet. He had become very fond of his young sister-in-law since they had been forced to spend so much time together during the last few dreadful months. Looking at her, he could see that strain and grief had etched tiny new lines in her face. And he could see she had been crying.

'Catherine, my dear! You look upset. Is there anything I can do for you?'

'No, John, thank you. It's just that the baby has completely forgotten me. I should have realised that he wouldn't know me after I'd been away from him for such a long time. It was stupid of me to think that he'd be exactly the same as he was before I went to France.'

'They change very quickly at that age. Not that I have much experience of babies, of course.'

'No,' said Catherine with a ghost of a smile, 'and, in truth, neither have I. Perhaps I should have insisted on taking him to France with me. Then he wouldn't have forgotten me and at least his father would have had the chance to see him before … before …' She bit her lip.

'Catherine, please, don't upset yourself any further. How were you to know that Henry would die? Now, come, let me tell you why I wanted to see you.'

He took her hand and tucked it companionably under his elbow as they walked together back down the corridor. When they reached the library, John opened the door and ushered her inside, then settled her comfortably in a chair near the fire.

'I wanted to talk to you about the decisions which Parliament has been making on your behalf,' he said, smiling at her, 'and you'll be pleased to know that you are to receive the sum of six thousand pounds a year.'

'That seems quite generous.'

'Of course,' John went on, 'deductions of seven pounds a day will be made for your keep here in the King's household at Windsor for as long as you reside with him. The remainder will be for your personal needs, clothes, shoes, your servants' salaries, and so on and you will still have more than three thousand pounds for that purpose.'

Catherine didn't react. It was something she hadn't thought about, assuming that things would just return to normal, that she would have a roof over her head and that food would appear on the table as it always had.

'You will, in due course, inherit several of the dower palaces which are, by right, the property of the dowager queens of England.'

'But I'll be living in Windsor, won't I? With the baby?'

'Yes, of course you will. The other properties are yours to visit whenever you choose. But you must realise, Catherine, that crucial decisions have to be made about the King's welfare and his physical well-being, his education, and so on. So a Royal Council has been established, with Humphrey in charge, to look after his interests.'

'But I'll be looking after him!'

John nodded. 'You are his mother, of course, but you can't possibly do everything for him, Catherine. That's where the Council comes in. But don't worry,' he added, seeing the concern on her face, 'the decisions they make concerning the King will require the agreement of all the council members. So, in theory, no one will have any undue influence over him.'

He knew that now he had to sound a note of caution. 'Catherine,' he said, 'you have been very brave in the last few months but perhaps not nearly so brave as you're going to need to be in the years to come.'

She frowned. 'Why do you say that?'

'Because your position in the royal household has changed. You're still the Queen but you are not the King's wife. You're now the King's mother and it's not quite the same thing. He is too young to champion you and protect you as a husband would. So if you are to serve him well you must be aware of every possible danger.'

'Are you suggesting that his guards and nurses are untrustworthy?'

He shook his head. 'No. Not at all. Just let's say that I know enough about human nature to realise that there are those who would try to gain power for themselves by having power over him. He's only a small child. One day he will learn wisdom, I'm sure of it, but it will be several years before he can make his own decisions and even then he will need guidance. I'm anxious that you're aware of the situation from the beginning.'

Catherine was becoming only *too* aware of the situation. 'Yes, but who do you think would want to harm him? Apart from my brother, of course. He won't bend the knee to a baby.'

'Not just the Dauphin, my dear, the threats could come from much nearer home. I'm thinking about anyone who seeks self-advancement. And I'm not talking about doing the King any physical harm. I think we have more to fear from those who might try to influence him, to manipulate him, seek to change his attitudes. He is young and very, very vulnerable. You are his main ally so you must make sure you're with him as much as possible.'

'That won't be difficult, John. He is my son. And I love him.'

'Of course you do, and in a few days he will have learned to recognise you and will have come to love you again, as he used to when he was younger.'

'Oh, *Mon Dieu*, I do hope so!'

'Yes, of course he will, Catherine. And you must work hard to make him.' He smiled at her. 'You must enjoy being with him. Play with him, feed him, get him used to having you back in his life again. Don't let Elizabeth Ryman have sole charge of him, nor any one of his nurses. You the King's mother, after all, so you will have to accompany him to Parliament very soon and he must feel comfortable with you before that.'

'Parliament?' Catherine looked surprised.

'He is the King.'

'But he isn't one year old until next month! Why does he need to attend Parliament? What if he cries?'

John shrugged. 'Then he cries. Catherine, the fact remains that, young as he is, he is still the sovereign. His presence in Parliament is needed to ratify, to sanction, to approve, to disapprove … well, almost anything, really. There is little or nothing that Parliament will do without the King's permission. Or, in this case, his presence. So, I'm afraid you will have to take him to Parliament from time to time. But make sure that you are the one who is with him … and no one else.'

Catherine shook her head in disbelief as John went on. 'Catherine, the truth of it is that the Members of Parliament will decide themselves what they want to do. But they do need to be able to claim that certain things were done in the presence of the King … and that he did not disapprove of their decisions.'

'But this is insane! He can't even talk yet, let alone ratify or sanction anything. And his head is certainly not big enough to wear the crown!'

'No, of course not, nor will he be able to carry the orb and the sceptre,' John agreed, smiling again. 'But there are scaled-down versions of all three being made especially for him.'

Ten days later, on the way to attend the State Opening of Parliament, Catherine found herself riding in a curious vehicle. It was a lofty two-wheeled cart fashioned to look like a throne, painted white and gold and drawn by four ornamentally caparisoned white horses, two either side of the central shaft and each with a knight of the realm walking at its head. Little Henry was sitting on her lap, wrapped up warmly and wearing a coronet of finely worked filigree gold, light as thistledown and lined with soft wool. To her great relief, he had become quite used to her again and sat quietly now, staring, fascinated, at the cheering crowds of people thronging the streets, his chubby hand curled around a small sceptre of solid gold which was perfect in every detail. Balanced in the palm of her hand, Catherine held a miniature orb for him, much as she might have held a toy ball in the nursery. Together, she and Henry travelled through the streets of London towards Parliament, accompanied by members of the aristocracy from all over England.

That night, in the moments before sleep, she recalled the faintly ridiculous way in which those scions of England's noblest families had crowded around to greet the young King, first bowing to him then fawning over him with silly expressions on their faces, like apprentice nursemaids. Even the Chancellor had looked on fondly as the infant King babbled and dribbled, then said that His Highness had spoken his mind quite clearly on several subjects, though by means of another tongue. There was applause at that, and much avuncular laughter.

Catherine remembered what John of Bedford had said about those who would want to influence the child in order to achieve their own ends. She wondered which of them it would be.

The Bishop of Winchester was hurrying to a meeting, one at which he hoped to influence the thinking of the other sixteen members of the ruling Council of England. Beaufort wished heartily that his late nephew had not been quite so adamant on his death bed. Henry could always be remarkably obdurate if he chose to. There was all that nonsense about the Cardinal's hat, for instance. When Pope Martin V had offered Beaufort a cardinalate nearly five years ago, Henry had absolutely forbidden him to accept it, stubbornly convinced that his uncle and the pontiff were plotting to take over the English church. Uncle and nephew had a serious disagreement over that and it wasn't until after Henry's wedding to Catherine that they'd patched up their differences.

What was on Beaufort's mind now was that, in his will, Henry had made it quite clear that after his death, John of Bedford must be made Regent of France. Since John was expected to be abroad more often than not, Humphrey therefore became Chief of the Council which meant that – by default – he was Regent of England: king in all but name.

To Beaufort's way of thinking, it would have been far better to send Humphrey off to France where he would have stood a fairly reasonable chance of getting himself killed. Bishop

Beaufort was no great admirer of the Duke of Gloucester. And what in Heaven's name, Beaufort fumed as he quickened his step, did the headstrong idiot think he was doing with the Countess of Holland? He was inviting disaster! Surely, surely, he couldn't be thinking of marrying the woman? That would be certain to incur Philip of Burgundy's wrath and risk ruining everything Henry had worked for, fought for, and indeed died for, in France. It was imperative that the Philip should continue to be an ally of the English and that was far more likely to be the case if the Countess Jacqueline remained married to the Duke of Brabant, however unsavoury a character he was.

He really must bring up the subject at today's Council meeting, though it would be devilishly awkward to do so with his arrogant nephew sitting at the head of the table. Perhaps it would be better to take a low-key approach and suggest other good reasons for keeping Burgundy in a sweet temper, rather than say anything about Jacqueline.

The meeting went on all day and Henry Beaufort felt exhausted by the end of it. He had spoken eloquently and convincingly about the need to keep the Duke of Burgundy kindly disposed towards England but it had taken all his debating skills, his guile, and his subtlety to get his way.

During the course of the afternoon, the Council voted for small changes to its own constitutional structure. After much debate, the members deemed it wise that, for what they saw as the best of reasons, the Duke of Gloucester's headship of the Council should be nominal rather than absolute. As the afternoon shadows lengthened, lighted candles were placed down the centre of the long table and the meeting eventually drew to a close. Entirely democratically, it had been agreed that henceforward the Duke's title would be 'Protector' rather than 'Regent'.

Gloucester was furious. It was quite clear in his mind that loss of authority on the Council also meant loss of his entitlement to rule the country He tried his best to recall exactly how he had come to be demoted and detected the cunning intelligence of his uncle but couldn't remember a single thing Bishop Beaufort had said which might have influenced the other members of the Council.

Humphrey of Gloucester had never particularly liked Henry Beaufort. That day, he began to hate him.

Chapter Eleven

Windsor Castle, December 1422

Jacqueline went in search of her cousin and, guided by the sound of a song being sung by a singer with a pretty voice and a pronounced French accent, found Catherine, dressed in a mourning gown of stark white, kneeling on the floor of the nursery, building a bridge of brightly coloured wooden blocks for baby Henry.

London Bridge is broken down,
Dance over my Lady lee;
London Bridge is broken down
With a gay lady ...

How shall we build it up again?
Dance over my Lady lee ...
How shall we build ...

'Oh, Henry, I'd nearly finished it!'

The King was taking great delight in knocking down the blocks, squealing delightedly as he did so. Jacqueline hesitated before trusting herself to speak.

'Catherine,' she said after a moment. 'Do you know what day it is?'

'Saturday, isn't it? All day. Sunday tomorrow.'

'And what had you planned for tomorrow?'

'Mass, of course, in the morning, but nothing special after that.'

'Ah, I thought as much. You realise, don't you, that it's my godson's first birthday tomorrow? I think we should celebrate the fact.'

'Yes,' said Catherine, sitting back on her heels as the King, with a wooden block in one hand, began banging all the other blocks with it. Catherine had to raise her voice to make herself heard. 'I know. It's the sixth of December: I hadn't forgotten. But, Jacq, it's the Sabbath. Besides, we daren't play party games with the baby while the court is in mourning.'

'The baby doesn't know that! Look, it's over three months since Henry died and over a month since the funeral. Why not just a quiet little celebration? Oh, come on, Catherine, it will do no harm. A small *fête d'anniversaire* in the afternoon, perhaps, with some of his little friends?'

'He hasn't got any little friends.'

'Well, we could ask the Countess of Westmorland to bring her young nephew the Duke of York. Then there's the Earl of Ormond's son, James, and little Thomas Roos.'

Catherine looked doubtful. 'They're all a few years older than Henry,' she said.

'No matter,' Jacqueline prattled on excitedly. 'Henry needs a few playmates. Oh, and Catherine, we could ask Edmund Beaufort to come, too. He's always seemed very fond of little Henry. And his sister, Joan, needs to get used to children if she's to marry James of Scotland and give him an heir to the throne. She could do with the practice!'

Catherine scrambled to her feet, smiling. 'Yes, let's do it!' Suddenly she looked forward to a small impromptu party the next day, with just a few other children and adults in the nursery. Jacqueline was right, it was important to celebrate Henry's first birthday, such a significant milestone in his young life.

Anton was summoned to the nursery be consulted about food for the occasion and suggested honey cakes and gingerbread for the children with savoury pasties for the adults, followed by date slices in spiced wine. It was only an informal little party and there wasn't time for elaborate preparations.

Before giving the baby over to the care of Joan Astley, Catherine asked her to find Elizabeth Ryman so that she could inform her of the plans for the following day. She expected

144

disapproval, of course, but she didn't care. After all, she was the Queen and she was not going to be dictated to by the woman. Elizabeth Ryman did seem to disapprove of everything Catherine did in the nursery, an unconvincing sympathetic smile thinly disguising her contempt, though she dared not openly criticise the Queen.

Next, Catherine went in search of Les Trois Jo-jo, to enlist their help in getting invitations written and delivered. The problem was that so near the Sabbath, there weren't many staff on duty in the castle so Joanna Troutbeck was dispatched to search for messengers and Joanna Belknap was sent off to round up as many clerks and scribes as she could. Belknap returned with a scribe and two clerks and Troutbeck had found three messengers lounging around in the stables, playing a card game with some of the grooms. They all listened attentively as the Countess Jacqueline explained what needed to be done.

All, that is, except Owen Tudor, whose attention wandered as he looked about him. It was the first time he had ever been into any of the private apartments in Windsor Castle and he could hardly tear his eyes away from the sumptuous tapestries and paintings that hung on the walls. The floor was covered, not with rushes and strewing herbs but with a thick woollen carpet of an intricate pattern. It must have come from the East, he thought, perhaps brought back from the Crusades. It was beautiful.

'So, that's the message. Have you all taken it down?' Jacqueline asked.

Owen hadn't but he dared not say so. He could copy it later from his friend Gilbert, with whom he shared a carrel and an ink horn in the library. He nodded along with the others and they were dismissed.

Just as they were leaving the room, Gilbert elbowed Owen in the ribs. 'The Queen,' he hissed. They stood aside, bowing extravagantly from the waist, as Catherine came back into the room, her mouth set in a determined line after a mildly unpleasant encounter with Elizabeth Ryman.

Owen, his eyes averted, saw the passing swish of a long white gown and was aware of the faint perfume of lavender. He sneaked a look after she had passed but was rewarded with nothing more than the sight of the straight back of a slim young woman with fair hair coiled about her head. She wasn't as tall as Owen had imagined her but she certainly carried herself well, he thought. So that was Queen Catherine.

The Dukes of Gloucester and Bedford were enjoying the rare opportunity of spending an informal evening together in the Palace of Westminster, intending to pass the night there before travelling back to Windsor in daylight the next day.

For Gloucester, it was an opportunity to talk to his brother privately about his concerns regarding Catherine. For Bedford, home in England for the coming Christmas holiday, it was an opportunity to talk to Gloucester about his concerns regarding Philip of Burgundy; he was quite certain in his own mind that having Philip remain loyal to the English crown was of crucial importance in maintaining a peaceful relationship with France.

The two brothers had enjoyed an excellent supper and there was ample wine left in the decanter, glowing ruby red in the candle light. Humphrey held it poised above two goblets.

'Will you join me?'

John nodded, smiling. His brother's well-known liking for Burgundy wine gave him a golden opportunity to introduce the subject he wanted to discuss.

'You know, it would be a pity to have to give up drinking this excellent wine,' he said, reaching out to take the goblet Humphrey was offering him.

'Why should we?'

'Well, I'm deeply perturbed about Philip of Burgundy,' John said. 'I understand that he turned down an invitation to join the Order of the Garter earlier this year.'

'He did. Not many people would do that!'

'Exactly,' said John, 'it's rather an insult to the English sovereign to decline it. But, worse than that, he didn't come to London for Henry's funeral. It wouldn't have been much trouble for him. I thought that was very disloyal. He could have combined it with a visit to his new sovereign, our young nephew. I hope he's not beginning to think that loyalty to the

Dauphin Charles is advantageous.'

'Let's hope not. Did he give a reason for his absence?'

'No, not that I'm aware of.'

'He's certainly making life difficult for my poor Jacqueline,' said Humphrey. John stiffened. The thorny subject of Humphrey's relationship with Jacqueline had been introduced into the conversation rather earlier than he had intended.

'In what way?'

'Well, he absolutely refuses to entertain any suggestion that her marriage to that ugly little pansy the Duke of Brabant should be annulled.'

'You can't expect him to, not with so much of his own inheritance at stake. But Burgundy's dangerous, Humphrey. And if you ever tried to marry Jacqueline, things could get very ugly indeed.'

'Thanks for the warning, brother,' said Humphrey. 'But I'll handle it my way. Relax. Don't worry.'

'Just think before you do anything rash.' John was frowning. 'Really, we do not want to annoy Philip of Burgundy. It could be disastrous for young Henry's future.'

'Talking of which,' said Gloucester, eager to change the subject, 'I wanted to talk to you about the Queen. Do you think she'll want to go back to France, now that Henry has died?'

'Why should she?'

'Isabelle did.'

'Catherine's sister?' John raised his eyebrows and Humphrey nodded.

'Well, she was a child bride if anyone was,' John said. 'Can't have been more than seven when she was married to Richard and she was widowed at eleven, so there was nothing to keep her here. Catherine is twenty-one now and she has young Henry. She'll want to stay if only for his sake. She dotes on the child.'

'But what if she wants to marry again?'

John wasn't surprised that Humphrey had broached the subject of Catherine's future but he thought it a little premature; she was still grieving piteously. He thought she'd be unlikely to rush into a second marriage.

'No doubt she will in time,' he said, 'but while we're still in mourning for Henry she is hardly likely to start behaving like an alley cat. Dear God, Humphrey, she is the Queen!'

'Yes, but she's also a damned attractive widow. She won't grieve for ever. And I do remember Henry boasting that she was panting for him as soon as their bedroom door was closed. Rather more than was proper for a princess, he said. Like mother like daughter, no doubt. Queen Isabeau was the most aristocratic slut in Europe, according to some. A whore with a crown. Anyway, Henry said Catherine gave as good as she got and, knowing Henry, she probably got it rather often.'

'Humphrey!' John was appalled. His brother was always inclined to talk smuttily in private but it was difficult to believe that he was talking about the young woman whom John had come to admire so much in the last dreadful months.

Humphrey had the bit between his teeth. 'Well, think about it. She's young, she's healthy, and I have it on her own husband's own authority that she enjoys bed sports. She'll find it difficult to restrain herself. Could be disastrous if she takes an unsuitable lover.'

'You don't know Catherine,' John said, remembering the nightmare journey through France to Calais with Henry's coffin. 'I have spent a great deal of time in her company in recent months and I found her to be devoted to Henry while he was alive, as she is now devoted to his son. Be assured, Humphrey, she won't behave with any impropriety at all. It is the last thing I'd expect of her.'

Humphrey shrugged and poured himself more wine. 'Time will tell,' he said. 'Only time will tell.'

Anton's honey cakes had all but disappeared, the adults had made short work of his delicious little savoury pasties, and four wine jugs stood empty on the table. Catherine was holding the one-year-old King of France and England splay-legged on her left hip while she fed him a gingerbread man. He held on to the sweet biscuit with both hands, not eating it but staring wide-eyed at all the people who were milling around his normally quiet nursery, playing guessing games, talking and laughing. A small see-saw had been set up in the corner of the room for the very youngest children and a side table was covered with a chequered cloth for board games. Edmund Beaufort was demolishing his third helping of dates in spiced wine when Catherine sensed him at her elbow.

'My Lady,' he said, 'you were so wise to bring a royal chef back from France with you. These dates are sublime!'

Catherine smiled. 'Good,' she said, 'I'm glad you're enjoying them.' She had an idea that the sixteen-year-old had probably been at the wine jugs but at least he wasn't making an exhibition of himself; not yet. He was at that amusing stage of tipsiness quickly reached by young men who think that they can hold their drink.

'Don't have any more of those spiced dates, Edmund,' she whispered, 'or you'll have to explain yourself to your mother!'

'She's not here,' Edmund whispered back dramatically, 'and when the cat's away, the mice can play! The nice, spicy mice can eat as many dates as they like!'

Catherine smiled. 'All right, my little mouse. But don't say I didn't warn you!'

Mouse? Her little mouse? Edmund flushed a dark red and he was aware of a pleasurable sensation in his loins. He remembered that, in his schoolroom, the very mention of the word 'mouse' had set the other boys sniggering behind their hands. Perhaps Catherine was trying to hint at something. He felt very confused.

Edmund's mother, Margaret, had been invited to the party, of course, but wouldn't countenance such a thing on the Sabbath, though she was the only one who had declined the invitation. 'It'll end in tears,' she predicted ominously. But everyone else had accepted with alacrity and now the crowded nursery was becoming overheated.

Jacqueline jumped up onto a bench and clapped her hands, calling for attention. 'Come, everyone, we're going to play hide-and-seek. Now I want the adults to go and hide first. Then, after a count of ten, the children have to go and find them. Then we'll do it the other way round.'

'Where can we hide?' called the Countess of Westmorland.

'Anywhere?'

'No, not just anywhere. Hiders must find hiding places here in the nursery or in the great hall or the inner ward but don't stay out there too long and get cold. And don't go near the kitchen, whatever you do, or you'll upset Anton! When you hear me ringing this bell, you must all come back here because it means that there will be some children who haven't found any grown-ups. Now, grown-ups – off you go to find a hiding place! I'm going to count down from ten before the seekers come to find you. Come on, children, help me to count. We're going backwards, remember! You'll need to concentrate!'

There was an undignified scramble as the adults ran off to find hiding places. Catherine stood watching them with an indulgent smile on her face and little Henry still saucer-eyed astride her hip.

'Ten … nine … eight … Wait! Wait! Aren't you playing hide-and-seek, Catherine?' Jacqueline asked.

'No. I must stay here with the King. He's too young to play!'

'We'll look after the King, Ma'am,' said Joan Astley. 'Why don't you go and enjoy yourself for once. I'll put him in his high cradle, where he can sit up and see everything that's going on.'

'Yes, go on, Catherine,' said Jacqueline. 'You go and hide. Go on. We'll start counting again. Ready children? Ten … nine … eight … seven …'

Catherine managed to squeeze herself into a narrow cupboard at the far end of the main hall, near the dais. It was where the domestic servants kept spare linen for the royal table and there was just enough room for someone as slim as Catherine to get inside. She crouched in the dark, feeling a little foolish, her heart thumping after the effort of getting away from her young pursuers before Jacqueline had reached '… three … two … one! Ready or not, they're coming!'

She heard someone approaching, an adult by the sound of the footsteps, rather than a child. Someone else looking for somewhere to hide. Bad luck, she thought, she had found this good hiding place first. The cupboard door opened and Edmund

Beaufort was surprised to find the Dowager Queen of England doubled up and crouching inside it.

'Your Highness! I … I'm …'

'Go away, Edmund, I found this place first!' Edmund seemed remarkably tall when viewed from the level of his knees. 'Go on, go away! Find somewhere else to hide!'

'But I'm a seeker!' he protested. 'And I've found you!'

'You can't be a seeker, you're not a child! Now, go away and let a child come and find me.'

'I'm being a seeker because there aren't enough children to go round.'

'Then help me up, please Edmund. I should get back to the nursery. I shouldn't be playing silly games like this, I've a child of my own to care for.'

She gave Edmund her hand and as he helped her to her feet, he made a clumsy lunge towards her, trying to take her in his arms. 'I'm not a child, you know,' he said, his face turning a dull red, 'I'm … I'm not a child. I'm a man. And I have found you. And I … I wish …'

'Edmund, you're drunk! How dare you!' Catherine pushed her hands against his chest and he stopped abruptly, hanging his head, looking for all the world as though he had been slapped.

'Edmund, you've gone too far. Don't you dare do that again!' She felt confused and frightened but she needed to remind the young man standing miserably in front of her that she was the Queen, a grown woman, five years his senior, a widow with a child of her own and all the responsibilities that went with her position.

'Sorry,' he muttered. 'I'm sorry.'

'What the hell is going on here?' A stentorian voice rang down the hall and Catherine looked up to see the Duke of Gloucester striding towards her, followed by his brother.

'Your Highness! Is this man bothering you?' he demanded.

'No … no … er, we were playing hide-and-seek,' stammered Catherine, her cheeks blazing with embarrassment; she wasn't at all sure what Gloucester had seen. 'I was hiding in the cupboard … Edmund was a seeker and he found me … he was helping me up …'

'Playing hide-and-seek!' Humphrey's face was purple. He turned to his brother. 'John, didn't I tell you …!' he began.

'Oh, Humphrey, I'm sure it's all harmless enough,' John protested calmly.

'And what are you doing here, young man?' Gloucester demanded of Edmund.

'I'm, um, well, I'm playing hide-and-seek too.' As he said the words, Edmund realised how very silly they sounded. He might have thought of a more reasonable explanation had he been entirely sober.

'Hide-and-seek? On the Sabbath? That is the most disrespectful …'

'My Lord,' Catherine interrupted him, drawing herself up to her full height though Gloucester still towered above her. 'You will kindly moderate your words. This was the most innocent of children's games. It is the baby's first birthday, so we were having a little party for him, that is all.'

'I see,' said Gloucester in an icy voice. 'And do you think it appropriate, my Lady, to celebrate the birthday of His Highness the King by hiding in a cupboard with a man?'

'My Lord, how dare you make such an accusation!' Catherine was upset now and very angry but Gloucester's fury had not abated. She looked helplessly at John of Bedford who was standing behind his brother and felt relieved when he gave her a broad wink and moved between them, taking charge of the situation.

'That is how the game of hide-and-seek is played, Humphrey,' he said. 'You should know that, you've played it often enough yourself.'

'But not on a Sunday,' Humphrey muttered resentfully. 'And certainly not when we're supposed to be in mourning.'

Catherine looked down at her white mourning gown. The bodice was covered with the baby's sticky gingerbread finger marks. Summoning all her dignity, she straightened her back, turned on her heel, and began walking towards the nursery with Edmund Beaufort trailing sheepishly behind her.

John of Bedford placed a restraining hand on his brother's arm. 'Try not to judge her too harshly, Humphrey. You said yourself only last night that she's young and, after all, it is the little one's first birthday. And it's Saint Nicholas' Day, too, a special day for children. They should be allowed to play together and exchange gifts. It's all part of the tradition.'

'She needs to learn to restrain herself,' muttered Gloucester. 'Or she'll never be a fit mother for the King. You wait and see, John. You just wait and see!'

Catherine's hands were shaking. Gloucester had followed her to the nursery where Jacqueline was still standing on the bench, shouting encouragement to excited adults and children alike.

'Jacqueline!' he barked. 'Get down from there, madam! What on earth do you think you're doing?'

'Tut, Humphrey,' said Jacqueline lightly. 'We're playing a game of hide-and-seek, that's all. It's a lot of fun.'

'Having fun is not something you do on a Sunday. Get down from there, for God's sake, and show a little decorum. This is no example for the children.'

John of Bedford spotted Catherine sitting in the corner of the room, anxiously plucking at the stained white fabric of her gown. 'I'm sorry, John, I'm so sorry,' she said, shaking her head from side to side.

'Catherine, please. Don't. Don't torture yourself. You have done nothing wrong.'

'But I have, I've defiled the memory of my husband. Your brother will never forgive me.'

'There's nothing to forgive, Catherine. Ignore Humphrey, I don't know what's got into him. I think he's feeling the strain of wanting to marry Jacqueline and not being allowed to.'

Catherine shook her head helplessly. 'I hope you're right.'

'Of course I am. Now, the party seems to be breaking up. Well, let's face it, Humphrey has rather ruined the atmosphere. I'm sure he'll apologise to you when he comes to his senses. So why don't you go and wash your face and change your gown. You'll feel better when you do. I'll say goodbye to everyone for you. I'll thank your guests for coming and see them to the door. Where's your maid?'

Guillemote was hovering on the edge of the fracas,

153

concerned for her mistress, and she quickly led Catherine away and back to her own chamber. It was quiet there and, after she had washed her face and changed into a clean gown, Catherine asked Guillemote to brush her hair, something she had always found soothing and relaxing.

Eventually, she felt calm enough to return to the nursery and what she found there surprised her very much indeed. The big room looked as though a whirlwind had passed through it, leaving a trail of half-eaten food, discarded pewter plates, empty wine jugs, and goblets. It was deserted, except for the tableau in the centre of the room. His Royal Highness the King of England and France was sitting in his high cradle. Bending over it and holding the baby's hand was a tall, dark-haired man with his back to her and, much to the child's obvious delight, he was counting Henry's fingers one by one.

'*Modryb y Fawd,*
Bys yr Uwd,
Pen y Cogwr,
Dic y Peipar ...
A ...

'*Jolie* cwt bach!' Catherine finished for him, wide-eyed and very close to tears as the baby crowed in delight.

Startled, the man spun round. 'Your Highness!'

Catherine stared at him as he bowed to her, gaining the impression of curling dark hair, intense brown eyes, and a wide, sensuous mouth. 'Who are you?' she asked.

'I'm Owain ap Maredydd ap Tudur ap Goronwy Fychan, Ma'am,' he said, then smiled disarmingly. 'But hereabouts I'm known as Owen Tudor.'

They looked at each other for a long moment.

Catherine was the first to recover her composure. '*Jolie* cwt bach,' she said again. 'How do you know this?'

'It's just a children's finger-game, Your Highness,' he said. 'All children know it in Wales.'

'Ah, Wales. My husband the King told me about that. Are you from Wales?'

'I have that honour, my Lady,' he bowed but kept watching her.

'Then you will tell me, please, what is this little game? I would like to teach it to my son. After all, he is the Prince of Wales.'

Owen's smile was a degree colder this time. If only she knew how much he hated hearing her use that title in relation to the heir to the English throne. But how could she, a French woman, possibly know how strongly it was resented, not only by him but by all the Welshmen who had fought for their freedom under Owain Glyndŵr, the man who had more right to the title 'Prince of Wales' than any son of an English monarch.

But he didn't want to lose his job and neither did he want to hurt her feelings. From what he'd heard, she had been through some unendurable experiences lately; the loss of her sister, her husband, and her father. Poor woman, he thought, feeling oddly protective towards her. He smiled.

'If it is your wish, Your Highness, I will be honoured to teach it to the King. Perhaps when he is a little older and has a few more words in his vocabulary.'

Catherine smiled back at him as she lifted the baby out of his high cradle. 'And then you will confuse him with new words in a new language, just as he is beginning to learn his first words in English.'

'And in French, of course.'

'No,' said Catherine, a shade too quickly. 'No, not much in French. It is not … how shall I say … it is not encouraged.'

Owen raised his eyebrows. 'Really? Then I can assure you, my Lady, that no one is going to encourage him to learn Welsh! It is an ancient and beautiful language but considered very crass in the English court.'

Joan Astley bustled in through the open door. 'Oh, Your Highness, I'm so glad you're here, I thought the baby was with the Countess Jacqueline but I have just seen her with the Duke and she said she thought the baby was with me.'

'Please, Joan, don't worry. His Highness was quite safe. He was learning a little finger-game in Welsh from this gentleman.' She turned to Owen. 'I'm so sorry, what did you say your name was again?'

'Owen, Ma'am, Owen Tudor.'

'Owen Tudor,' Catherine repeated. 'Well, thank you, Master Tudor. As you said, the King will need to be a little older before he learns the rhyme but I would like you to teach it to him.'

'I would be honoured to do so, Your Highness.'

Catherine handed the baby to Joan Astley and Owen bowed low as she left the room. As he straightened up and looked at her retreating figure, he had a curiously protective feeling towards her, though he wasn't at all sure why.

Chapter Twelve

England, Christmas 1422

Grand boughs of green holly had been brought in to decorate the Great Hall of Windsor Castle, and mistletoe hung discreetly in certain doorways. The great Yule log was turning slowly to ashes on the fire but because of the recent death of the King, the festive season was being celebrated with only modest feasting. Nevertheless, in the castle kitchens, Anton was supervising the roasting of geese, swans, chickens, wild boar, and suckling pigs to satisfy the appetites of the royal family and their guests.

While the court was still in mourning, Owen and Gilbert were often glad to escape from the restrained atmosphere of the castle to the more convivial surroundings of the tavern at the sign of The Swan, where Owen found himself much in demand to lead the raucous singing of carols with his crwth. Gilbert, who had unexpectedly proved himself to be a very capable tabor player, was intrigued by the strange Welsh instrument which he had never seen before but he was delighted by the sounds it made when Owen drew a horsehair bow across the strings. The two were quick to realise that as long as they were prepared to accompany the singers, they wouldn't have to pay for a single tankard of ale all night.

'Thish is the life,' Gilbert observed.

'It is, isn't it?' agreed Owen. 'But they'll soon stop buying ale for you when you start getting the rhythm wrong. Behave yourself! Slow down.'

'Yes, you're right. I'll just finish this one.' Gilbert drained his tankard and set it down heavily on the table. 'Hey, Owen, let's play another carol.'

'Which one do you fancy?'

'"The Whore's Bed."'

Owen grinned from ear to ear. 'The what?'

'No! Sorry. I'm sorry. "The Boar's Head". "The Boar's Head Carol",' Gilbert enunciated carefully. His eyelids were beginning to droop.

Owen let out a great whoop of laughter. 'Come on, then, my drunken friend. "The Whore's Bed Carol" it is!'

They were nearing the end of the last verse when Maredydd sauntered into the tavern with some of his friends from the guard room. Hearing the familiar sound of the crwth, he was pleased to see his young cousin leading the singing, ragged though it was. Then again, in Maredydd's opinion, the English were useless singers. He pushed his way towards Owen and Gilbert, just as the noisy revellers had reached the chorus.

'You're late tonight!' Owen mouthed at him above the din. Maredydd shrugged. He'd come to search for Owen in order to pass on some news but that would have to wait until Owen and Gilbert had stopped being the centre of attention. He found a space on a bench near the fire and sat down.

Gilbert was the first to give up. He slumped down on to the bench beside Maredydd. 'I can't do it anymore,' he said. 'I must be getting old.'

'What, at twenty-six? Nonsense!' said Maredydd scornfully. 'Wait 'til you get to my age! You've just drunk too much, that's all.' Gilbert nodded, putting his elbows on the table in front of him. Within minutes his head was cradled on his arms and he was fast asleep.

Owen had to battle through "The Contest of the Ivy and the Holly" on his own before the singers would let him go but finally they did, clapping him on the back and pressing yet more ale on him. He shook his head, smiling, and pushed his way through the crowded room to join his cousin and the somnolent Gilbert.

'How is he?'

'Asleep. Says he's getting too old for it.'

'What? He's only three years older than I am!'

'Oh, to be twenty-three again,' Maredydd said, rolling his eyes. 'I'm sure poor old Gilbert would agree with me.'

'No doubt he would if he was sober enough,' said Owen. 'Anyway, what news from the guardroom?'

'Well, it's only a rumour, but some of us might be going to Holland fairly soon,' Maredydd confided. 'At least, that's what they say. There's nothing official yet.'

'Why Holland?'

'The Duke of Gloucester is getting a battalion together. It's some quarrel about the Countess Jacqueline's disputed lands, as I understand it.'

'But that doesn't concern Gloucester, surely,' said Owen. 'I mean, what reason would he have to invade Holland?'

'A perfectly good reason,' said Maredydd, draining his tankard and wiping his mouth on the back of his hand. 'It seems they're getting married.'

'Gloucester and the Countess Jacqueline? But she's married to someone else, isn't she?'

'Not any more, apparently. Must have had an annulment.'

'I wonder if the Queen knows,' mused Owen.

'The Queen? Why should you wonder if the Queen knows?'

'Well,' said Owen hesitantly, 'I don't think she's quite as *au fait* as she might be with what's happening at court. She seemed to be hinting as much when I was speaking to her.'

'When *you* were speaking to her? *You* were speaking to the Queen? *Duw Mawr*! Good God! I've heard everything now!'

'She's very charming,' said Owen, ignoring the blasphemy in both languages.

'I'll wager she is!' Maredydd laughed. 'But don't worry about telling your new friend, the Queen, about this. She will have heard already. Everyone has.'

The Queen had not heard. Jacqueline had not told her the news because Humphrey was quite adamant that it was none of his sister-in-law's business and warned Jacqueline that it should be kept from her. Catherine was a widow now, he pointed out, so she could be dangerous. She had no husband to occupy her mind and her baby son was well looked after so he didn't really need her. With time on her hands, Humphrey said, Catherine's thoughts might well turn to political manoeuvrings. After all, her mother had been well known for it and there was no reason to suppose that Catherine would be any different. Since she didn't recognise the authority of the Avignon Pope, she could well try to interfere with their plans.

As far as Jacqueline was concerned, she had finally received papal dispensation to proceed with her marriage to Humphrey and she didn't give a tinker's cuss which pope had granted it. She stared time and time again at the piece of parchment in her hand and pressed the papal seal fervently to her lips. It was Pope Benedict's written agreement to the annulment of her marriage to the Duke of Brabant, based upon her assertion under oath that the marriage was a sham and had never been consummated. Thank God! At last! She had read it and re-read it. By now, she knew the short message by heart and yet she couldn't stop reading it. This was what she had spent so many months hoping for, scheming for, planning for, praying for, and now it was here, delivered by papal messenger direct from Avignon.

She couldn't risk anything going wrong, even if it meant distancing herself from Catherine, but it was difficult to keep the secret from her, particularly when they shared the same seamstress. The purchase of a length of white silk was carefully entered into Jacqueline's wardrobe accounts ledger and its purpose recorded as the making of a gown for the Garter ceremony. Even if Catherine had seen it, she would have had no reason to question it.

Catherine also accepted the fact that her cousin was away from court for a few weeks before Easter, because Jacqueline had always said that Humphrey wished to take her to visit his dear friend, the Abbot John Whethamstede at St Albans.

It had thrilled Jacqueline to be welcomed to St Albans as the Duchess of Gloucester. It almost blotted from her mind the indignity of the little hole-in-the-corner marriage ceremony she had recently gone through with Humphrey. Though she had longed to be married by Archbishop Henry Chichele in the great cathedral at Canterbury, Humphrey had other ideas. He was impatient at the idea of wasting time and money by going through the organisation and extravagance of a cathedral wedding, however much Jacqueline might want it. And he was keen to become the Count of Holland, Zeeland, and Hainault at the earliest opportunity.

The first Catherine heard of the marriage was when Elizabeth Ryman came into the nursery one April afternoon. The King was on his mother's knee and she was dandling him up and down to the rhythm of a nursery rhyme.

Baa baa, black sheep, have you any wool?
Yes sir, yes sir, three bags full.
One for the master and one for the dame
And one for the little boy who lives down the lane.

By now Joan Astley had joined in with the singing and the baby was laughing out loud and bouncing excitedly on Catherine's knee, wanting more.

'My Lady!' Elizabeth Ryman had to raise her voice to make herself heard. 'Your Highness! I have a message for you! His Grace the Duke of Bedford wishes to see you urgently.'

Kissing the fine baby on the tip of his nose, Catherine handed him to Joan Astley.

'I won't be long, my little one,' she promised him, standing up and straightening her skirts. 'Very well, Mistress Ryman. Thank you. Where is His Grace?'

John of Bedford had been shown into her private apartment and Guillemote was serving him a goblet of wine when Catherine arrived.

'Your Highness! Catherine, my dear,' he said, rising from his chair and bowing low over her outstretched hand. 'It's kind of you to see me and I'm sorry to demand an audience with you in this way but we must talk. It's urgent,' he added, as Guillemote withdrew.

'Is it about my allowance?'

'Your allowance? No, no Catherine, your allowance remains as it was agreed by the Council. It is sufficient for you, isn't it? If not, I can go back to them to see if they will increase the amount.'

'No, it's quite generous, and I'm grateful. So what …?'

'My brother Humphrey,' he began 'and your cousin

161

Jacqueline ...'

'They haven't come to any harm, have they? They're all right?'

'Well, yes, they're all right.' He paused. 'They've been married.'

'What? Married!' Catherine was astounded. 'But they can't have! Have they had permission?'

'They've had the permission of the Avignon Pope. Pope Benedict has seen fit to grant an annulment of Jacqueline's marriage to the Duke of Brabant.'

'But Benedict is not the Pope. Pope Martin in Rome is the only Pope. Benedict has no authority, no right to do that!'

'Exactly,' said John, 'but much depends on where you stand with regard to the division in the Holy Roman Church. I agree with you but clearly Humphrey and Jacqueline believe that Pope Benedict has every right to grant an annulment of her marriage. Well, they must do. They were married some weeks ago, I gather, before they visited St Albans.'

Catherine dreaded the answer to her next question. 'Does my cousin Philip know?'

'Yes. Oh, yes, he knows. And he is, apparently, furious. He has challenged Humphrey to a duel. And Humphrey is hot-headed enough to take up the gauntlet. They'll kill each other.'

'Oh, *mon Dieu*,' Catherine rose from her chair and began to pace the room, realising the potential gravity of the situation. 'I foresee trouble.'

'Yes, very big trouble. I can't see a way out of it. Except ...'

'Except what?'

'Well, that ... I don't know. It depends on you. After all, you are the only one who knows all the people involved in the argument. Really knows them, I mean. Could you intervene somehow, do you think? They might listen to you.'

'And they might not!'

Catherine sank down onto a bench against the wall. What could she do? Where was she to begin? Humphrey wouldn't listen to her, she knew that. And Jacqueline would agree with anything Humphrey said. The situation was too urgent to allow her the time to make the journey to France to see Philip of

Burgundy in person and he would never be persuaded to come to England. Besides, he most certainly wouldn't listen to a woman.

It didn't matter where Philip stood morally with regard to the schism in the Church because politically he would always side with whichever Pope refused to grant Jacqueline an annulment of her marriage. It was in his interests that she should remain married to the Duke of Brabant. He'd be likely to do anything in order to protect his own inheritance. Philip would, without doubt, contest the decision of the Avignon Pope.

Yet again, she regretted Henry's passing; not only for reasons of her own grief but because her marriage to him had represented a strong alliance between their two countries. That alliance had weakened with his death; the bond was fraying rapidly. It must be re-made for her son's sake and another dynastic marriage was the only way to do it. She looked hard at John of Bedford before speaking, knowing that once she had made her suggestion, there would be no retracting it.

'You know, John, you've asked me to help and, you're right of course, something must be done. Philip must be pacified. But you are the one who can best rectify this situation, not I.'

There was a look of despair on John's face. 'There's nothing I can do.'

'Yes there is. Now, listen to me, John: Cousin Philip was my Aunt Margaret's only son, which rather grieved my uncle, John the Fearless, I'm afraid. Philip was the one boy among six girls that lived. So he has several sisters.'

'Surely you're not suggesting, are you …?'

'Yes, I am. Because the only way to strengthen the bond between England and Burgundy is through another marriage and now that Humphrey appears to have married Jacqueline, there is no one else. Thomas has died. You are the only one, the only unmarried brother.'

'But … they say those Burgundy girls are as plain as owls!'

Resisting the temptation to laugh at his indignation, Catherine laid her hand on John's arm. 'You know, sometimes a royal marriage works out well. My own marriage did, even though it was arranged under the terms of the Treaty of Troyes. And there is no reason why such a marriage shouldn't work out well for you, too. Believe me, Philip's sisters are not a bit like owls. They're very charming young women. You must have met them when Henry and I were married.'

'Well, I suppose I must have seen them, but I had no reason to remember them particularly. Besides, my dear Lady, you were the centre of attention on that day!'

Catherine smiled her thanks for the compliment before she went on. 'Now, there are two whom you might consider marrying, Agnès and Anne. Agnès is still a little young but Anne is now nineteen years old and has never been betrothed.'

'That's probably because she's ugly,' he muttered.

She tapped his hand lightly in mock rebuke. 'Now, my Lord, don't be ungracious. Anne is funny, witty, and a wonderful companion. She was quite often at court in the year before I married. Henry and I always enjoyed her company because she made me laugh. And she is very, very loyal.'

'Does she bring a reasonable dowry?'

'I imagine so, the family is not without wealth. But, John, a dowry isn't everything. Henry dropped his demand for a dowry before we were married and that was the one thing which made our marriage possible. Don't make difficulties for yourself. This is the only answer, I promise you.'

There was a discreet knock at the door and Guillemote came back into the room with a small plateful of honey cakes which she set down beside John's goblet of wine. As she bobbed a curtsey to him, John remembered how he had once followed her down a corridor and admired her trim waist, her strong, square shoulders, and her gleaming dark hair. Perhaps a pretty face wasn't the only measure of an attractive woman and he remembered thinking that the Frenchwoman would make some man a good wife. Perhaps Anne of Burgundy would make him a good wife, a loving wife, and if everything Catherine had said about her loyalty and companionship was true, he would certainly be a lot less lonely than he had been of late. And if nature had not endowed Anne with great beauty, she would at least be grateful for a husband. Whatever happened, he would have to try to pacify Philip of Burgundy, so if he were to ask for his sister's hand in marriage, the man would surely back down from his threats towards Humphrey.

'Do you know, Catherine,' John said slowly, 'I think you might have had a very good idea.'

She smiled again. 'It's the only way out of the problem. And I think you should go to France as soon as possible.'

Safe on his mother's lap and within the protective circle of her arms, the King watched, fascinated, as mummers re-enacted the story of St George. Young Henry wasn't at all sure about the dragon, a fearsome-looking creature made of green woollen material stretched over a willow frame. Beneath its exaggerated body, two pairs of feet and legs in green hose and shoes were plainly visible but the child's attention was riveted by the long red tongue which lolled out of the creature's mouth and by the dreadful roaring noises it was making. He was thrilled with terror of the beast and cuddled ever closer to his mother.

The guests and servants of the royal family thronged the grounds of Windsor Castle in celebration of St George's Day. In the Upper Ward, archers were demonstrating their skills, jesters, and minstrels mingled with the crowds and there was an appetising smell of roasting ox on the fresh April air. High above the Home Park, a pair of magnificent peregrine falcons wheeled and swooped under the expert handling of the King's Falconer.

Owen Tudor and Gilbert Wilkins were watching the display and joined in the enthusiastic applause as the Falconer finally hooded his birds. They were thoroughly enjoying themselves. On the dancing green, some young people were whirling around in an impromptu dance to the accompaniment of a pipe and tabor. Owen would like to have joined in and cursed the fact that he had left his crwth in the dormitory, but he applauded the minstrels and the dancers before he and Gilbert moved on towards the crowd gathered around the mummers' wagon.

'Huh!' Owen said dismissively, stopping to watch from a few yards away. 'The English don't know anything about dragons!'

'That one looks a bit fierce from what I can see,' said Gilbert. 'Except for its feet. I didn't know that dragons wore shoes, did you?'

Owen wasn't listening. 'I should write a mummers' play about the Welsh dragon,' he mused. 'I should write about the way the red dragon of Wales killed the white dragon of the Saxons and the ancient prophecy which says that he still sleeps under Dinas Emrys, waiting for the call to slay the English. And when the call comes and that battle is won, a Welshman will sit upon the throne of England.'

'A Welshman on the throne of England?' Gilbert snorted his derision. 'Pigs might fly, my friend! Mind you, the Welsh enjoy a bit of fisticuffs, from what I've heard.'

'Not unless we're roused. We're very peaceable in the main. We'd rather be writing poetry than fighting.'

'Then why do you do it?'

'I told you. We only react when other people attack us.'

'People like us English, you mean?'

'No, not you personally, Gilbert. You're a very peaceful soul. I'm talking about greedy English landowners who aren't satisfied with what they've got and covet what rightly belongs to us. They lie to us, too. We have to protect ourselves.'

'Surely an Englishman wouldn't lie?'

Owen gave his friend an incredulous look. 'What? You think an Englishman wouldn't lie? Well, you ask my cousin Maredydd about his father's neighbour, Baron Reginald Grey, the sly bastard! He was the biggest liar of all. He was asked to pass on a message from the King, asking Maredydd's father to fight with the King's army in Scotland. Henry IV that was, of course, when he came to the throne –'

'But Maredydd's father was Welsh,' Gilbert interrupted. 'Would he have fought for the English King?'

'Owain Glyndŵr? Yes, of course he would, in a just cause. He was a very fair-minded man; a lawyer, trained in London at the Inns of Court. But Grey withheld the information, so the message never reached him. And then Glyndŵr was accused of treason! That's when all the bad blood and resentment led to the insurrection: it was like bursting a boil.'

'Resentment?' asked Gilbert. 'Why?'

'Because the English have been aggressive towards us for centuries, trying to get the upper hand, insulting us, attacking us, and passing laws to deprive us of our rights. And we've never regained those rights, either.'

Gilbert picked his teeth thoughtfully with a sliver of wood. Owen was a good friend but a bit misguided. A Welshman on the throne of England? A *Welshman*? Never! He hadn't given very much thought to the relationship between England and Wales until he met this fiery Welshman who seemed to care about it with such passion. The Scots could be awkward, too, from what he'd heard. He was rather glad that he was English and didn't have to prove anything – except superiority to the French, of course.

The mummers' play came to an end and, grinning broadly, the players walked hand in hand to the front of their wagon to acknowledge the applause of the crowd. St George posed in triumph with his foot on the neck of the dragon which lay prone at his feet, two pairs of green shoes sticking out from under it. The mummers bowed low to the young King, the Queen, and the other members of the royal party.

As she applauded the performance, a sudden thought struck Catherine and made her laugh out loud. Queen Isabeau would surely love to have a dragon as a pet. From what she'd heard recently, her mother had now added a leopard and a monkey to her collection of exotic animals which already included a positive menagerie of dogs, cats, and birds. Catherine had a mental picture of her mother leading a big green woolly dragon around the gardens at St Pol. She wouldn't need St George to protect her from the beast, it certainly wouldn't have the temerity to eat Isabeau!

Rising from her seat and handing young Henry to Joan Astley to be carried, she inclined her head to the mummers, smiled, and raised her hand in acknowledgement of their entertainment before beginning the short walk back to the castle with her ladies. Standing to one side as the Queen came towards them, Owen and Gilbert bowed low.

'Good afternoon, Your Highness,' said Owen as they

straightened up again. The Queen looked in his direction and her face lit up with pleasure.

'Good afternoon, Master Tudor,' she said. 'I trust you are well?'

'Indeed, Ma'am, thank you.'

Gilbert stared at Owen, open-mouthed in astonishment. The Queen knew him by name!

Chapter Thirteen

England, Summer 1423

In Catherine's later memories of that summer in Windsor, the golden days stretched out behind her, long and lovely, each one bringing her new strength to face her life as a widow. When she wasn't with the baby, she was rediscovering the pleasures of music, playing her harp and learning new songs. The songs were sadder now, songs of yearning, of love and loneliness and she sang them with feeling, remembering how she and Henry had found such pleasure in singing together.

Now the remaining Henry in her life was growing to be a happy, healthy child, curious about the world around him and learning new lessons every day. Earlier in the year, the Council had appointed Richard Beauchamp, the highly respected Earl of Warwick, to be the young King's guardian with particular responsibility for his education. Catherine felt quite happy about this but, remembering John of Bedford's advice, she spent as much time with her little boy as she possibly could, taking great delight in looking after him, feeding him, playing with him, teaching him, and watching him grow. The King was eighteen months old now and, as long as he held onto his mother's hand, he could walk quite well.

Edmund Beaufort watched the two of them for a long time. They were on their own, unattended by either guards or nursemaids. Mother and toddler walked slowly hand-in-hand in the sunshine, safe in the inner ward of the castle, she anxiously watching in case he should fall, he trying his baby best to walk like an adult and looking to her for approval. Edmund's heart was close to melting. He had never quite got over the gawky embarrassment of the episode with the Queen in the cupboard six months ago, on the occasion of the King's first birthday. He still flushed a dull red when he remembered it but nothing had ever been said since. The trouble was that what he had blurted out at that time was the truth. He might be five years her junior but he was not a child and he had some very un-childlike feelings towards his sovereign lady.

Catherine caught sight of him. 'Edmund!' she called. 'You're back from France. How lovely to see you. Come, let's find somewhere to sit in the shade and talk. You seem to have been gone a long time.'

'Just eight weeks or so, Your Highness. We arrived back in Windsor quite late last night. It's good to see you again. You're looking well.'

'I am, thank you. And look at the King! See how well he walks! Hasn't he grown since you last saw him?' She bent down to pick up the baby and swung him up astride her hip. 'We've run away from his nurses, Edmund. We don't have time on our own very often, do we, Henry?' The child was sucking his thumb and regarding Edmund solemnly as he and the Queen settled themselves on a sunlit bench against the wall. 'Now tell me, Edmund,' she said, 'what news of the Duke of Bedford and his new Duchess?'

Edmund, with his sister Joan and their mother, had been in Paris to attend the wedding of John of Bedford to Anne of Burgundy, a hastily arranged affair but an alliance which seemed to have placated the bride's brother. There was no more talk of the challenge to a duel with Humphrey and everyone breathed a little more easily.

'The Duke and Duchess are well, my Lady, and everyone was delighted at the marriage,' said Edmund. 'My mother remarked that she had never seen so many smiling faces in one place.'

'When was the wedding?'

'On the thirteenth of May at Troyes, in the church of St Jean-au-Marché.

Catherine smiled broadly. 'Oh, I'm so pleased. That is where Henry's father and I were married almost exactly three years before them. I do hope they'll be happy. I'm sure they will;

Anne is delightful and I've become very fond of John since he's been my brother-in-law.'

'Ah, that reminds me. I almost forgot. The Duke particularly wanted to be remembered to you, Your Highness, and he asked me to tell you that you were right. Just that. He didn't say what you were right about but he asked me to be sure to tell you. I'm glad I remembered.'

'I'm glad you remembered, too,' said Catherine. She knew what John meant, that he had found his new bride to be an amusing, witty, and pleasant companion, just as Catherine had described her. She sincerely hoped they would be very happy.

It seemed to be the season for weddings. In early September, the Duchess of Clarence was telling Catherine delightedly about the plans for the wedding of her daughter, Joan.

'And since she is to become Queen of Scotland, she will have the finest wedding money can buy,' said Margaret emphatically. 'Her uncle Henry Beaufort will pay for it. And willingly.'

'Well, he can certainly afford it and he does seem to be fond of them both.'

'I've asked him to conduct the ceremony as well,' said Margaret. 'I trust we will be graced with your presence among the guests?'

'Nothing would give me greater pleasure. After all, I was instrumental in getting the King's agreement to the match.'

Margaret smiled at her. 'They are both very grateful to you, my dear. In fact, the whole family is delighted that you were able to help.'

'Believe me, my Lady, it was a pleasure. A very great pleasure indeed,' said Catherine, recalling the night of her coronation and hiding a rueful smile.

Then towards the end of October, the Earl of Warwick requested an audience with her. She liked Richard Beauchamp; his wife, Elizabeth, had died not long after Catherine herself was widowed and she had always felt that his sympathy and condolences were very genuine. Today, his face was wreathed in smiles as he bent to kiss her hand.

'Your Highness,' he greeted her, 'I wanted you to be among the first to know of my great good fortune. I am to be married again!'

'Married? Then I am delighted for you, my Lord!' She was quite surprised at the news since she hadn't heard the castle gossip about the determined widow who had made a beeline for the good-natured Earl the moment he was out of mourning for his late wife. 'Who is the lady who will have the privilege of becoming the new Countess of Warwick?'

'The Lady Isabella, the widow of my cousin, the Earl of Worcester, Ma'am. She's a fine woman, a very fine woman. I'm greatly honoured that she has agreed to be my wife.'

'Indeed. And I've no doubt that she, too, appreciates the honour that you have done her in asking for her hand in marriage.'

'Well, we aren't in the first flush of youth, my Lady,' said the Earl who was still just on the right side of forty. 'At our age, companionship is just as important as any other feelings we might have for each other. That and, of course, the consolidation of our lands and properties.'

Catherine nodded. 'Of course. Does she bring a large dowry?'

'Property, Ma'am,' said the Earl, matter-of-factly. 'A considerable amount of land in the West of England as well as the lordship of Glamorgan which is, of course, a very large area.'

'Indeed? And where is that?'

'In Wales, my Lady, in the south of that country, along the coast.'

'Ah. And is that anywhere near Monmouth, where my late husband was born?'

'Not far, Ma'am, no, not far at all. It's a pleasant four or five days' ride from Monmouth Castle. But you must remember that you, too, have property in Wales. It was part of your dower settlement.' The Earl, a member of the Council, was quite familiar with the provisions which had been made for Catherine. 'You have your dower palaces and manor houses of course,' he went on, 'but you also have dower lands in

Anglesey and Flintshire as well as in Leicester and Knaresborough.'

'I know Leicester, of course, but the others? Are those in Wales?'

'Not Knaresborough, Ma'am. That's in Yorkshire, not too far from York, which you are already familiar with. But Flintshire is in the north of Wales, on the English border and Anglesey is a large island just off the North Wales coast.'

'You'll pardon a Frenchwoman's lack of knowledge, my Lord. This is still something of a foreign country to me.'

'Of course, Ma'am, perfectly understandable. But you should travel to see these places and familiarise yourself with them. After all, they are yours and they are fully staffed, ready and waiting for your visit.'

'Yes, of course. I should. Perhaps next spring, when the weather improves.'

Joan Astley was dressing His Highness the King for the State Opening of Parliament. He had quite a vocabulary of words by now, though to Catherine's great disappointment the first word he ever said was 'Joanie'. Now the King was yelling 'No, no, no!' at the top of his voice as Joan tried to button him into a crimson velvet gown. Having succeeded, she turned her attention to the little cap he was to wear on his head. The ingenious design incorporated a miniature crown in its turned-up brim. 'Who is Joanie's little kinglet, then?' she whispered in his ear as she contrived to give him one last small hug without creasing the crimson velvet.

'Is His Highness ready, Joan?' Catherine asked as she came into the nursery followed by the Earl of Warwick.

'He is, my Lady, but I don't think he likes his clothes very much.'

'I'm not surprised,' said Catherine. 'I don't like them either.' She had no idea who had made the decision that the child should be dressed up like a big doll. She suspected Elizabeth Ryman, probably acting on the instructions of Humphrey of Gloucester. It was just easier not to interfere.

'I think His Highness looks very fine,' said the Earl of

Warwick, putting his face close to the baby's and adopting the faintly silly tone of adults trying to arouse a baby's interest. 'And he'll look even more the king when he has his orb and sceptre, won't you, sire?' The Earl held out the miniature gold sceptre to Henry who grabbed it from his hand. He looked at it for a moment and then tried to put it in his mouth.

'No, no, Your Highness, you mustn't eat it!' said the Earl, trying to pull the King's hand away from his mouth. Henry clenched his little fist around the heavy, solid gold sceptre and, with a sudden movement, hit the Earl over the head with it, just above the eye, really quite hard. The Earl flinched and bit his tongue before smiling as though nothing had happened.

'My Lord!' Catherine was all dismay. 'Let me see your forehead. Oh dear, I'm afraid you're going to have quite a swelling there. I'm so sorry. I'm sure His Highness didn't mean it.'

'No, of course he didn't, Ma'am. Please, don't give it a moment's thought.'

'I have a little paste of comfrey root, my Lady,' said Joan Astley. 'I always keep some to hand in case the King should happen to fall and cut himself. If His Lordship will permit me to apply a poultice of it to his forehead, it will help to take the swelling down.'

They entered Parliament an hour later with Queen Catherine walking a few steps in front of the Duke and Duchess of Gloucester. The whole procession was led by His Highness the King, still brandishing his miniature gold sceptre, in the arms of the Earl of Warwick whose good-natured countenance was rather marred by the rapidly darkening bruise around his half-closed eye. An amused murmur ran around the chamber of the House as everyone tried to guess how the Earl, so soon to be married to a famously domineering wife, had come by such a painful-looking swelling.

Catherine did not attend the Earl of Warwick's wedding to the Lady Isabella, though she was pleased to hear that the bridegroom's black eye had disappeared in time for the ceremony at the end of November. By then, Catherine had taken his advice in the matter of her dower lands. Other than what the Earl had told her, she really had little idea of precisely what constituted her inheritance.

She informed Sir Walter Hungerford that she would like to know more about her properties and where they were situated. Sir Walter was delighted to realise that she was taking an interest in her future in England and suggested that a list of her dower lands should be drawn up, including facts and figures, staffing levels, tenants, rents, and income for each one. Perhaps he could even arrange to have copies made of some precious maps, so that she could study all this information at her leisure. He thought that two of the royal clerks could begin work on the project immediately so that she could soon have a document which would help her pinpoint exactly where her properties were and the value of each one.

Several days into the job, Gilbert got up from his chair, yawned, and stretched his back luxuriously. 'Do you think the Queen will ever visit all these properties?' he asked.

'I'd like to think that she will visit Anglesey,' said Owen, 'though it will take her weeks to get there, with all the cartloads of belongings she'll be taking with her.'

'That's where you come from, isn't it?'

'Yes, a place called Penmynydd. It means "top of the mountain" but the strange thing is that it's in the flattest part of the whole island!'

'I always said the Welsh were illogical,' said Gilbert, though he had never said so before and had no idea why he said it now.

Owen ignored him, remembering the long journey south nearly a year ago. 'It took me months to get here,' he said. 'I wasn't in any hurry, mind. Just as well, really, because I met a man in Shrewsbury who slowed me down quite a bit. We decided to travel together and he talked nearly all the way about his dreams of becoming a glover, of all things, in London.'

Gilbert laughed. 'He probably believed that old chestnut about the streets being paved with gold,' he said.

They had all but finished their work a few days later when Sir Walter Hungerford came bustling in to the Library.

'Quick!' he said. 'Quickly, tidy the place up, for heaven's

sake. Her Highness the Queen is on her way to see you.' He bent to pick up some stray scraps of parchment off the floor. Owen and Gilbert began gathering together quills, ink, parchment, and powder. Owen was trying to rub an ink stain off his middle finger when the door opened again.

'Your Highness,' Sir Walter Hungerford bowed extravagantly. He hoped that, behind him, Owen and Gilbert were doing the same. He hadn't had time to remind them and good manners were so important. He wouldn't want to upset the Queen.

'Good afternoon, Sir Walter.' Queen Catherine entered the room with her ladies. 'Please, would you introduce the two gentlemen who have been working on my documents. I look forward so much to seeing what they've been doing.'

'Of course, my Lady. This is Master Gilbert Wilkins. He has been in our service for five years now and is highly skilled in the copying of maps. And this is Master –'

'Master Tudor! I didn't know that you were one of the gentlemen Sir Walter recommended so highly.'

Sir Walter Hungerford's jaw dropped as he saw the Queen's dazzling smile directed at the clerk. It almost seemed as though there was no one else in the room. Owen Tudor bowed again. 'I was deeply honoured, Your Highness, to have been chosen for the work. Both Master Wilkins and I felt very privileged to be of service to you.' He was at pains to encompass his colleague in his response.

'Then tell me, Master Tudor,' said the Queen, 'is the work finished yet?'

'Indeed, Ma'am, we finished it today. We were going to ask Sir Walter to present it to you in the morning.'

'But I want to see it now. Please, show me.'

Sir Walter stood to one side as Owen and Gilbert spread out sheets of parchment on a table for the Queen to inspect. She exclaimed with pleasure at the maps, wanting Gilbert to show her exactly where Westminster was, where Knaresborough was in relation to York, and where Glamorgan was in relation to Monmouth. She wanted to know where Flintshire was, then Anglesey.

176

'Master Tudor should tell you about Anglesey, Ma'am,' said Gilbert. 'It is his home.'

'Is that so, Master Tudor? Then, please be so kind as to show me where your home is.'

'This is the island, my Lady, just off the coast of North Wales.' Catherine bent over the map and, standing so close to Owen, she was surprised by a strong urge to stroke the soft dark hairs on the back of his wrist where he had pushed up his sleeve. She followed his finger as it traced the route to Penmynydd.

'My home is almost in the centre of the island. Gilbert has inscribed the English name on the map but the Welsh name for Anglesey is Ynys Môn. The Island of Mona.'

'Is that so?' Catherine, aware of the effect that Owen Tudor was having on her, kept her head down, hoping she wasn't blushing. 'How interesting. And is it very beautiful?'

'Very beautiful, Ma'am. In fact, it is a well-kept secret that when Our Lord created Wales, he made the most beautiful country he possibly could, with high mountains and deep lakes, with delightful little streams trickling down the valleys.' Owen, enjoying the rapt attention of the Queen, began to embroider the tale. 'Yes, the Lord crafted this wonderful country so lovingly that the Archangel Gabriel questioned whether any country could possibly be so perfect and whether there were any disadvantages in living there. The Lord replied that, sadly, there was one disadvantage: the people who lived in Wales would have the world's most obnoxious neighbours!'

There was a long, embarrassed silence. Every face in the room was totally impassive until the Queen had reacted to Owen Tudor's joke. He watched her face as his own creased into a huge smile. Then, after a pause, the Queen laughed delightedly. 'Oh, you mean the English! Yes, yes, of course, the English are the ... what was it? ... the obnoxious neighbours! Master Tudor, it is very wicked of you to say such a thing!' She laughed again and, reassured, her ladies tittered behind their hands. Gilbert let out a huge guffaw and even Sir Walter emitted a sound which rather resembled a neighing horse.

'I trust you are pleased with the work, my Lady,' he said,

thinking that he would really have to have a word with the Welshman. How dare he tell cross little jokes to Her Royal Highness the Queen like some court jester! Who did he think he was?

The Queen had noticed his look of annoyance. 'I'm delighted with the work, Sir Walter. It is exactly what I needed and, please, don't think badly of Master Tudor. I did enjoy his amusing story. Indeed, it might even apply to France and her neighbour Spain! You must remember that he and I are both foreigners in England.' She turned to Owen and Gilbert. 'However, thanks to you two gentlemen, I now have a very much clearer idea about my new, adopted country. I'm very grateful to you both. Good afternoon to you.' She turned to leave the room as the three men bowed again.

As soon as she and her ladies had left, Sir Walter rounded furiously on Owen. 'What on earth possessed you to tell the Queen that stupid story?' he fumed. Then, as Owen grinned engagingly, so Sir Walter's anger suddenly subsided and again he made the curious neighing sound which passed for laughter. Really, he thought, the Welshman wasn't the kind of person you could stay angry with for long. No wonder the Queen was so charmed by him.

Sir Walter was to remember the expression of pleasure on the Queen's face a few weeks later when Sir William Gifford, the seneschal of the castle, approached him with a problem. Gifford was a thin man with hunched shoulders, his face lined with the constant worry of staffing and running a huge household. He relied heavily on those staff members who held responsibility for various aspects of castle administration and worked well with their teams. He was delighted with the work of Anton, the French chef, and perfectly happy to leave the ordering of food supplies and the organisation of the kitchens to him, particularly now that the problem with his spice merchant had been resolved. The merchant in question had been cheating the system for years, growing proudly plump on the proceeds of his crime. It had taken a bit of clever financial investigation on the part of a shrewd castle clerk to identify the felon but when the merchant had been exposed for the trickster he was, Gifford was pleased to be able to tell him to his fat face that legal proceedings were already under way and that he could expect to be pilloried.

Now Sir William Gifford's problem was a very different one. In this case, Richard Hinton, the Clerk of the Queen's Wardrobe and one of his most trusted castle servants, had become increasingly blind over the past few years and had finally told him that he could no longer continue with his duties. Things had come to a head two days ago. The Queen had asked Hinton to procure some fine silk in her favourite sage green with a view to having a gown made for her niece Joan's forthcoming wedding to James of Scotland. Hinton had infuriated her by purchasing an inferior quality silk in light blue. Being a man who had hitherto always prided himself on his work, he had been deeply upset about the incident. He simply hadn't been able to appreciate the poor quality of the fabric nor tell the difference between the two colours.

Sir Walter was concerned. 'Has Hinton tried bathing his eyes in beer?' he asked. 'They say it is very beneficial.'

'He has. And it seems that his wife has also persuaded him to try warm bat's blood, but it's difficult to come by and he has had no great relief from it.'

'You'll be needing another Clerk of the Wardrobe, then. Had you anyone in mind?'

'No. That's why I wanted to talk to you.'

'Perhaps we should discuss it with Her Highness,' said Sir Walter. 'I will request an audience with her.'

They went together to see the Queen the following afternoon. The Clerk of the Queen's Wardrobe was a senior staff position and a sensitive appointment, because whoever held the office would have to see a great deal of Her Royal Highness. It was crucially important that she should approve the choice and be able to trust the incumbent to oversee not only the purchase of fabrics, furs, and personal effects but also to be accountable for the safety and care of her jewellery, plate, and valuables and to supervise the work of her seamstresses, laundresses, and personal staff. It was a position of great responsibility.

Catherine welcomed them warmly. 'Sir William,' she said as the seneschal bowed low over her hand, 'I haven't seen you for some time. Is there a crisis in the household?'

'I'm afraid there is, Ma'am. We've come to see you about the Clerk of your Wardrobe.'

'Master Hinton? I'm very displeased with him. I had intended talking to you about it.'

'My Lady, it appears that he is rapidly going blind and there is little that can be done about it. This is the reason ...' he didn't finish his sentence before the Queen interrupted him.

'Going blind! But he said nothing. The poor man. Has he tried bat's blood?'

'Apparently so, Ma'am. It seems that he has tried all known remedies but to no avail.'

'Then that's why he's been behaving so strangely of late. I should not have been so quick to judge him. It's really not his fault that he's losing his sight.'

She rose from her chair and walked to the window, weighing up the problem in her mind. Turning back, she said: 'If he has to leave my service because of his blindness, Sir Walter, there must be a way of offering him a small pension. If there's a problem, it can come from the account which pays for my personal staff.'

'That's good of you, Ma'am. Yes, I'm sure we can help him. He's been in the service of the royal family for so long that we can't see him destitute. In the meantime, it's rather urgent that we find you a replacement.'

'You have someone in mind?'

'There doesn't seem to be anyone obvious, my Lady, and it's a sensitive appointment.'

'Indeed. It has to be someone I like and can trust.'

All three were silent for a moment, Sir Walter and Sir William desperately trying to think of a solution to the problem and the Queen trying to quell the sudden, violent beating of her heart. When she felt more in control of herself, she spoke.

'The two clerks who worked on the reports I requested on my dower properties seemed very efficient, Sir Walter,' she said, as casually as she could.

'Yes, Gilbert Wilkins is a certainly good worker,' said Sir Walter. 'If a little young for this job. It needs someone with authority.'

'Is he younger than Master Tudor?'

'No, Ma'am, Tudor is the younger of the two. I wouldn't have thought him particularly suitable,' said Sir Walter. Then he remembered the expression he'd seen on the Queen's face when she realised that Tudor had been working on her property reports. 'Of course,' he said quickly, 'if your Highness has any preferences in the matter, then we must accommodate them.'

'Tudor!' exclaimed Sir William Gifford. 'Not Owen Tudor? That was the name of the clerk who discovered that the chef was being cheated by his spice merchant. A very clever piece of investigation.'

'Yes, I heard about it,' said Sir Walter. 'Very clever.'

'Rather an unusual name, I thought. That's why I remembered it.'

'It is unusual,' Sir Walter agreed. 'Welsh, originally.'

'Welsh?' Sir William looked doubtful. 'Oh, I hadn't realised that. You can't trust them, you know. Dishonest. Cheat you as soon as look at you.'

Catherine couldn't believe what she was hearing. 'That is nonsense, Sir William,' she protested. 'Why should any one race be more dishonest than another? It's individual people who are dishonest. Only a moment ago you were admiring Master Tudor for discovering that the chef was being cheated by his spice merchant. But now you know he is Welsh, you assume him to be dishonest! I cannot see the logic in that. Master Tudor has proved himself to be both honest and capable in the last few weeks. I was very impressed with his work on my property reports.'

Sir William paused. That had been quite an outburst and he had no desire to annoy his Sovereign Lady any further. 'But would you be prepared to employ him as your Clerk of the Wardrobe, my Lady?' he asked, sounding doubtful.

'Yes, of course I would,' Catherine said firmly. 'Keeping wardrobe accounts is not so very different from keeping kitchen accounts, is it?'

'Perhaps not, Ma'am.'

Sir Walter Hungerford sounded a note of caution. 'As long as you're sure that his little jokes won't irritate you, my Lady. He seems to be of a rather playful disposition. That attitude might not be suitable in a position of authority.'

Catherine tried to look stern but came close to failing. If only these two decent, straight-laced old gentlemen knew how she longed for some gaiety in her young life, the opportunity to laugh.

What she said was: 'If you're suggesting Master Tudor for this appointment, Sir Walter, then I think he will do very well.'

Sir Walter, who was actually suggesting no such thing, hesitated. 'If you're sure, your Highness.'

'I am quite sure, Sir Walter. Please be so good as to speak to him immediately and inform him of his new appointment. Thank you, gentlemen.'

Catherine inclined her head to dismiss the two men. When they had left the room she picked up her little bell and rang for Guillemote.

'Guillemote,' she said slowly when her maid came running to do her bidding, 'I think I've done something I might live to regret.'

'And what is that, my Lady?'

'I have suggested the name of Master Owen Tudor for the position of my Clerk of the Wardrobe.'

Guillemote saw the radiant expression on her mistress's face. 'Well, Ma'am,' she said, 'the prospect seems to make you very happy!'

Chapter Fourteen

England, Spring 1424

There had been so little travelling since the late King's death that Sir Walter had almost forgotten what it was like. At one time, the court would journey regularly to stay for a few weeks at one or other of the great royal residences outside London, providing an opportunity for the King to meet his people throughout the country, people who were the source of his revenues. As a rule, there was one visit a year to Leicester, usually at Easter, and Christmas at Kenilworth had always been a source of great delight to the late King.

But the Queen now wished to break with tradition and spend the festive season somewhere different. Hertford seemed a good choice. It was an old, established castle some twenty-five miles to the north of London, well-appointed and comfortable. Catherine and her young son had been escorted there by Bishop Henry Beaufort and they were joined by the Duchess of Clarence, her son Edmund, and her daughter Joan. A few days later, the Duke of Gloucester arrived with the Duchess Jacqueline, and the final guest completed the royal party on Christmas Eve. He was James of Scotland, soon to be married to Margaret's daughter. Catherine was delighted to see them both. They planned a February wedding in London and, whenever she wasn't with her betrothed, Joan was either being fitted for some item of her bridal trousseau or closeted with her mother, putting yet more detail onto the plans for the ceremony and the elaborate celebrations afterwards.

Catherine left them to their lists and menus and went in search of Jacqueline. She had broken off a sprig of mistletoe from a bunch which hung in the great hall of the castle and, privately, she suggested to Jacqueline that she should pin it to her garter. It was well known, she told her earnestly, that mistletoe enabled a woman to conceive a child if she really wanted to. Jacqueline whirled around to face her, beaming with joy.

'Catherine, I don't need to! I didn't want to tell you until I was absolutely certain but I know now that there will be a baby, come summer.'

The two women hugged each other ecstatically, both delighted at Jacqueline's good fortune. All in all, it was a very happy Christmas.

The court remained at Hertford for nearly two weeks after Epiphany but Catherine wanted to be back in Windsor well before Candlemas in early February to allow plenty of time to prepare for Joan's wedding on the twelfth of the month. The safe packing and transport of her boxes and coffers for the return journey had been entirely the responsibility of the new Clerk of the Wardrobe and he felt mightily relieved when it was all safely on its way back to Windsor. He wondered yet again why one woman needed so many clothes. And not only clothes: among the items in Owen's care were the Queen's personal plates, knives, spoons, and goblets, tapestries, and all her jewellery. Shoes, too. God's knees! How many pairs did she have?

Guillemote, who had been a great help to Owen, pointed out that life on the road was always difficult for the Queen's personal staff. There was never any guarantee that there would be adequate provision of rooms for bathing and hairdressing, not to mention laundering and making running repairs to clothes. At least now that they were back at home, there was a place for everything.

'And everything in its place!' said Guillemote, her hands on her hips, surveying the familiar royal storage rooms at Windsor. Everything had been unpacked and put away and now all that was needed was a decision from the Queen about what she would like to wear for her niece's wedding.

'Such a shame about the blue silk,' muttered Guillemote.

'Entirely the wrong shade.'

'What shade of blue does Her Highness favour?' asked Owen, looking up from the ledger he was working on.

'She doesn't favour blue at all, she never thinks it suits her, even though she has blue in her eyes. Though sometimes they look more grey than blue so perhaps that's the reason why. Well, anyway, I doubt very much that we will be able to get what she wants in good time to have it made up into a gown for her to wear at the wedding.'

Owen got up from his seat. 'Have you got a sample of the colour Her Highness likes, Guillemote? You know, a little scrap of fabric. Anything like that. Then I'll see what I can do.'

Next morning, with a small offcut of sage-green silk in his pocket, Owen shivered as he stood on the river steps at Windsor. It was bitterly cold on the water so early in the day but at least the journey could be made quickly by boat. Acting on a hunch, he had summoned a wherryman to take him on a private errand.

Owen entered London Bridge from the Southwark end where trade was already brisk in the jumble of little shops on either side. He wrinkled his nose against the stench of weed, slops, and dead animals in the river below, looked around, and then made his way towards half a dozen shops grouped between the stone gate and the drawbridge on the west side. He had glimpsed a sign bearing the image of a gloved hand. On a trestle table in front of the shop, the glover's assistant was busying himself with laying out his master's wares in various colours, designs and sizes.

'Rhodri Fychan! *Sut wyt ti, 'ngwas i*?' Owen said, delighted at having so easily found the friend he was looking for. He banged him heartily on the back. Rhodri turned.

'Owain ap Maredydd! How the devil are you?'

'Owain ap Maredydd no longer, my friend. I'm Master Owen Tudor now, I'll have you know. A fine gentleman of the English court and in the personal employment of Her Royal Highness the Queen. Her Clerk of the Wardrobe, no less.'

'Never! Oh, hoity-toity! So *that's* how to get on in this world. Change your name, is it? I could be Master Roderick

Vaughan, then!'

'You could, but you'd be the same old Rhodri Fychan to me. How are you?'

'Happy as a pig in sh … sh … Shrewsbury!' said Rhodri, grinning. 'Mind you, leaving Shrewsbury was the best thing I ever did. D'you know, I earn nearly two pounds a year more here in London. And the girls are prettier!'

'And just as willing, I'll wager!'

'Aye, twice as willing!' agreed Rhodri, leering. 'And you? Have you got a girl, yet?'

'No! No such luck,' said Owen rather abruptly as the image of a young woman with blue-grey eyes and braided fair hair came, unbidden, into his mind's eye. 'Now, Rhodri, I'm here on the business of Her Highness the Queen.'

'And what sort of gloves does Her Highness want?'

'Rhodri, I'll be honest with you. She doesn't want any gloves. But – and it's a big but – I will ask her if you and your master may wait on her when she is next at the Palace of Westminster and show her a selection of your wares. On the one hand, she might want your gloves. On the other hand, she might not.' Owen laughed at his own unintended pun. Rhodri hadn't noticed.

'Really? Really! You wait 'til I tell the master. He's bound to give me a pay rise if you can find him favour with the Queen!'

Owen put a restraining hand on his friend's arm. 'First you've got to do *me* a favour.'

'Anything, Owain, anything. Just tell me.'

'Right. Information. You can tell me who is selling the best silk in town at the moment. And at the best price.'

Rhodri looked nonplussed. 'I don't know,' he said, 'I don't know much about silk but I'll find out for you. Wait here.' He disappeared inside the shop and came out a minute or so later with an older man who was rubbing his hands together obsequiously. 'Owain, this is my master, Thomas de Gloucestre. He is a master glover but his family have been in the cloth trade for many years. He thinks he can help you.'

'Is it silk you're after, Master Tudor?' the man asked. Owen nodded. 'Well, as it happens, my own brother-in-law is a silk trader. And a very reasonable man. He has modest premises in Queenhithe and has just begun importing silk from France. From the town of Lyon, he tells me.' He was looking intently at Owen. 'Perhaps, if it is for the personal use of Her Highness the Queen, she would be pleased by the thought that the silk is imported from France.'

'Perhaps she would. Now, if you'll be so good as to tell me where to find your brother-in-law's shop, I'll pay him a visit.'

'It's a warehouse, Master Tudor, just behind Brook's Wharf in Queenhithe, near the sign of the bear. Tell him I sent you and I'm sure he'll give you a good price. And might I venture to hope that Her Highness would be interested in the purchase of some fine gloves in the near future?'

'Of course, of course.' Owen was already moving away. 'Yes, the next time the court is in Westminster, I will let Rhodri know. It could be very soon.'

'*Diolch i ti, 'rhen gyfaill!*' Rhodri doubted that his friend had heard his shout of thanks. It was lost on the breeze from the river.

The silks on offer were of a high quality at a reasonable price and Owen was delighted to find one in almost exactly the shade he was looking for. When asked how much he needed, he realised that he had absolutely no idea so he bought all the trader's remaining stock of it and returned to Windsor with a neat package under his arm.

Now he had to involve others in the conspiracy, Guillemote, Les Trois Jo-jo, and two of the royal seamstresses, Molly Betts and Madge Wilkin. Disappointingly, there wasn't quite enough of the sage-coloured silk for a gown, but Madge Wilkin suggested that, to make the fabric go further, they might use the silk for the bodice and make alternate skirt panels in silk and cloth of gold. Molly Betts thought that they might complement the gown with a matching houppelande to go over it, made of cloth of gold and lined and trimmed with miniver to keep Her Highness warm in the draughty church of St Mary Overie during the wedding ceremony. Later, when she wished to remove the houppelande for the wedding feast, the gown would be revealed in all its glory. Owen, completely out of his depth, couldn't imagine the finished ensemble. He just had to trust that the women knew what they were doing. With very little time in which to complete the work, Madge and Molly started on it immediately with a team of four senior apprentices and the six women hardly slept until they had produced two sumptuous matching garments.

Unaware of this, Catherine asked for several of her formal gowns to be brought to Windsor from the Great Wardrobe near St Paul's where they were normally stored so that she could decide what to wear. Owen made sure that these were delivered promptly and displayed neatly for the Queen's inspection but Guillemote had kept the new clothes to one side with some idea of producing them at the right moment, as though in a jongleur's conjuring trick.

Finding it difficult to make a decision, Catherine finally picked up the white embroidered silk she had worn for her coronation and held it against herself. 'This will do quite well for the wedding, won't it? It's hardly worn.' She looked at Guillemote. 'What do you think?' she asked. 'Shall I wear this?'

'It might need a little alteration here and there, my Lady. Your coronation was three years ago and you've had a child since then. You've probably put on a little weight. Besides, white always makes you look pale.'

'Then I've nothing to wear!' wailed Catherine. 'There's nothing else I like half as much. Guillemote, what am I to do? Is there time to have this altered?'

'Wait, my Lady, wait. I have a little surprise for you!' Excitedly, Guillemote disappeared into the room next to the garderobe where the conspirators were waiting. She almost snatched the new gown out of Madge Wilkin's hands and took it to show to Catherine.

'Ma'am, I think you might like this,' she said, curtseying.

Owen ached to see Catherine's face. He hadn't realised how much he wanted to please her until this moment. Then he heard a great shriek of joy.

'Oh, Guillemote! It's the most beautiful thing I've ever seen! Look at this silk! It's exactly the right colour. And the cloth of gold panels in the skirt … that looks so lovely. Who made it? Give it to me. Let me try it on. Oh, I do hope it fits!'

'Molly and Madge made it, my Lady, and I promise you it will fit because they took their pattern from a gown you were wearing only last week.'

'But the colour, Guillemote! It's wonderful. Who found this beautiful silk?'

'Ah, that was the new Clerk of the Wardrobe, Ma'am. Master Tudor.'

'Master Tudor?' Catherine paused, her eyebrows raised, blushing with pleasure. 'But how did he know what to buy?'

'He made it his business to know, Ma'am. He was anxious to please you.'

'He has pleased me very much,' said Catherine, holding the gown to her cheek. 'Very much indeed. I am delighted.'

Listening in the next room, Owen turned away from the two jubilant seamstresses to hide the extent of his own elation.

'Yes,' he whispered to himself, clenching his fists. 'Yes, oh yes, oh yes!'

Catherine turned several heads as she arrived at church for the wedding of King James of Scotland to Joan Beaufort. The bride's mother looked up in surprise from the paternoster beads which she had been fingering nervously and the Duchess Jacqueline's eyebrows almost reached her hairline at the sight of Catherine. Duke Humphrey stared at her for rather longer than was polite. Catherine merely inclined her head towards the high altar, crossed herself, and muttered a silent prayer. Then all eyes turned towards the side door of the church as the bride entered, looking very nervous and pale on the arm of her brother, Edmund.

The ceremony was conducted by Bishop Henry Beaufort, beaming with avuncular pride as the bridal couple made their vows. Naturally the wedding feast was held in the great hall of the palace of Winchester, the Bishop's London home in Southwark but one of Catherine's many gifts to the bridal couple was a second celebration a few days later, this time in the King's name, at the palace of Westminster. The royal chef, Anton, rose to the occasion and had been at his most imaginative and extravagant. The seventy guests feasted on beef, mutton, capons, chickens, boars' heads, and waterfowl, beautifully presented and accompanied by a plentiful supply of the finest wines of France. Minstrels and jongleurs played and danced for the guests while jesters took turns at amusing them with sly stories of innocent brides and inexperienced bridegrooms.

The royal dais remained undisturbed when the floor was cleared for dancing but other tables and benches were pushed against the walls. The King and new Queen of Scotland, hand in hand, led the guests on to the floor as the minstrels in the gallery struck the first chords of the Pavane, the simple processional dance which could involve every single guest.

Catherine took the opportunity to slip away to the nursery where the King had been having a late afternoon nap. He smiled sleepily at her and she kissed the soft fair hair on top of his head. Now she watched as Joan Astley fed him and dressed him again in his best crimson velvet and set on his head the little crimson cap which incorporated a small crown. After carrying him down the long corridor, Joan then set him down on his feet for Catherine to lead him into the great hall. He was walking very confidently now, but still wanted her to hold his hand.

The floor was crowded with dancers when a bugler's fanfare from the minstrels' gallery brought the proceedings to an abrupt halt. The little King entered the room with his mother to a burst of affectionate applause as the dancers stood to one side to allow them to pass. The bride dropped a deep curtsey to Henry, the groom bowed low, and the other dancers followed their example.

Catherine led Henry to the centre of the dais where a very distinctive chair had been set out for him. Fashioned like a small throne with a restraint across the front of it for safety, it was high, substantially higher than any other chair in the room, ensuring that the supreme monarch, though not yet three years old, would sit head and shoulders above all the wedding guests.

Catherine couldn't quite reach it so she accepted the Earl of Warwick's offer to lift the child into the chair, watching anxiously in case her son, wriggling and kicking in protest, should give the Earl another black eye.

Some of the more senior palace servants, including Owen and Gilbert, had been invited to join the dancing, and Owen stared about him at the enormous display of wealth in the room. Here were kings, queens, princes, princesses, dukes, and duchesses, all trying to outdo each other in their finery. Now that the short February afternoon was drawing to a close and lighted candles were being brought into the room, there was a sparkle everywhere, in jewellery, in candlelight, and in the wine. Owen took two large goblets from a trestle table behind him and offered one to Gilbert.

'Drink a toast, my friend,' he said loudly over the music. 'You won't see a sight like this too often in your lifetime.'

Gilbert nodded. 'Impressive, isn't it?' he agreed. 'All that jewellery. All those fine clothes. Mind you, I think you have the most interesting shoes.'

'Why do you always notice people's shoes?'

'Well, yours are about the longest and most pointed in the whole room. How on earth do you avoid people treading on them?'

'With great difficulty,' said Owen, grimacing. He was already beginning to regret having worn his fashionable new shoes for the occasion. Never mind, he wasn't going to go and change them now. He'd just have to be careful.

Sitting on the royal dais, Edmund Beaufort had drunk at least half a jugful of wine. Now he sat with his hand cupping his chin, staring morosely at Catherine as she moved among the wedding guests. Edmund had never seen her looking so beautiful. Her hair and skin against that sage green were so very lovely and it did seem to bring out the startling colour of her eyes. He despaired of ever becoming close to her. He had dreamed about her several times recently and awakened with a start, sweating and wet. He blushed silently.

Humphrey of Gloucester was watching him. Ah, so that was the lie of the land, was it? The Beaufort boy was staring at

Catherine like a love-sick calf and not caring who saw him. No wonder. That burgundy wine was strong enough to fell a grown man, let alone an inexperienced boy of seventeen who hadn't even developed a proper beard. What Catherine needed, thought Humphrey, was an older man to pleasure her, a man of the world. It wasn't difficult to imagine how she would look if she took off that green and gold gown but how welcoming she would be to a lover? What would she be prepared to do to please a man? Really, he thought, it was all most unfortunate. He could have had Catherine for himself except that when he'd first lusted after her she had been married to his brother, and now that she was a widow and free to re-marry, he was saddled with a wife of his own. He cast a sidelong glance at Jacqueline. Full of concern for the coming baby, she wasn't exactly ardent towards him these days – so she could hardly chastise him for his thoughts and he was a red-blooded man, after all. Could that explain why he found Catherine so alluring today? Or could it be that she really was attracted to Edmund Beaufort and wanted to attract him to her in return? Surely not. Still, Humphrey felt he should keep an eye on the situation.

The King was safely restrained in his high throne, the object of much cooing and calling from the peers and peeresses of the realm who crowded around him, vying for his attention. So Catherine had left him in the care of the Earl of Warwick and gone to sit on a low bench with some of her ladies, well below the royal dais. Several of the wedding guests had relaxed their customary formality and were mingling with the more senior members of the household.

The liberal provision of wine meant that, little by little, the palace staff lost some of their inhibitions and began to enjoy the dancing. Amid much laughter and merriment, Owen and Gilbert found that they danced exceptionally well with the seamstresses Molly and Madge, except that Madge kept treading on the pointed toes of Owen's shoes. It didn't seem to matter. Well not, that was, until they came to the Galliard.

Owen loved to dance the Galliard. Most of the other dancers moved away once they recognised the first few notes, knowing that it was a dance best performed by the more experienced among them. Against the rhythm of a triple beat, the pattern of steps included five athletic leaps into the air for the male dancers, who would attempt to jump as high as they could, each time changing the way they landed back on their feet.

Standing with Molly and Madge, Gilbert watched from the sidelines. He certainly wasn't going to attempt a dance like that, even though both women were urging him to. 'Go on, Gilbert. You can do it. If Owen can, then surely you can!'

Owen was enjoying himself. By now, many of the other dancers were standing to one side and watching him, clapping to the rhythm of the music.

So nearly all eyes were on him when he fell.

Gilbert had been right. Owen had tripped himself up over the ridiculously long pointed toes of his shoes. He tried to save himself but failed utterly and hit the floor with a painful thud in front of the bench where the Queen sat. Her ladies screeched in horror, jumping to their feet. The music stopped as everyone turned, aware of an accident, to see what had happened.

What they saw was Owen lying full length on the floor with his head in the Queen's lap.

He remained lying there for a long moment, looking up at her: in this light her eyes were the colour of Ogwen Valley slate. Aware that he was staring at her, Catherine feigned a little scream and her hands flew to her neck in a gesture of horror but her overwhelming feeling was that his face was just as pleasing when viewed upside down.

In trying to break his fall, Owen had twisted his wrist quite painfully and when he'd got to his feet and bowed apologetically to the Queen, he allowed himself to be led away by Molly Betts who said she had a small supply of precious mandrake root made up into an ointment. She applied it skilfully to Owen's wrist, chattering as she did so.

'Her Highness didn't seem to mind very much, did she? You could swear she liked having your head in her lap like that.'

'Oh, I don't think so, Molly.'

'But you're wrong, Owen. She could have made much more of a fuss than she did. She could have had you put in the stocks for making such an exhibition of yourself.'

'Molly, I was not making an exhibition … I was … I was merely dancing.'

'Hmm,' said Molly, giving him a quizzical look.

In the Great Hall, dancing had begun again after the diversion of Owen's fall but the Countess of Westmorland was so scandalised that she felt she had to say something to the Queen. 'Your Highness, that coarse fellow took advantage of your good nature. You should have had him thrown out of the room.'

'Oh, I don't think so,' said Catherine mildly. 'It was merely an accident. Master Tudor wasn't trying to hurt me in any way. Besides, I wouldn't want to make a scene and spoil the day for the bride and groom.'

'But Ma'am, he is a servant!'

'I am aware of that, my dear Countess. But even servants have accidents. They can't always be blamed for it.'

'Ma'am, you cannot allow yourself to show favour to a man like that. You are the Queen. Of course, you are French and perhaps you don't quite understand. So let me explain. You see, not only is he a mere servant but … but …'

'But what?'

'He isn't English.'

'Neither am I.'

'But Ma'am, he's … he's …' the Countess could scarcely bring herself to say the word, 'he … he's *Welsh*.'

'Indeed he is.' Catherine paused then rose from the low bench where she had been sitting and turned to face the Countess. 'So, let me understand you clearly, *Madame*. I must not forgive the fact that this poor man had an accident because he is Welsh. Is that it? Or because he's a servant? Or because he's a Welsh servant?'

'Your Highness, please let me explain, I beg you. You are probably not aware … but the … the Welsh are not like us. They are rough, barbarous people, barely on the edge of polite society. We English have been forced to build strong castles, at great expense, to subdue them. And they speak the most outlandish tongue that no decent person could possibly

194

understand. Your own husband, the late King, was constantly troubled by them. Really, I wonder you tolerate having one of them in your household!'

Catherine paused again for a long moment, then took a deep breath. When she spoke, her voice was low and her tone was measured. She was desperately trying to keep control of herself.

'Countess, do not presume to tell me anything about my late husband, the King. His Highness counted several Welshmen among his friends and he valued the unstinting service they gave him on the battlefield, particularly at Agincourt. And let me tell you something else – Master Tudor is an excellent servant, quite one of the best on my staff. He is polite, he is well-spoken, he is agreeable, and he goes to considerable lengths to ensure that I am well served. I have no wish to quarrel with you, Countess, but if you think I should single out Master Tudor for punishment just because he is Welsh, then, to your eternal shame, Madame, you are a bigot!

She turned on her heel and walked swiftly towards the door, conscious that all eyes were on her. Her heart was hammering and she was shaking with anger. How dare that stupid, arrogant woman say such things! Owen was worth twenty of her!

Catherine almost ran to her bedchamber, slammed the door, and threw herself down on the bed, her mind in turmoil. Within a moment, the door opened again to admit Guillemote.

'My Lady, are you all right?'

'No, Guillemote, I am not all right. I am furious.'

'The Countess spoke out of turn, my Lady, I'm sure she will apologise.'

Catherine looked at Guillemote. Slowly, her heart was resuming its normal rate and her breathing was becoming calmer. 'Guillemote,' she said, 'I am just as furious with myself as I am with the Countess.'

'But, my Lady …'

'No, Guillemote, please listen. I have to talk to someone. The Countess is a stupid, vain, shallow woman and a complete bigot. As I told her in no uncertain terms, if I remember correctly!' She gave a rueful smile and sighed. 'I don't regret that. I only regret that I could hardly control my feelings. I

195

might have given myself away in front of all those people, people like the Duke of Gloucester, heaven help me ... my cousin Jacqueline ... the Duchess of Clarence ... not just the Countess of Westmorland ... Oh, that dreadful woman! Do you think she might have guessed what I was really so furious about?'

'Master Owen Tudor, Ma'am? The way she was talking about him?'

Catherine nodded. 'Yes, Master Owen Tudor. Guillemote, I couldn't bear to hear that stupid woman criticising him. He's a wonderful man, thoughtful, charming, funny, considerate. He makes me laugh, he takes me out of myself. He makes me forget how cold the English people are, how much I worry about Jacqueline, how very hurt I feel every time Mistress Ryman takes the baby away from me. Owen Tudor is the only friend I have ... except for you, my dear Guillemote.'

'Thank you, my Lady.' Guillemote paused. 'Of course, Master Tudor is also very handsome. Last summer, I happened to see him swimming in the river with his cousin and some of their friends from the garrison.'

'Swimming?' Catherine's eyes widened. 'Was he clothed?'

'No, Ma'am, he was wearing nothing at all. And I noticed ...' Guillemote hesitated, then decided that she knew her mistress well enough to venture a little risqué humour in an attempt to cheer her up. 'I noticed that he has ... er ... well ... you remember what we French used to think?' She paused, then her words came out in a rush, 'He has a very fine tail!'

'Guillemote!'

Guillemote's smile was both fond and sympathetic: she put her hand on Catherine's arm, genuinely concerned for her. 'And you're in love with him, my Lady. I have long suspected it.'

Catherine's tears welled and spilled over as she nodded. 'Yes, Guillemote, I think I must be. Deeply in love.'

'And ... if he feels the same way about you, my Lady, you could both be deeply in trouble.'

Chapter Fifteen

Summer 1424

'*Wel, sut wyt ti'r hen lwynog*!' Maredydd asked as he moved up to make room for Owen to sit next to him on their favourite bench in the tavern. 'How are you?'

'Llwynog? Fox? Why am I a fox?'

'Because I haven't seen you for such a long time. You must have been up to something crafty, something cunning. A little vixen, is it?'

'Oh yes,' Owen exaggerated. 'The most beautiful little vixen you ever saw. Small, fair-haired, blue eyes, you know, big here, small here.' He outlined the shape of a woman's body lasciviously with his hands.

'Get on with you. You won't find one like that around here, more's the pity!' Maredydd drained his tankard and wiped his mouth. 'I was just going to buy another one of these. D'you want one?'

'Aye, why not?' Little did Maredydd know, Owen thought, that he had already found her, though she was so far out of his reach that she might as well live on the moon. He watched as his cousin bought more ale and knew that he could never tell him or anyone else how he felt about Catherine. She would always have to remain a secret, locked in his heart.

'The trick with women,' Maredydd confided, setting two tankards down on the table, 'is to go for the grateful ones.'

'The grateful ones? Why?'

'Well, it's simple, isn't it? They hang on your every word, obey your every command, and anticipate your every little whim … just for the joy of having you pleasure them. It's true. Ask any ugly woman and, if she's honest, she'll tell you it's true.'

'So, the uglier the better, eh?'

'Not necessarily. Just as long as she's grateful. You know, a bit like the Duchess of Gloucester.'

'She's not ugly.'

'No, perhaps not, she's comely enough, I suppose. But if you compare her with her cousin, the Queen, I'd say she comes a pretty poor second.'

Owen's heart lurched. He agreed wholeheartedly with Maredydd but dared not risk betraying his own feelings about the Queen.

'So, you're saying that the Duchess probably feels grateful to the Duke for pleasuring her?'

'Well, she's forever fawning over him. An arrogant bastard, that one. Proud as a dog in a doublet.'

Owen changed the subject. 'Any more news about his plans to invade Holland?'

'No, not yet. The Duchess is whelping, isn't she? They'll wait until that's all out of the way before they make their move. I hope they don't wait too long, though. I'm to go with them and I'm not getting any younger!'

Jacqueline had been so excited, so happy throughout the spring and had developed an endearing little habit of patting her swelling belly and talking to the child within. Catherine often found her looking down at herself and saying such things as: 'You little rapscallion! You wait until I tell Papa how hard you're kicking me!' And all the while her face was wreathed in smiles.

There was nothing to worry anyone. Then, one sultry night in July, Jacqueline, attended by the midwife, Margery Wagstaff, and two of her assistants, smiled nervously at Catherine. 'Not long now,' she said. 'Stay with me for a while.'

These were the dog days, the hottest and most oppressive of the whole year. The air was still but, despite the stifling heat, a fire was kept burning in Jacqueline's bedchamber so that a small cauldron of hot water was constantly available to the midwives. It made the room unbearable and for two long days and nights, poor Jacqueline sweated and strained and cried out in agony. For hours at a time, Catherine sat by the bed, holding her hand and trying not to mind how painfully her cousin's fingernails were digging into her. Humphrey retired to the north tower of the castle where he was completely unable to hear his wife screaming. His son would be born eventually and there was nothing he could do. This was women's work and no man had any business being anywhere near it.

The midwives tried everything they knew but the baby wouldn't come. Margery Wagstaff massaged ointment into the taut skin across Jacqueline's swollen belly then shushed the others while she listened for a heartbeat. She felt for the child's head but could only feel its buttocks. She tried to encourage the baby to move by opening and closing drawers and cupboard doors to simulate the opening of the womb. She smeared pepper under Jacqueline's nose to make her sneeze. And still the baby wouldn't come.

'This one's going to be a lazy little tyke, Your Grace,' she said, teasing, to keep Jacqueline's spirits up. 'He likes taking his time so he's always going to be late for appointments. You'll have to train him well!' Jacqueline smiled weakly between the searing pains of contraction. The child could be as lazy as he liked once he'd been born, she didn't care. She just prayed that he'd be here soon.

Catherine stayed with Jacqueline and did whatever she could to help. She soaked a cloth in cooling rosewater and gently cleaned Jacqueline's face where it was streaked by rivulets of sweat running through the pepper grounds around her mouth. Poor Jacqueline had sneezed pitifully but to no effect and the baby was still firmly in her womb. The midwives had used all the techniques they knew and they began to talk of past experiences they could draw on. They even discussed whether, as a last resort, they would summon a doctor to cut the baby out. Catherine begged them not to.

'She'll surely die, if you do that!' she whispered urgently. 'You must not! The Duke will be very angry.'

So Jacqueline's agony continued and Margery Wagstaff urged Catherine to snatch a little sleep. As the hours went by, the midwives made several more attempts to turn the baby but without success. Out of earshot of his mother, they muttered to each other that if the child wasn't already dead, he soon would be. He was having too much of a battle to be born. They had completely failed to turn him, so there was nothing for it but to haul him out as best they could and hope against hope that both he and his mother would survive. Getting a grip on a small leg, Margery Wagstaff looked around in desperation.

'I'll have to baptise him as soon as he's out,' she said. 'It's urgent. We might lose them both. There's no time to get a priest. Get me the holy water. Does anyone know what he's to be called?'

The midwives shrugged, no one had told them that. 'Richard is quite a nice name,' one of them suggested. Margery looked down at the small body which she was trying to manoeuvre into the world. 'Oh, God. Bad luck. This one's a girl and by now it doesn't matter what I call her. Get me the holy water. Now! Just get it!'

'Tacinda is a pretty name for a girl,' said the youngest midwife, as she handed Margery the bowl of holy water. 'My sister called her little girl Tacinda. I really like it.'

'Tacinda it is.' Margery dipped her bloodied fingers into the water and made the sign of the cross on the forehead of the small baby girl. '*In nomine Patris ... et Filii ... et Spiritus Sancti ...*' The child was dead. She had never moved, never cried, never breathed. She had probably been dead since becoming entangled with the umbilical cord which was still knotted around her little wrinkled neck.

Catherine had slept like a stoat, wary, half-listening for the cry of a new-born baby, but she'd heard nothing. By the time she came back into the room, Jacqueline had lost consciousness and the midwives' most urgent task was to keep her alive. Two of them were trying to prop her up on pillows to ease her breathing while they cleaned her and changed her blood-soaked bedding. Margery Wagstaff took away the limp, lifeless body of the baby. She would wash the little one and lay her out, in case her poor mother should want to see her. Never having lived, she had not been given the last rites, but at least she had a name to take with her to the grave. The midwife muttered a prayer over Tacinda's tiny corpse.

Catherine wept.

Humphrey had to be told, of course, and Catherine cast around in her mind for the best person to tell him. If only John of Bedford were here, he would know what to do, but John was still in Picardy after the latest in a string of recent victories in France. Margaret would have been another ally but she, too, was away from court. There was nothing for it but to tell Humphrey herself.

She realised, afterwards, that she should have taken a few minutes to prepare herself, to wash her face and comb her hair at least. Her eyes were red with weeping for her cousin and the dead child and her hair was matted with sweat. No doubt her gown, too, was creased and stained.

When she found him, Humphrey was with a group of a dozen or so friends in the north tower. The sound of high-pitched laughter and the music of psalteries reached her before she had even opened the door. Lolling in a cushioned chair, Humphrey had a wine glass in one hand and when he saw Catherine he gestured with the other hand to stop the music. Her appearance prompted a flurry of bows and curtsies among his companions and, kicking away his footstool, Humphrey rose to greet her, barely lifting a disdainful eyebrow at her dishevelled appearance. He bent over her hand and pressed it a little too warmly to his lips.

'Your Highness. I am delighted to see you. You bring me news of my son?'

She looked at him in disbelief. Was that all men cared about? Siring a son? Had he not thought that his wife had gone through exactly the same birthing agonies to bring him a daughter? And didn't he care enough to ask how she was? Catherine tried hard to control herself.

'I'm sorry to be the bearer of bad tidings, my Lord,' she said. 'The baby was a girl.'

He frowned. 'Was?'

'Yes. She didn't survive. She was such a pretty little thing but she was stillborn.' Catherine swallowed hard to keep the tears at bay. 'Jacqueline has endured three days of agony and to no avail. I'm sorry, Humphrey.'

'I'm sorry, too, my Lady. How is the Duchess by now?'

'Very weak, my Lord but, with God's grace, she will survive.'

'Then I won't disturb her rest,' he said. 'Please give her my condolences. I will visit her in due course.'

She felt more uneasy than usual about Humphrey. He had not once sent a message to enquire about Jacqueline during the whole time she had been in childbed and now it was as though he was enquiring after the health of someone he barely knew. 'Come, my Lady,' he said, 'why don't you join us for a little while? You must be tired. The music will soothe you. Look, we have some marchpane and we can call for more wine.'

'Thank you, no.' Catherine felt physically sick at the thought of marchpane and was barely able to trust herself to speak. 'I must … I must … get back.'

He bowed again, extravagantly, and Catherine turned on her heel. The sooner she was out of that room, the better. She was angry, angry, angry. Angry with Humphrey for his attitude and his superficial friends; angry with a God who allowed a much-wanted baby to die, strangled in her mother's womb; angry with herself for being so close to losing control.

By the time she reached her own rooms, the tears were coursing freely down her cheeks but she didn't much care who saw them. Guillemote put an arm around her shoulders to steady her and helped her towards a chair.

'The baby died, Guillemote. The baby died. Oh dear God, why do babies die when so much love awaits them if they live? Why, Guillemote? Why? And poor Jacqueline. So much pain!'

'There, my Lady, sit for a moment while you compose yourself and I will find you a clean gown. And why not let me wash your hair? You know how it always calms you.'

Catherine sat meekly in her shift, while Guillemote washed her hair in her favourite soap of Marseilles, rinsing it several times with infusions of rosemary leaves until the water ran clear. It dried quickly in the warmth of the July day and

Catherine began to relax under her maid's practised hands.

'How is the Duchess by now, Your Highness?'

'She was sleeping when I left her, Guillemote. She will need to sleep for several hours to regain some of her strength. Though it will take her a very great deal longer than that to get over losing her baby.'

'No doubt the Duke will visit her when she wakes. That will make her feel better.'

'I expect he will, though he seemed rather preoccupied with his friends when I saw him. Tell me, Guillemote, do you know who they are? His friends?'

'Oh, his usual clique I expect, Ma'am. You know, people like John Robessart, Sir John Kirkby, some of his Italian friends, too, I shouldn't wonder. They like their wine and their music.'

'There was a woman there, too, a woman with a high-pitched laugh ... dark hair ... a crimson gown ... I had never seen her before.'

Guillemote paused uncertainly and then said: 'That would be Eleanor Cobham, Ma'am.'

'Eleanor Cobham? I don't know the name. Who is she?'

'She's one of the Duchess of Gloucester's ladies, I believe.'

'Then what was she doing with the Duke?'

'I wouldn't like to say, Ma'am, but there has been gossip.'

'Not about her and the Duke?'

'I'm afraid so, Ma'am. There, now. I have finished dressing your hair. Take a look in your mirror, my Lady. Are you pleased with it? Yes? Well, now let me help you into your robe de chambre while I go to the wardrobe. Shall I bring out the new yellow gown for you to wear?'

Guillemote was babbling, trying to divert Catherine's attention and discourage her from asking any more questions about Eleanor Cobham. Gossip among the castle servants was rife. The Cobham woman was quite brazenly flaunting her friendship with the Duke. No one knew if he had bedded her yet but even if he hadn't, it would only be a matter time before he did. Or so the gossip went. Catherine was bound to hear it eventually.

Leaving her mistress sitting at her dressing table, trying to come to terms with what she had just heard and with everything else that had happened that afternoon, Guillemote went in search of the yellow gown. She knocked at the door of Owen Tudor's small office next to the big wardrobe room. He was sitting at his table, working on a new duty rota for the laundresses. He looked up and smiled as Guillemote came into the room.

'*Bonjour*, Guillemote. How are you? What can I do for you?'

'Her Majesty's new yellow gown, please, Master Tudor. It's stored in Cupboard Three, I believe?'

'It is. And you may take it with pleasure as soon as I have entered it into the Wardrobe Acquisitions ledger. It's brand new so I don't want to lose track of it. And what, pray, is that grubby garment you've got there?'

'It needs to be laundered. Her Highness was wearing it while she attended the Duchess of Gloucester at her lying-in. It's a bit the worse for wear.'

'Has the Duchess had her baby?'

'Aye, a dead one. And a girl at that.'

Owen rose from the table, concern in his face. 'That's dreadful news! I'm so sorry to hear it. How is Her Grace?'

'Exhausted, from what the Queen said.'

'And how has the Queen taken it?'

'Rather badly, Master Tudor. She's very upset. I think perhaps she'll never stop weeping.' Guillemote looked up at him, her brown eyes narrowing, wise as a monkey, an idea forming in her mind. As casually as she could, she said: 'I ... er ... I need to run another errand before I return to the Queen. I wonder whether you'd be kind enough to take the yellow gown to her and tell her I have been delayed? I shouldn't be long.'

Unaware of the maid's subterfuge, all Owen could think of was that he would see Catherine. He took the yellow gown and draped it over his arm. Guillemote watched him as he walked quickly up the corridor. She would take her time going back.

Owen stopped outside the Queen's private rooms and

knocked at the main door. There was no sound from within. Cautiously, he pushed open the door and put his head around it. There was no one there. He entered the antechamber, closing the door behind him, and looked around for somewhere to leave the gown where the Queen would be sure to see it. The place was as quiet as the grave.

'*C'est toi,* Guillemote? Is that you?' Coming from an adjacent room, the voice was muffled but Owen was in no doubt whose voice it was. Panic seized him and rooted his feet to the spot. He realised that he was quite, quite alone with the Queen.

Catherine was puzzled. She thought she'd heard a sound but, surely, Guillemote would have answered her call. She went to the door of her bedchamber and opened it to see Owen standing in the middle of the outer room, her yellow gown over his arm. Emotion overwhelmed her. Here, above all others, was the one person she most wanted to see.

'Master Tudor! Owen!'

'Your Highness, I … I … Guillemote asked me to bring your gown. But if you're alone … I could always come back …'

'No, please. Come in. I'm pleased to see you. I'm very, very pleased to see you. I need you. That is … I need … I need to talk to you … to …'

She held out her hand and he reached out to take it. The yellow gown fell to the floor.

Afterwards, they couldn't remember who had made the first move. All they knew, all they cared about was their tremendous need, each for the other. They clung together, half laughing, half crying, muttering endearments in French, in Welsh, snatching shallow breaths and little kisses, not quite knowing what was happening and yet certain that what was about to happen was inevitable.

Catherine's robe de chambre fell from her shoulders and she stood before Owen clad only in her shift. He held her at arm's length and looked at her for a long moment, his eyes drinking in every detail of her, the way her head was set on her long neck, the creamy pale skin of her shoulders, the breasts high and proud against the fabric of her shift. She could hardly bear it. 'Don't,' she whispered. 'Don't stare at me like that. Please, just … take me. I've waited too long. Come, my love, please.'

She pulled him towards her bedchamber. Stumbling, awkward, he tore at his clothes, his doublet, his undershirt. Lifting her arms, Catherine drew her shift up over her head and Owen caught his breath at the beauty of her body. He cursed the inconveniences of buttons and laces, of hose and shoes.

At last, he measured his naked length against hers, savouring the sensation of her skin against his, the smell of her hair, rosemary and lavender. He was rigid with desire for her and she, her eyes closed, was moving her head slowly from side to side, moaning softly from somewhere deep in her throat. Feeling his hand on the smooth skin of her thighs, pressing them apart, she moved willingly under him, her hands clasped behind his head, her body arching to receive him. Then they became one, moving together in a primeval rhythm which seemed to last for an eternity yet was only a brief moment in time. They had ceased to be queen and commoner, mistress and servant; they had become man and woman, Adam and Eve.

Owen and Catherine. It was all that mattered.

Guillemote found the yellow gown and Catherine's robe de chambre on the floor when she returned an hour or so later. She picked them up and folded them carefully. There was no sound from beyond the closed doors of the Queen's bedchamber.

Chapter Sixteen

Winter 1424 - Spring 1425

Every time she looked at Owen, Catherine was overwhelmed by the realisation that her desire for this beautiful man was equally matched by his for her. Torn between the enormity of what had happened to them and the need to guard their secret, they were at great pains to behave normally in public, to all outward appearances still mistress and servant. But on chilly autumn nights, as logs crackled in the small grate in Catherine's bedchamber and with the door firmly locked, Owen loved to lie on a goatskin near the hearth with his head in her lap, gazing into the flames and listening, fascinated, to stories of her childhood and her life in the convent. He felt he almost knew the gossiping Sisters Consolata and Madeleine and he felt genuinely grateful to Sister Supplice for having been so loving and protective towards Catherine, the little girl who'd been first neglected and then exploited by her own family.

How different from his own upbringing. He told her tales of his early childhood on the island of Anglesey, growing up as a member of what had once been the most powerful family in North Wales, Tuduriaid Penmynydd, the Tudors of Penmynydd. He explained to her why their loyalty to their kinsman Owain Glyndŵr had cost them their authority, their lands, and, for some, their very lives in the face of incessant English military aggression. Then he amused her with stories of the itinerant Welsh bards, the praise they would lavish on their wealthy patrons, the extraordinary beauty of their love poems, and the subtlety of their poetic insults to each other. He sang to her the songs of his homeland in a language foreign to her ear but delightful in his singing. He painted word pictures for her of his native island, the sunlit strand of the Menai Strait against the majesty of mountains in the distance, across the water.

The beauty of natural things had always been something Owen took for granted but now he was full of wonder, he looked at everything through new eyes. He greeted every sunrise with a glad heart and the joyful certainty that the coming day would bring him some proper purpose to be in the Queen's presence, even if only for a few moments. His life now revolved entirely around her. They both delighted in the little things they learned about each other and, at every opportunity, they made love joyously and generously. Everything was perfect, except that they dared not speak their love aloud.

Delighted that her royal mistress had found a measure of happiness at last, Guillemote did everything she could to ensure that Catherine and Owen were able to spend time together undisturbed and she guarded their precious secret as jealously as they did themselves. Guillemote had no way of knowing whether this *affaire de coeur* was really only a passing fancy on Catherine's part; she was, after all, her mother's daughter and Queen Isabeau had been well known for her amorous dalliances. But there was a new lightness in Catherine's step, a note of laughter and gladness in her voice, and Guillemote vowed to guard that for as long as it lasted. So this new love was at the very centre of all their lives, a beautiful, fragile thing, stoutly defended from the outside world.

Now it was Catherine's turn to keep a secret from her cousin. Jacqueline had remained very ill, confined to bed for many weeks, lying pallid and listless against the pillows, her eyes dull with sadness. Catherine almost despaired of ever seeing her once-playful cousin laugh again. Yet she did recover slowly and eventually she was able to walk a little in the garden, leaning heavily on Catherine's arm while they talked of the future. Soon, Jacqueline said, Humphrey would have persuaded Parliament to provide financial backing for his attempts to pull an army together. Soon, she claimed, Humphrey's troops would march on Holland to defeat those who had deceived her and soon, she added, Humphrey would have every right to call himself the Count of Holland, Zeeland,

and Hainault.

Catherine said nothing but prayed that Humphrey would fail to raise the money to enable him to carry out his ill-advised, insane plans. She was also desperately anxious that Jacqueline wouldn't overhear any gossip about her husband and Eleanor Cobham before the whole affair blew over, as it surely must. She wouldn't have Jacqueline hurt for all the world. She had suffered enough.

By October, Humphrey, as Warden of the Cinque Ports, had managed to assemble a fleet of some forty ships and Jacqueline had taken her leave of Catherine and travelled to Dover to join her husband as he prepared to sail for Holland with a scratch army. When news of Humphrey's intentions reached John of Bedford, he hurriedly made the crossing from France, hoping to persuade his brother to change his mind but, stubborn as well as reckless, Humphrey would have none of it.

So John of Bedford was forced to stay on in England through the turn of the year, in order to take the reins of government and to chair the Council during Humphrey's absence. He did both with great efficiency and in an unusually calm atmosphere.

Henry Beaufort fell into step beside his nephew as they were leaving a Council meeting towards the end of April. 'I thought this morning's meeting went very well,' he remarked with his hand on his hat to keep it on his head in a gusting wind. 'Things are so much easier when you are in charge.'

John smiled. 'It's kind of you to say so, my Lord Uncle,' he said, 'but Council members all have the same concern at heart and that is to govern the country efficiently in the name of my young nephew, the King. But yes, you're right, things do seem to be going well at the moment.' He sighed deeply before continuing. 'My only regret is that my dear wife remains in France. We were forced to spend Christmas apart and I haven't seen her for several months. I miss her very much. I hope it's not too long before Humphrey gets back from Holland and is able to take charge of things again.'

'We're better off without him,' muttered Bishop Beaufort. 'He's far too ready to pick a quarrel and he's very selfish. By the way, did you know he had taken a mistress?'

'Really?' said John, unconcerned. 'I wouldn't worry about that. It's probably no more than a dalliance. Does Jacqueline know?'

'I shouldn't think so. The wife is always the last to find out. I don't know how he keeps it a secret, though. I'm told she's one of Jacqueline's ladies – I use the term loosely. So she's gone to Holland with them, of course.'

'Does the Queen know about it?'

'I've no idea. But you know how women love to gossip.'

'I told you, didn't I,' said John, 'that I'm intending to spend a few days in Windsor next week? So I shall see Catherine and I look forward to that with great pleasure. At least I've got some good news to give her after this morning's meeting.'

'Yes, she'll be pleased to hear the Council's plans for Baynard's Castle. I think she's finding Windsor a bit restricting. There's still a battalion of women surrounding young Henry and they don't seem keen to let her near him.'

John was not pleased to hear that. He felt strongly that the only way for a little child to learn about life was at his mother's knee and Henry must be allowed to be a child before he was forced to be a king. He would talk to Catherine about it.

Bluebells nodded their pretty heads among the damp grass under the trees and the scent of wild garlic was everywhere as John and his small entourage rode towards Windsor. Pale sunshine filtered through the branches and a blackbird whistled like a Billingsgate barrow boy from a branch above their heads. John loved springtime in England, he loved the freshness of it, the smell and the sound of it, and it felt good to be riding through the English countryside on a gentle morning like this. True, there was a certain sadness in being parted from his beloved Anne but he intended to return to France as soon as he could. In the meantime, he always looked forward to seeing Catherine.

As he approached her private apartment, the door opened and he narrowly avoided colliding with a man who stepped adroitly to one side and bowed.

'I'm sorry, Your Grace,' he said politely. 'Please excuse

me.'

John nodded at him and smiled. Where had he seen him before? He was rather a pleasant-looking man: dark hair curling over his forehead, dark eyes, and a friendly demeanour. He must ask Catherine. He was probably one of her servants.

Seeing her, John promptly forgot to ask who the man was. She was looking well; she had lost that strained, haunted look. He was delighted by that.

'Your Highness. Catherine, my dear, I am so pleased to see you.' John bent to kiss her hand, savouring the familiar faint perfume of lavender. She really was a very beautiful woman, he thought. Gone were the rounded, girlish looks and in their place was a more mature beauty, exquisite skin, a fine profile, though she could never claim to be anything other than a Valois with that slightly elongated nose. But her eyes! They were lovelier than ever today. She looked … somehow … fulfilled.

'John! I'm glad you were able to come. You're looking well. Tell me, how is my cousin Anne? Have you heard from her?'

'My dear wife is well, thank you, though I have been parted from her for too long. She delights me. Everything you said about her was true. She is my treasured companion. She makes me laugh!'

Catherine smiled. 'Yes, that's very important. Come, let's sit and catch up with what's been happening to us both since we last met.' They talked, like the old friends they were, for some time before John remembered that he had some good news for her.

'Now, tell me, Catherine, how would you like a fine home of your own, where you could be your own mistress, rather than live at court?'

Catherine was instantly on her guard. 'Why would I want to do that? I wouldn't go anywhere unless I could take little Henry with me. John, remember the Book of Ruth, "whither thou goest, I will go." That's how I feel about my son. I won't leave Windsor while he is here.'

'It's not a matter of your leaving Windsor, Catherine. Not at all. Let me explain. There were several important items on this week's Council agenda and two of them concerned you. One was that Dame Alice Boteler has been appointed governess to the King.' Catherine made as though to interrupt. 'No, let me finish. It's a good appointment, really. She's a sensible woman and will see to it that the King is taught courtesy and good manners. These are imperative for a young man to learn, especially a king.'

'I can teach him those things.' Catherine's expression was mutinous.

'Catherine, you know as well as I do that your son is public property. Everyone wants a say in his upbringing. Don't break your heart over that. Trust Dame Alice. Believe me, she has wisdom and is infinitely preferable to several other women who might have been given the job.'

Catherine gave a sigh of resignation and John continued. 'The other piece of news should cheer you up, Catherine. The Earl of March has died, a victim of the plague, I'm afraid.'

'The plague? Surely not!'

'Please, dear Lady, don't be alarmed,' John said, then crossed himself fervently. 'The Earl was in Ireland so there is no risk of infection here in London.'

'That is small comfort. And did you say that this is supposed to cheer me up?'

'No, no, of course not. But, sadly, the Earl was a gambler and lost much of his personal fortune, so his property now reverts to the crown and the Council has decided that it will become a dower residence. As the Dowager Queen, you may live there by the grace and favour of your sovereign son if you wish, on condition that you keep the buildings and gardens in good repair. That is all that will be required of you. And it is a very elegant house,' he added.

'But where is it? How far from Windsor? From Westminster?'

'Very near to Westminster. It's on the riverbank, close by the Priory of the Black Friars. And if the court should happen to be at Windsor, and you wished to see the King, it's no great distance by river barge. It is very convenient. It's called Baynard's Castle.'

'Ah, yes, I have seen it from the river. But if I went to live there, I still think that I would miss my son unbearably. Not that I see a great deal of him as it is.'

John looked at her dejected face. He was very aware that, as a foreigner, she was still regarded by some with suspicion. There was not much he could do to change that attitude and not much comfort he could offer her. He sighed and took her hand in his.

'My dear Lady, he is the King. He is not as other children are and he never can be. Believe me, if it was what you wanted and I could arrange it, you and he could live together happily in the country, away from the pressures of court and of Parliament. You could churn your own butter ... keep a goat ... Henry could have a puppy ...'

'He'd prefer a kitten.'

'Oh, a kitten, then!' There were limits, even to John's patience. 'Come Catherine, believe me, Baynard's Castle is ideal for you. You'll be in London, at the centre of things. It will be entirely yours. Your home. People will come there only at your invitation. And it is so very convenient. My dear, you only need go next door to choose your gowns!'

Catherine turned sharply to face him. 'What do you mean by that?'

'Baynard's Castle is right by the Great Wardrobe. That's where all the royal family's most valuable possessions are stored. The ceremonial Robes of State are kept there, tapestries, furnishings, plate, some silverware and jewellery as well as furs and everyday clothes. It's heavily guarded, of course.'

'But my gowns aren't kept there, are they?'

'Some are, I imagine, certainly the ones you wear for formal occasions.'

'Then it could be quite a convenient place to live.' Catherine's mind was racing. Here was a chance for her and Owen to spend more time together without raising suspicion. He was, after all, her Clerk of the Wardrobe and would need to visit the great royal storeroom quite often. What could be more natural? And, though Henry would remain at Windsor in the care of Elizabeth Ryman, she could still see him easily enough.

The Ryman woman was making her increasingly nervous,

appearing in unexpected places, seeming to be watching her, spying on her. But she would have no business in Baynard's Castle and no excuse to visit it, other than by Catherine's express invitation, so there would be no possibility of her stumbling upon Catherine and Owen in a private moment. Yes, a move to Baynard's Castle suddenly seemed to be the solution to most of Catherine's problems.

'D'you know, John,' she said slowly, 'I think Baynard's Castle might suit me very well.'

John of Bedford sighed and shook his head. Women were such strange creatures. Stubborn as mules and quoting from the Bible one minute and then, as soon as you mentioned their gowns and fripperies, they became compliant and biddable. He would never understand them.

Catherine hadn't planned that Henry should have a kitten, at least, not until John of Bedford had assumed he might like a puppy. But when she suggested to him that he might like a pet cat, his little face lit up with pleasure so he was allowed to choose one from a litter which one of the stable cats had produced. One of the lads who slept in the hayloft had been feeding the mother cat and said the kittens must be about two months old by now, perhaps more. It had been perishing cold when they were born, anyway; he remembered that. So three of them were brought into the nursery in a hay-lined box and Henry stroked their soft heads while he decided which one he wanted as a pet.

'This one,' he said, gently lifting out a pretty brown tabby. 'Look, Maman, Virgin Mary did that mark.' Tenderly, he traced the M in the markings on the little creature's forehead with his finger and the kitten didn't seem to mind a bit. Catherine wondered where on earth he'd heard the story about the Virgin Mary.

Joan Astley glanced apologetically at the Queen. 'He likes tales of the saints and the Holy Family, Ma'am,' she said. 'He's always asking for them, so I told him the story about the Virgin Mary and how she blessed the cats in the manger at Bethlehem for keeping the Christ child warm.'

'Warm little Jesus,' said Henry solemnly, still holding the tabby kitten very gently in his arms. 'Little Jesus cold.'

'What will you call her?' asked Catherine.

'Doucette,' said Henry.

'That's a good name. She is very sweet.'

'Let's hope she's good mouser,' said Owen unsentimentally when Catherine told him about the kitten later that night. 'Cats are a lot more valuable when they're good mousers. Worth a groat. It's the law in Wales.'

'You have laws about cats?' Catherine asked in disbelief.

'Indeed we do. Our laws were made by an old king called *Hywel Dda*, Howell the Good.'

'A relative of yours?'

'Oh, yes. Long, long ago. Many generations. But his laws still hold good. He said that a new-born kitten is worth a penny until it opens its eyes, then tuppence until it kills its first mouse then, when it's a good, adult mouser, it's worth a groat.'

'How strange!'

'Not at all strange. Everything has its value. Hywel Dda made laws about women too, I'll have you know, Madame!' Owen added, playfully patting her bare rump. Catherine squealed in mock terror and ran around the room, jumping onto the bed to escape him. But he was quicker than she was and, collapsing with laughter, they rolled around on the big bed, playful as puppies, Owen easily gaining the advantage.

Suddenly he relaxed his grip and looked down at her with infinite tenderness. 'And in Wales, *Catrin*, we value our women very highly. We respect them as people, we don't treat them as chattels. You should thank your God, *cariad,* that you are loved by a Welshman!' He grinned at her and made as though to let her go but she wriggled and squirmed her way under him, pulling him down towards her, her mouth searching for his. Cariad he had called her; his own dear love. She was too preoccupied to tell him so, but she already thanked God that she was loved by this particular Welshman.

Spring is always a good time for making a fresh start and it was on a bright day of sunshine and showers that Catherine, with

215

some of her ladies and a small retinue of guards, embarked on a journey down river from Windsor. As the royal barge drew level with the great Priory of the Black Friars, she saw the walls of Baynard's Castle rising steeply, almost sheer out of the water. They put her in mind of the white cliffs which rose vertically out of the sea at Dover and she immediately had a strong feeling of new beginnings, of imminent happiness.

Stepping onto the landing stage and climbing the steps into the castle itself, she felt oddly welcome, a feeling she couldn't quite put her finger on, except that she had taken an instinctive liking to the great, solid, square bulk of the place. She felt she would be safe and secure within its walls. It was not a new building but the rooms which had been allocated for the private use of the Queen and her staff had been cleaned thoroughly and the walls hung with new tapestries. She could almost have sworn that Guillemote had been there before her, fussing and filling vases with spring flowers, just to make her feel at home, except that Guillemote had remained in Windsor with an unpleasantly heavy cold.

The Queen's ladies exclaimed in delight at the elegance of the furnishings and admired the graceful reception rooms in the twin hexagonal towers with their panoramic views of the Thames. To one side of the castle a charming garden was bordered by the river and behind it, a maze of little cobbled streets and alleyways clustered at the foot of the hill which led up to the parish church of St Andrew. Just to the north of the church was the huge outline of the building which housed the Great Wardrobe of the royal family. Between them, the Castle and the Wardrobe dominated the whole area and the little church of St Andrew-by-the-Wardrobe seemed to unite them. Catherine was captivated. Here she and Owen could be together almost as much as they liked. He would be as pleased as she was by the prospect of moving to Baynard's Castle and she could hardly wait to tell him all about it.

By the time the homeward-bound royal barge took the final bend in the river, the great round tower of Windsor Castle was outlined against the glowing red of the setting sun dipping towards the horizon in the west. Catherine, her eyes closed, was allowing herself to look forward to the future, day-dreaming contentedly until Joanna Troutbeck tapped her arm to draw her attention to a flurry of activity on the river bank.

'My Lady, look! We're almost home but there's something going on.'

Catherine sat up with an immediate feeling of foreboding. She shaded her eyes and looked in the direction of Troutbeck's pointing finger. There were foot soldiers, archers, and buglers milling about as though they were waiting for something to happen.

'Who are they?' she asked. 'What livery are they wearing?'

'I'm sure I don't know, Ma'am,' Troutbeck replied. 'It's getting dark and my eyesight is not what it was. I'll ask one of the boatmen.'

'I think it's the livery of the Duke of Gloucester, Your Highness,' said the boatman, resting on his oar. 'Looks like he's back from Holland.'

'But he can't be! He can't have come back so soon! Can he? Oh, I do hope it's good news!'

Catherine was the first to alight from the barge as soon as it had been moored. She hurried into the castle and immediately went in search of her cousin. Guillemote, her poor nose red and streaming, intercepted her.

'My Lady, it's the Duke of Gloucester,' she said, sniffing piteously. 'He has returned from Holland.'

'Yes, yes, Guillemote, so I see. So, where is the Countess Jacqueline? Where is my cousin?'

'She is not with him, Ma'am.'

'Not with him? Nonsense! She is his wife: of course she's with him.'

Guillemote shook her head and sneezed violently. 'She is not, my Lady. Really. He has been here for three or four hours now and she is not with him. He and his retinue arrived unexpectedly and he's arranging for the last of his soldiers to be paid. That's what they are waiting for. But the Countess Jacqueline is not with him.' Guillemote sneezed again. 'Really, my Lady. She is not here.'

Catherine was amazed. Why on earth would Humphrey have

left Jacqueline behind? Was she still in Holland? Surely not.

'Guillemote, take my cloak, please. And take an infusion of lemon balm for that sneezing. I must go and find His Grace the Duke and ask him when my cousin Jacqueline will be arriving.' Catherine undid the clasps on her cloak and let it slide from her shoulders. Guillemote caught it and folded it over her arm as she watched Catherine hurrying away, in search of her brother-in-law. She sneezed again and shook her head. Her mistress would find out soon enough that Humphrey of Gloucester had returned home with Eleanor Cobham in tow.

Owen looked in at The Swan that same cool spring evening, hoping to meet Gilbert there. He was on his way back to Windsor from a visit to the royal cordwainer, with whom he had been haggling over the price of leathers for Her Majesty's summer shoes. But, sitting in his familiar place on a bench by the table in front of the peat fire, there, large as life, was his cousin Maredydd. He looked tired and travel-stained.

'God, this is good,' he said, quaffing a long draught of ale. He set the tankard down on the table and gave Owen a huge smile. 'That Dutch beer is as weak as priest's piss. *Sut wyt ti 'rhen gyfaill*?' He wiped his mouth on the back of his hand, as he always did. It was as though he had never been away. 'How are you?'

Owen was grinning with delight at seeing him. 'What the devil are you doing here? Shouldn't you be fighting with the Duke of Gloucester in Holland?'

'Oh, you haven't heard the half of it! You wait 'til I tell you what a complete waste of time it all was. But while you're on your feet, get us another mug of ale, I've finished this one.' Maredydd drained his tankard noisily and wondered where on earth he'd begin to tell Owen the story, the saga of impetuosity and mismanagement which had governed Duke Humphrey's fruitless campaign to lay claim to his wife's lands in Holland.

He watched Owen take the empty tankard to the alewife, chatting and laughing with her while she replenished it. He had done well, Maredydd thought, to have risen so high in the service of the Queen in such a short time: and he was much

218

better off than he would be as a gentleman-at-arms. That could be heartbreaking.

Maredydd mulled over the events of the last few months. He had set out with high hopes, feeling like a mercenary but proud at the same time that his skills as a professional soldier had been recognised. The pay had been good to start with and the Duke had promised yet more money in the event of a triumph in Holland. Triumph? What a joke! Gloucester had made a real pig's ear of the whole campaign. There was no preparation, no leadership, and absolutely no discipline at all. Naturally, rumours were rife among the soldiers who wanted to know why they were being kept hanging around idly instead of fighting. They heard the rumour that the Duchess Jacqueline's own people had turned against her, questioning both the wisdom and the legality of her marriage to an Englishman, particularly when that Englishman had brought an army with him to strengthen his claim to her lands. As the troops waited for orders that never came, they heard a buzz of gossip from the messengers that the correspondence they were carrying between Gloucester and Philip of Burgundy was bitter and vindictive. So the soldiers started laying bets on whether Burgundy would come to Gloucester's assistance and those who had wagered against the likelihood won hands down. Then, to cap it all, came the news from Rome that Pope Martin V had issued a declaration that the Duchess Jacqueline's marriage to the Duke of Brabant was still binding, which meant that her subsequent marriage to the Duke of Gloucester was illegal. All in all, it had been a fine kettle of fish and doomed to failure from the start.

'But what I found most difficult to understand,' Maredydd added, having told Owen the whole story, 'was that Gloucester was always thought of as a good soldier. They say he excelled at Agincourt, before he got an axe in his thigh. But in Holland, he was like a dithering virgin. He had absolutely no control over his troops. We senior ranks were entirely without leadership, waiting for orders that never came.'

'So where was he?'

'Enjoying a dalliance with a certain Madame de Warigny, from what I understand, the wife of an equerry.'

'I thought he was enjoying a dalliance with Eleanor Cobham?'

'He was: still is. Perhaps she had to be with the Duchess when they were over in Holland. I don't know. But she was certainly hanging around him all the time on the journey home. A real slut, if you ask me. Persistent, too.'

'So where's the Duchess now?'

Maredydd shrugged. 'She's still in Holland. Under house arrest in Ghent, apparently, and not allowed to leave. That's the story, anyway. But I don't think it mattered much to Gloucester, to be honest with you.'

'Heartless bastard!'

'Dangerous bastard,' said Maredydd. 'I wouldn't trust him an inch. He might have been a great soldier once upon a time but he certainly isn't now. He's weak in some ways but he's also an arrogant, ambitious arse-licker. That's a lethal combination.'

Humphrey never mentioned Jacqueline's name in Catherine's presence and she kept out of his way as much as she could but he had no sooner set foot over the threshold of Windsor Castle than he was back to his old, imperious ways again, dictating how things were to be done, ignoring her wishes, and undermining what little authority she had. She wondered whether he would have been quite so domineering if John of Bedford had not returned to France.

The King's large staff of protective women, under the command of Elizabeth Ryman, never left Henry's side and Catherine was always painfully aware that every time she tried to pick him up or hold his hand to guide his footsteps, one of them would approach her and offer to take him, as though generously sparing her the effort of looking after her own little boy. Her frustration knew no bounds and she often had to guard her tongue against an entirely unladylike refusal of their kind suggestions. Day by day, she saw less and less of her son and she found herself longing for the day when she, and all the members of her household, including her Clerk of the Wardrobe, could move to Baynard's Castle.

In the meantime, the King was required to attend the State Opening of Parliament and this was the one place where no one could question either Catherine's authority or her relationship to her son. She was the Queen, the King's mother, and she always accompanied him on State occasions.

He no longer needed to sit on her lap because by now he had been taught to sit up straight in his own chair. She watched the Duke of Exeter lift her little boy onto the huge Throne of State and had to admit that Dame Alice Boteler had achieved miracles with her young charge. Henry sat without fidgeting through an interminably long speech given by his great-uncle Bishop Beaufort.

He looked a little more interested when his uncle, Humphrey of Gloucester, addressed the Members, though he couldn't possibly have understood the veiled remarks which Humphrey made about Henry Beaufort, criticising legislation which the Bishop had sanctioned while he, Humphrey, had been away in Holland and implying that His Grace's allegiance to the throne was not what it might be, hinting at disloyalty and treachery. There were rumblings of dissent from the floor of the House but Humphrey seemed remarkably unconcerned. As the ceremony drew to a close, he smiled as he lifted his royal nephew off the Throne of State and set him on his feet. He then led him out into the sunshine where a crowd of people pushed and shoved each other to get a glimpse of their young sovereign.

Not wanting to get too near Humphrey because he didn't trust himself not to punch his nephew's arrogant face, Henry Beaufort let the procession move ahead of him. He was seething with anger. A group of the Bishop's closest friends hung back with him, cautioning him. Gloucester was not to be trusted, they said, even more so since the debacle in Holland. They had heard rumours that he meant Beaufort actual physical harm. He was stirring up trouble, they warned, and it could end in bloodshed.

Outside, the sun glinted on the little coronet of gold on the King's head as Humphrey of Gloucester bent down and lifted his nephew up as far as he could, moving him to right and left to acknowledge the approbation of the crowd which had gathered to catch a glimpse of him. Then he set the child astride

221

a piebald horse, an animal of seemingly uncertain temperament, which rolled its eyes alarmingly. Grooms on either side of its head kept it under control.

Catherine saw what was happening and she was terrified. She pushed through the group of people surrounding the King and tugged at Humphrey's sleeve. 'My Lord, that animal is far too nervous to have a young child on its back.'

'Don't worry, my Lady, he will be perfectly safe.' Humphrey busied himself with checking the girth of the saddle.

'But he hasn't learned to ride! This is not his hobby horse in the nursery, you know.' A note of hysteria had crept into Catherine's voice and she tugged again at Humphrey's sleeve. 'He has never been astride a real horse before!'

Humphrey turned and patted her shoulder condescendingly. 'Oh, but he has, my Lady. You must not concern yourself about such things. Since the King has no father to guide him, I have personally seen to it that he learns horsemanship from an early age. And, aye, this horse is a fair courser, but he'll have to get used to the feel of a decent mount under him. He is the King. It will be expected of him.'

He gave her a wintry smile then turned and waved again to acknowledge the shouts of the crowd. Catherine could do no more than clench and unclench her fists in anger and frustration. Her son had been taken out of her hands yet again and she had been made to feel foolish and fussy. Her natural maternal concern for the child's safety had been ignored by those who claimed to know better.

'But, my Lord ...' her protestations were drowned out by the shouting of the excited crowd.

'God Save the King! God bless our young King! God bless Harry and St George!'

Humphrey slapped the horse's rump and it started forward nervously, restrained by the grooms. Henry's legs, much too short to reach the stirrups, were splayed out on either side of the saddle and he clung on to it for dear life with a terrified expression on his face. The crowd elbowed each other out of the way, craning their necks to catch a glimpse of the King. 'Look! Look!' they called to each other. 'He's just like his father! A born horseman!' Humphrey walked ahead of his nephew, waving at the crowd, goading them on to even more excitement while the piebald horse tossed its mane, champing at the bit.

The Duke of Exeter was well aware of the danger facing the King, though he didn't challenge Gloucester's actions: he merely positioned himself alongside the horse. Catherine thanked God and crossed herself when she saw that Exeter's arm was raised protectively behind Henry's back to support him if he should fall. In this way, the ragged procession made its erratic way through Cheapside in the direction of Kennington, where the royal party was to pay a short official visit.

Catherine demanded that a horse be found for her and kept up with the procession every step of the way. If her son was going to fall off that skittish animal, she was going to be there to pick him up and comfort him. Mercifully, he didn't and the royal party arrived safely at the Palace of Kennington. The Keeper, Sir John Waterton, awaited them, ready to greet them formally but Henry was still astride the horse, clinging to the saddle, and Catherine would make small talk with no one until he was safely on the ground, however rude they considered her behaviour. It was only when she had seen him slithering off the skittish mount and into the waiting arms of the Duke of Exeter that she could relax. She ran to Henry and hugged him.

'Did you see me ride, Maman?' he demanded, his trepidation having quickly evaporated in the excitement of the moment. 'My uncle of Gloucester says I will be a great horseman one day. But the horse wasn't going very fast.'

'It was going fast enough, my little soldier!' she said. 'You were very, very brave.'

'Your Royal Highnesses,' said Sir John Waterton, bowing extravagantly to Catherine and Henry. 'You are most warmly welcome here at Kennington. It is a great honour you do us in staying for a few days.'

Despite an aching back, Catherine straightened up and gracefully extended her hand. 'Thank you, Sir John. I look forward to being here with my son the King who, as you see, is developing great skills as a horseman. He has surprised us all.

Now, if he and his governess and his nurse could be shown to his rooms, please, he will need to rest before supper. He has had a tiring day.'

She, too, was exhausted and once Guillemote had helped her out of her outdoor clothes and into a comfortable robe, she sat for a moment in her room and took stock of events. She worried desperately that little Henry was being moulded into a soldier king while he was far too young to know what was happening. He was a quiet, sensitive child and could well grow up to inherit his father's fondness for books, rather than his skills on the battlefield. She also knew that she herself had been relegated to the shadowy fringes of her little boy's life. There was no longer a role for her in the upbringing and education of her firstborn.

Almost unawares, she had started thinking of Henry as her firstborn because she was also sure by now that he would have a brother or a sister within the next six months. When she was at this stage in her first pregnancy, it had been a cause for great celebration, she was carrying the King's child, the much-wanted, long-awaited heir to the thrones of England and France. She had fulfilled the wishes of her royal husband and everyone rejoiced. She was the means by which the great Lancastrian line of kings would continue.

But things were very different this time and one thing was clear: she had no idea how she was going to keep it a secret but nobody at court must ever know about this baby. She was still the Queen, the Dowager Queen, the mother of the King, and yet, like any common kitchen wench, she had been got with child by a servant.

Chapter Seventeen

Summer 1425

Though Catherine had always felt relaxed and comfortable at Windsor, by now she was glad to be away from there because by every action, every instruction he issued, Humphrey made it abundantly clear that she was no longer a person of any importance in her son's life. He had established himself as the authority to whom everyone should defer; his decisions were final. The King's mother was of no consequence and John of Bedford was still in France so Humphrey was the King's sole guardian, the Duke Protector. There would be no argument.

Wary of almost everyone around her these days, Catherine couldn't rid herself of the suspicion that Elizabeth Ryman was spying on her and reporting back to the Duke, so she was pleased to think that she would see a great deal less of her in future.

It also pleased her that she need have nothing more to do with Eleanor Cobham, the woman who had usurped Jacqueline's place at Humphrey's side. Catherine had taken a deep dislike to her and found it difficult to decide whether that was simply because of what had happened to Jacqueline or because there was something in Eleanor's dark, haughty face that defied anyone to question her position in the Duke's life. He was rarely seen these days without Eleanor somewhere near him, hanging on his every word, an expression of adulation in her calculating eyes. She was, beyond question, a beautiful woman, but it was the kind of chiselled beauty which had a hard edge to it. More than once, she had tried to claim friendship with Catherine, calling her 'my dear', as though they were on intimate terms. It took all Catherine's self-control not to claw the woman's face.

So she was pleased to be in charge of her own small household and she enjoyed the responsibility of making decisions in the day-to-day running of Baynard's Castle. Guillemote was with her, of course, as were Les Trois Jo-jo and her domestic staff. She'd had to leave Anton behind in the King's service, though he did promise to keep her supplied with her favourite cakes and biscuits. She remembered how his culinary genius had been thwarted during the visit to York, four years ago, when news came of the Duke of Clarence's death. She had wanted to celebrate her pregnancy then, something she certainly couldn't do now. The circumstances were very different. This time, she dared not arouse suspicion.

Owen's joy that Catherine was to bear his child was overwhelming but knowing what her pregnancy could mean to them both if it became public knowledge engulfed him in horror. Woe betide them if Gloucester should ever find out. He'd find a reason to pack Catherine off to a nunnery at the very least and Owen himself would probably lose his head.

They locked themselves into Catherine's bedchamber, telling Guillemote that they must not be disturbed under any circumstances. Guillemote, having heard Catherine vomiting in the garderobe twice since Sunday, had a shrewd idea why.

'We can't stay in London, Catrin,' said Owen. 'We must get as far away from court as we possibly can.'

'But I like Baynard's Castle, I feel safe here now that we've settled in. And it's only a short river journey to Windsor if I should wish to see Henry …'

'Cariad, look at me,' Owen took both her hands and pressed them together, covering them with his own. Then he kissed the tips of her fingers, his face very close to hers. Raising his eyebrows, he gave her a quizzical smile. 'Catrin, your pregnancy is the logical conclusion of what you and I have been doing to pleasure each other, isn't it?' She dropped her gaze and nodded, smiling despite her anxiety. 'And the logical conclusion of your pregnancy is that you will give birth to a child. Yes?'

'Yes.'

'And you can't do that here in London, can you?'

'No.'

'Very well. You cannot take the smallest risk that someone will guess that you're pregnant. Imagine what Humphrey of Gloucester would do if he found out! So I think it's high time you visited some of your dower properties in Wales, don't you?'

'Wales? But it is such a long way away from here!'

'Exactly. So, let's make some plans.'

It was a pleasant day, sunny with a light breeze off the Thames, so, with very few pressing duties to attend to, Henry Beaufort took a small mounted guard of half a dozen men with him as he set out to conduct some private business north of the river. During the morning he called on his vintner and they spent a thoroughly enjoyable hour together while the Bishop tasted a number of newly imported wines. Having made his choices, Henry placed his order and concluded his business. Then he took his leave and, climbing the mounting block outside the vintner's premises, thought it odd that the man closed the door behind him rather more quickly than was polite. It was only then that he became aware of a gaggle of wharf men gathering outside the tavern at the sign of The Crane and they were inching threateningly towards him. He was on his horse in an instant and his guards quickly took up their positions around him.

'Oi, Bishop! Over 'ere!' Despite himself, Henry looked towards the group of wharf men. There appeared to be about twenty of them, armed with long staves of wood which they began to bang rhythmically on the ground as they moved to form a semicircle, getting closer. The tall man who was shouting with his hands cupped around his mouth was clearly the ring-leader.

The captain of the guard manoeuvred his horse into a more defensive position near the Bishop's black stallion. 'Leave them to us, my Lord Bishop,' he said, 'we'll soon see them off.'

Henry held up his hand to silence the man, though his heart was thudding with fear. 'No, let's hear what they have to say. I

227

need to know what's going on.'

'You don't scare us, Bishop!' shouted the ringleader. 'You nor your guards neither. And you'll never get us to work with them foreign bastards. They've got to go. English workers need the jobs.'

'Out, out, out! Foreign workers out!' chorused the group, beating the rhythm of their chant on the ground with their staves. 'Out, out, out! Foreign workers out!'

'Wait!' shouted Henry. 'Wait! Listen to me! I understand your concerns but I assure you that restrictions have been placed on the movements of foreign merchants and those in their employment. The Council has passed the legislation.'

'Yeah, but it hasn't stopped them, has it? It's all your fault, you two-faced cheat. You say one thing to them and another thing to us. We should have listened to the Duke. He was right.'

'Out, out, out! Foreign workers out!' The mindless chant continued among those at the back of the group who couldn't quite hear what was going on at the front.

'Are you a man of God, Bishop?' asked the ringleader, mocking.

'Of course!'

'So if we threw you in the dock you'd float, wouldn't you? Your angel wings would 'elp you to swim. Come on, lads! Let's shove 'im in the dock. 'E won't drown. God is on 'is side!'

Henry was terrified now as one of the wharfmen ducked suddenly forward and grabbed his horse's bridle. The agitated animal started neighing with fear, jerking its head away from the assailant, spittle gathering in the corners of its mouth. The guards flailed from left to right with their short swords and when the captain drew blood the crowd fell back a few paces before one of the thugs turned his long wooden stave and prodded Henry's horse in the rump with the sharpened end. The black stallion reared up, pawing the air in terror and nearly unseating Henry who clung on to its mane, trying to force its head down. The crowd scattered and the horse, seeing a gap between them, darted forward.

Henry was still clinging on as the frightened animal, given its head, cantered past the Vintners' Hall, through the Vintry,

228

and on to Three Cranes Lane, sending startled street traders running for cover and scattering cabbages and parsnips in its wake. Riding furiously at the gallop, one of Henry's guards managed to overtake him and grabbed the loose bridle, heading off the horse until it was forced to stop, rolling its eyes and side-stepping fretfully. Henry slid out of the saddle, trying to hide the uncontrollable trembling in his legs.

'My Lord Bishop,' said the Captain, riding up alongside, 'are you hurt?'

Henry, temporarily winded, shook his head.

'The church of St Michael Queenhithe is no great distance, my Lord. Perhaps you could rest there for a while. You must be feeling badly shaken.'

'No … thank you … no,' Henry panted, bent double as he tried to catch his breath. He had heard that the new incumbent at St Michael's was a skinny, sanctimonious prig who kept an empty cellar and Henry was badly in need of a drink. No, he would bypass St Michael's.

'St Andrew-by-the-Wardrobe is almost as near,' he said to the captain as he straightened up, his breathing rather less painful now. 'I know the Rector there. He's a good man. He'll give me a glass of decently strong mead, at least.'

The Reverend Marmaduke de Kyrkeby was already entertaining a guest when Bishop Beaufort was shown into the room. 'Ah,' said Beaufort as they rose to greet him, 'de Kyrkeby and Gray. I couldn't have asked for more! I can't tell you how pleased I am to see you. Both of you. Let me sit down. I need a drink. I've just had the most distressing experience.' He sat, heavily, and the other two clerics started fussing around, finding a goblet and filling it.

'There, my Lord Bishop,' said Marmaduke de Kyrkeby, handing him a generous measure, 'that will steady your nerves and calm you down. Now, tell William and me exactly what happened.'

The Rector of St Andrew-by-the-Wardrobe was an inch or two shorter than Bishop Beaufort. His greying hair was thinning on top of his head but still grew in a profusion of curls where his plump neck showed above his collar. William Gray, the newly nominated Bishop of London, might have been his twin brother, with the same receding hairline and was comfortably full in his skin. The three men had always been relaxed and easy together, contemporaries who had struck up a friendship on meeting for the first time in Oxford as undergraduates and had remained friends ever since their student days. Beaufort's royal blood had ensured his rapid rise through minor orders to an early prebendary at Lincoln, quickly followed by the deanery of Wells. William Gray, too, had pursued a successful career in the Church, culminating in his recent nomination as Bishop of London. On the other hand, de Kyrkeby, never an ambitious man, had remained in relatively minor orders throughout his career, settling happily at St Andrew's, where he had served as Rector for many years. It was a fairly wealthy parish and provided sufficient income for his modest needs. His only temptation was a glass of good wine and he gave in to that fairly frequently on the grounds that, since it was his only vice, it was hardly likely to cause The Almighty much offence.

'A most excellent vintage, my old friend,' Beaufort said, reaching out to accept a second glass. 'Tell me, Marmaduke, what do you know of your charming new neighbour at Baynard's Castle?'

The Rector's eyes twinkled. 'Her Grace, the lovely Queen Catherine? William and I were just talking about her. I know very little, I fear. I should have called upon her before now to pay my respects and bid her welcome to this lovely part of London. How very remiss of me!'

'I have never had the pleasure of meeting her,' said Bishop William Gray, 'but I'm told she is delightful and very easy on the eye.'

'She is,' agreed Henry Beaufort. 'I'm pleased to say that I have come to know her quite well. Indeed, I'm delighted to say that though I am merely her uncle by marriage, she has the grace to call me by that name. And she is, I assure you, as charming as everyone says she is. Would you like to meet her?'

'Very much!'

'Let's go now, then,' said Beaufort, impetuously. 'Baynard's Castle is such a very short walk from here. Leave your wine, both of you. It's a decent vintage, so it won't hurt it to mature for another hour or so.'

Beaufort had recovered now, after his frightening experience in the Vintry, though there was still a worm of worry at the back of his mind. That thug had said something about listening to 'the Duke'. He can only have meant Humphrey of Gloucester. The debonair, handsome Humphrey was popular with Londoners and Beaufort had been warned that he was stirring up trouble.

Guillemote was busy folding some of Catherine's gowns and putting them carefully into coffers. She was frowning, deeply troubled by recent developments. Catherine and Owen had taken her into their confidence and told her of the coming baby. They would go to Wales, they said, where Owen had friends. But Guillemote wasn't at all sure where that was, nor was she sure what clothes the Queen would need when she got there.

Owen had already made lists of what needed to be packed in the way of jewellery and tableware. Now it was Guillemote's turn to pack her mistress's gowns, undergarments, and shoes, just as she would have done for any journey to any one of the crown's residences outside London. Except that there wasn't a lot of point in packing too many of Catherine's gowns, well, not the ones that couldn't be let out as her waistline spread. Perhaps the seamstress, Molly Betts, would have to be let into the secret.

Catherine was with Owen in her private solar, his arm across the back of her chair, her head on his shoulder as they discussed their problem for the hundredth time. Owen was deeply worried about arranging the journey to Wales, though he hadn't said so. Perhaps Ludlow would be a better place. But, wherever they went, they'd have to leave soon. Catherine, twitchy as a cat, nearly leapt out of her seat when there was a quiet knock at the door.

'Just a moment,' she called, patting her hair into place.

'Your Highness, you have visitors,' said the castellan as Catherine opened the door a crack, screening Owen from possible prying eyes. 'His Grace the Bishop of Winchester is here with two of his colleagues and has asked if they can see you. That is if it's convenient.'

'Bishop Beaufort! Yes, yes, of course. Tell His Grace that I will join them shortly.'

'Very well, Ma'am.'

Waiting in the Great Hall with the Reverend Marmaduke de Kyrkeby and Bishop William Gray, Henry Beaufort had noticed the coffers and boxes stacked against the wall.

'Is someone on the move?' he asked when the castellan returned. 'Can't be the Queen moving out, she's only just moved in.'

'I understand that Her Highness intends visiting some of her dower properties, my Lord Bishop,' said the castellan, as he showed them into a large, comfortable room overlooking the river. 'Those coffers will be loaded in preparation for her journey when we have more details of her itinerary and a date for her departure.'

Henry Beaufort frowned. There was too much going on these days that he didn't know about. He certainly hadn't heard about Catherine's plans to visit her dower properties, though he did remember Walter Hungerford telling him some time ago at a meeting of the Council that she had expressed a desire to do so. He wondered where she was intending to go. Wallingford, perhaps? Hertford again? Leicester?

'Wales,' she answered firmly when he asked her a little later.

'Wales?'

Marmaduke de Kyrkeby put his hand over his mouth to hide a smile when he saw his old friend Henry Beaufort's face. He looked astounded.

'Yes, Wales, my Lord Uncle. I have two dower properties there, one on the Isle of Anglesey and one in somewhere called Flintshire.'

'Yes, of course. I was aware of that. But nobody has ever actually visited them. They're in North Wales, after all.'

'Then there's all the more reason to go there,' said Catherine. She looked at her late husband's uncle, then across at his two friends sitting side by side, the Rector of St Andrew-by-the-Wardrobe and the Bishop of London. She had been pleased to meet them both and delighted that Henry Beaufort had made the spontaneous gesture of bringing them to see her. He had always been kind. Catching her eye, he gave her a quizzical glance.

'Why have you decided to do this now, my dear?' he asked gently.

'It's … well … it's as good a time as any, my Lord Uncle. You know, travelling is always more pleasant in the summer months. I shall return before the winter sets in, certainly in time for Christmas.'

'But you don't have to go there at all. You could visit your other dower lands nearer home. You wouldn't be so far away from your son.' He was testing the water, probing her decision to journey such a distance with no obvious necessity to do so. There was something here that was not quite right. There had to be an explanation for this apparently sudden decision, this reckless scheme.

'Now tell me, my dear, the real reason why you're doing this.'

Catherine broke down. She covered her face with her hands and sobbed. She sobbed for the unknown fate which awaited her and her unborn child. She sobbed that in her nightmares there were men shouting and horses going too fast as they carted Owen from Newgate to Tyburn, where he would pay the ultimate price of his love for her. The tears had been stopped up for too long, now they flowed like a stream.

At first, none of the clerical gentlemen knew what to do. They looked at one another helplessly and questioningly over Catherine's bowed head while her shoulders shook. Tentatively, Bishop Beaufort reached forward to put a comforting hand on her arm but she pulled back as though he'd burned her with a hot poker.

'Catherine, what is it? Tell me, please tell me. I'm sure there must be something I can do to help.'

'No, no, there isn't,' Catherine gasped between shuddering breaths. 'Really, there isn't.'

There was a tentative knock at the door and, when it opened, Guillemote's head came around it. 'Excuse me, my Lord

Bishop,' she said. 'Forgive me, but I thought I heard crying. I wondered ...'

She didn't finish the sentence. Henry Beaufort crossed the room in three strides and grabbed her arm, dragging her back towards Catherine. 'Why is your royal mistress so upset?' he demanded, shaking her in his anxiety. 'Do you know anything about this?' Guillemote's glance darted from one to the other like a frightened animal. She didn't know what to say.

Catherine was knuckling the tears from her eyes. 'It's all right, Guillemote, don't worry. Look, I need to speak to my royal uncle alone. Would you be kind enough to show the Rector and the Bishop into the library and find some refreshment for them, please. They might like a goblet of the Saint-Pourçain ...

'That would be most acceptable, if it's not too much trouble,' said the Rector, beaming.

Catherine smiled shakily. 'It's no trouble at all. And I believe there are still some honey cakes left.' Marmaduke de Kyrkeby and William Gray followed Guillemote out of the room and Henry Beaufort turned to Catherine, all concern. 'Now, my dear, please tell me what is troubling you.'

Catherine took a deep breath. If she told him about the baby, the secret would be out. There could be no going back. Could she trust him? Would he keep a secret? She had no idea but her instinct was to confide in him.

'I am with child, my Lord Uncle,' she said quietly. There was a long pause while he took in what she had said. Through the open window, she could hear the waters of the Thames slapping gently against the side of a boat and a moorhen's rattling call in the reeds at the river's edge echoed in the quiet room. Still Henry Beaufort didn't speak. When he did, his voice was low and quiet.

'You are with child?' She nodded dumbly. 'But your husband the King ... is ... dead. So who ...?' He didn't finish the sentence.

'Does it matter?' She turned to look at him, pleading.

'Yes, it does matter. Very much, I'm afraid. Is he at court?'

'In a manner of speaking, yes.'

'What do you mean by that? He's not a commoner, is he?'

'No, no. Not at all. He is high born. He is a noble man of ancient lineage. The blood of princes runs in his veins.'

Henry Beaufort went cold. 'Not Humphrey of Gloucester, surely!' He couldn't endure the thought that his bombastic, arrogant nephew had lain with the widow of his own dead brother; sullied her, impregnated her. 'Not Humphrey!'

'No, not Humphrey, Uncle. Never Humphrey. Never.'

'Thank God! Who, then? Not Edmund? Not my nephew Beaufort?'

'No, no, not Edmund. He's very young. I couldn't think of him like that.'

'Then tell me, Catherine, in God's name, tell me. Who else has the blood of princes in his veins? Who has done you this wrong?'

She hesitated again. Getting up, she walked over to the window and looked out onto the calm waters of the Thames, thinking, trying to come to a decision. She had told him so much already that she needed to tell him everything but she must make him understand. She turned to face him.

'It wasn't wrong, my Lord Uncle. I went to him readily with my heart full of love. And he to me. We are deeply in love and we have been, these many months. We are both very happy and we cherish the wonderful secret of our child.'

'Catherine, I beg of you. Please tell me, who is the father of this child?'

She took a deep breath. 'Owen Tudor, my Lord Uncle.' Beaufort looked at her, shaking his head, not recognising the name. 'Who?' he asked again.

'Master Owen Tudor. He is my Clerk of the Wardrobe and serves me well.'

'So it appears!' Bishop Beaufort slumped into a chair and put his head in his hands. He remembered the name now, and recalled that Walter Hungerford had mentioned it admiringly, though he couldn't quite remember why. After a long moment, he looked up at her. 'Catherine,' he said, 'Owen Tudor is a servant.'

'As it happens, yes, but …'

'Queens do not lie with their servants.'

'Perhaps not. But he's not a common servant. His grandmother was the daughter of a Welsh prince and his is an old and honourable family, the noblest in Gwynedd. That's in Wales,' she added lamely.

He rose and took a few steps towards her, looking into her face. 'And that impresses *you*, Your Royal Highness? A princess of the royal blood of France? You, the daughter of a king? The widow of a king? The mother of a king? That impresses *you*?'

'Everything about him impresses me, my Lord Uncle. He has made me very happy. He is my best friend at court, my only friend. You see, I am denied access to my son. I'm allowed no part in his upbringing and yet I cannot bring myself to leave him and return to France. The English are very cold towards me. I am made to feel that I am not wanted here. The only time I am ever really happy is when I'm with Owen. He makes me laugh, he helps me forget my worries. He looks after me, cares for me. I would be very lonely without him.' She looked up at Henry Beaufort, her eyes anxious and tearful. 'But now that I am to have his child, Uncle, I'm very frightened of what will happen.'

Beaufort put his arms around his nephew's widow then, his heart full of compassion, letting her cry quietly against his shoulder. Suddenly feeling very old, he remembered standing like this, over a quarter of a century ago, with his arms around another tearful young woman who had just told him about her pregnancy. Perhaps he should have married Alice, despite her quarrelsome family, but he'd chosen the church instead. He knew that Alice would never have loved him in the way that his own mother had loved his father.

He smiled at the sudden memory of his mother: she had been a Katherine, too, the Lady Katherine Swynford, mistress of the great John of Gaunt, Duke of Lancaster. With no hope of ever being his wife, she had given the Duke a lifetime of devotion. Then, as a widower in old age, John of Gaunt had scandalised everyone by marrying his Katherine, and their four bastard children were declared legitimate and given the surname

236

Beaufort. Henry himself was the second of them and his childhood memories of his parents' devotion to each other still informed his concept of love. Perhaps, he thought, it was only the very luckiest people who experienced that kind of love once in a lifetime. He looked down at the top of Catherine's head: she was still standing, though quieter now, within the shielding circle of his arms. Who was he to deny her the right to such a love?

Confiding in Henry Beaufort, however difficult, had been the right thing to do. He promised to return to Baynard's Castle the next day, having persuaded Catherine not to do anything until he'd had a chance to think things over. He really didn't see the necessity for her to travel all the way to North Wales, a dangerous and uncomfortable journey at the best of times. No, her secret could be just as well kept a lot nearer home.

'Monmouth,' he said as they sat around a table in Catherine's private solar. By now they'd been joined by Owen Tudor and, despite himself, Beaufort could see what his nephew's widow admired in the young man. He was very personable, well-spoken and intelligent, and he clearly adored Catherine. He was rather tall, too, and looked capable of taking care of her, but what pleased Beaufort most of all was that he seemed honest and trustworthy. Owen's dark eyes and sensuous mouth impressed the Bishop not one jot but he nevertheless acknowledged that Owen Tudor was a handsome man. Women liked that sort of thing, he knew.

'Monmouth, Your Grace? But it is not one of Her Highness's dower properties.'

'It isn't. You're quite right.'

'Then, why ...?'

'Because it is right and proper that the King's widow should wish to see the place where her late husband was born,' replied the Bishop. 'Besides, it will keep my nephew Humphrey's nose out of your business. If Humphrey thinks that the Queen is spending some weeks at Monmouth, he won't question the fact. But we'll be laying a false trail. You will both have gone somewhere else, not far away, where no one would dream of looking for you, a place where the baby can be cared for and left to be brought up in loving family surroundings when the Queen has to return to court.'

They were both looking at him questioningly, waiting. 'And yes, Master Tudor,' Henry Beaufort added with a twinkle, 'you'll be pleased to know that your baby will be born in Wales.'

Owen laughed softly. '*Diolch i Dduw*,' he said. 'Thank God for that.'

'So,' Henry Beaufort continued, pleased with his plans, 'you've entrusted me with your secret, now I must tell you mine. There are several people who know what I'm about to tell you, but I'd still appreciate it if you kept the information to yourselves. The fact is that I have a daughter, just a little older than you are, Catherine. Her mother was Alice, the Earl of Arundel's niece, and I didn't marry her because … oh, well, it doesn't really matter. It all happened a long time ago and much water has gone under the bridge since then. I wanted the baby named Joan, after my sister, but I understand that she prefers to be known as Jane these days. She is married to a good man, Edward Stradling, who seems to be responsible for almost everything that happens in South Wales.'

'South Wales?'

'You can't have everything your own way, Master Tudor,' said Beaufort, though his eyes were still twinkling. 'You can't have my nephew's widow and a baby and a birthing place for her in North Wales, simply because that's where you come from. Just be grateful that there's a way out of this mess.'

'Yes, my Lord Uncle,' said Catherine, 'we're very grateful to you. It does sound like the solution to our problems, even though it is quite a long way to travel.' Impulsively, she leaned forward and kissed the older man.

'It would have been even further to North Wales,' grumbled the Bishop, pretending to sulk but pleased by the sensation of a young woman's soft mouth on his cheek.

It was warm for early September and Catherine was grateful for a cooling breeze off the sea. She lay in a large, comfortable bed in an airy room overlooking the formal gardens which fell away in elegant graded terraces towards a secluded cove on the South Wales coast. For all its luxury, the castle of St Donat's was very much a family home and she was sleeping well, entirely relaxed while she awaited the birth of her baby.

The journey to Bristol had been tiring but, by the time they reached the town, Catherine had made a subtle transition which, to all appearances, altered the nature of her relationship with Owen. Gone were the jewels, the formal gowns, and in their place, she dressed very much more simply, in the manner of a country gentlewoman. It delighted Catherine to realise that no one recognised her; she knew no one whom she met so there was no threat, no risk of anyone discovering their secret. She and Owen, relishing the heady sensation of appearing together in public for the first time, strolled around the bustling port of Bristol, enjoying the colour and the noise, exclaiming at the sights they saw, and listening to the foreign merchants blabbing away in a dozen different languages.

They walked the length of Broad Quay before they found the little ship they had been told to look for, the *Rose of Lundy*, lying at anchor. To the crewmen who were making her ready to sail, Owen and Catherine were simply wealthy passengers who had a few more servants than usual and needed to be ferried to the South Wales coast.

Sir Edward Stradling awaited them on board and greeted them effusively. He was a man some ten or eleven years older than Owen, tall and well-built with dark eyes and greying hair. They were to discover that he had a prodigious energy and was forever bustling about some business or other. For now, he was almost falling over himself to make them welcome and comfortable aboard the *Rose of Lundy*, where he appeared to be quite well known.

'Oh, yes, I travel on this ship regularly,' he explained, fussing with a warm blanket for Catherine's knees. 'She's a good little coaster; cuts a fine feather in the Severn Sea when the winds are favourable. We'll have you in Colhuw in no time!'

'What brings you so frequently to Bristol?' Owen asked.

'Business. Last year, I was appointed High Sheriff of Somerset and Dorset and I serve as a Justice of the Peace in Somerset from time to time.'

'Then shouldn't you live in Bristol?' asked Catherine.

'Oh, no, Your Highness,' said Sir Edward, then bit his tongue and looked around to see if anyone had heard what he'd called her. No one had. He was sworn to secrecy about her identity. 'I'm so sorry! I forgot!' he whispered and then went on. 'No, I can't live in Bristol because I am also Chamberlain of South Wales. And I need to get to Devon from time to time. I can see the Devon coast across the channel from my garden and sometimes it looks so close that I feel I could almost reach out and touch it. So you see, St Donat's is really quite a convenient place to live, given a decent ferry which sails regularly on those routes between Wales and the west of England. Besides which, my dear wife Jane is so very happy living where we do.'

'I look forward to meeting her,' said Catherine. 'I'm fond of her father. He has been very kind to me.'

'And, indeed, to me,' Sir Edward Stradling nodded with great enthusiasm. 'So many appointments are within the gift of my father-in-law and he is most generous. Marrying his daughter was the best day's work I ever did!'

Catherine was quite surprised by that, not by the fact of it but by the way it had been so readily confessed. 'And you have a son?' she asked.

'Indeed. Our young Henry. He's two years younger than your son, my Lady, His Highness the King ...' Again, his hand flew to cover his mouth as he realised he might have divulged dangerous information.

'Please don't worry, Sir Edward,' Catherine smiled. 'There's no one listening.'

They arrived at the little port of Colhuw on the Glamorgan coast towards the end of that afternoon and Catherine was glad of a sturdy, sure-footed Welsh pony to carry her up the steep incline away from the sea. Several carts and horses awaited the party near the ancient collegiate church of St Illtyd to take them the last few miles of their journey west to the castle of St Donat's. By the time they had been made welcome and comfortable, she was ready to sleep and sleep and sleep.

They couldn't have been better cared for. Catherine half-opened her eyes now and looked towards where Lady Jane Stradling, the very picture of patience, sat in the window embrasure, quietly sewing while her royal guest slept. As soon as she realised that Catherine was awake she was on her feet and at the bedside, her sewing abandoned.

'Your Highness! You're awake!'

'Yes, and as hungry as a hunter,' said Catherine.

The baby was born two months later, with little trouble, in the big bed in an airy room overlooking the sea; a contented child, who appeared to be solemnly regarding the world through eyes the colour of forget-me-nots.

'A girl!' said her delighted father, when he was allowed into the bedchamber to see her. 'Isn't she beautiful? Oh, Catrin, look at those tiny fingers! Aren't they perfect? I've always wanted a daughter.'

'Yes,' said her equally delighted mother. 'A girl. Tacinda.'

'What? Tacinda? Is that to be her name? I rather hoped that, if we had a girl, we might call her Marged. Margaret, after my mother.'

'No, not Margaret after your mother, nor Isabeau after mine. I'd like her to be Tacinda. I'm sorry, Owen, but I've quite set my heart on it. Do you really mind?'

'No, of course not, cariad. You're both safe and well and that's all that matters to me. That's much more important than what we call her. But ...' he hesitated. 'But ... Tacinda? What sort of name is that? Why have you chosen it?'

Catherine looked down at the child with forget-me-not eyes and blinked back sudden tears. 'It's the name the midwife gave Jacqueline's daughter. And we owe that poor little baby a lot, Owen. She was the one who brought us together.'

Owen's arms went around them then, the two most important people in his life, his beloved Catrin and their baby daughter. His heart was brimming over with love and pride but it ached at the thought that he would only ever be able to acknowledge them both in private. And if that was going to be difficult for him, how would Catrin ever forget that she had been forced to leave her precious baby in the care of strangers?

Chapter Eighteen

Winter 1425-1426

Waiting to disembark, the Duke and Duchess of Bedford stood on the deck of the *Trinity Royal*, their eyes screwed up against the biting wind, looking down at the flurry of dockside activity which greeted the arrival of the great ship at Dover. The gangplank, slippery as an eel, slid out of place yet again, accompanied by shouts and curses. John ground his teeth in frustration at the delay. He and Anne were both bundled up in warm, fur-lined cloaks and leather gloves but the cold still gnawed at their bones and every hour counted in their attempt to reach the Palace of Westminster before the weather closed in. Of having to be in England, John could at least look forward with pleasure to spending Christmas with his wife in convivial company and to seeing his young nephew, the King. Much to their regret, he and Anne had no children of their own.

To be honest, he would rather have stayed in France which felt more and more like home to him but, with the authority vested in him as first in line to the English throne, he'd had no option but to return in order to intervene in the ridiculous ongoing quarrel between his brother and his uncle. This visit was in response to an urgent message from Henry Beaufort in which the Bishop claimed that Humphrey was behaving erratically, in a way which threatened to endanger the life of the King. There was nothing for it but to respond to Beaufort's request. Not knowing how long he would have to stay in England in order to settle the quarrel, John had brought his wife with him. He'd spent last Christmas without her and could not endure the thought of being parted from her again.

They managed to reach Merton Abbey without any more

delay and were pleased to find that Henry Beaufort had ridden out from London to meet them. But any thought of travelling further was frustrated by deep, drifting snow which had begun falling from leaden skies. A journey to Westminster to join the King and his mother would only have been undertaken by the foolhardy so, forced to remain in Merton, the three of them passed the festive season quietly together, though pleasantly enough.

The bad weather and bitter cold persisted for several days, which gave Henry Beaufort ample opportunity to acquaint John with what had been happening over the past three or four months and Bedford was appalled by the stories of Gloucester's rumour-mongering and aggressive behaviour. He heard how things had come to a head in a confrontation on London Bridge at the end of October when uncle and nephew, with their respective guards, had only just been kept apart by the intervention of Archbishop Chichele who managed to convince them that the young King's interests were not best served by such an irresponsible display of bad temper by his uncle and great uncle, the two most powerful princes of the blood in England.

'So you were both involved in that confrontation?' John asked, not wanting to apportion blame until he was certain where it lay.

'Indeed we were,' said Beaufort, 'and I confess I feel ashamed at that. But I'd had enough of Humphrey's behaviour. He'd gone too far this time. He couldn't be allowed to get away with what he did.'

John raised his eyebrows. 'And what was that?'

'Well, there were several things, but the main one was that he abducted the King,' Beaufort paused to let the seriousness of the allegation have its effect.

'Abducted the King? You mean ...'

'He took the boy from his nursery, jammed some sort of makeshift crown on his head, then he and some of his cronies rode with the King through the streets, showing him to the people ... waving at them ... getting the child to wave. Humphrey is popular with Londoners. They were very ready to cheer him.'

John was appalled. 'What in God's name did he think he'd achieve by doing that?'

'Oh, that's easy. He did it to remind them that he's the most important man in England, seen to be responsible for the King and therefore responsible for the country.'

'It's almost unbelievable.'

'Not these days. Humphrey's behaviour is unpredictable to say the least.'

'And where was the King's mother?' John of Bedford wanted to know. 'Where was Catherine when all this was happening?'

'In the country,' said Henry Beaufort, without offering any further explanation. 'Though she has recently returned to court.'

'Let's call for some more logs for the fire,' said John. 'We have a great deal of talking to do.'

Since the marriage of her daughter, Joan, to James of Scotland, the Duchess of Clarence had become a very great deal closer to her son, Edmund Beaufort. So she was delighted to welcome him when he arrived at Westminster some ten days before Christmas, to spend the festive season at court. She felt pleased that the somewhat gauche youth appeared to have grown up at last and become rather a dashing young man. It would be a great deal easier to find him a suitable wife, the Duchess reflected, if the girl in question also found him physically attractive.

She watched him now as he led Queen Catherine into the dance to the opening strains of the *Farandole*, the pair of them a picture of elegance. She had always been fond of Catherine and nothing would have pleased her more than to welcome her as a daughter-in-law. Despite the difference in their ages, she mused, Catherine and Edmund would make an excellent match. Five years was nothing between husband and wife, even when the wife was the older of the two. She could still bear children and a marriage between the two of them would make Edmund stepfather to the King and any child of their union would be the King's half-brother or sister. The idea had a lot to recommend it.

Other eyes were on them, too. Humphrey of Gloucester led the chain of dancers weaving in and out of the line in which Catherine stood, opposite Edmund. Instead of linking arms as he should have done when he passed her, he slid his arm around her waist and Catherine grimaced involuntarily. Eleanor Cobham saw the clumsy grope and gritted her teeth. While Humphrey remained married to Jacqueline of Holland, Eleanor was very conscious of her vulnerable position in his life. It wouldn't take much to make him look elsewhere and the Queen was a very beautiful woman. Moreover, she was a widow now and, if Humphrey managed to divorce his wife, well, it was not unknown for a man to marry his brother's widow. It would certainly strengthen his claim to the throne. The chief weapon in Eleanor's armoury would be to nail him down by conceiving his child but, try as she might, she still had no luck at all in this endeavour, despite her fervent prayers to the Virgin Mary on the one hand, and her consultations with the witch, Margery Jourdemayne, on the other.

Duke Humphrey was in predatory mood tonight, full of festive high spirits, surrounded by attractive women and exactly where he wanted to be, at the centre of attention. At times like these he found that Eleanor could be very tiresome. Still, he reflected, she didn't own him and she could hardly raise any kind of objection to his behaviour while he still had a wife. He didn't often think about Jacqueline these days though he had received several letters from her, desperate pleas in which she swore she loved him more than life itself and begged him to return to Holland, to raise another army and rally to her cause.

He couldn't, of course, and wouldn't. Even he was forced to admit that his manoeuvres in Holland had been far from successful. Besides, he wasn't at all sure that he wanted to return to Jacqueline just at the moment. Eleanor warmed his bed perfectly acceptably, and there were other fish in the sea if he should tire of her. Of course, there were one or two who, for various reasons, were unattainable, but Humphrey loved a challenge, particularly when it came to the conquest of a haughty beauty.

Catherine irritated him though, particularly since she was, by any yardstick, the most attractive woman at court but she had made it quite clear that she would not welcome his advances, always making a point of asking after his wife whenever they spoke. He watched her now, elegantly performing the *Saltarello*, seeming to enjoy dancing with Edmund Beaufort and any oaf with half a brain could see that Beaufort was entirely besotted with her. Perhaps what Humphrey had foreseen a few years ago on the occasion of the King's first birthday party had finally happened. Perhaps, now that Beaufort had grown considerably in stature and sophistication, Catherine had begun to find him attractive. Perhaps she had already succumbed to his charms.

If that was the case, then he must do everything in his power to prevent a marriage between the pair of them. The last thing he wanted was a series of unwanted brats at court who could claim to be half-brothers and -sisters of the King. That would weaken his own position considerably and he had to prevent it happening at all costs. The ideal situation, of course, would be to marry Catherine himself but, as long as he was married to her cousin, that was out of the question. A great pity! In the meantime, he must do something to come between the Queen and young Beaufort and nip any relationship in the bud.

The King was sitting in his nursery at Leicester Castle, solemnly practising nodding his head and then shaking his head. And again, nodding his head and shaking his head. His uncle of Bedford had told him that he would have to do both these things when he went with his mother to the Great Hall at Leicester, where he would have to sit up straight on the throne in front of a lot of very important gentlemen in Parliament and nod his head or shake his head, depending on whether his uncle of Bedford said 'Do you agree, Your Royal Highness?' or 'Do you not agree, Your Royal Highness?' He would try very hard to get it right but there wasn't a lot of difference between 'Do you agree?' and 'Do you not agree?'. Just one little word, really. He would try to remember that even though 'not' sounded like 'nod', he should really shake his head when he heard that word. And his uncle of Bedford said he would give a little nod himself when he wanted Henry to nod, so he would have to keep watching him. It was very difficult. Sometimes his head would hurt with trying to remember very difficult things like that.

Anxiously, Catherine watched her little son now as, with his back ramrod-straight, he perched on the edge of the great throne with an over-large crown on his head and a serious expression on his face. In front of him stood his uncle, Humphrey of Gloucester, and his great-uncle, Bishop Henry Beaufort. Between the two of them, as though to keep them apart, stood Archbishop Henry Chichele, a scroll of parchment in his hands, droning his way through an interminably long statement. Standing to one side of the group, John of Bedford made sure that he was in the King's line of sight, in case the child should be uncertain whether to nod or shake his head.

Bedford couldn't afford any mistakes. Not this time. It had taken him nearly three months to arrange a venue at which he could get his brother and his uncle together so that this nonsensical situation could be resolved. If one man was available, the other was not, and he was genuinely concerned that they would do each other physical harm, so much so that he had banned the wearing of swords at this session of parliament, though he knew that some members had concealed sticks and clubs under their cloaks. Already the wags were calling it 'The Parliament of Bats'.

He was furious with his brother Gloucester for fabricating and spreading malicious stories which effectively accused Bishop Beaufort of treason against the crown. These accusations were being categorically denied now, in the lengthy statement being read out by Archbishop Chichele on behalf of Bishop Beaufort. The Bishop had sworn on oath that he had never plotted to assassinate King Henry V. From where he stood, John of Bedford could see Beaufort's face, seething with fury at the injustice of the accusations and, though the whole concept was entirely ridiculous, Bedford knew that it had to be established without question as a falsehood in front of the full Parliament and, crucially, ratified by the King.

At last, Henry Chichele reached the end of the statement and looked up. Taking his cue from the Archbishop, John of Bedford turned and moved into position in front of his nephew. He spoke very clearly.

'Thus His Grace the Bishop of Winchester denies absolutely and in every regard that he did ever, at any time, plot the downfall of your royal father King Henry V or of your royal grandfather King Henry IV. He is, has always been and always will be a loyal subject and a faithful servant of the crown and of the Royal House of Lancaster. He swears this upon oath and implores Your Highness to believe what he has said. So I must ask you …' and here John of Bedford paused and looked hard at his nephew, '… do you agree, Your Royal Highness?'

Henry was nervous. He'd heard so many long words but had he heard the little word 'not'? No, he didn't think he had but he wasn't really sure. He looked uncertainly at his uncle of Bedford and saw that he had raised his eyebrows and was nodding, almost imperceptibly. Yes, he was supposed to nod.

He nodded so vigorously that the crown was almost dislodged and a low murmur of relief ran around the Great Hall from the assembled Members of the full Parliament. Now, perhaps, the foolish behaviour of these two princes of the royal blood could be brought to an end. It had been disrupting the governance of the country for far too long. But Bedford had not finished.

'Then Your Highness, might I suggest that the Bishop of Winchester and the Duke of Gloucester should indicate their mutual willingness to work together for the greater glory of England under your just and benign rule by shaking hands?' He paused. 'Do you agree, your Royal Highness?'

Oh, there were those long words again! The little boy was uncertain. He'd nodded last time, perhaps he was supposed to shake his head this time. He was about to do so when remembered that he must look at his uncle for guidance. Bedford's heart skipped a beat as he raised his eyebrows and inclined his head slightly.

The King nodded as vigorously as his crown would allow.

'Then, my Lords,' said Bedford, feeling as though his spine

had turned to water, 'perhaps you will do His Highness's bidding?'

With a condescending smirk on his face, Gloucester held out his hand and the Bishop steeled himself to shake it. The assembled Members of Parliament breathed a collective sigh of relief.

An uneasy truce had been achieved during those long weeks in Leicester but John, though mightily relieved, had the sense to realise that there were still loose ends to be tied up.

'Of course,' he pointed out over a modest supper with Anne and Catherine that evening, 'that's probably the end of Uncle Henry's political life.' Both women looked at him questioningly.

'Why do you say that?' Catherine asked.

'I'm afraid I've had to ask him to relinquish his Chancellorship,' said John. 'He didn't like that one bit.'

'Then why did you ask him to?'

'Because Humphrey insisted upon it before he'd agree to the reconciliation. Everyone knew how angry he was when he found out that Uncle Henry had been made Chancellor in his absence but, of course, no one expected him back from Holland quite so quickly.'

'Uncle Henry must have been very hurt.'

'He was. But don't worry,' John smiled, 'he went with good grace and I have a plan for him that will soften the blow considerably.' His wife looked at him, beaming with pride. 'I have persuaded him that having less responsibility will give him more time to undertake a pilgrimage. I know he has long wanted to follow the *Camino de Santiago*. I have suggested that he should travel with us when we return to France so that he can start his pilgrimage from Calais.'

Anne of Burgundy clapped her hands, her face lighting up with pleasure. '*Ah! Une idée excellente!*' she exclaimed. John reached out and, still smiling, grabbed hold of his wife's wrist to curb any further excesses of enthusiasm before kissing her fingers.

Catherine smiled, too, as she watched them, pleased by their evident affection for each other and by her own part in bringing them together. Theirs was a good marriage and the ties between their native countries were stronger because of it.

If only she'd been able to help in some way to patch up the bitter squabbling between Beaufort and Gloucester. She worried particularly about how that quarrel affected her son, ever since she'd heard that Henry had been snatched from his nursery by his Uncle Humphrey, though she suspected that he'd simply been handed over by Elizabeth Ryman. But, she reflected, it was pointless feeling guilty about it because there was little she could have done at the time to help her son since she had been going through the agony of parting from her daughter. Poor little Tacinda. When Catherine was alone, she often crossed herself and prayed that the baby was being lovingly absorbed into the family of Jane and Edward Stradling. The whole abduction episode had convinced her that she must spend as much time as she could with Henry, the child whom she was allowed to acknowledge. It dulled the pain of being parted from the child with forget-me-not eyes.

Seeing John of Bedford and his wife together made her realise how much she missed Owen. He had been detained in London by Sir John Norris, the newly appointed Master of the Royal Wardrobe who was insisting on reorganising the way things were done. New brooms always swept clean, Owen had said wryly when he told her that he was wanted in London while she would be in Leicester. Of course, she could have insisted that her Clerk of the Wardrobe should accompany her but there was wisdom in being apart from time to time; it did deflect suspicious interest in their relationship and, really, Guillemote could manage quite well on her own. Catherine had not seen Owen for several weeks.

Their secret was still safe with the handful of loyal servants who'd had to be entrusted with it but she ached for Owen's company and the opportunity to talk to him about the uncertainties that were crowding her mind. She had been dreaming, too, her old recurring worry-dreams of shouting men and galloping horses, though it was easy enough to put those down to sleeping in a lonely bed.

Despite her delight at being near the King, life in Leicester was fairly dull for Catherine, though she did take great pleasure in spending time with her cousin Anne, gossiping happily in French and catching up on what had been happening since Catherine was last in France.

She pressed for news of her brother, Charles. The Dauphin, said Anne, remained in the southern town of Bourges. She'd heard that he desperately wanted to be crowned in accordance with French royal tradition in the cathedral at Rheims but, since Philip of Burgundy and John of Bedford controlled the whole of northern France including Rheims itself, the frustrated Charles was forced to remain where he was.

Then Anne told her that Queen Isabeau, now excessively fat, was spending more and more time at St Pol with a positive menagerie of malodorous pet animals.

'Ah,' said Catherine with a peal of laughter, 'I'll wager she hasn't got a dragon! There was a very fierce one in a mummers' play at Windsor not so long ago. I wonder if she'd like to have that. It was made of green wool and was wearing green shoes. Little Henry was very frightened. Mind you, Anne, I think that red dragons are very much more attractive than green ones.'

She didn't explain why she thought so.

Humphrey, who clearly felt himself the victor in the conflict with his uncle Henry Beaufort, had resumed his chairmanship of the ruling Council which controlled the day-to-day business of the Commons. He saw this as his opportunity to safeguard his interests by introducing a bill which called for the creation of a parliamentary statute making it an offence for a dowager queen of England to re-marry without the knowledge and specific permission of the reigning sovereign. Humphrey was damned if he was going to allow the possibility that a pack of the Queen's half-blooded brats by Edmund Beaufort would be able to threaten his own claim to the throne though, of course, he wouldn't state that publicly as a legitimate reason for wanting to introduce the bill.

To his fury, the Commons threw it out.

This pleased John of Bedford, who really couldn't see the

necessity for such legislation. After all, the idea of the King withholding his royal permission for such a marriage was preposterous. The King was not yet five years old.

So why, John wondered, had Humphrey deemed it necessary to introduce the bill? Did he know something about Catherine that John was unaware of? John aired his concerns to Henry Beaufort and was surprised when his uncle laughed.

'Ah,' he said, 'that means that Humphrey is suspicious. He thinks that the Queen has her eye on a second husband and I wouldn't be at all surprised that he's noticed the way my nephew Edmund Beaufort looks at her! And of course, far be it from me to say so, but it could be that his feelings are reciprocated.' Bishop Beaufort had a twinkle in his eye and couldn't see any harm in misdirecting John's curiosity.

On considered reflection, John decided not to tell Catherine about what had happened in Parliament, it would only upset her and make her feel even more alienated from the English court than she already was. What she didn't know, she wouldn't grieve over. After all, the Commons had rejected Humphrey's bill, so it wouldn't make any difference to her, and if she was becoming fond of Edmund Beaufort, well, good luck to her, she deserved to find a little happiness.

Privately, Catherine thought that Henry was far too young to be knighted but John of Bedford was of the opinion that conferring a knighthood upon him would bring the Leicester Parliament to an appropriate conclusion. Catherine wasn't going to argue so, before they left for the closing parliamentary session in the Great Hall of the castle, she made young Henry twirl around two or three times before she was satisfied that he was perfectly presented.

'But, Maman, I am the King. It doesn't matter how I look!'

'It's precisely because you are the King that it *does* matter,' she contradicted him. 'Dame Alice Boteler wouldn't let you go to Parliament looking like a hobbledehoy, now would she? But since Dame Alice is unwell and confined to her bed, I will make the decisions! And I think you'll do nicely.' Then she smiled and bent to hug her little son. He stiffened in her arms, uncertain how to react to a gesture of affection.

That Whit Sunday morning John of Bedford duly knighted his nephew the King who, in turn and using a lightweight sword with a blunted edge, dubbed thirty other new knights. His mother watched him with pride and even his Uncle Humphrey beamed his approval.

There was one last item on John's agenda. As part of his solution to the current problems, he had already made an approach to Pope Martin in Rome. Once safely back in Calais with his wife and his uncle, John intended to procure for Bishop Beaufort the coveted cardinalate which had been denied him for so long. He knew that the one thing which would restore Beaufort's good spirits and leave him with some tangible gain from this whole sorry mess would be to further his ecclesiastical ambitions. He liked to imagine his uncle's face, beaming with pleasure beneath the broad red brim of a cardinal's hat.

Chapter Nineteen

London, 1428

His cousin was the most nervous of bridegrooms and, as he hurried up Crane Street towards the church of St Michael Paternoster Royal, Owen couldn't for the life of him understand why Maredydd, a royal gentleman-at-arms and a soldier of many years' distinguished service in battle, should be reduced to a quivering jelly at the thought of getting married. If only Owen had the opportunity to marry where his heart lay, he would be jubilant.

Maredydd's bride, Emma Maunsell, was pleased to boast of her family's relationship to Richard Whittington, who still held pride of place in the hearts of Londoners though he had been dead these five years and was buried in this very church. Emma was from Whittington's mother's side of the family and had been brought up in rural Gloucestershire, an area which offered few opportunities for a woman with lofty marital ambitions, particularly a woman who was not in the first flush of youth. So, taking advantage of her excellent family connections, Emma had moved to London and lodged with the remaining members of the Whittington family in their elegant home. Here she hoped to meet the right people and make a good marriage to an aristocratic English husband. She had not yet achieved her objective when she was introduced to Maredydd by a mutual friend. As soon as she set her shrewd blue eyes on him, she came to the conclusion that she had spent far too long worrying about the wealth and position of a prospective husband rather than taking advantage of what might be her last opportunity of being made to feel like a beautiful, desirable woman. She had accepted his proposal of marriage with grateful enthusiasm.

All heads turned in her direction as she arrived at the door of the church and gave her future husband a dazzling smile. There was tenderness in his eyes as he led her towards the altar where they took their vows, Maredydd in a strong baritone with a perceptible Welsh accent, Emma a little more quietly with her gentle West Country burr.

By the time they came to the giving of rings Owen was grinding his teeth in frustration at the unfairness of it all. Why couldn't he be standing there with Catherine? They had been lovers for more than three years now, they had a baby daughter, and yet they still had to keep their relationship secret. They dared not compromise Catherine's position at court but Owen knew that having to leave Tacinda had come close to breaking her heart.

He'd had to let Maredydd into the secret eventually and he would never forget the look of incredulity on his cousin's face. They had been sitting together in The Swan as they had done so often in the past, though not so much these days, now that Maredydd was betrothed to Emma.

'Well, I'd better get back to her,' Maredydd had said loftily as he rose to leave. 'You should get yourself betrothed, you know, Owen. There's nothing like a good woman to bring out the best in a man.'

'I know that,' said Owen and then, despite himself, added: 'I already have one.'

'What?' Maredydd paused before fastening his cloak, suddenly interested. 'You dark horse! You've never told me about this! What's her name?'

'Catherine.'

'Catherine? Catherine who? Do I know her?'

Owen blushed in confusion now and reverted instinctively to his mother tongue. '*Y Frenhines*,' he said.

'*Y Frenhines*? The Queen? What? You … and the Queen! Oh, yes, very funny. Come on, Owen, don't take me for a fool. How can you expect me to believe that?'

'Because it's true.'

'What, you and the Queen? Don't talk such utter rubbish …'

'*Mae'n wir*, Maredydd. It's true, I promise you.'

'You're … you're, what, having an affair? That's absurd. Edmund Beaufort is giving it to her. Everyone knows that. It's common knowledge.'

'*Taw, Maredydd, paid a siarad Saesneg,*' Owen attempted to silence his cousin. 'Don't speak English for God's sake, and lower your voice or everyone will hear you and nobody must know. Nobody!''

Maredydd saw the expression on his cousin's face. 'Dear God,' he said, wonderstruck. 'It's true, isn't it? I'll say nobody must know! How long has this been going on?'

Owen steered Maredydd roughly towards a quiet corner of the big room and pushed him down onto a bench. Maredydd was shaking his head back and forth like a man stunned by a heavy blow.

'You all right, mate?' On his way to the bar, his friend Will Simpkin stopped in his tracks at the sight of him.

'Yes, thank you Will, he's perfectly all right,' said Owen. 'Just had a bit of a shock, that's all. Just a bit of … er … news. He'll be as right as rain in a moment.'

'If you say so.' Will shrugged then moved away.

'News? It's the most amazing piece of news I've ever heard in my life! You and the Queen!'

'*Fi a'r Frenhines,*' Owen insisted. 'Please, Mared, don't speak English. Someone is bound to hear you and then the cat will be well and truly out of the bag.'

'Some cat!' said Maredydd, as the blood slowly started returning to his face. 'How long has this been going on? All right …' he held up his hand to silence his cousin, '*Ers pryd mae hyn wedi bod yn mynd 'mlaen?*'

Relieved at having persuaded Maredydd that the subject was more discreetly discussed in Welsh, Owen answered his question by starting the story from the very beginning. He left nothing out, from the initial attraction between himself and the Queen which they had both tried so hard to suppress, right through to the flight to Wales and the birth of little Tacinda.

'Tacinda? What sort of name is that?'

'It's what Catrin wanted.'

'Catrin!' Maredydd was shaking his head again. 'I can't

believe that you even call the Queen by her first name, let alone in Welsh. And as for sharing her bed …! You do share her bed, do you? I mean, you don't just have her up against a wall when you get the chance?'

Owen's nostrils flared and he suddenly wanted to smash his fist into Maredydd's face but he controlled himself. 'No, Mared. She's not like that, and, yes, I do share her bed whenever I have the chance. Sadly, that's not as often as we'd both like.'

'Well, dear God, I've heard everything now. You know what this means, don't you? You could lose your head if the wrong people get to know about it.'

'Oh, yes,' said Owen. 'I'm very aware of that. So you must promise me faithfully that you won't tell a living soul. Not even Emma.'

'No, not even Emma,' Maredydd nodded his agreement. He changed his mind about leaving and sat quietly for the rest of that evening, subdued. Every now and then he'd look at Owen and shake his head in disbelief. He was going to take a long, long time to get used to the idea of his cousin's royal lover.

'Your Highness,' said Guillemote, opening the door into Catherine's room, 'the priest with the curious name is here. He would like to see you if it is convenient.' Catherine smiled; there were some things about which Guillemote was peculiarly stubborn, she knew the man's name perfectly well.

'Is he on his own, Guillemote?'

'Yes, my Lady.'

'Then show him in, please. Oh, and I suppose you had better bring him a goblet of wine. He never refuses one.'

She couldn't put her finger on what it was about Marmaduke de Kyrkeby that made her like him instinctively and trust him implicitly. Perhaps it was the twinkle in his eye, his readiness to listen to her opinions, or just the fact that Henry Beaufort thought so highly of him. He and Catherine, together with Bishop William Gray, had formed a close friendship over the last two years since Catherine had come to live in Baynard's Castle. She was always pleased to see them both.

'Do sit down, Rector,' she invited him. 'Now, tell me, to what do I owe the pleasure of your visit?'

'Your Highness, I have a letter from Bishop Beaufort, no, I'm sorry, Cardinal Beaufort. I must get used to calling him that. Thank you,' he said as Guillemote set down a goblet on a table at his elbow. 'Mind you,' he went on, 'his cardinalate hasn't changed him, he still writes as he always did. Very entertainingly. And on this occasion he has particularly asked me to give you his compliments. I couldn't ignore the opportunity to come and deliver them in person!'

'That was kind of you.'

'It was a good excuse for me to visit you, my Lady,' de Kyrkeby smiled, opening a leather scrip he'd been carrying and taking out a small roll of parchment. 'By the way, as well as asking after you, he has also asked me to enquire after someone called Tacinda. A small child of your acquaintance, I believe? He seems keen to know that she is well.'

Catherine's heart somersaulted and she caught her breath. 'Are you sure that's what he said?'

'Of course, look, see for yourself.' He held out Beaufort's letter. She took it from him and looked at the Cardinal's neat, well-formed handwriting. The name leapt out at her from the page. Tacinda. Why had he mentioned her in a letter to Marmaduke de Kyrkeby? Unless … unless … perhaps Henry Beaufort was giving her the opportunity to confide in his old friend the Rector of St Andrew-by-the-Wardrobe, should she wish to.

Her eyes scanned the letter without seeing it while her mind raced. It was another of those moments when, if she spoke the truth, she would never again be able to deny it. And yet there was something about the Rector which made her want to confide in him.

Catherine looked up. 'She's my daughter,' she said.

The Rector paused in the act of raising his goblet to his lips. 'Your daughter?'

'Yes, my daughter. Bishop Beaufort … I'm sorry, Cardinal Beaufort … seems to want me to tell you about her.'

'Then perhaps you would be wise to do so, my Lady.'

She never regretted it. She talked and talked, her words tumbling out in a jumble at first, a mixture of French and English, difficult to understand. Then she calmed down and de Kyrkeby was able to get a better picture of a lonely young woman away from home in a foreign environment where no one seemed at all interested in her welfare, falling in love with a young man who had befriended her. It seemed the most natural thing in the world to him, except that she was no ordinary young woman. She was the Dowager Queen of England and she was in love with a servant. Thinking back, he realised that this must have been the cause of her distress on the occasion when he first met her. He remembered how Henry Beaufort had taken charge of the situation. He seemed to be doing so again, from a distance.

'And the child is the result of your … er … friendship with Master Tudor, Ma'am?'

'She is. And it has broken my heart to leave her. I think of her every minute of the day and pray for her often.'

'Then with your permission, my Lady, I, too, will include the little one in my daily prayers.'

'I would be so grateful if you would. You see, I'm forced to trust her welfare to others, though I take great comfort in the fact that she is in the care of Cardinal Beaufort's daughter.'

'He did well to suggest it. D'you know, I remember his daughter being born. It was something of a cross for him to bear at the time and he was mightily torn between the child's need for a father and his own need for the holy mother church. These are not decisions lightly made, any more than your decisions have been easy. Of course, had you been able to marry the child's father, things would have been very different for you.'

'I can't marry Owen, Rector,' said Catherine. 'It would cause uproar. Besides, we have only a very small oratory here at the Castle and the chaplain knows nothing about our relationship, so even if it were possible …'

'Quite so. Quite so,' the Rector nodded. 'But would you be happier about your situation if you and Master Tudor could marry?'

'Of course. It's the one thing I want above all others. But it's

260

impossible.'

'No, not impossible. Your late husband the King is dead and you are therefore free to marry again. You can marry whomsoever you choose and, indeed, wherever you choose. You could undertake a clandestine marriage in a barn if you wish, it's just as binding as any. It is your commitment to each other that's important.'

'But the church is important to me, too. I wouldn't want to be married anywhere else but it would be difficult to do that in secret.'

'A clandestine marriage is for anyone who has a good enough reason not to make it public and you, my Lady, have every reason not to make it public. But that doesn't stop you being married in church. The Church only requires that a couple should be married by a parish priest in the presence of three witnesses. And I, my Lady, am a parish priest.'

Catherine's eyes were shining. 'So, are you saying, Rector, that if you were to perform the ceremony, Owen and I would be married in the eyes of the Church?'

'That is exactly what I'm saying, my dear Lady, and it would give me great pleasure to arrange it. Perhaps that's the outcome Cardinal Beaufort hoped for. No one else needs to be involved, other than your witnesses. Tell me, do you have three trustworthy friends who would be prepared to witness the ceremony?'

'We have. Oh, yes, we have several very loyal friends. And nothing would make me happier than to be married to Owen in the eyes of God.'

'Then you shall be, my Lady, as soon as you wish.'

The boot was on the other foot. This time, it was Maredydd who stood to one side with the ring in his safekeeping while his cousin Owen made his marriage vows. They had assembled behind the locked doors of the little church of St Andrew-by-the-Wardrobe, a small group headed by Catherine and Owen with the Rector, Marmaduke de Kyrkeby. To one side, beaming with pleasure, stood the Bishop of London, William Gray. Behind him Guillemote and Les Trois Jo-jo were in attendance.

Having made Catherine's new gown for the occasion, Molly Betts and Madge Wilkin were there, too, as was Maredydd's new wife, Emma. Owen had relented at last, allowing Maredydd to let her into the secret and she had been elated at the news. It was just like marrying into the Royal Family, she said excitedly, having the Dowager Queen of England as her husband's cousin-in-law! Emma was still keen on maintaining her excellent connections, however convoluted.

The service was a simple one. The Rector took Catherine's right hand and placed it in Owen's left hand then her left hand in his right, hand-fasting them together by binding them symbolically with a narrow length of rich gold brocade. Then came the vows, and when Catherine, in her pretty Parisian accent, swore to honour him as her husband for the rest of her days, Owen looked at her in wonder, hardly able to believe his ears. Marmaduke de Kyrkeby unwound the length of gold brocade and turned to Maredydd for the ring.

The Rector guided Owen's hand as he first placed the ring lightly on the tip of Catherine's thumb, saying 'with this ring I thee wed.'

Then over the tip of her index finger, '… in the name of the Father …'

Then half way down her middle finger, '… and of the Son …'

And finally, fully onto her ring finger, '… and of the Holy Spirit.'

Close to tears, Catherine resisted the urge to add '… and *Jolie* cwt bach!'

There the ring remained. Catherine and Owen were man and wife.

She wouldn't able to wear the ring, except in private, but she was delighted to be able to show it off at the modest reception in Baynard's Castle after the ceremony. Guillemote had been allowed to tell Anton, swearing him to secrecy, and the little French chef had excelled himself in the preparation of food for the occasion, so pleased was he to hear the news. He joined the guests at Catherine's invitation. 'It is very different from your first wedding, Your 'Ighness,' he said. 'I remember it well.'

'Ah, yes, but the food is even better, since there are fewer guests to cater for.'

'It 'as been my privilege to prepare it for you, my Lady.'

He had been very surprised, he told Catherine, when Guillemote had confided in him, because even the scullions in the royal kitchens were placing bets on whether she would marry Edmund Beaufort. Owen, he thought privately, was a much better-looking man.

'I will tell all my staff that the rumours are not true, my Lady, and that you are not in love with Edmund Beaufort.'

'No, Anton, don't do that,' Owen said quickly. 'It suits our purpose very well for people to think that the Queen and Edmund Beaufort are close. It deflects attention away from us.'

'*Mais oui*! Yes. Yes, of course! So, I will say nothing. Nothing!' Anton beamed, tapping the side of his nose conspiratorially. 'Your secret is safe with Anton. I will tell no one. And please, let me wish you both every 'appiness.' He bowed deeply as they smiled and turned away to talk to Maredydd and Emma.

Guillemote tapped Anton on the shoulder. The two had remained friends ever since coming over from France together in the royal entourage which accompanied Catherine nearly eight years ago, after her first marriage. For Guillemote, gossiping with Anton was like slipping her feet into an old, comfortable pair of shoes.

'The Queen knows, does she, about what 'as been going on in Parliament?' Anton asked when they'd been chatting together for several minutes.

'And exactly what *has* been going on in Parliament, Anton? And why should it worry my mistress?'

'Well,' he confided, 'I only 'eard about this the other day, when the scullions were blabbing in the kitchen about the Queen and young Edmund Beaufort. They were saying that the Duke of Gloucester 'as been busy getting a new law through Parliament, forbidding any widow of the King to re-marry without special permission. Everyone thought it must be because of Beaufort.'

'Ah, so the Duke at it again, is he? I know he's already tried it once, in Leicester, but the Commons rejected it. Now he's trying to get it through a second time.'

'But this time, 'e seems to 'ave succeeded,' said Anton. 'One of my apprentices told me last week. He was quite certain. And it is more than 'is job is worth to tell me a lie! I would dismiss 'im from my kitchen!' Anton paused dramatically and looked around him before whispering in Guillemote's ear. 'The Duke of Gloucester doesn't know anything about the Queen and Master Tudor, does 'e?'

'No. Of course he doesn't. Everybody who knows about it has been sworn to secrecy and no one would ever let the Queen down.'

'*Mon Dieu*, I 'ope not. I 'eard that anyone who would dare to marry a dowager queen without the reigning monarch's consent could lose 'is 'ead!'

'The reigning monarch's consent?' Guillemote laughed out loud. 'Ridiculous! The reigning monarch is only six years old! He won't be seven until next month. I don't think that's much of a threat to Owen Tudor, do you?'

Anton gave an eloquent shrug. 'I'm not so sure,' he said. 'Small children will usually do what they're told and the one who tells King 'Enry what to do is his uncle of Gloucester. And I would not trust 'im further that I could throw a pig by the soapy tail.'

Guillemote woke with a raging sore throat on the morning of the King's birthday and sneezed violently several times. The problem with living in England, she reflected, was that it was always so damp. She never had these wretched colds when she lived in France, where she remembered that even the weeks before Christmas seemed pleasantly balmy compared with the icy December winds which were howling in from the North Sea this morning, straight up the River Thames and into the dormitory she shared with Molly Betts and Madge Wilkin in Baynard's Castle. She sneezed again.

'*Gesundheit!*' Molly had learned the word from her association with a corn-trader from Cologne.

'Oh, Molly,' Madge groaned, 'don't quote your lewd foreign friends from Queenhithe here, please. Go and tell Her Highness that Guillemote isn't well enough to go to Windsor today while I make her an infusion of lemon balm.'

'*Merci*, Madge,' Guillemote croaked. She would be sad to miss the occasion of the young King's birthday, such a significant one too, but she was better off staying where she was, trying to keep warm.

The Queen agreed that a small boy's birthday party was really no place for Guillemote that afternoon. 'Not that he's a small boy any more,' she said to Owen, as she got ready to leave for Windsor. 'He's seven years old today, no longer an infant. Now officially a child. He'll be jousting next!'

Owen smiled. He watched as she removed her wedding ring and placed it carefully in the small tortoiseshell box on her dressing table where she always kept it when she wasn't able to wear it. Then he helped her into a warm, hooded, coney-lined cloak for the river journey to Windsor. He'd like to be going with her but that wasn't possible. He would have to content himself with seeing her off from the wharf at Baynard's Castle and watching until the barge carrying the Queen and her ladies had rounded the bend in the river.

As the familiar curved tower of Windsor Castle came into view, Catherine remembered the King's first birthday. Strange, she thought, but that was the day when she had first met Owen, too, and so much had happened since. Who would ever have thought that the young man she had found playing finger games with her baby would become the father of her second child. And she remembered Jacqueline, trying to make the party go with a swing and only succeeding in angering Humphrey of Gloucester. Poor Jacqueline. She had received several letters from her, begging for news of Humphrey, and had done her best to answer them without mentioning Eleanor Cobham.

'Your Majesty,' Humphrey rose from his chair to greet her when she arrived at Windsor, pressing her hand warmly to his lips, as he always did. She wanted to snatch it away.

'I trust you are well,' he said. 'This is an important day for all of us.'

'Birthdays are always important,' she agreed. 'Everyone loves a birthday.'

'Indeed,' he replied, leading her to a comfortable, cushioned bench in the window embrasure. 'But, of course, it is a particularly important milestone for the King. That's the main reason why I wanted to see you privately beforehand. I wanted to make you aware of some decisions made by the Council at a meeting which took place only last week.'

He sat down next to her. 'You realise, of course, my Lady, that having reached his seventh birthday, His Highness must no longer be treated as an infant. So he will have no further need of the women who have been charged with his welfare up until now. The Council has decided to dispense with their services.'

'You mean Dame Alice is to be dismissed? But Henry is very fond of her ...'

'Dame Alice and Mrs. Ryman, who has done a remarkably good job, incidentally, for which she will be amply rewarded. His nurse goes, too. What's her name, er ...'

'Joan Astley, my Lord. Is Joan to be dismissed?'

'She is. It is all for the best, I assure you. You'll see. We cannot have the King being brought up as a little ninny, can we? He will share his studies in the schoolroom with other boys and he will have men around him at all times to teach him by example.'

Catherine hesitated. 'And I? Where do I stand in all this?'

'Well, naturally, my Lady, nothing can alter the fact that you are his mother. But I think you ought to try not to influence him unduly.'

'But he is my son.'

'Of course, and as I said, nothing can alter that fact. But he is the King and he must be trained for kingship. To that end, the Earl of Warwick, while remaining his legal guardian, will also assume overall responsibility for his education. He was always the right man for the job, loyal, knowledgeable, and wise. Comes from good English stock. Though, having said that, his command of French is excellent. That will be a useful advantage when the King is crowned and takes over the throne of France.' Catherine swallowed hard but didn't rise to the bait.

She could have taught her son to speak French like a native, had she been allowed to.

'But what of his personal needs? Who will make sure that he's clean? Comfortable? Properly fed?'

'His Highness will have four knights of the body and four esquires of the body. Good men, all of them, as they should be for what we're paying them, but the Council deems it money well spent. His health will be the personal responsibility of Master John Somerset and the Frenchman, Anton, will remain in charge of the royal kitchens. The plans are all in place and, from Monday onwards, no one ...' and here he looked pointedly at Catherine, '... no one will be allowed to question them.'

She felt quite faint. This hard, male-dominated regime would be immensely difficult for Henry, she knew, and there would certainly be no place for his mother in the new scheme of things.

'I ... I don't think he'll be happy, my Lord.'

'Oh, you think not? Madam, of course he'll be happy. He's the King and that is the shape of his future from Monday onwards.' Then he smiled one of his rare, remote smiles and lightened his tone. 'But today is Saturday and we will celebrate with a small birthday party for His Highness so that he can get to know the boys who will share his lessons in the schoolroom. Nobly born boys, of course, every one of them.'

Catherine smiled in return but immediately regretted dropping her guard when Humphrey turned to her suddenly. 'Of course, you can have access to Henry at any time, you know. You have only to ask me ... I could make life a lot less painful for you. You just need to return those feelings which you must know I could so easily have for you if things were different.'

He had his hands on her shoulders now and his face was close to hers, too close, his lips a shade too red. She could smell his breath, a faint whiff of wine, barely disguised by tincture of myrrh. Her utter revulsion almost paralysed her as he bent his head to kiss her. Then, fury lending her strength, she shook him off, leaped to her feet, turned, and slapped him as hard as she could. He reeled back and his hand flew to his cheek.

'Don't you dare! Don't you ever, ever, dare to do that again!'

'But, Catherine …' he began.

'May I remind you, my Lord, that you address me as *Your Royal Highness*!' She stood in front of him, her hands on her hips, her eyes ablaze. 'And as for you, Your Grace,' she snarled, 'if you ever lay a hand on me again, I'll … I'll …' She didn't finish the sentence, partly because she could think of no threat severe enough and partly because her blind fury was subsiding. She swallowed hard but it was quite some time before she felt in control of herself again. Humphrey remained silent, rubbing his cheek.

'Very well, then,' she said at last. 'You were talking about arrangements for the King's future welfare. Well, it all seems to have been arranged, doesn't it? I dare say it's all been thought out very carefully.'

'It has,' Humphrey sounded subdued. 'And it is all for the King's ultimate benefit.'

He seemed to be expecting her to say more. She couldn't. After several moments she took a deep breath. 'Now, if there's nothing more, I wish to see the King.'

'Of course, Your Highness.'

She didn't really know what to expect but she found that the nursery had been colourfully decorated and there was already a party atmosphere. Some boys of Henry's age were playing a guessing game in the corner of the room and a big trestle table nearby was laden with jellies, cakes, and biscuits, including Henry's favourite honey cakes and gingerbread men. She saw him before he saw her, across the room and in solemn conversation with young Thomas Roos. Her heart contracted painfully.

'Your Highness!' she called. 'Henry!' He turned towards her.

'Mother,' he said. He had never called her that before. She had always been his 'Maman'. He was clearly learning his lessons and learning fast.

'*Joyeux anniversaire, Henri!*' She could easily have wished him a happy birthday in English but she wanted to keep one special thread of their relationship unsullied. Mother and son looked at each other uncertainly, neither quite knowing what to say next.

'How are you, my Lady?' Henry blurted out, at exactly the same instant as his mother said: 'How is your kitten, Henry?'

'Doucette? Oh, she's not a kitten any longer, Mother. And she has been sent back to the stables to live with the other cats. My uncle Humphrey of Gloucester says I am to have a dog for my birthday. A setter. They are very good hunting dogs, Uncle Humphrey says.

'Really? And what will you call your dog?'

He looked uncertain. 'I think I shall call him Gelert. It's a Welsh name and one of the gentlemen-at-arms once told me a story about a dog with that name. He said it was a prince's dog and I was the Prince of Wales before I became King, so it's a good name for my dog. But Uncle Humphrey says I should give him an English name. So I don't know what to do. My head hurts sometimes, when I have to decide really important things.'

Catherine wanted to stuff her fingers in her ears and scream. If she heard 'Uncle Humphrey says' just once more, she was sure she would lose control.

How she got through the remainder of the afternoon, she would never know. What she did know was that heading downriver towards Baynard's Castle, towards Owen and home, was the best feeling she'd had in a day of huge emotional swings. Eyes closed, she let her thoughts drift to the rhythm of the oars, thoughts of curling up with Owen in front of a cosy fire in her bedchamber. She might ask him to tell her the story of the dog ... what was it ... Gelert? She loved listening to him telling her stories of the old Welsh myths and legends as he lay on the hearth, his head pillowed in her lap while she twirled tendrils of his dark hair around her fingers.

It was wiser not to tell Owen about Humphrey's outburst, she decided: he would be too angry and, since he was powerless to do anything about it, there was nothing to be gained by it. But she would tell him all about the party and he would make her laugh and then he would pick her up in his arms and set her down gently on the deep goose-feather mattress. Then, when they had made love, they would find peace and sweet, restful sleep. She longed for the moment so much that she could almost smell the wood smoke spiralling upwards into the chimney.

'My Lady, wake up! Wake up, Your Highness! Look, look, smoke! There's smoke coming from the castle! It's on fire!'

Suddenly the smell of smoke was very real. She opened her eyes to see the outline of the Dominican Priory of the Black Friars thrown into relief by the eerie, red light which came from the building beyond it and lit up the whole river ahead of them. Her ladies were on their feet now and shrieking hysterically, in danger of capsizing the boat and the barge men were shouting at them to sit down or they'd all be in the water. The choking, acrid smell of smoke was everywhere and sparks cracked up into the black December night from the huge bonfire which had been Catherine's home. Ignoring the oarsmen, she was on her feet and in the prow of the boat, screaming.

'No! No! For God's sake ...! No!'

She didn't care who heard her. Dear God, she couldn't bear it if she had lost Owen in the inferno which was Baynard's Castle.

The wooden structure of the Castle's own wharf had already collapsed and its charred remains were floating in the choppy water. Rowing furiously, the oarsmen took the boat further downriver and managed to tie up at Paul's Wharf, safely out of the range of flying sparks.

'Your Highness! Stop! Stop, my Lady! Stop!' Joanna Belknap shouted at Catherine as she scrambled off the barge, missed her footing on the wharf, and slid in the mud of the river bank, soaking her feet and the hem of her gown. Hardly aware of it, she clawed her way up onto the path in the direction of Baynard's Castle. Her heart was pounding in her ears and the one thought in her mind was that she had to get to Owen. He must be in there, somewhere. She must find him.

'I wouldn't, my Lady, if I were you!' said a firm voice as a hand caught her arm and swung her round to a stop.

'Let me go! Let me go, immediately. I must get to my home.

I must …' with a wild look in her eyes, she was beating her fists on the man's chest.

'You must do nothing that will endanger your life, my Lady. If you attempt to go any further, I will not be answerable for your safety.' She looked distractedly at the man who held her arm in such a firm grip and tried to pull away from him again.

'Please, please, you must let me go.'

'Your Highness, don't! The place is an inferno. No one will come out of there alive. The fire has been raging these several hours but I think most of your staff are safe.'

'Most of my staff …? What do you mean by that?'

'Everyone who was able to escape has already done so and made for Chertsey House. Please, allow me to escort you there. It is in chaos, of course, but things are slowly being brought under control.'

She saw that he wore a heavy cross about his neck, though in every other respect he looked like a wharf labourer. His round face was streaked with soot and what little hair he had was plastered down with sweat. He must be from the Benedictine Order of Chertsey Abbey in Surrey, whose London lodging was Chertsey House.

'Father Abbot … I'm sorry … I didn't realise …'

'Please, my Lady,' he said. 'Try not to distress yourself. I know this has come as a great shock to you.' He turned to Joanna Troutbeck who was labouring along the path, panting with the effort. 'Do try to persuade Her Highness to come with me,' he said.

'Yes, my Lady. That is a very good suggestion. Let's all go there. Come with us.' Catherine turned to see two bargemen helping her other ladies through the mud.

'Oh, Troutbeck, what will I do? What if … what if Owen …? I can't bear it.' Meekly, with Troutbeck and the Abbot on either side of her, she allowed herself to be led back towards Chertsey House which, with its door wide open, was throwing a welcoming beam of candle light across a tiled floor and onto the path. A great babble of raised voices came from within.

Fearful of what she might find, she tried to remember what

271

the Abbot had said. He thought most of her staff were safe? Most of her staff? Why not all her staff? What of Owen? What if he was … it didn't bear thinking about.

'Cariad.'

Relief flowed through her and she thought her legs might give way. She turned and there he was, close behind her, calling her by the special name that only the two of them knew, in a voice so low that no one else could hear it.

'Owen! I thought … I thought … oh, God, I thought you were dead.'

He took a step back and made a formal little bow. 'Thank you, your Highness, but no, I am quite safe.' Dear God! Of course, he was still being cautious. Who knew who was watching them? Even in this life and death situation, they were still sovereign and servant. She wanted to throw her arms around his neck but she had to pretend that she was merely concerned for his safety as a member of her staff, nothing else.

'Master Tudor, I'm … I'm so pleased that you're safe. So pleased. And what of the other members of my staff, are they, too …?

She saw the look on his face and knew that something was terribly, terribly wrong.

'Who?' she asked. 'Who is dead?' She could see that he didn't trust himself to speak.

'Tell me, Owen, Tell me! Who is dead?'

'Guillemote, my Lady. I'm so sorry.'

'Guillemote? No, don't be absurd. She simply had a sore throat this morning and I said she should stay in bed. You are mistaken. She's not dead. She can't be dead.'

'Yes, Ma'am. I'm afraid she is. She is the only one … everyone else appears to be safe.'

'No, no, you're wrong. You must be wrong. Why do you lie to me about Guillemote?'

Owen risked being seen with his face disrespectfully close to the Queen's. 'Catrin, believe me, I wouldn't lie to you about something … someone so important to you. I tell you, Guillemote died in the fire. I did my best but … but it wasn't possible to save her. Guillemote is dead, Catrin. Guillemote is

272

dead. You must believe me.'

'Dead,' she repeated, dazed but still unbelieving. 'Dead? But why is Guillemote dead?'

'Because she tried to retrieve something,' he said. 'Something ... I'm sorry, my Lady ... she appears to have gone back to get ... to get something from your room.'

'Oh God,' Catherine had begun wailing. 'Oh God, not Guillemote. Not my Guillemote! Not my darling, darling Guillemote! What will I do without her? *Non*! *Sans elle je ne vis pas*!'

She and Guillemote had known each other all their adult lives. Their relationship transcended that of a queen and her servant. They were friends, the dearest of friends. She lifted agonised eyes to Owen.

'What did she go back for?' she asked in a small voice. 'In God's name, what made her go back?'

'This,' he said and held out his hand. In his palm lay the little tortoiseshell box in which Catherine always kept her wedding ring.

Chapter Twenty

Summer 1429

The requiem mass was attended by all the friends who had loved the little French woman, had benefited from her advice over the years, and had occasionally felt the sharp edge of her tongue. Anton was inconsolable and wept copiously and noisily throughout the funeral. Catherine's grief was almost unbearable. She knew she had been inclined to take Guillemote for granted and hadn't realised what a close, devoted friend she had always been, through all the years they had known each other. After the funeral, she wrote a long letter to Queen Isabeau, asking her to break the news to Guillemote's parents and urging her to tell them of their daughter's bravery and unswerving loyalty to her mistress.

The fire which had killed Guillemote had completely gutted Baynard's Castle, forcing Catherine and her small household to move back to Windsor. True, she now lived in the same building as Henry, but she was no nearer her son for that. He spent his days in the schoolroom and in the chapel, or honing his skills at archery, swordsmanship, and horsemanship. When she wished to see him she had to make a special request to the Earl of Warwick. Money for her keep was deducted from her allowance and she felt as shunned as a leper.

Apart from her cherished wedding ring, almost all Catherine's clothes and jewellery had gone in the fire, but at least that gave her an excuse for seeing Owen under the pretence of having to discuss the replacement of items from her wardrobe. So, in private, he comforted her and told her the whole story of Guillemote's last hours. Remembering that she hadn't accompanied Catherine to Windsor, he had looked for her among the large group of Baynard's Castle servants who had congregated in the churchyard in front of St Andrew-by-the-Wardrobe, well away from the fire. She was nowhere to be seen. Perhaps, he reasoned, if she'd been feeling ill when the fire broke out, she was trapped somewhere near where she slept. He slipped away from the group and risked going back into the Castle to look for her. He knew that she shared a dormitory with Madge and Molly not far from Catherine's bedchamber, so he worked out the best route back into the building towards the place where he was most likely to find her, if she was still alive. Then he saw her, at the top of the service stairs. Her thin nightgown was ablaze and she was stumbling, retching and coughing in the choking atmosphere. He tore at the fabric of his sleeve and held it over his mouth, reaching out as far as he could with his other hand in an attempt to pull her towards him. Guillemote reached out, too, but their hands never met and she threw the little tortoiseshell box towards him just as the wooden staircase collapsed beneath her and she had fallen, screaming, into the flames below. There were tears in his eyes as he recalled the tragedy. He put his arms around Catherine and held her very close while she wept for her dead friend.

She could no longer bring herself to leave her ring in the tortoiseshell box when it was not on her finger. She now wore it on a long chain around her neck, tucking it between her breasts and under her gown where no one could see it. She knew it was there and that was all that mattered. Owen knew it was there, too, and took great delight in retrieving it from its hiding place when they had a chance to be alone. They had fallen back into the habit of largely ignoring each other during the day and spending as much time together as they could in the evening and at night, entrusting one or other of Les Trois Jo-jo with the responsibility of making sure they were not disturbed. The three Joannas had offered to share Guillemote's duties between them, rather than run the risk of a new maid being unable to resist the urge to gossip about the Queen.

As time went by, more and more people had to be let into the secret of the marriage and there was the constant worry about what would happen if Humphrey should ever find out about it but, after his outburst in Windsor on the day of the King's seventh birthday, Humphrey had tended to avoid Catherine as far as he could. For the moment, the smoke-screen story of Edmund Beaufort was still working well enough since, nowadays, Edmund spent a great deal of his time in France where he was not called upon to confirm or deny his relationship with the Dowager Queen.

A kind of numbness had settled over Catherine since losing Guillemote and she seemed disinclined to make plans of any kind. She lived for the evenings when she could be with Owen, to tell him about her day, to dream with him about the future, and to make love in the big four-poster bed.

As creamy white blossom began to hang heavy on the hawthorn in late spring, she knew with certainty that she was pregnant again. The knowledge came as no great surprise to her though, she reflected, she had only herself to blame. If she had been capable of resisting Owen it would never have happened but her body responded to him in a way which seemed entirely outside her control. He had only to look at her in a certain way and she was beyond salvation.

But another baby posed a problem. She wasn't entirely sure when it would arrive – Guillemote had always been so good at making these calculations – but she was fairly sure that it would be during early November. That meant going into hiding again but at least she would have a reasonable chance of regaining her figure before having to appear in court for the Christmas festivities. Perhaps she was wrong to be too worried.

'So which of your dower properties would you like to visit this year, my Lady?' asked Owen with a broad grin when she told him. It didn't seem so much of a crisis this time, not for either of them. They had managed to maintain a cloak of absolute secrecy over Tacinda's birth and, if they were very careful, there was no reason to suppose that this birth would be any different.

'Owen, I really don't mind. As long as it's a healthy baby which will be born safely and as long as I don't suffer pain like poor Jacqueline did. But I must keep this child, Owen, somehow. I must. I've had two babies, Henry and our little

Tacinda, and I haven't been able to keep either of them.'

'But we had no option but to keep Tacinda's birth a secret, Catrin. We had to.'

'Yes, of course we did, and God knows when I'll ever see her again. But I never see Henry either. He might as well have been stolen from me and given to the gypsies. They've used me, Owen. They've used me to provide an heir for the English throne, like some sort of brood mare. That's all I'm good for. But I'm not giving up another baby. This time, I must have the pleasure of watching my child grow up to look like his father.'

'And so you shall, cariad,' Owen smiled, hugging her close to him. 'We'll find a way. And if we have another little girl, I hope she grows up to look exactly like her mother!'

They decided on Hertford Castle. Catherine's preference would have been Wallingford but the King and his entourage would be spending the summer there and Catherine didn't want to be anywhere near the court as her pregnancy progressed. The gimlet-eyed Eleanor Cobham wouldn't miss a thing.

So most of the crates and coffers for the royal family's summer progress were sent to Wallingford with the King but several were held back to await Catherine's departure to Hertford. Humphrey was still keeping his distance from her so no one questioned her decision to spend the summer away from court. No one seemed to care where she went, so she didn't expect to be disturbed or called to account. She looked forward to long summer days with Owen and their small, loyal group of servants.

Before she left Windsor, Catherine received a disquieting letter from her mother in answer to her own letter informing Queen Isabeau of Guillemote's death. The letter began with a few platitudes rather than genuine sympathy, since the Queen had never really understood her daughter's fondness for the girl who was, after all, no more than a servant.

Suddenly Catherine sat bolt upright and called to Owen. 'Listen,' she said, 'to what my royal mother writes from France.' She smoothed out the parchment on the table and tried to translate from the French as she went along.

'Maman writes that my brother Charles is at Chinon with his

entourage and is being pestered by a mad peasant girl who says that she has a divine mission to save France from the English invader and to put the Dauphin on his rightful throne! A girl! And a peasant girl at that!'

'Really? And what makes her think she can do it?'

'She says she is being commanded by God, through the saints. According to Maman, she claims that St Michael speaks to her regularly and he is often accompanied by St Margaret and St Catherine.'

'Quite a crowd,' observed Owen mildly. 'And what do all these saints want her to do?'

'Apparently, they want her to lead Charles and his army into battle against the English.'

'A girl, eh? At the head of an army. And what does your brother make of it?'

'Maman says that he has arranged for her to be examined by a committee of bishops and doctors, to determine whether she's a genuine heretic or just a crazy girl.'

'Or a visionary,' said Owen. 'You never know.'

'Don't be ridiculous, my sweet,' said Catherine. 'She's probably mad. Then again, if Charles is crowned King of France, it puts a completely different complexion on things, doesn't it? What happens to Henry? And where should my loyalties lie? With my son or with my brother?'

She didn't want to think about it. Well, not until after the baby was born.

Owen left for Hertford a day or two in advance of Catherine, to ensure that that the household was running smoothly by the time she arrived. Had Catherine left at the same time, she would have missed Cardinal Beaufort altogether.

'My Lord Uncle,' she greeted him warmly when he was shown in to see her. 'This is indeed a pleasure. I had thought you were in Scotland.'

'I was. But my homeward journey didn't take as long as expected,' said Henry Beaufort, holding both her hands in his and smiling broadly at her. 'Which pleases me greatly, my Lady, since it affords me the opportunity of seeing you. How are you? And how is that husband of yours?'

'My dear husband,' she said, savouring the word which she wasn't often able to use, 'is well. And I have you to thank that I have a husband at all!'

'I was glad to help. You know, we really should think of offering him rights of denizenship. For services to the Royal Family.'

'Would you do that? He would be very pleased.'

'Indeed, I shall personally endorse it. Life would be a great deal easier for Master Tudor if he wasn't a Welshman. He has absolutely no rights at all under English law and it has to be said that he has rendered excellent service to the Royal Family. He has even helped to increase their number!' The Cardinal gave her a mischievous look, his eyes twinkling. 'And who knows,' he added, 'he could increase that number yet again, so it is as well you are married!'

She smiled, feeling both embarrassed and reluctant to burden him with the disclosure of another pregnancy. After all, he was a man with issues of national importance to concern him.

'I understand,' he went on, 'that my old friend Marmaduke de Kyrkeby was more than pleased to help you both in the matter of your marriage.'

'He was, and Owen and I were very glad of it, though keeping it a secret is a constant challenge.'

'Gloucester doesn't know, does he?'

Catherine frowned. 'No, Humphrey knows nothing about us and those who share our secret are very discreet though, of course, we all have to try to stay one step ahead of him. But, largely thanks to you my Lord Uncle, Owen and I are very happy. Tell me, have you any other good ideas up your sleeve?'

'No, sadly. No good ideas but several concerns, I'm afraid.'

'Concerns?'

'Catherine, it would be less than honest of me not to tell you that things are really bad in France at the moment. And there is something I need to discuss with you. Come, let us sit down.'

They sat together at a table near the window. Henry Beaufort leaned forward on his elbows and made a steeple of his fingers. 'My dear, my concerns are about the King,' he said. Catherine waited for him to go on, watching his face. 'It's high time he was crowned King of France.'

'But he hasn't yet been crowned King of England. Shouldn't that come first?'

'Yes, of course it should. But there are very worrying things happening in France and we need to stamp our English authority on the people as soon as we can. Your brother Charles is being influenced by a young woman they call *La Pucelle*, the Maid.'

'Ah! So, Maman was right! She wrote to me and told me that this girl wants to lead Charles' armies against the English. But, surely, that can't be true! She's probably a clever little strumpet, a camp follower who craves the company of soldiers.'

'Whatever she is, she has found a way of influencing your brother. She's given him a sign that she knows the secrets of his innermost soul and he believes her. She claims to hear voices that tell her what to do. They say the Dauphin offered her a sword but her voices told her not to accept it, that instead she should look behind the altar in the chapel of St Catherine de Fierbois where she would find the sword she was to use.'

'And …?'

'And there *was* a sword there. No one had ever seen it before. It was exactly where her voices told her it would be. Now the people are starting to believe that she will yet see your brother crowned King of France. And, what is worse, they are quoting a popular prophecy saying that France has been lost by an old woman but will be recovered by a young girl. It is a prophecy which is, apparently, widely believed.'

'And when they say 'an old woman' … do they mean …?'

'Your mother, the Queen. After all, it was Isabeau who worked so hard to bring about the Treaty of Troyes. So, yes, I'm afraid they do mean Queen Isabeau. And the young girl they talk of is Joan.'

'Joan?'

'La Pucelle. Joan of Arc.'

When Catherine arrived at Hertford a few days later, she could hardly wait to tell Owen that he was to be granted rights of denizenship. He received the news in silence.

'But, aren't you pleased, Owen?' she asked, puzzled.

Owen sighed. 'Yes, of course I'm pleased,' he said as he took her arm and led her towards a cushioned seat in the window embrasure. 'Just think, now that I have the same rights as an Englishman, I could marry an English woman if I wanted to.'

'But you are married to me!' Catherine was indignant.

Owen put his arms around her and held her close. 'Yes, cariad, and you are the only wife I will ever want,' he assured her. 'But just think, your devoted husband will now be allowed to enter an English town on the Welsh border on any day of the week, not just on market day. And if that border town is Chester, I won't have my head cut off if I'm still there after sunset!'

Catherine's eyes were widening as Owen smiled wryly and shook his head. 'Yes, it's true, Catrin. The English have made some sickening laws for dealing with the Welsh, particularly in the marcher towns. But I will have as many rights as an Englishman now and, yes of course, I'm pleased about that. It's just that they're so damned high-handed about these things, so condescending. I wonder what Ednyfed Fychan would have said about their so-called generosity ... or my grandfather, Tudur ap Goronwy. I am a descendant of princes, after all.'

'Ah, but Welsh princes,' said Catherine. 'That doesn't impress the English.'

'Well, it should,' said Owen, 'they were all great men. But let's forget that now. The most important thing is that you are here with me and we're together again. So tell me, what else did Cardinal Beaufort have to say for himself?'

He listened to her tirade about La Pucelle with his head on one side and a quizzical look on his face. He didn't appear to feel any particular indignation about the girl. That, too, surprised her.

'But she is a charlatan, Owen, she must be!'

'What makes you so sure of that?'

'She says she hears voices, she communes with the saints, she ... she wears a man's clothes!'

'You can't lead soldiers into battle wearing a gown,' said Owen mildly.

'Yes, but Owen, she says that she will save Orléans and that she will see Charles crowned in the cathedral at Rheims. She claims to be able to foretell the future.'

'There are those who can. Don't question it. They are able to interpret things which are beyond our understanding. Perhaps there's no more than that to this little French girl.'

'Little French girl? Owen, she's a monster!'

'Cariad, let's wait and see what happens. Until you've had this baby there is absolutely nothing we can do about it anyway. So let's wait and see.'

'The baby isn't due until November,' said Catherine. 'Anything can happen between now and then.'

They lived quietly in Hertford throughout that summer like country gentlefolk, their days following a pleasing, undemanding pattern. They took every opportunity to be together, being looked after by Les Trois Jo-jo and a small domestic staff who were more like family members than servants. Catherine sat in the shade and grew plump as a partridge while Owen tried his best to keep the bad news from France away from her. From time to time, a horseman would arrive with a message for Her Majesty and Owen always felt a little apprehensive as he broke the seal. He didn't often worry Catherine with the contents of the message but this time it was different.

It was particularly hot, even for August, and Catherine was lying on their bed clad only in her shift when Owen brought her a letter from Cardinal Beaufort. He couldn't keep this one from her, the news was much too important. She lay there, trying to cool her face with a fan while Owen read aloud to her, his anxiety increasing with every word.

Your Royal Highness, my dear niece,

I write in haste on the eve of my departure for France, a visit made necessary by the continuing success of 'La Pucelle' in battle. By now she has raised the English siege on the town of Orléans and her campaign upon the Loire has culminated in a series of successes, most notably a great victory at Patay where her forces defeated our English army under Sir John Fastolf.

I have to inform you that she then saw your brother Charles crowned in the cathedral at Rheims in July ...

'What? What?' Catherine sat bolt upright. 'Owen, read that again ... He can't be saying that Charles has been crowned King of France!'

'He is saying exactly that,' Owen said grimly and started reading again. 'Where was I? Oh, yes ...'

... she then saw your brother Charles crowned in the cathedral at Rheims in July and the people of France rejoice in this as the fulfilment of the ancient prophecy which I spoke of when we last met. Of course, under the terms of the Treaty of Troyes, your brother the Dauphin has no claim to the throne of France so it is now imperative that your son, by the grace of God His Highness King Henry of England, should take his rightful place upon the French throne at the earliest opportunity. This must be preceded by his English coronation and preparations are already in hand for this, though no date has yet been set. However, I entreat you to hold yourself in readiness for it. I earnestly look forward to your company in the abbey church at Westminster on what will be, I'm sure, a very great occasion in the sight of God.

Catherine listened, aghast, as Owen finished reading the letter. Her mind was racing. Her brother Charles had been crowned King of France, effectively usurping her own son.

'This puts you in a very difficult position, Catrin,' Owen said, frowning.

'Difficult? Impossible! Should I go back to France as the King's sister? Or stay here as the King's mother? Owen? Owen, for God's sake, what am I to do?'

'You can do nothing for the moment, cariad. You are six months pregnant and you're not going anywhere. Certainly not until after the baby is born. Do you want to endanger your health? Do you want the world to know about us?'

Catherine slumped back onto the bed. She had thought herself quite safe here in Hertford Castle, relaxed in the knowledge that her baby would be born before November and that everything would be back to normal by Christmas. But now she would be expected to return to court in time for the coronation so her world was torn apart by doubt and uncertainty. Now she demanded to see every message that arrived, frantic to know when the coronation would take place.

Towards the end of September, the expected message was delivered. She was summoned to attend the coronation of her son, King Henry VI of England. It was to take place in the abbey church at Westminster on St Leonard's Day, Sunday the sixth of November.

Owen was desperately worried. The services of a midwife had been engaged and Catherine should have commenced her period of lying-in before the birth but, tense as a bow string, she would not take to her bed. She spent her time writing letters, including one to the King, pleading ill-health but telling him that he could rely on his mother to attend his coronation unless her illness worsened. She was deliberately vague about the nature of that illness. Then there were letters to Cardinal Beaufort, the Duke of Gloucester, and the Earl of Warwick to assure them that she would do her best to be present in Westminster on the sixth of November, if her physician would allow it.

She was on the horns of a dilemma. On the one hand, she needed a reason for her possible absence from the coronation if, indeed, she was unable to attend it. On the other hand, she didn't want it to look as though she was making excuses for her inability to attend, in case that was seen as loyalty to her brother and the throne of France.

However much she wanted to be in London, Catherine knew that there was nowhere safe to stay. Windsor Castle and the Palace of Westminster were denied her in her advanced stage of pregnancy. Owen suggested that they should travel as far as St Albans, just a day's journey from London, where they could stay until the child was born and Catherine was well enough to travel. The Benedictine monks at the monastery were skilled in the use of herbs if there were any problems and there were plenty of inns in the town, a popular destination for pilgrims. If they, too, were to dress as pilgrims, they could travel incognito.

Catherine leaped at the idea of wearing a disguise but she wanted to avoid St Albans at all costs, knowing that the powerful Abbot Whethamstede was a close friend of Humphrey's. They couldn't take that risk. She wanted to get as near Westminster as possible so that if the baby still hadn't arrived by St Leonard's Day then, in their pilgrim disguises, they would be able to lose themselves among the crowds and catch a glimpse of Henry as he passed on his way to the abbey for his coronation. She would at least be able to see her son, even if he was unaware of her presence.

It all began as something of an adventure. Dressed as inconspicuously as possible, Catherine and Owen left Hertford Castle with just four guards, the midwife, Margery Wagstaff, and Les Trois Jo-jo. Their plan was that the little cavalcade would split into three groups as they neared London, one going to Windsor where Joanna Courcy was to say that the Queen had journeyed to Westminster and the other going directly to Westminster where Joanna Belknap was to say that the Queen was too ill to attend the coronation and had travelled to Windsor. Only Joanna Troutbeck and the midwife, Margery Wagstaff would remain with Catherine and Owen. They were taking a tremendous risk.

Their few belongings were loaded onto a cart and the Queen travelled in a curtained, horse-drawn litter while those attending her were on horseback. Everything went according to plan. With the town walls of London in sight, the procession slowed to a halt and Catherine and Owen, with Margery Wagstaff and Joanna Troutbeck, disappeared into a roadside inn, emerging a short time later dressed in pilgrims' clothing. From now on, they would move innocently along the road with Catherine riding side-saddle on a placid, elderly mare being led by Owen.

To Margery Wagstaff's way of thinking, Her Highness should be in her bed like any sensible woman and not dressed up in disguise and running about the countryside. She looked askance at the rest of the little pilgrim group with their broad-brimmed hats and commodious russet-coloured gowns. All except Catherine wore them pulled in and secured around the waist either with a girdle or a rosary. She wore hers loose and carried her rosary separately. She had slipped her wedding ring onto her finger. Those who were on foot carried stout walking sticks and they all had pilgrims' scrips across their shoulders.

'I can't imagine what I must look like in these clothes,' said Catherine in a quiet voice, trying to find a comfortable position in the saddle.

'You are beauty's self when you're wearing nothing at all,' said Owen, smiling back at her, 'but that's for me to know and no one else! Come, Catrin, the most charming thing you ever wear is a smile. So, cheer up! It's not far to go now.'

The small party claimed the right of pilgrims to stay at the monastery of the Carmelite Whitefriars for the remainder of that week and the morning of the coronation dawned bright and warm for the time of year. With still no sign of the baby, Catherine and Owen felt confident enough to undertake the short journey to Westminster and join the huge crowds which were gathering outside the abbey church. Joanna Troutbeck and Margery Wagstaff trudged along behind them and Catherine was again riding side-saddle with Owen walking alongside, leading her horse by the bridle.

Abbot Richard Harweden caught sight of them as they passed below the window where he was sitting in the Benedictine monastery. He was resting the badly wrenched ankle which was keeping him away from the coronation ceremony. To him, the pilgrim group looked like the Holy Family approaching the inn at Bethlehem: the little mare carrying the pregnant woman was scarcely bigger than a donkey, the man leading it was as dark-haired as any Nazarene, and the woman had the face of a Madonna. He was intrigued.

In front of the high altar inside the abbey church, Archbishop Henry Chichele solemnly anointed the King with consecrated oil from a stone ampulla contained within a receptacle shaped like a golden eagle, making the sign of the cross several times, over Henry's head and shoulders, his back, his elbows and the palms of his hands. Henry did his best to sit up straight as the heavy crown of St Edward was placed on his head but he was grateful for the comforting hand of his great-uncle Cardinal Beaufort on the nape of his neck, just in case.

Outside, his mother was frantic with anxiety for him. He wouldn't be eight years old for another month and she had seen the crown and felt its weight. She was sure it would be too much for her little boy.

At last, the coronation ceremony came to an end and the great west door of the abbey church was thrown open. Two buglers stepped forward to sound a fanfare heralding the newly crowned King's approach and Catherine's startled horse suddenly threw up its head in alarm, taking a few nervous steps sideways until Owen got it back under control. Feeling a sudden, stabbing pain, Catherine gritted her teeth and said nothing. If it was the baby, then it might be several hours before she needed to worry too much and she was desperate to see her first-born as he emerged from the abbey church.

Then, to the noisy delight of the waiting crowd, Henry appeared at the top of the abbey steps with his uncle the Duke of Gloucester, his great-uncle Cardinal Beaufort, his guardian and tutor the Earl of Warwick, and Archbishop Henry Chichele. They stood together under a baldaquin of blue silk held aloft by four gentlemen-at-arms in ceremonial livery, acknowledging the roaring welcome they were being given.

Henry looked bewildered and so very small and vulnerable with the great crown of St Edward wobbling uncomfortably on his head that Catherine thought her heart would break. She should be there with him. With tears streaming down her face, she waved and called to him as loudly as anyone but he would never have recognised any member of the pilgrim group, even if he had been able to pick them out in the huge crowd. The Duke of Gloucester waved once more, then began to usher the King and his entourage towards Westminster Hall and the coronation banquet.

Owen felt a tug at his sleeve and turned quickly, wary of cutpurses. There, dressed in the black habit of the Order of St

Benedict, stood a monk from the monastery of Westminster. He reached up to Owen's ear, to make himself heard. Owen listened and nodded, smiling. 'Come,' he said to Catherine as he tried to manoeuvre her horse through the crowd, 'there isn't much more to be seen and we are being offered the traditional hospitality of the Benedictines.'

The familiar scents of beeswax and incense worked a soothing magic on Catherine as she and Owen, with Joanna Troutbeck and Margery Wagstaff, were ushered into the monastery. Suddenly, all was cool and quiet where there had been heat and noise. The boisterous shouting of the crowd had given way to the distant sounds of monks at their devotions. Leaning heavily on a stick as he waited to welcome them, Abbot Richard Harweden was even more intrigued by the pilgrims now that they were at close quarters. He almost felt as though he knew the woman; perhaps she looked like some painting or icon he'd seen somewhere in the past.

Wary of using their proper names, Owen made the introductions. They were, he said, just members of a group of simple pilgrim worshippers who, now that they had witnessed some of the excitement of the coronation, were planning to travel to Canterbury.

'Then you must rest first,' said the Abbot, 'and take some refreshment. Brother Wilfred will show you to the refectory.' He was looking thoughtful as they thanked him and followed Brother Wilfred out of the room.

Babies always arrive in their own sweet time, whether or not this is convenient for their mothers, and this was certainly true of Thomas Owen Tudor. He chose to make his presence felt as Catherine sat with the others at a long table in the refectory, causing her to bend double in pain. Margery Wagstaff immediately took charge of the situation by having her moved to a small room near the monastery's infirmary. The infirmarian was keen to help in any way he could and prescribed mugwort to be bound to the pilgrim mother's left thigh. Margery humoured him but respectfully shooed him out of the room when Catherine's contractions became more frequent. As soon as the monk had left, Margery removed the mugwort. She always suspected it of causing a patient to haemorrhage.

'What do men know about it!' she said contemptuously, throwing the mugwort onto the fire.

'Of course,' Catherine panted between contractions, 'they have something here which would help me very much and something which I could have demanded from them at one time.'

'And what might that be, my Lady?'

'The girdle of the Virgin Mary. It is kept here in the monastery but only allowed out for royal births. That's no good to me now, of course. I daren't let them find out who I am.'

'Then we'll have to do our best without it, my Lady,' said Margery.

'It won't be the first time,' said the Queen, managing a wry smile.

Catherine's baby was born later that evening, leaving her feeling drained. It hadn't been a particularly difficult birth but she was exhausted by the tension of the last few weeks, by the journey from Hertford, and by the emotional strain of having to watch Henry from a distance. She was fast asleep when Margery Wagstaff went to find Owen.

'You have a son, Master Tudor,' she said. 'And your wife is sleeping. I would be obliged if you didn't wake her.'

Owen wanted to hug the woman, despite her rather forbidding demeanour. He would have wanted to hug anyone who was anywhere near him, he was so overjoyed. Then he saw the expression on the midwife's face and she spoke before he could frame the question he knew he must ask.

'He's a handsome babe,' she said 'and contented enough. But he has a club foot. He won't be able to lead a normal life. It doesn't worry him now but it will trouble him later on when he starts walking and he will never be able to run and play like other boys.'

The most difficult thing Owen Tudor had ever had to do in his life was break the news to his wife of their beautiful baby boy's disability and explain to her that it would worsen as he grew, affecting his ability to walk. At first, she refused to believe him but Margery Wagstaff gently explained to her that though the twisted foot didn't look too bad at the moment, once the little boy started growing, he would only ever be able to move about on crutches.

Once she realised the implications of what she was being told, Catherine gave vent to her distress. It was bad enough, she wept, that she and Owen had to behave like fugitives but at least they stood a chance of staying one step ahead of their persecutors. The little one could never do that, not if he couldn't even walk unaided.

What was wrong with her? Had she offended God in some way? Why could she not have a husband and children like any other woman? She had looked forward so much to this baby and been so glad to be able to give Owen a son. But what good was a son to him if the child had to be looked after constantly and carried everywhere? A man needed a son he could rely on, not an invalid he had to care for.

Catherine was inconsolable.

Abbot Harweden's painful ankle gave him good reason to keep his distance from the pilgrims but they continued to puzzle him and Brother Geoffrey, the infirmarian, had told him that the woman had become hysterical in her grief at giving birth to a disabled child. He still had a strong feeling that somehow he knew her, but who *was* she? *What* was she? The Abbot suspected that the pilgrims were not exactly as they appeared to be and he had the reputation of the monastery to consider. One couldn't be too careful. Still, he had to shoulder some of the blame for the situation since he'd been burning with curiosity about the woman. He shouldn't have been so inquisitive. Perhaps he should not have invited the pilgrims to avail themselves of the monastery's hospitality if the woman was quite so close to her time but had he not done so, he would have been guilty of disobeying the rules of St Benedict. The situation was very difficult. The more Abbot Harweden thought about it, the more he realised that he must talk to the woman's husband. He ordered that Owen should be summoned to a meeting in the chapter-house the following morning.

'Forgive me for not rising to greet you,' he began as Owen was shown into the room, 'but my wretched foot is still rather painful and I try to keep the weight off it. Now, tell me, how is your goodwife feeling today?'

'My wife is asleep,' said Owen. 'I'm afraid the birth of our son was not without its problems and she has exhausted herself with weeping. She is very upset.'

'It's quite understandable,' said the Abbot. 'Brother Geoffrey tells me that the child has a disability and is likely to become halt as he grows up. Is that so?'

'Sadly, yes. At least, that is what the midwife says, though the child doesn't seem at all distressed at the moment.'

'No, but he will find things difficult as he begins to grow.' Abbot Harweden gestured towards his own bandaged foot, resting on a low stool in front of his chair. 'My current indisposition makes me doubly sympathetic towards those whose feet trouble them.' Owen gave a wan smile before the Abbot continued. 'Of course, as Benedictines, we will do our best to help. After all, we have taken a vow not only to shelter pilgrim travellers but also to heal the sick where we can. In fact, I have a particular interest in the disability which affects your child. He has a club foot, has he not?'

'Yes,' said Owen, 'he has and I don't know what's to be done about it. Though perhaps, Father Abbot, with your experience of healing, you could suggest something to help him? That would be of great comfort to my wife.'

'As it happens, we had a foundling here some five years ago who had the same disability. Of course, it is not possible to cure the condition but I have a theory that if the baby's leg can be artificially straightened during the period of initial growth, it can help considerably. In fact, I had some success with that foundling child by restricting his leg in a wooden frame and, indeed, he seemed not nearly so halt as he might have been.'

Owen brightened considerably. 'Could you, perhaps, do the same for my son?' he asked.

'I could certainly try,' said the Abbot. 'Of course, he will always have to use crutches to aid his walking and will need sedentary employment when he grows up. And if you were to leave him here in order for me to supervise his treatment there would, of course, be the small matter of a contribution towards his care and his keep.'

'There will be no difficulty with that,' said Owen, 'but the situation is not exactly straightforward.' He paused for a moment as he came to a decision. 'Tell me, Father Abbot, are you a man who is able to keep a secret and divulge it to no one? On your honour as a man of God? It is a very important secret.'

There was nothing for it; Owen had to confide in the Abbot and had the situation not been quite so grave, he would have laughed at the expression of amazement on the Abbot's face when he was told the identity of the woman who had so recently given birth in the monastery's infirmary.

When he'd got over his initial shock, Richard Harweden was pleased that he hadn't been mistaken in recognising Her Royal Highness the Queen, knowing that he knew her from somewhere other than a half-remembered painting. He thought her a lot less like the Madonna now and more like Our Lady of the Sorrows but knowing who she was altered his assessment of the situation considerably. He was aware that being embroiled in this amount of subterfuge could have a seriously damaging effect both on himself and on the monastery if the wrong people got to know about it. But when he was told that Cardinal Beaufort was fully aware of the Queen's rather irregular domestic situation, he realised that kindness towards the pilgrim mother might be of great benefit after all.

At heart a compassionate man, Abbot Harweden pointed out to Catherine and Owen a few days later that the baby would never be able to live a normal life at court or anywhere else and that, in their circumstances, they would have the greatest difficulty in giving him a successful upbringing. He gently suggested that the baby should be taken into the care of the monks, as though he had been a foundling. This would guarantee him both a good education and the best possible treatment for his disability.

So it was arranged that young Thomas Owen Tudor would be brought up as a Benedictine and taught to read and write. Only Abbot Harweden would ever know that the Queen had promised the monastery a generous endowment towards his keep. In due course, even if he chose not to become a monk, the young man could be employed copying manuscripts in the scriptorium at the Abbey, where there would be little need for him to put weight on his deformed foot.

Everyone agreed that this was the best plan for the baby and Owen finally managed to convince Catherine of the good sense of it by reminding her of her own upbringing in the convent at Poissy and the unstinting love of Sister Supplice.

Nevertheless, when the time came, it took all his mother's strength and courage to walk away from her third child.

Chapter Twenty-one

London, 1430

Things changed after the coronation. Now that the King was exclusively under the tutelage of the Earl of Warwick, Humphrey's position had altered slightly and Catherine feared that, with more time on his hands, he would find another outlet for his energies, one that could spell trouble.

She felt she had good reason to worry. It was well over a year since Pope Martin V had finally declared Humphrey's marriage to Jacqueline unlawful and therefore invalid, which meant that Humphrey had been free to marry his mistress Eleanor Cobham and had done so, almost immediately. That in turn meant that the Cobham woman was now entitled to call herself the Duchess of Gloucester and had given herself such airs and graces that Catherine could hardly bear to be in the same room.

Those who had been fond of Jacqueline considered the marriage doomed from the outset. The gossips whispered that Eleanor had regularly used the services of the witch Margery Jourdemayne to supply her with potions and perfumes to attract the Duke. It could only end in sorrow, they said, but Eleanor had achieved her goal. The only thing that would have made the new Duchess of Gloucester even more triumphant would be the birth of a child but Margery Jourdemayne had failed her in that. Nevertheless, Eleanor was as beautiful and intelligent as Humphrey was cultivated and debonair and they were an impressive couple. They both loved music and dancing, poetry and parties and Humphrey had undertaken the conversion of a manor house at Greenwich into a pleasure garden which he and Eleanor called *La Pleasaunce*. Here they entertained musicians, scholars, poets, physicians, philosophers, and writers from all over the world. It was an adult, sophisticated alternative court, away from the child King's household at Windsor.

Catherine never craved an invitation to *La Pleasaunce* and the fact that the Gloucesters spent so much time there meant that she had some respite from her constant worries about keeping her marriage a secret from Humphrey. In any case, she would much rather remain at Windsor, where at least she had a chance to see Henry occasionally despite the fact that the boy was subjected to a relentless regime of education and training for kingship.

Now that the King's English coronation had taken place, planning had begun for his French coronation though no date had yet been set for this. Nevertheless, a large and costly royal entourage of over three hundred people left for Calais on St George's Day in April in preparation for the occasion. Catherine did not travel with them.

There was a good reason for her reluctance to visit France. Owen could hardly believe her when she told him. 'Not again!' he protested, though he felt a small thrill of pride that he was so easily able to get her with child.

Catherine couldn't pretend that she wasn't worried about expecting yet another baby but, seeing the expression of joy on Owen's face, she had no wish to dampen his delight. He seemed to thrive on the prospect of fatherhood.

'There's nothing for it, Owen, but to stop sleeping in the same bed,' she said sternly.

'It's not the sleeping that's causing it, my sweet, it's what we do when we're awake that's the problem.'

'That doesn't strike me as a good enough reason to stop doing it,' she said and kissed him.

'Then you can only expect to go on producing babies for the rest of your life, my Lady.' Owen wagged his finger at her in mock severity before taking her into his arms. 'And this time, cariad, I will move heaven and earth for you to keep the child. It doesn't matter what it takes.' Then he held her at arm's length and looked at her with a questioning twinkle in his eye. 'And where would your naughty Highness like to spend the summer this time, eh?'

She couldn't help but smile. He would sometimes call her by that silly name when he was teasing her, teasing her until she begged him to bring her to the pinnacle of her pleasure.

'I don't really mind,' she said, 'as long as I can get the news from France. We'll need to be somewhere near London, so that I can keep up with what's going on.'

Most of Catherine's dower properties were a good distance from London, too far for messengers to travel with ease, so the choice was a difficult one. It was quite by chance that they hit on the best solution.

Owen had been invited to St Paul's, where Bishop William Gray had agreed to christen Maredydd and Emma's first baby, a girl named Margaret, after Maredydd's mother. Maredydd could hardly contain his excitement but Emma, not yet churched, was not present, and neither was Catherine who was nervous about being associated with Owen on an occasion like this. But she joined him afterwards at the small, private reception in Maredydd and Emma's new home near St Paul's Cross where, naturally, the talk was all of babies. They laughed about the lack of choice when it came to naming little girls, since both Owen's mother and Maredydd's mother had been called Margaret. Then, in the company of trusted friends, Owen let slip the fact that there might soon be yet another Margaret in the family, though he was deeply worried about where Catherine could give birth to her coming child without raising suspicion. That was when Bishop William Gray made a suggestion.

'The manor house at Great Hadham would suit your purpose very well, Your Highness,' he said to Catherine. 'It is the country home of the Bishops of London and is fully staffed throughout the year. Sadly, I have limited time to spend there but I would be delighted if you and Master Tudor would like to make use of it. All I will tell the staff is that you're my guests: they don't need to know who you are. But, my Lady, won't you be missed at court?'

'No,' said Catherine shortly. 'Most of the court has removed to France for the King's French coronation. And in any case –

forgive me for saying so, Your Grace – no one cares where I am as long as I don't get under anyone's feet. I will not be missed.'

Great Hadham was less than two days' journey from London, some thirty miles to the north east, beyond Epping Forest, at a sufficient distance from London to discourage casual visitors but close enough for Owen to attend the Royal Wardrobe if he was required to. The house, on a bend in the River Ash, was modest but comfortable and Catherine and Owen were both delighted with it. Bishop Gray accompanied them on the journey there, anxious to see them settled in comfortably.

It seemed a good place for a child to grow up and, determined not to be forced to abandon yet another baby, Catherine and Owen planned their strategy carefully. From now on, the family would base themselves at Great Hadham and, from time to time, Catherine would put in a token appearance at court. In her absence, the child could be safely left in the care of the Bishop's staff and two reliable nurses.

News from France filtered through sporadically. Henry's coronation was repeatedly postponed and the cost of maintaining the royal retinue, as well as an army of over a thousand men-at-arms and nearly six thousand archers, was spiralling almost out of control. Then news came that Joan of Arc had been taken prisoner by the forces of Philip of Burgundy who promptly sold her to the English. Not knowing what to do with her and wary of her reputation, her English jailers chained her up in a cage like an animal. The Dauphin did not lift a finger to help her.

'I can't understand that,' said Owen. 'Your brother Charles owes that girl everything. Why does he just sit back and let her be punished?'

'Well, think about it, Owen. If Charles really is being accepted as King of France, he doesn't want his people to think that he owes his throne to Joan of Arc's diabolical skills.'

'And what happens when young Henry is crowned King of France?'

'God alone knows. I have no idea. And until this baby is

born, I have no option but to lie low and wait to see where the future lies, whether my son or my brother is eventually recognised as King of France. And as for La Pucelle, well, it seems she is a witch and a heretic. She can't be sent to a convent because no convent will ever accept her. There's only one alternative, and that's burning.'

'Oh, Catrin,' Owen shook his head. 'She's probably just a poor, misguided young woman.' What Catherine had predicted was probably exactly what would happen but clearly she didn't associate the fate of the Maid of Orléans with what had happened so tragically to her own maid. Owen would never forget the terror on Guillemote's face as the wooden staircase collapsed. Being burned to death was an obscenity, whether it happened by accident or design.

They made excited plans as they whiled away the chilly spring evenings at Great Hadham, lounging on the hearth in front of the fire discussing whether to name the coming baby after their parents.

'I'm not sure I like the name Isabeau for a little girl,' said Owen. 'I'd much prefer Marged.'

'But if we named her after your mother, we'd use the English version of the name and call her Margaret, wouldn't we?'

'What if she's a boy?'

'Well, we've already had one of each, so she could be … or he could be. I don't know. My father was Charles but the most common name in the Valois family has always been Louis.'

'If we're going for family names,' said Owen, 'we could call him Ednyfed. Or perhaps Caradog. Lovely old Welsh names.'

'But the poor child is going to live in England so he won't thank us for giving him a name like Cad … Crad … what did you say?'

'Caradog. Caractacus in English.'

'Well, we are certainly not going to call him Caractacus!' Catherine laughed. 'Listen, Owen, I've been thinking. We have every reason to be grateful to young Edmund Beaufort, haven't we? After all, we've spent years putting Humphrey off the scent by letting him think that Edmund is nursing a grand passion for me.'

'Well, he certainly was at one time.' Owen was punctuating his sentences with little kisses on the soft skin at the nape of her neck. 'Perhaps he still is. And you have to admit that he has excellent taste in women!'

Catherine made as though to push him away. 'No, seriously, my love, we owe him a favour, don't you think? So, all right, if the baby is a girl we'll call her Margaret but if it's a boy, why don't we name him Edmund? It's a perfectly good name and the reason for giving him that name will be our secret.'

Owen smiled, kissing her nose this time. 'Why not?' he said. 'You're right, cariad, it's an excellent name.'

Edmund Tudor first saw the light of day three months later. He was the bonniest of babies and both his parents doted on him from the moment of his birth. Catherine was never happier than when she had him in her arms and Owen was never happier than when he had his arms around both of them.

At last, thank God, this was the baby they would keep: and they would keep him at all costs.

They spent the remainder of the year at Great Hadham, contentedly learning to live as a family, and it was the most profound pleasure Catherine had ever known. She and Owen delighted more than ever in each other's company and now there was another dimension to their happiness. They both doted on their baby son. Catherine even began to let herself dare hope that they might send for their daughter, Tacinda, but Owen had to point out to her that, if they did, the little girl would be confused and bewildered. She didn't know them, she had never known them. For her sake, it was far better she should remain with the Stradling family in St Donat's.

All too soon, it was time for Catherine to return to Windsor. She couldn't absent herself for too long, it would only arouse suspicion. She would return for a few weeks, just to make her presence felt and dispel any possible gossip.

With the King and so many courtiers in France, life in Windsor was as dull as ditchwater so when word came that

Cardinal Beaufort was in England and intending to visit the castle, the whole place went into a frenzy of preparation. Floors were swept, tapestries cleaned, and mouth-watering smells wafted from the kitchen.

Almost as soon as he arrived, Cardinal Beaufort went in search of Catherine, delighted to learn that she, too, was in Windsor. It always gave him immense pleasure to see her and he was glad to find her looking so happy. He was not a bit surprised to learn that she'd had another baby and chuckled when she told him why he'd been named Edmund after his nephew.

'A brother for little Tacinda,' he said, smiling broadly.

'Yes,' said Catherine, 'and a little half-brother for the King, too, though I don't know whether they'll ever meet.' She said nothing about the child she'd had to leave in the care of Abbot Harweden at Westminster because she didn't know whether the Cardinal was aware of the nature of the 'illness' which had kept her away from her son's English coronation and she saw no reason to tell him. Besides, the memory was still too raw and painful for discussion. She changed the subject.

'Tell me, what news of my son, the King? And why have you returned to England, my Lord Uncle?'

'His Highness is well, my Lady, and sends you his most respectful greetings. He is still in Rouen but there is no prospect of a French coronation at the moment. As for me, well, I am back in England with my begging bowl, to raise yet more money. I have to persuade the Council to provide sufficient funds for another army. We need some two and a half thousand men to recapture Rheims. It has been in French hands since your brother's coronation. But first we have to resolve the problem of the heretic girl.'

'La Pucelle?'

'Yes, the Maid. Joan of Arc. She remains in prison and I'm afraid she's become something of a heroine to the French, a symbol of national pride, and it would be madness to put her to death without a very good reason. Still, until that is done, I see no prospect of crowning your son. I confess I don't look forward to it but I'm afraid she will burn.'

Owen kept quiet on the subject of Joan of Arc because he didn't want to worry Catherine more than he had to. She was deeply concerned about the situation in France. Owen could accept that Joan was a simple peasant with a deep faith and an absolute belief in what her 'voices' told her, though Catherine, torn between her love for her son and a lingering loyalty to her family in France, was not so sure. Well, blood was thicker than water, thought Owen, but perhaps the saints really did talk to Joan. Who had the right to say they didn't? He knew of people not unlike her in Wales, people who lived in harmony with the rhythms of Nature. Was this girl any more than that? And if her convictions were religious, then it was only another way of looking at things.

Above all, he understood Joan's patriotism, the strength of her desire to see a French king on the throne of France and the English invaders retreat from her beloved homeland. Every Welshman understood that, particularly a kinsman of Owain Glyndŵr.

At the head of an army only half the size of the one he'd requested, Henry Beaufort returned to France in time to see Joan of Arc accused of heresy. He presided at her trial in Rouen and found the proceedings deeply interesting from the standpoint of theological argument. The Maid couldn't be guided by heavenly voices, her accusers reasoned, because it was a well-known fact that the saints spoke only to priests and then only in Latin, certainly not in the rough patois of Domrémy, Joan's home village. Yet this simple country girl seemed possessed of a powerful intellect. When asked if she presumed herself to be in God's grace, she answered that if she was not, then she prayed that God would put her there and that if she was, then she prayed that God would so keep her. It was the most elegant of replies and astounded her accusers but it didn't stop them from lying to her. They promised that she could attend confession if she would agree to wear women's clothing but, when she did, they refused to let her go to church. Sick and exhausted by months of imprisonment, Joan's last small gesture of disobedience was to put on men's clothing once more and, for this, she was accused of immodesty and

302

defiance of the teachings of the church. She was sentenced to die at the stake on the thirtieth of May.

Beaufort's mind was in turmoil. He had genuinely admired the way in which the nineteen-year-old Maid had conducted herself at her trial, with her simple grace and quiet conviction that she was being given divine guidance. Now, watching her slight body being lashed to the stake in the market square at Rouen, he felt a different, very powerful emotion. With half-closed eyes he saw the huge bonfire being lit and resisted the urge to stuff his fingers in his ears so as not to hear the crackle of dry wood as the flames took hold. It was difficult to ignore the baying of the huge crowd that had gathered to watch the burning. He tried not to look directly at Joan as she stood with a cross held between her outstretched hands, her lips moving in prayer. He knew he would never forget the sight of her and he would remember the stench of burning human flesh for the rest of his life.

Six months after Joan's death, Henry Beaufort held the crown of France above the head of his great-nephew in the cathedral of Notre Dame in Paris. It was the sixteenth of December, just ten days after the King's tenth birthday. Beaufort should have felt elation, pride, supreme happiness; this was the ultimate achievement, this was the crown of France which he was placing on Henry's head, the height of his late father's ambition. And yet all Beaufort felt was a hollow emptiness. He was getting very old now, nearer sixty than fifty, and he realised that England had been at war with France throughout his lifetime and that this, this very crown which he now held in his hands, was what all the fighting had been about. All he could think of was the appalling waste, the lives lost, the bodies maimed, the families ruined, the children left fatherless and a brave young woman burned at the stake. Henry looked up as the crown was placed on his head and was surprised to see tears in the Cardinal's eyes. The boy assumed that they were tears of joy.

Huge crowds of people thronged the streets of Paris, singing and dancing; wine ran in the fountains and there were pageants and *tableaux vivants* everywhere. The Duke of Bedford with the

Earls of Warwick and Salisbury were at the head of the large delegation of English aristocrats who had come to France with Henry in preparation for this great day and all the lords of the royal house of France were represented, with the exception of the Duke of Burgundy. He nowhere to be seen and neither was Catherine's brother, Charles.

The obese, ageing Queen Isabeau sat in the royal palace of St Pol, stroking a lapdog and waving as the coronation procession passed her window, trying to catch the eye of her grandson who was the embodiment of the union with England which she had worked so hard to bring about. She wondered why his mother was not with him.

Entirely unaware of what was happening in Paris, Catherine had no desire to be anywhere other than Great Hadham. She was happy here, comfortable, relaxed and, above all, secure. Here she could be with her husband and her baby son and had almost convinced herself that this would be where her little family would spend the rest of their lives. They had few visitors but, occasionally, trusted friends would come to see them, friends like Bishop William Gray who was travelling from London to Lincoln and broke his journey to call on them. He strode into the hall to be greeted by Owen, who had seen him arrive.

'Your Grace. I find it very strange to be welcoming you into your own house!'

'My own house no longer, Master Tudor. That is why I'm here. I have something to tell you. Is Her Highness at home? And is she well?'

'Well enough, if a little tired. She has gone to fetch baby Edmund so that she can show him off to you.'

'I shall be delighted to see him. Is he walking yet?'

'No, not quite, but he gets around very quickly on all fours!'

'Just you wait, you won't be able to keep up with him before long,' said the Bishop. 'Your Royal Highness, what a pleasure to see you!'

Catherine, baby Edmund on her hip, had come into the room, delighted to see Bishop William Gray and eager for his news. 'To what do we owe the pleasure of this visit, your

Grace?' she asked as he bowed low to greet her.

He straightened up, looking suddenly doubtful. 'I … I'm not sure that you will see it as a pleasure, your Highness, but for me it is a very exciting prospect. I am being moved to Lincoln. A great honour …so many opportunities.'

'Congratulations are in order then, Your Grace,' said Owen.

'Indeed, thank you, Master Tudor. I must confess I'm very thrilled. But it does, of course, mean that I will no longer have any right to this house. It is not my personal property, it belongs to the church, so I will have to relinquish it. That is why I wanted to see you.'

'Does that mean …?' Catherine didn't finish her sentence.

'I'm afraid, Ma'am, it does mean that, personally, I will no longer be in a position to offer you hospitality and security here in Great Hadham. Robert Fitzhugh, my successor will, I'm sure, be honoured if you should want to stay here, but that all rather depends on whether you want him to know of your circumstances. It is entirely up to you.'

Baby Edmund chose that moment to exercise his lungs, wanting to be the centre of attention. He let out a long, piercing wail, causing his father and the Bishop to smile indulgently and disguising the fact that his mother wanted to wail just as loudly herself. She couldn't bear the thought of leaving Great Hadham, she had never been so happy in all her life as she had been here. Now her happiness was being threatened yet again. She couldn't face the upheaval of another move, hounded from place to place, never settled, never at peace. She couldn't go back to Windsor and run the risk of Humphrey or Eleanor finding out about baby Edmund, and she was certainly not going to give him up. Owen caught sight of her face just as she began to bite her quivering lip.

'You mustn't worry, Catrin,' he said quietly, putting his arm around her shoulder. 'We'll find somewhere just as good.'

William Gray was appalled. Thrilled at the prospect of moving to Lincoln, he had not realised the impact his news would have on the little Tudor family. He knew they had been happy at Great Hadham but he hadn't realised quite how much of a blow this would be for them. Catherine, white-faced, was avoiding his gaze.

'I'm so sorry, Your Highness. Please don't upset yourself! I hadn't thought … that is, I'm very glad you've been so happy here … but I didn't realise …'

He was profoundly embarrassed. But he did, at least, have a suggestion to make: it was an idea which had occurred to him on his journey from London.

'Are you acquainted with Bishop Philip Morgan, my Lady?' he asked.

Catherine took a deep breath, shifting the baby's weight onto her other arm. Now that Owen's hand was under her elbow, steadying her, she managed a smile. 'Yes, I do know him slightly. He serves on the Council. Cardinal Beaufort speaks highly of him.'

'Yes, he's the Bishop of Worcester and of Ely. He's a good man, wise and very experienced. When he was younger, he also served as army chaplain to your late husband the King. He was with him in Normandy.'

'Ah, yes,' said Owen. 'I heard my cousin Maredydd speak of him. He, too, served in Normandy with the King. He said he'd more than once heard Bishop Morgan grant absolution in Welsh on the battlefield. So he's now the Bishop of Ely, is he?'

'Indeed he is, Master Tudor. He was Phillip ap Morgan when we knew him at Oxford but he dropped the "ap" part of his name, just as you did. He was studying Civil Law at Queen's College when I was there. And that's where I first met Cardinal Beaufort, of course. De Kyrkeby, too. We all knew each other as young men. I think he might be just the man I need to talk to.'

Catherine, still feeling stunned, wondered where all this was leading but William Gray explained that he knew the opportunity to use another house, much like this one, was within the gift of the Bishop of Ely.

'Hatfield,' he said. 'Bishop's Hatfield. I'll write to Bishop Morgan …'

Since time was not pressing and since he wanted to be absolutely certain that he was doing the right thing, William Gray decided instead to pay a visit to Bishop Morgan. He was sure that, face-to-face, he'd find it easier to explain the reasons for his request and the need for great secrecy. Bishop Morgan, a man of kindness and sensibility, was fascinated to hear of the widowed Queen's romance with a kinsman of the Welsh freedom fighter Owain Glyndŵr. He had once met Catherine but couldn't really claim to know her, though he had known her first husband quite well and had received several royal commissions from him. He also remembered that Henry Beaufort had told him of his avuncular affection for her.

So Bishop Morgan was honoured and delighted to be able to help, which meant that, after Catherine had eventually become resigned to the situation, the move from Great Hadham to Bishop's Hatfield went ahead remarkably smoothly.

'Plain sailing, then,' said Owen, looking around him after they had moved in. 'Guillemote would have been proud of us! Everything is unpacked and in a sensible place.' He put an arm around Catherine's waist and tapped the end of her nose playfully. 'And the place for you, your naughty Highness, is in bed. On your own this time. Go on, cariad. You must be tired.'

Catherine managed a smile. 'I don't want to be on my own, Owen. I don't feel well but I really want to know that you're lying beside me.'

'I'll always be beside you, cariad, wherever we are. You know that.' He was true to his word. They were preparing to sleep in an unfamiliar bed but, for each of them, the sweet familiarity of the other's body worked its usual magic.

This time Owen was extremely worried about her, she looked gaunt and tired and he noticed some streaks of grey at her temples.

'It's too soon, cariad. Little Edmund is not yet a year old. You're wearing yourself out with child-bearing. We must be more careful.' Catherine reached out for him and nuzzled his neck.

'Too late for that! Edmund's little brother is already on his way.'

'His little sister Marged, you mean?' He smiled, teasing her.

'Oh, Owen. If she's a girl, she'll be Marged. Margaret,

307

anyway. I promise you.'

Catherine hadn't really recovered after the move to Bishop's Hatfield and felt profoundly tired. So when the time came, she spent longer lying-in than she had with any of her other children. Les Trois Jo-jo fussed over her and the midwife, Margery Wagstaff, was pleased to point out that this was the proper way for pregnant women to behave, not rushing around the country in fancy dress. She put up with their good-natured scolding, knowing she was in good hands.

The Feast of St John the Baptist came and went and, according to the midwife's reckoning, the baby was overdue. Then, in the second week of July, Catherine went into labour. She, who thought she had inherited her mother's gift for bearing children with ease, now met the excruciatingly painful experience of a breech birth. She remembered Jacqueline's torment and prayed that it wouldn't be like that for her. Thus far, she had avoided the worst consequences of the curse of Eve but now the pain was almost unbearable and she thought it would never end. Oh, for the Virgin's girdle, Our Lord's foreskin, anything, anything to ease the agony. Margery Wagstaff paused before massaging her hands with oil of wild thyme for another attempt to turn the baby. She reached into her apron pocket and pressed a smoothly polished brown-coloured stone into Catherine's hand.

'What is it?' Catherine asked weakly.

'Jasper, my Lady. It will help you. I'm doing everything I can at this end, so just push down when I tell you to and pray to the blessed Saint Margaret. And hold this piece of jasper in your hand. Hold it tight. Jasper is well known to ease the pains of childbirth. I have used it many times. With great success,' she added.

Catherine started screaming then and Owen, who was pacing anxiously up and down in the room below, fell to his knees and prayed as he had never prayed before, for her safety and the safe delivery of her baby. He would be kind to everyone, he would give to the poor, he would listen attentively to the sermon every Sunday, he would be polite to the clergy and forego the pleasures of the ale house. If only she would be safe, he would do anything, give her anything, agree to anything, if only she would be safe. Please, God. Dear God. Please, God.

Then everything went quiet. That was worse. Women often died in childbirth. Please, God. Dear God. Please, God.

Then he heard the most wonderful sound in the world, the indignant squalling of a newborn baby. His baby. His daughter? Marged? Who cared, as long as mother and child were both alive and well.

It seemed an age before Margery Wagstaff appeared at the top of the stairs. She was beaming.

'That was a tough one,' she said, 'but your wife is all right. And so is your son!' Owen took the stairs two at a time and hugged her, catching her off balance and giggling. He didn't care. He didn't trust himself to speak.

Quietly, he opened the door of the bedchamber and looked in to see Catherine lying with her eyes closed, her skin almost as white as the pillow she lay on. The baby, red-faced and wizened, lay sleeping in the crook of her arm. He approached them as quietly as he could, knelt at the side of the bed, and watched them for a long moment. He was overwhelmed. He would never, ever, let Catherine go through that again. She opened one eye.

'That,' she said 'hurt a lot.'

Owen smiled at her. 'It's a boy. We didn't think of a name for a boy.'

'He's called Jasper.' Catherine's voice was weak but determined. 'His name is Jasper Tudor.'

Chapter Twenty-two

France and London, Autumn 1435

Henry Beaufort understood why Pontius Pilate had washed his hands. There comes a point, he thought, at which the wise man must withdraw from a situation over which he no longer has control. True, no one was about to die on the cross, but enough fine young men had died anyway. There had been too much war, too much death. He was tired of it. All he wanted was to live out his old age in the knowledge that France and England were at peace. He wanted to wash his hands of the whole disastrous pantomime which was the Congress of Arras and go home to England.

It had all started so well. Cardinal Beaufort had welcomed the invitation to attend a big diplomatic congress in northern France, the first since the Treaty of Troyes fifteen years earlier and long overdue. It was with high hopes that he had set out for Arras at the head of a distinguished delegation of Englishmen and he was particularly proud that the group included his nephew Edmund. They were all anxious to see a peaceful outcome to the Congress.

Beaufort, as much a diplomat as a clergyman these days, was well aware of the deterioration of the relationship between England and Burgundy. Things had gone from bad to worse, he reflected, in the three years since John of Bedford's wife had died. Anne, the apple of her husband's eye, had been visiting the sick at the Hotel de Bourbon in Paris during an epidemic of the Plague and had herself become a victim of it. John was inconsolable. Not only that but, while Anne was alive, she had held together the uneasy peace between her husband and her brother, Philip. Since her death, their relationship had disintegrated rapidly.

Face to face with the Duke of Burgundy at the negotiating table in Arras, Henry Beaufort invoked the terms of the Treaty of Troyes and insisted that the French must recognise the English King, Henry VI, as King of France and pay due homage to him. The French argued that Henry VI had no valid claim to the French crown, since his father Henry V had died before inheriting it and could not therefore pass it on. Charles VII, they insisted, was now the King of France.

Things had come to an impasse. That's when Henry Beaufort had stormed out of the congress, followed by every Englishman in the room.

With the English delegation gone, Philip of Burgundy and King Charles swiftly agreed to the terms of an entirely new treaty, the Treaty of Arras, under which Charles would acquire all the territory hitherto in the possession of the English. In return, Charles promised retribution for the death of John the Fearless, to pay for masses for his soul and to erect a monument in his memory.

Revenge is a dish best eaten cold and Philip had nurtured a prodigious appetite for it over a long period. He had sworn an oath that he would remain in mourning until his father's murderers were brought to book and he had stayed true to his word. For sixteen years he had worn nothing but unremitting black, ever since the fateful day when John the Fearless was slain on the bridge at Montereau.

Now there appeared to be solutions to all Philip's problems because, in addition to the favourable outcome of the Congress of Arras, he had received a message to say that his erstwhile brother-in-law John of Bedford lay gravely ill at Rouen. If John should die, and with the weak-willed and lazy Charles on the throne, Philip himself would be the most powerful man in France. He would run the country. He began to sense that his moment of glory was near.

For some time after Jasper was born, Catherine remained quite ill and made only a very slow recovery from that difficult birth. She'd been thin and listless with a poor appetite and a hollow, rasping cough that would not respond to any treatment until Owen remembered that his mother had sworn by a remedy which she attributed to the Physicians of Myddfai. He remembered the foul taste of hemp agrimony mixed with boiled milk but it had cured many of his own childhood coughs and colds and now, praise be, it finally seemed to be curing Catherine. Under Owen's watchful eye and with the help of Les Trois Jo-jo, she had built up her strength and now positively revelled in the joys of a happy family life with a loving husband and two lusty little boys, Edmund, who was five, and four-year-old Jasper. Well wrapped up against a slight breeze, she watched them play games of tag and hide-and-seek with their father in the golden October sunshine. It was such a joy to see them racing about the garden on their sturdy little legs, shrieking with pleasure.

She sometimes felt, though, that they were really only half a family. She would have been so very happy to see their big brother Henry helping Edmund to ride a horse, perhaps, or teaching Jasper a new game. And she would have taught them all to be gentle with their sister Tacinda and their disabled brother Thomas. Tacinda was nearly ten years old, she realised with a shock. How she would love to see her little girl. Who did she look like? Did she have reddish-coloured hair like her brothers, or her father's dark curls? Did she enjoy wearing pretty clothes? Had she inherited the Valois nose? Were her eyes still forget-me-not blue? She would dearly love the child of her imagining to have some substance.

Still, she told herself, getting up abruptly from her seat in the shade of the chestnut tree and brushing down her skirt, it didn't do to live in the past and there were many, many women who would be envious of her two healthy young sons. The Cobham woman, for instance: from what Catherine had heard, she still hadn't managed to conceive. She still couldn't bring herself to think of her as the Duchess of Gloucester. That had been Jacqueline's title.

Leaving Owen and the boys to enjoy their games for a little longer, she began to walk back to the house and saw Joanna Troutbeck hobbling towards her. Poor old Troutbeck, she thought, she wasn't getting any younger. She must try to persuade her to take things a little more easily.

'Your Highness, you have a visitor,' Troutbeck panted. 'Cardinal Beaufort is here to see you.'

'My Lord Uncle! I didn't know he was in England. What a surprise! Thank you. Thank you, Troutbeck, I can't wait to see him!'

Standing for a moment to catch her breath, Joanna Troutbeck watched Catherine as she turned and hurried down the path to the house. She didn't think the Queen would be too pleased to hear what the Cardinal had to tell her.

Catherine knew immediately that something was gravely wrong. Henry Beaufort dispensed with the niceties of royal protocol and simply took both her hands in his. 'My dear,' he said. 'I have some very sad news.'

'Who?' she asked flatly.

'My nephew John of Bedford.'

'John? No, surely. He's not dead? He can't be dead!'

'Yes. I'm afraid so. He died last month after a long illness and has been laid to rest in the cathedral at Rouen. It was a magnificent funeral. If that's any comfort to you,' he added, knowing that it probably wouldn't be.

'But … but John's an Englishman. Why wasn't he brought home? Henry was brought home. It wouldn't have been difficult. Why was John buried in France? Was that because his new wife insisted upon it? She should not have been allowed to. They hadn't been married long. He should have been brought home.'

'Hush, Catherine, hush.' Beaufort kept hold of both her hands in an attempt to calm her. He knew that Catherine had never met John's new wife, Jacquetta of Luxembourg, but she must have realised that this second marriage had been undertaken for political reasons. It was not the love match John had known with his first wife.

'It was his wish, Catherine,' he said. 'John knew France as well as he knew England. And you must remember that Anne is buried in France. I'm sure that's the reason why. Perhaps he wanted to feel near his beloved Anne.'

Anne, the solemn, funny cousin who could always make Catherine laugh, and tall, gentle John, who had been so kind to her. She couldn't imagine how her world would be without them. She pulled her hands away from Beaufort's warm grip and covered her face.

Owen hurried in from the garden, summoned by Joanna Troutbeck who knew that his wife would need him. At a glance, he realised the gravity of the situation and crossed the room to take Catherine in his arms. 'Who?' he mouthed at Cardinal Beaufort over her head. 'John of Bedford,' replied the Cardinal in a voice barely above a whisper.

Owen nodded and knew that Catherine would need all the comfort he could offer her but, as she sobbed against his chest, he also realised that this death was much more than a bereavement. It meant that, if anything should happen to Catherine's son Henry, the only remaining royal uncle, Humphrey of Gloucester, would inherit the throne. He couldn't help feeling apprehensive.

Cardinal Beaufort, too, was very aware of the issues involved but for the moment it was enough to sit with Catherine while she listened tearfully to his account of John's funeral. Later, he told them both about the outcome of the Treaty of Arras. Catherine's irresolute, feckless brother was now the King of France and her son's claim to the French throne was utterly repudiated by the French. With John of Bedford's death, Philip of Burgundy's power had increased greatly in France, as had Humphrey of Gloucester's in England.

Listening to the Cardinal, Owen could almost smell trouble ahead.

A memorial service for the Duke of Bedford was held in the abbey church at Westminster in November, attended by scores of his friends. He had been a popular member of the royal family and many in the Abbey congregation smiled at each other's remembered anecdotes about his kindness. Cardinal Beaufort delivered the oration and struggled to control his voice. Though he had never regretted his decision to choose the church over parenthood, his nephews had been like sons to him.

It was not in the natural scheme of things, he thought, for parents to bury their children, and now here he was, presiding over the memorial service for the latest of the brothers to die. It wasn't an easy thing to do. They'd gone now, all except Humphrey. Henry Beaufort was tired of death.

Catherine was finding the service difficult, too. Travelling separately, she and Owen had returned to the Palace of Westminster as soon as they could but now that they were back in London, they dared not be seen together. They had left Edmund and Jasper behind in Hatfield, being looked after by Joanna Courcy and two nurses: Catherine's wedding ring was again on the chain around her neck and nestling in its old hiding place. As she listened to Cardinal Beaufort's oration extolling his nephew's virtues, her own memories were of John's kindness when he accompanied her on the agonising journey through France and England with her husband's coffin all those years ago. She would sorely miss him. She prayed that he was reunited with his beloved Anne.

The court was still in mourning for John during the first week of December and the King's fourteenth birthday came as a welcome relief. Catherine was pleased to be at Windsor with him and included in the celebrations, modest though they were.

Anton, with his usual deftness of touch, had created a splendid banquet for the occasion and forty people sat down to the meal. The King was seated between his mother and the Duchess of Gloucester, who monopolised the conversation. She talked incessantly, punctuating her conversation with a laugh which tinkled down a descending scale. She positively sparkled. Catherine, sitting on the other side of Henry, felt quite dowdy and wished heartily that she was in Bishop's Hatfield with her husband and children.

But then this, too, was her child. Only fourteen years old but solemn beyond his years, Henry was already burdened by the perceived responsibilities of kingship. He had shown no emotion at the recent death of his uncle, assuming that to do so would have been frowned upon. He was being groomed assiduously for his role in life and, in true royal fashion, he had mastered the art of making inconsequential conversation.

'So, tell me, my Lady,' he said to his mother between mouthfuls of his favourite marrowbone pudding, 'can we expect you to be at Windsor for Christmas?'

'If I am to interpret that as an invitation, then certainly,' said Catherine. 'It is always the greatest of pleasures for me to spend time with my son.' With all my sons, she thought to herself. Spending Christmas with Henry would mean being away from Edmund and Jasper during the festive season and she knew how excitedly her little boys were looking forward to it. Perhaps she could smuggle them into Windsor, so that she wouldn't have to divide her heart in two.

'Of course,' Henry was saying pompously, 'I look forward to Christmas as a time to celebrate the coming of Our Lord. I eschew the more frivolous aspects of the festival, though the carol singing is enjoyable enough.'

Catherine longed to tell him to let go, to relax and make the most of his youth while he could. But what she said was: 'Of course. That is the sign of a truly pious nature.'

'I often think,' Henry went on in the same exaggerated tone, 'that Christmas is a time for little children and, since there are none in this household, perhaps our celebrations are rather subdued.'

It seemed like a God-given opportunity to tell him about his brothers and his sister. Catherine grasped the nettle.

'My Lord,' she began slowly, 'I have something to tell you which I think you would like to hear ...'

'Then Catherine, my dear,' came a voice from Henry's other side, 'I'm sure we would all like to hear it, particularly if it means we can share in the King's pleasure!'

Catherine could have kicked herself. She should have realised that the Cobham woman's ears would be flapping. 'Oh, it's nothing of any great consequence,' she said. 'Just an idea I'd had for a Christmas entertainment. It will keep for another time.'

Her opportunity came though, a few days later when Henry, aware of his mother's liking for music, requested the pleasure of her company for an hour during the afternoon to listen to some of the newest compositions by Master John Dunstable,

317

who had recently returned from France, but when Catherine was shown into the room where Henry was waiting for her, she found him entirely alone.

'My humblest apologies, Mother,' said Henry as Catherine curtseyed. 'But I'm afraid that Master Dunstable has succumbed to an illness which confines him to his room. From what I hear of his health, I doubt that he will be able to entertain us this week.'

'No matter, my Lord,' Catherine answered. 'We could, perhaps, make good use of this opportunity to talk. We haven't talked together for a very long time.'

'Several years,' said Henry with a wry smile. 'Perhaps that's because you're so rarely at court. Tell me, Mother, why do you choose to stay away? It would be pleasant to see you more often.'

Catherine looked at him. The moment had come. 'Henry,' she said after a long pause, 'you had better sit down. This is going to take a long time and I hardly know where to begin.'

She left nothing out. Shaking with emotion, she told him of the abject loneliness and misery she had endured after his father's death, about the rejection she had met on all sides, about the Duke of Gloucester's dismissive arrogance and about the extraordinary kindness shown her by the Clerk of the Wardrobe who became first her friend and then her husband. Then she told him about his sister and his brothers.

Henry listened in shocked silence, his eyes never moving from her face. He stopped her for a moment while he rang a small bell and ordered a jug of wine and some honey cakes from the kitchen. Waiting for them to arrive, he walked over to the window and stood there for a long time, looking out, saying nothing, his hands locked together in an effort to control their trembling as he came to terms with what he had been told.

Slut! The word screamed in his head and it took all his self-control not to scream it at her. How could his own mother descend into such depravity? How could she fall so far from grace? He could scarcely believe that she had consorted with a servant, allowing that servant to lie with her and violate her body. Slut! Slut! Slut! Surely, his mother was no better than a

318

whore!

And yet she had married the man in good faith and in the eyes of God so who was he, even as a king, to gainsay that?

The cakes and wine were brought in and set down on the table. Henry dismissed the footman who brought them with an impatient wave of his hand and sat down again. At length he spoke.

'So, you and Master Tudor are married, Mother?'

'We are. We have been at pains to keep our marriage secret, of course, because Master Tudor would be in terrible danger if certain people were to know about it. But yes, we were married in the church of St Andrew-by-the-Wardrobe.'

'When you lived at Baynard's Castle?'

'Yes. Seven years ago.'

'You don't wear a ring.'

Catherine took hold of the gold chain around her neck and fished out her wedding ring from its hiding place beneath the bodice of her dress. 'I have a ring, but I cannot always wear it.'

'I see. But Master Tudor is a servant, Mother.'

'He is.'

'And he is Welsh.'

'Indeed. He is both those things. He is also a man of honour and integrity and descended from a noble family which included princes of ancient lineage who ruled in these islands long before the Normans came here.'

'But the Welsh are idle, ignorant people. Dirty, too, my Uncle of Gloucester says.'

'My son, you must make up your own mind about your Uncle of Gloucester. I feel quite certain of my own opinion of him. He is not a kind man.'

Henry felt he ought to defend Gloucester but could not think how. If only he could break down the barrier of mutual distrust between his uncle and his mother, the two most important people in his life.

'Did you know that my Uncle of Gloucester has taken over Baynard's Castle since the fire?' he asked. 'He is having it rebuilt and intends to use it as his London residence.'

'So I understand. I hope he will be very happy there. I

319

certainly was.'

Henry paused; clearly his mother had no further interest in her old home. He changed tack. 'You said I had brothers, well, half-brothers anyway. What are their names?'

Catherine smiled. Now she felt happier, speaking about her children and, as she talked, so Henry relaxed visibly and some colour returned to his face. He had really been shocked but now he felt quite excited to hear about his younger brothers. Brothers! And until this very moment, he had thought himself an only child.

'I wish you had told me this before, my Lady. I feel that a great deal of time has been lost. I would like to have had the opportunity to meet my brothers before this.'

'But Henry, you weren't really old enough to be told. And don't you see why I've never said a word about it? Don't you understand why I've been to such lengths to hide it, staying away from court for months at a time so that no one would ever know? It's because my dear husband would be persecuted for his audacity in marrying the Dowager Queen without your permission. There is a law which prevents it and he has broken that law. It is likely that he would be imprisoned, perhaps even ... even beheaded. I could never, ever run that risk.'

'But I would positively forbid it, Mother. And I am the King.'

'Yes, of course, Henry, but ... but there are others who act in your name. And I'm not sure that you're always aware of it. They've been doing it since you were a small baby. The Council ... the Duke of Gloucester ...'

'Surely, my Uncle of Gloucester wouldn't ...'

'Your Uncle of Gloucester is capable of anything, Henry. Believe me. Anything. I must ask you to promise that you will never, ever tell him anything about this. Perhaps I have already been too rash in entrusting you with the secret but I wanted you to know. Please, please for the love of God, give me your word that this will go no further than this room. Please, Henry. I am very worried for Owen and I would never forgive myself if anything happened to him. He is very, very dear to me.'

'Very well, Maman. I give you my word.' Henry nodded

with his eyes closed. It didn't escape Catherine that he had called her by the old name. Then he opened his eyes again and gave her a shy smile. 'I would very much like to meet my brothers.'

'Then you shall. Oh, my dear son, you shall! We must arrange for you to visit us at Bishop's Hatfield very soon. It's too much of a risk to bring them here to Windsor. I will go back to Hatfield for Christmas and tell them all about their big brother who will come to see them in the spring. They'll be so excited. So will I. I can hardly wait!'

Catherine held out her arms to her eldest son as though it was the most natural thing in the world and he, somewhat taller than she was by now, put his arms around her. It was the first time they had embraced each other since he was a small child.

Christmas at Hatfield was an enchanting family occasion and Catherine, feeling as though a huge weight had been lifted from her shoulders, enjoyed herself immensely. The entire household attended mass on Christmas Eve and again on Christmas morning, before sitting down to a gargantuan mid-day feast of goose and pork.

Afterwards, Owen took his crwth from its case, tuned it carefully, and played carol after carol interspersed with a few jigs and dance tunes to amuse Edmund and Jasper. They played games, too, Blind Man's Buff was the most popular but, when it ended in tears, Catherine handed the boys over to Joanna Courcy to put them to bed.

She went upstairs to wish them goodnight and help them say their prayers. Little Jasper was already fast asleep and she wouldn't wake him but she had a special secret to tell Edmund about a big brother he never knew he had, the big brother who would be coming to see him in the spring. Listening wide-eyed to what his mother was saying, Edmund thought that perhaps next time he said his prayers, he would ask God to make it Christmas every day.

Owen was lying full-length on the hearth rug when she came downstairs again, his chin on his hand, gazing into the dying embers of the fire. When she joined him, he sat up and took her hand in his.

'Did you have a happy Christmas, cariad?'

'The happiest ever. The happiest Christmas of my life. Come, the fire is dying. Let's go to our bed.'

'Yes, you've had a long day, my sweet. Are you tired?'

She gave him a sidelong glance and smiled.

'Not in the slightest,' she said.

Chapter Twenty-three

London, Summer 1436

Spring came and went and still the King had still not made the journey to Bishop's Hatfield. He needed an excuse for his visit and couldn't think of one. There were so many people who had to be informed, so much organisation ahead of the journey. His advisers politely pointed out that he had never visited his mother when she had been away from court on previous occasions and questioned his wish to do so now. Henry was an honest young man to whom truth, integrity and piety were everything. He couldn't bring himself to tell a lie, not even a small one. It was easier just not to go to Hatfield.

Catherine had said nothing more to Edmund. Small boys have short memories and the secret she had told him before he drifted off to sleep on Christmas night had been forgotten as quickly as the taste of the festive plum duff. Now, at the height of summer, it was as if she had never said anything.

It was time for a visit to Windsor and there was a pressing need to make that visit sooner rather than later because, despite Owen's avowed intention not to let her go through the agonies of a difficult child-birth again, she was expecting yet another child. She had certainly inherited her mother's fecundity. It seemed that Owen had only to give her a sideways look, let alone anything else, and she would become pregnant, but she had neither the heart nor the inclination to refuse him. Torn between joy and trepidation at the prospect of another birth, she had to admit to herself that she was feeling far from well. While she still could, she would be wise to leave the boys in Hatfield with Owen and pay a fleeting visit to court, discharge her social duties there and get back to the family as soon as possible. Then she would be among people she loved and trusted and could concentrate on building up her strength for her confinement.

The King was delighted to see her. Since their epiphany before Christmas last year, when she had told him everything, his attitude towards her had changed completely. Nowadays, he was her affectionate son. Gone was the unnatural formality of the past and, when they were alone, he was eager for news of his brothers. He assured his mother that her secret was still safe with him and he smiled when she told him that his little brother Edmund was pestering to be given a pony. Jasper, she said, wanted to learn to play the crwth, just like his father, except that his hands were too small to handle the instrument. They were both growing up very quickly.

Henry was growing up, too, she thought, noticing traces of a soft, downy beard on his cheeks. They'd have to find a wife for him soon, he was already old enough to be betrothed. And when he was married to a suitable royal bride, there would be no argument about who would inherit the crown of England. Not France, just England. She and everyone else knew that her late husband's dream of a dual monarchy would never happen now; not since last year's Treaty of Arras. France and England were drifting further and further apart.

Windsor was still the comfortable, relaxed family home it had always been and there were few formal commitments for her to worry about. She was surprised, though, to receive an invitation to spend a day at La Pleasaunce with the Duke and Duchess of Gloucester, to celebrate Her Grace's birthday. Catherine's first instinct was to panic and her second was to refuse. She could plead illness, insanity … anything rather than spend a whole day with a man whom she loathed and a woman who undoubtedly loathed her. She wondered why she had been invited. She wanted to run back to Hatfield.

It was Henry who persuaded her. He, too, had been invited to the birthday celebration so, in the warmth of an August morning, accompanied by two dozen guards and a handful of smartly dressed courtiers, mother and son set out for Greenwich in the royal barge. They made an early start to take advantage of a high tide and as La Pleasaunce came into view they heard the sound of pipes and tabors, already playing as guests arrived.

La Pleasaunce was unashamedly devoted to pleasure. The manor house, large and elegant, was surrounded by river walks and gardens with shrubs and flowers, where secluded little arbours provided every opportunity for dalliance and secret amours. For this occasion, a large pavilion had been erected on the river bank and decorated with pennants which were fluttering in the gentle breeze off the water. Inside the pavilion, seated in regal splendour on a dais at the far end, the Duke and Duchess received their guests, only rising from their seats to welcome His Royal Highness the King as he entered with his mother.

Having first curtseyed to him, the Duchess made an enormous fuss of Henry and, having bowed, the Duke patted his nephew's shoulder in a proprietary way. Then the Duchess turned to Catherine. 'Your Highness,' she said in a condescending tone, 'my dear. I'm so glad you could come to our little party. My Lord, why not introduce the Queen to some people she might not have met? After all, it's some time since we had the pleasure of her company at court. There must be several people she doesn't know.' She turned away to concentrate her attention on the King.

Catherine, with Humphrey's hand a little too intimately in the small of her back, found herself being shepherded from one group to another and being introduced to people she didn't know and in whom she had no interest, making small talk for the sake of it. After an hour, she knew she shouldn't have come. With so many people in the pavilion, it had become unbearable in the suffocating August heat and she really wanted to sit down, even if only for a moment. She was grateful for the concern of a tall, fair-haired, rather elegant older woman whose duty seemed to be to look after the guests. She noticed Catherine's discomfort, helped her to a chair, and snapped her fingers at a footman to bring some wine.

'You're very kind,' Catherine said. 'It's so noisy and I was really feeling quite faint in this heat. I'm better now, thank you so much.'

Smiling, the tall woman curtseyed before moving away. 'It

was my pleasure, Your Highness,' said Margery Jourdemayne.

The Duchess of Gloucester had asked Margery to call on her the following week, a routine visit to enable Eleanor to stock up on her supply of Margery's expensive skin creams and perfumes.

'Come in,' she called in response to a knock on her door. 'Ah, Margery. I haven't seen you since my birthday celebration. It was good of you to help out with the guests. Did you enjoy yourself?'

'I was glad to be of service, Your Grace, and I enjoyed it very much,' said Margery. 'It was a great success. Perhaps even more of a success than you realise.'

'What do you mean by that?'

'As it happens, I spent a little time seeing to the needs of Her Highness the Queen. I was able to find her a chair and a glass of wine when she said she was feeling faint. She was clearly very uncomfortable.'

'Well, it was rather hot in the pavilion.'

'Your Grace ...' Margery paused, to gain the maximum impact for the statement she was about to make. 'The Queen is pregnant.'

'What!' The Duchess dropped a bottle of Hungary Water and spun round in her chair, open-mouthed. 'Pregnant! How can she possibly have become pregnant?'

'Presumably, Ma'am, in much the same way as any other woman becomes pregnant.' Margery could have bitten her tongue. The Duchess' nerves were very raw on the subject of pregnancy but she appeared not to have noticed Margery's *faux pas*.

'Yes, but ... but who by? Has she married while she's been away from court? Surely not! We'd have known! Or has she been sleeping around? The slut! Who with? Not with Edmund Beaufort. Can't be. He's in France. Besides, he's married to Eleanor Beauchamp now and she's breeding like a rabbit by all accounts.' She looked stunned. 'Margery, how do you know that the Queen is pregnant? Did she tell you?'

'Oh, no, Ma'am. She didn't need to. I could tell by looking at her. She was showing all the signs. Despite the cut of her gown I could see that she's … well, she's thick in the waist and there were shadows under her eyes. Her face was blotchy, too. It's always easy to tell, especially in the summer. Yes, I would say she has a baby due in about four months.'

'You're sure, Margery?'

'As sure as I can be, Ma'am.'

'Dear God. Wait until I tell Humphrey.' She waved her hand in dismissal then paused. 'Oh, and Margery …'

'Yes, Your Grace?'

'Find out who the father is.'

Margery Jourdemayne had reckoned without the loyalty of Catherine and Owen's friends, none of whom would ever have dreamed of betraying them. But she knew that, eventually, someone would need money badly enough to tell her. She didn't have long to wait before she was approached by a groom from the royal stables at Windsor whose gambling debts had got him into trouble. Once he had said the name 'Master Tudor', it didn't take Margery long to find out everything and she lost no time in conveying the information to the Duchess of Gloucester.

Eleanor longed to pass on such an explosive secret to her husband but, knowing his unpredictable moods and painfully aware of her own inability to conceive, she pondered the wisdom of telling Humphrey about Catherine's pregnancy and the existence of her other children by Owen Tudor. She had no wish to be compared unfavourably with the Queen when it came to the vexed question of fecundity but, having come to the conclusion that Humphrey would probably find out about it eventually, she waited until he appeared to be in a genial frame of mind and then chose her moment with care.

She immediately regretted having said anything, so alarming was his reaction to the news. He turned a dull red with fury and sweated so profusely that she genuinely thought he had done himself serious harm. He paced up and down the room, swearing and smashing his right fist into the palm of his left hand.

'Humphrey, don't upset yourself so much, you'll only make

yourself ill.'

'Shut up, madam. Let me deal with this. I won't have women meddling in affairs of state.'

'But it's not an …'

'Eleanor, it is! Don't you see, you stupid woman, that there are now other possible heirs to the throne? The King's half-brothers? They all have the same mother, for God's sake, and she's still the Queen of England, for all that she's been shagging like a bitch on heat with that great oaf of a Welshman. I knew she was a slut for all her simpering and whimpering over my brother Henry. I knew it! She's just like her slut of a mother. Well, I've got to make it impossible for those bastards of hers to inherit anything. I must get them from her somehow. Does the King know about them?'

Eleanor was cowed by her husband's rage. 'Er … M-Margery didn't say. Perhaps he does.'

'Aye, he's probably in on the secret as well. I seem to be the only person in England who didn't know about it. Well, this is where I show them what happens when they make a laughing stock of Humphrey of Gloucester. I'm damned if I'll let them get away with it.'

Catherine was back in Hatfield with Owen in time for Michaelmas and they were returning from a family walk in the late September sunshine. Edmund was astride Pegasus, his new pony. With a firm hold on the bridle, Owen walked alongside, patiently explaining to his son that since the pony was named after the great winged horse of the Greek gods, it was rather inappropriate to call him 'Peggy'. Holding his mother's hand, Jasper trailed a kite along the ground because there wasn't really enough wind to fly it.

'*Hâf bach Mihangel*,' Owen said contentedly. 'St Michael's little summer. I've always loved this last short burst of warmth and sunshine before the winter sets in.'

Catherine smiled. 'But the fireside has its delights in winter,' she pointed out. Her husband gave her a sidelong glance. 'There's only one place I like better,' he said. Owen and Edmund went to stable Pegasus while Catherine took Jasper back to the house. Edmund begged his father to be allowed to stay with his pony for a little longer, to feed it some windfall apples he'd found. Owen, ruffling his son's hair affectionately, left him and his pony in the care of one of the older grooms. He took the short cut from the stables back to the house through the service door to the kitchen and was alarmed to hear raised voices coming from the hall.

He found Catherine surrounded by a group of half a dozen people, some of whom he recognised, some he didn't. There were guards, too, in royal livery. Surely, that was the Countess of Suffolk, Alice de la Pole and, if Owen wasn't very much mistaken, her husband's infamous henchmen, Sir Thomas Tuddenham and John Heydon. At the centre of the group's attention, Catherine had her arms protectively around Jasper, clutching him to her.

'Owen, thank God!'

'What the devil is going on here? What do you people think you're doing?'

'We've come for the Queen's children,' said Sir John Tuddenham, a big bruiser of a man. 'On the King's orders.'

'Well, you can't have them,' said Owen. 'They are my children too, you know, and I absolutely forbid it. You are not taking them anywhere.'

Tuddenham's lip curled in scorn. 'No jumped-up little Clerk of the Wardrobe can forbid *me* to do anything!' he said. 'I'm certainly not taking orders from you.'

'But he is my husband,' Catherine protested, hysteria rising in her voice. 'And I am the Queen. I will not let you have my children.'

'The King's orders take precedence,' snapped Alice de la Pole.

'Here's the warrant if your ... er ... *husband* wants proof,' said John Heydon, producing a piece of parchment. Owen made a lunge for it but Heydon held it aloft between thumb and forefinger.

'So you can read, can you?' Heydon asked rudely, dangling the warrant deliberately in front of him.

'You insolent ...!' Owen ripped the warrant from Heydon's

hand. Yes, that was the royal seal, there was no mistaking it. But it was not the Great Seal. It had clearly come from the palace but not necessarily from the King himself. He broke the wax, unfolded the warrant, and began to read. 'I don't recognise the hand,' he said.

'No doubt it was dictated to a scribe,' said the haughty Lady Alice. 'Be that as it may, the King wants his brothers brought to court. Immediately.'

'Yes, so it seems. Why do think that might be, my Lady?'

Owen was stalling, very uneasy as he tried to understand the situation. If it genuinely was an edict from the King, then it had to be obeyed without question. He knew that the Lady Alice's husband, the Earl of Suffolk, was steward of the King's household. He was a decent enough man by all accounts but Owen had heard that when it came to loyalty, he tended to run with the hare and with the hounds and he was known to be one of the Duke of Gloucester's cronies. Of course, Owen could perhaps offer to take the boys to court himself, or at least to travel with them. That would put Catherine's mind at rest.

'My Lady?' he prompted the Countess again. 'Why do you think the King wishes to have his brothers brought to court?'

Alice de la Pole drew herself up to her full height and looked down her long, thin nose. 'I really do not know. I am simply carrying out the instructions of the King,' she said. 'I would not be so impertinent as to question them.'

'The Countess doesn't have to give you a reason,' snarled Tuddenham. 'We have undertaken to get the King's brothers back to London as soon as possible. On His Highness's own orders. You can't argue with that. You've got an hour to get them ready for the journey.'

'No!' Catherine's scream was spine-chilling, primeval, a vixen baring her teeth, defending the last of her cubs against a predator. Even Tuddenham was momentarily taken aback.

'No,' she screamed again, 'you can't have them. You will not have them!'

The captain of the guard moved menacingly towards Catherine and reached out to pull Jasper away from her. Owen sidestepped, placing himself in a defensive position in front of his wife and child. Catching him unawares, another guard came from behind him, grabbed his arm, and swung him round, flooring him with a huge punch to the side of the head. Reeling from the blow, Owen went down heavily and lost consciousness.

Now Catherine's screaming became louder and more incoherent as, wailing pitifully, Jasper was roughly torn from her grasp and handed to Alice de la Pole, who held his small arm in an iron grip. 'Where's the other one?' she demanded.

'You shall never have him!' shouted Catherine. 'Never, never!' At that precise moment the door opened and another guard dragged a bewildered Edmund into the room.

'Found this one in the stables,' he muttered as Catherine flew at her child, trying to take him protectively into her arms. She was roughly pulled away by another guard. She beat her fists on her captor's chest, screaming at him and weeping. He gripped her wrists, easily overpowering her. Unconscious, Owen lay prone under the heavy boot of a great thug dressed in royal livery.

Alice de la Pole still had hold of little Jasper's arm and he, bewildered at being dragged away from his mother, was crying loudly. With her free hand, she reached into a small bag at her waist and took something out of it.

'Oh, for heaven's sake, child, stop that caterwauling,' she said impatiently. 'Here, why don't you have some nice marchpane.'

Catherine froze with horror. Marchpane! Her body went limp and when the guard relaxed his grip on her, she crumpled to the floor.

The countryside was still bathed in the late sunshine of St Michael's little summer, and the birds still sang, but en route for London, Jasper was crying, frightened and upset because his mother had been screaming so horribly. Edmund was crying too, because he didn't understand what was going on and he didn't want to leave Peggy.

'Be quiet both of you, and stop snivelling,' said Alice de la Pole, raising her voice against the shouted commands of the escort party. The horses strained against the traces as the driver whipped them into a gallop.

Katherine de la Pole, the Abbess of Barking, didn't much care for her sister-in-law. After all, her brother William had married Alice chiefly for her money, which he'd badly needed at the time. By now, though he was still saddled with Alice, his fortunes had changed, thanks to royal patronage. Katherine de la Pole, too, had reason to be grateful to her brother's patron, since the post of Abbess at Barking was in the King's gift. Having no great interest in life at court, she took great pride in her work at the abbey and was pleased to have so little contact with her sister-in-law. There was no love lost between them.

So she was surprised when Alice arrived unannounced one day in late September with two small boys, aged around five and six, demanding that they should be accommodated in the abbey for a few weeks while their parents resolved their problems. On asking who the children were, the Abbess was told that their father was a senior household servant at Windsor and the boys were the result of his unfortunate *affaire de coeur* with one of the ladies of the court.

The Abbess thought it sounded an unlikely story but it was her duty in the eyes of God to give shelter and succour to the children. Moreover, Alice had provided a substantial sum of money for their keep. Fifty-two pounds and twelve shillings would cater very adequately for their needs for some considerable time to come. She took the boys by the hand and led them away to be cared for by her nuns, according to the Rules of Saint Benedict.

Chapter Twenty-four

Winter 1436

Catherine's health went rapidly downhill in the weeks that followed. The brutal seizure of her children had been impossible to bear: she felt her heart had been ripped from her body. Under Owen's gentle questioning, old suppressed memories of her own childhood abduction grew as vivid as her nightmares and she was wild with grief and worry. The prospect of the new baby did nothing to cheer her and her face had taken on a hollow, haunted look. All her physician could suggest was to leech her but Owen thought she was thin enough and pale enough already, without the greedy attention of those little black blood-suckers.

Her unpredictable moods swung between moments of absolute fury and long periods of utter misery. At her angriest, Owen would find her pacing the floor, swearing that she would go to London to find the boys but when he managed to convince her that she really wasn't well enough to travel, she would dissolve into hopeless tears. She would spend her afternoons lying on their bed, exhausted and staring blankly at nothing. He often found her there and, if she wasn't sleeping, she was weeping silently.

Owen tried to hide his impotent fury. This was an abduction, plain and simple, and it was Gloucester's doing. Why else would the de la Poles and their brutish associates have had anything to do with it? If he was to find his sons, he knew he must go to London himself, to get some answers. Maredydd, though he was too old for active service, still had his ear to the ground and Emma was a celebrated gossip. If anyone knew anything about Edmund and Jasper, they would.

Catherine wouldn't hear of him leaving her. She wept and clung to him, convinced that if he went, he would never return but she was far too ill to travel with him.

Owen took Joanna Troutbeck into his confidence. There was nothing for it but to go to London alone, to see what he could find out. The only way to do it, he said, was to steal away at dead of night while Catherine was sleeping. He couldn't bear the thought of leaving her and knew that he wouldn't be able to if, yet again, she begged him to stay. So he had to entrust Troutbeck with the responsibility of telling her that he had left. There was no other way.

First, he swore her to secrecy then told her that he wanted her to arrange to take Catherine to London in a comfortable horse-drawn litter, with an armed escort group in royal livery.

'Royal livery, Master Tudor? Surely that …?'

'Yes, Troutbeck, royal livery. They are guarding Her Royal Highness the Queen and it no longer matters who knows that. There is no need for subterfuge any more, not now that the Duke of Gloucester has learned our secret.'

Owen had a hollow feeling of nervousness in the pit of his stomach but he knew that there were no other options. He was making the best, the only possible plans for Catherine. 'Once you reach London, Troutbeck, you are to make for the monastery of the Benedictines at Bermondsey, south of the river. They are accustomed to caring for royal patients at Bermondsey from what I understand. It's something of a tradition. Catherine will be well cared for there and, please God, nursed back to health.'

Seeing the worried expression on Troutbeck's face, Owen patted her hand reassuringly before he continued. 'As soon as I reach London, I will go to see the Abbot and make the necessary arrangements. Then, when you bring Catherine to Bermondsey, Troutbeck, let her believe that you're bringing her to me. Lie to her, if you have to. And, God willing, we can be together again when she's better. With our boys. Just as we were.'

'There'll be another child by then, Master Tudor.'

'Yes, there will. A girl, perhaps. Oh, and Troutbeck, please secure the services of the midwife, Margery Wagstaff. She pulled Her Highness through when Jasper was born so she'll be in good hands there, too.'

Sick with apprehension, he turned away, not trusting himself to say more. 'Just … just look after Catrin for me,' he blurted out, '… when I'm gone. Please.'

Owen allowed himself one more night with his dear wife, who slept quietly in the crook of his arm, her head on his shoulder, entirely unaware of his plans for her. Overwhelmed by *hiraeth* for all that they had meant to each other, Owen hardly slept at all.

In the small hours of the following night, he got up and dressed himself quietly without disturbing Catherine who was exhausted after a painful bout of coughing. He knelt beside her and watched her in the dim light. She was breathing quietly now with her eyelids, pale as parchment, closed over her lovely eyes. His Catrin. He had never loved her more than he did in this moment of parting. Catrin, his wife, his dearest love, more precious to him than anything. He wanted to touch her cheek but didn't dare run the risk of waking her. So he bent his head, closed his eyes, and prayed that he would find the children. He knew that if he didn't, he would lose her.

He let himself out of the house as quietly as he could, grateful for a dry, moonlit night as he prepared for his journey. It was almost dawn and he would make good time as soon as it was light in the east. Swinging himself up into the saddle, he turned his horse's head towards the south. He had to trust the animal to stay on the road because he could see nothing through a veil of tears.

At first, Abbot John Bromley of Bermondsey took some persuading that Master Owen Tudor was a representative of Her Royal Highness the Dowager Queen Catherine. He claimed to be her Clerk of the Wardrobe, no less. Travel-stained and weary, Owen was not at all the kind of person whom the Abbot would have expected to be the bearer of a message about the Queen's illness and her need for treatment. The man couldn't even rightly describe what was wrong with Her Highness, except that she was excessively melancholy and her worries were having a devastating effect on her health.

Owen delved around in his scrip for evidence of his credentials and was relieved to find a receipt from the royal cordwainer for a pair of Her Highness's shoes. Astounded, the Abbot realised that this dirty-looking messenger really was who he claimed to be and that he genuinely *was* making arrangements on behalf of the Queen. And he'd assured him that Cardinal Beaufort would be certain to visit the patient, as might her son the King. How exciting to think that the monastery would soon have another royal patient! It had been a long time since the last one. He must make plans.

After leaving Southwark, Owen headed back across London Bridge, straight for St Paul's Cross and Maredydd and Emma's house. They were delighted to see him though Maredydd had heard nothing about the children and knew nothing of their whereabouts. Even the sociable, gossipy Emma had heard nothing and they were both appalled by Owen's account of Edmund and Jasper's abduction and how Catherine's health had deteriorated so rapidly because of it.

'Melancholy,' said Maredydd. 'Bile. That's what causes it. Black bile. She should drink a spoonful of the juice of the mallow each morning, boiled in water. Saffron is beneficial, too, they say.'

'Who says?'

'*Meddygon Myddfai*,' said Maredydd. 'Surely you haven't forgotten them? The Physicians of Myddfai are much talked about here in London nowadays. People say there's nothing they can't cure.'

Owen brightened visibly. Of course he remembered. And that was the answer. The celebrated Welsh physicians would cure Catherine of the black bile that tormented her, he was sure of that. He would take her to see them, just as soon as he had found Edmund and Jasper.

He took his leave of Maredydd and Emma, thanking them for their many kindnesses, waving aside their apologies for not being able to offer him a bed for lack of room in their small house.

In Bermondsey two weeks later, Abbot John Bromley ordered a great peal of bells to be rung for Her Highness the Queen and monks were summoned from all parts of the monastery to greet her.

Expected to process into the monastery church of St Saviour and kneel before the crucifix to pray, Catherine somehow managed to get through a service and endured some interminable singing by a group of choristers. One of the older boys looked so like little Edmund that her heart raced and for a moment she almost believed it could be Thomas. Then reason prevailed. Thomas was growing up as a foundling in the monastery at Westminster, not here in Bermondsey. She prayed then that Troutbeck had been right when she'd promised that Owen would come to Bermondsey soon, with news of the boys. As the service came to an end, Abbot Bromley gave Catherine his blessing and sprinkled holy water over her. He didn't seem to notice that she could barely stand.

At the Abbot's table after the service, the royal guest picked politely at a small amount of the food on her trencher before pleading extreme tiredness. Joanna Troutbeck helped her to bed in the best room the monastery could offer where, lulled by the scent of beeswax and incense, she fell immediately and soundly asleep.

Wanting to reflect on the events of the days gone by, Owen was taking a late-night walk by the waters of the Thames. He had found himself board and lodging at a nearby inn and had left his horse with the ostler there. It was good to be back in London, even though it was necessary to be circumspect in moving about the town, trying to pick up scraps of gossip. It had been good to see Maredydd, too, and it was rather touching that he had become a family man in middle age and had filled his small house with children, six daughters, his days of sowing wild oats long gone. He seemed very happy but had confided in Owen his only regret which was that, having had more experience with the sword than with the pen, he would find it difficult to make a record for posterity of the brave exploits of his father, Owain Glyndŵr. And because Emma couldn't see the point of educating girls, his daughters were hardly likely to do so either.

Suddenly, Owen was on the ground, pinned down and winded by the weight of an attacker.

'What the hell …?'

It was pitch dark and he couldn't see his assailant. Neither could he tell how many men had attacked him.

'Orders, mate. You're to come with us. We've got a nice little college in mind for you and we're going to bang you up in there for a couple of weeks, just to give you a bit of education.'

'What? Are you arresting me? What for? What have I done?'

'You're Welsh and you're out of doors after dark. That's enough.'

'But I've got my letters of denizenship! I've had them for four years. I have as many rights as an Englishman.'

'You'll never be fit to lick the arse of an Englishman! Once a Welsh bastard, always a Welsh bastard. Besides, you've been messing about where you shouldn't 'ave been, 'aven't you? Thinking yourself good enough to screw 'Er 'Ighness the Queen! Ha! There's a law against that, you know, you ignorant Welsh bastard.'

The thick-set thug who had been kneeling on him got up suddenly and yanked Owen up with him, bending his left arm painfully behind his back. Another seized his right arm and he was unceremoniously frog-marched up Newgate Street and thrown into the notorious building at the end of it.

Whittington's College, of course! That was the name the wags of the London underworld had given to Newgate Jail since it had been rebuilt with money bequeathed by Richard Whittington. Lying in the dark on a slimy stone floor, Owen realised what his attackers had meant by 'a nice little college'. He wondered as he lay shackled in filth and darkness, grimacing at the stench of the place, what Emma, so well connected to the late Lord Mayor, would have made of it.

In Bermondsey, Catherine awoke to the sound of the monastery bell. Joanna Troutbeck smiled at her.

'Good morning, Your Highness. You've slept well. It's nine

338

of the clock.'

'Good morning! Was that the bell ringing for Terce, Troutbeck? Why, surely, it's almost time to wish me "Good Afternoon"!'

'No matter, my Lady. You have rested. That is all that matters.'

'Indeed I have and I feel refreshed. Troutbeck, please, fetch my robe. I would like to dictate a letter. Perhaps you will …'

'No, Ma'am, I don't feel confident enough in my writing. I will ask if one of the monks take your dictation.'

'Yes, of course. I'm sure Abbot Bromley will recommend someone. In the meantime, I think I could manage to eat a little frumenty.'

The letter which Catherine later dictated to Brother Osbert was addressed to Cardinal Beaufort. His London residence was also in the parish of Southwark and she suddenly wanted to see him very much. Once the message had been dispatched she knew that if he was in London, she wouldn't have long to wait.

The Cardinal was shocked at the sight of her though he tried not to show it. Pregnancy was distorting her slender frame and she looked as though she harboured a monster which was consuming her from within. She was emaciated and gaunt and though Troutbeck had done her best, she lacked poor Guillemote's talents as a hairdresser and Catherine's once-glorious hair was coarse, lacklustre, and streaked with grey.

'Your Highness! Catherine, my dear. I came as soon as I received your message. I had no idea that you were in Bermondsey. I would have been here to welcome you …'

'My Lord Uncle! I'm so pleased to see you.'

'How are you, my Lady?'

'I am very unwell. My babies … they've … they've taken them away from me and I don't know where they or Owen are. I fear the worst.' Catherine had hoped to control her tears but found she couldn't.

Henry Beaufort laid his hand very gently on her head as she wept and his heart ached for her in her grief. So, everything he had had heard was true. It was widely rumoured that Humphrey of Gloucester had somehow found out about Catherine's

339

marriage and, in his fury, had ordered that her children should be seized. Beaufort, who could scarcely believe that anyone would do such a monstrous thing, also knew that Owen was a marked man, wanted for the crime of marrying the Queen without royal consent. But he did have some information which he knew would please Catherine and he was certain of it because, though he had come by it in a roundabout way, at least he had it at first hand.

He had met William de la Pole, the Earl of Suffolk, a few days ago at a policy meeting of the King's Council. Henry was wary of Suffolk; not for nothing was he nicknamed 'Jackanapes'. He knew the man for a boaster and he naturally mistrusted anyone who was friendly with Gloucester. Making sociable conversation after the meeting, Henry had casually asked after de la Pole's sister, Katherine, and de la Pole had boasted that she was in charge of the King's half-brothers these days. That had struck Henry as very odd but he'd presumed that there was a good reason for it. Now he knew.

He put his finger under Catherine's chin and lifted her face to look at him. 'Don't upset yourself too much, my dear Lady. I do have some good news for you. I know where your children are and they are in good hands.'

Catherine clutched at his sleeve. 'Oh, please, tell me. Tell me. Where are they? Who is looking after them?'

Beaufort patted her hand reassuringly. 'They have been taken to the abbey at Barking and are in the care of the Abbess. I know her quite well. She is a good woman. She'll make sure that the children are well looked after and will come to no harm.'

Catherine was crying with relief and gratitude, unable to speak.

'But, as for your husband … well, I'll see what I can find out. I will make enquiries.'

'Oh God,' Catherine sobbed, 'I can't bear to think that he might … he might be …'

'My dear Lady, if you feel strong enough, you would do well to write to the King, your son, as soon as possible for your husband's sake. It is your best hope. I feel sure that His

340

Majesty's tender love towards you will not permit him to see you suffer like this. It would break his heart …'He took Catherine's hand, held it gently between both of his and added '… as it breaks mine.'

The Cardinal helped her to compose the message to the King and promised that he would have it delivered as soon as he could. Catherine signed it and he pressed his ring into the warm sealing wax, feeling certain that the King would come to Bermondsey in search of his mother at the first opportunity.

It was hopeless. As long as he was here in Newgate, Owen would never know whether Catherine had reached the monastery at Bermondsey in safety and could only pray that, if she had, her health would improve under the care of the Benedictine monks. He must find a way of escaping from this hell hole and find the children, then he would take them all to Wales, first to Myddfai where Catherine would be fully restored to health by the famous physicians, then to Anglesey, among his people, where she and the children could enjoy the wild beauty of the mountains and be enchanted by the music and poetry of the bards. He tried, in his memory, to hear those half-forgotten rhythms and sweet cadences once again but they were drowned out in the darkness by the ugly noises of men snoring, cursing, and shouting abuse.

How ashamed his great kinsman Owain Glyndŵr would have been to think that a member of his own noble family had been jumped on from behind and wrestled to the ground like a common cutpurse. And how distraught Catherine would be if she could see him now, a prisoner, lying shackled on this stinking floor in the dead of night.

The King didn't notice that the monastery had been scrubbed and waxed in his honour but he pleased Abbot Bromley greatly by agreeing to attend midday mass when he arrived at Bermondsey a few days later. On his knees in the little church of St Saviour, Henry prayed silently but fervently for his mother's return to health. Then he visited her in her room and was shocked by what he saw.

341

Catherine lay on her bed, deathly pale and still but she struggled to sit upright when her son entered the room.

'Maman, please, don't. Stay where you are comfortable, don't move. My learned uncle the Cardinal told me that you were ill but I didn't realise … I thought … perhaps …'

'I am gravely ill, Henry,' said Catherine, falling back on to her pillows. 'I am sorely troubled both in mind and in body. I have been suffering these several months with something … lethargy … a painful cough … no one seems to know … the doctors try to leech me and Owen tries to stop them …'

'How is he? How is Master Tudor?'

'I don't know. I don't know how he is or where he is. I can only pray to God that he is alive. All I know is that he was trying to bring me news of our boys, Edmund and Jasper. I know now that they are being cared for in the Abbey at Barking but I'll never get well again as long as I am parted from them. It was so cruel …'

Henry grimaced. He knew something of his uncle's persecution of his mother and her husband, she had told him of it herself. But the Duke of Gloucester was still a figure of authority in his young life and, not quite fifteen years old, he was not entirely sure how to deal with the problem.

'You're wearing your wedding ring now, Maman, quite openly.'

'Oh yes, there's no pretence any more. Everyone knows that Owen and I are married in the eyes of God and His holy church.'

'And my brothers are acknowledged.'

'Yes, acknowledged, but stolen from me. And how I wish that I could see my husband and my children together.' Tears came unbidden. 'All my children. I know you would love your brothers as I do and I know they would love you. As I do,' she added, so quietly that he strained to hear her. 'As I have always done.'

Awkwardly, Henry took her hand in his. 'I know, Maman,' he said. 'I should never have lost sight of that love, even though matters of kingship came between us.'

'Henry, it wasn't just matters of kingship. Everything, everyone came between us … forced us apart. I should never have allowed it, I should have been stronger. It's all my fault. I should have listened to your father and not flown in the face of a prophecy.'

'Prophecy?'

'Prophecy, yes. Your father wanted you to be born in Westminster, he tried to insist upon it but, when the time came, he was in France and I … I was in Windsor. I didn't think it mattered. That's when everything started to go wrong … it's my fault. It's all my fault.'

'Shhh, Maman. What was the prophecy?'

'Oh, I can't remember the exact words. Something like "… Henry, born at Monmouth, shall small time reign and much get; but Henry of Windsor shall long reign and … and … lose all. But as God wills, so be it".'

'But that wasn't a Biblical prophecy so it doesn't count for anything. My father should not have taken any notice of the ramblings of some old soothsayer. It is clearly not God's will, Maman, we should ignore it.'

'But I could so easily have ensured that you would be "Henry of Westminster" and not "Henry of Windsor". Don't you see? It's my fault. I was arrogant and selfish. And now I'm paying for my selfishness.'

'Then let us pray, Maman, that our Blessed Lord will forgive you. For my part, I will try my best not to be the "Henry of Windsor that shall long reign and lose all".' Come, Maman, dry your eyes now and close them. You must rest. I will come to see you again soon.'

Catherine was exhausted and longing for sleep but it was denied her. She was tormented again by the words of that old prophecy. Her son had said that he would try his best not to be the Henry who would lose all but, already, her brother Charles had claimed the throne of France; the Treaty of Arras had reconciled all the warring factions of the French royal family but excluded the English. France was lost and everything that her first husband had fought for and died for was slipping away … slipping away into darkness and oblivion.

343

It was soothing throughout Advent to be aware of the monks in the chapel of St Saviour celebrating mass five times a day. Advent coincided with the period of Catherine's lying-in and she was close to her time now. Margery Wagstaff seemed quite certain in her prediction of a Christmas baby though she had confided in Joanna Troutbeck that she was very concerned about the Queen's health. This time, Catherine found it easy to comply with the midwife's instructions to stay in her bed. She couldn't have got dressed up as a pilgrim and gone running about the countryside any more than she could have flown out of the window into the cold December air.

She wrote again to the King, anxious to greet him on his birthday. She also wanted to make him aware of the terms of her will, which she was dictating to the nun brought in to provide some relief for Margery Wagstaff. Sister Annunciata wrote in her elegant hand:

The last will of Queen Catherine, made unto our sovereign lord, her son, upon her departing out of this world ...

The nun looked up. 'But, Your Highness, we pray for your complete recovery.'

'Sister, I thank you for your prayers. Believe me that I, too, pray. No one prays more earnestly than I do for the chance to see my children again, and my dear husband. But, unless I see them soon, I fear I will die. So it is sensible, surely, to leave some indication of my wishes after my death. Now, please ... continue ...'

Sister Annunciata bent to her work again, the silence broken only by the sound of her quill scratching across the parchment and Catherine's quiet, rambling voice.

Right high and mighty prince and my entirely beloved son ... I commend me to your Highness ... that before the silent and fearful conclusion of this long, grievous malady, in the which I have been long and yet am, troubled and vexed ... by the visitation of God (to whom be thanks in all his gifts) ...

After a long pause, Sister Annunciata looked up to find Catherine fast asleep. Oh well, writing wills was a depressing business. They could always continue it tomorrow if the Queen felt up to it.

By St Thomas' Day, the last will and testament of "Her Highness Queen Catherine, daughter of King Charles of France and mother of the King of England" had been written, signed, and witnessed. It made no mention of her husband, Owen Tudor, nor of their children. It was almost as though she was so accustomed to hiding this, her second family, that she dared not commit their names to paper, trusting her son the King to remember what she had told him.

Christmas came in a haze of warmth and goodwill and distant liturgical music. *Veni Emmanuel*, the monks sang in the chapel of St Saviour towards the end of Advent. Then, as Christmas Day dawned, she heard a carol she had never heard before, a gentle description of the Virgin mother singing to her baby. *I saw a sweet seemly sight,* came the voices of the monks. *Lully, lullay, baw, baw, my bairn, sleep softly now.*

Her own bairn came into the world on the first day of the New Year, 1437. Racked with pain and fever for two days and nights, Catherine's body had fought and sweated to deliver the child and she was left exhausted. Sister Annunciata took the baby and cleaned it, listening for a faint heartbeat. She was very afraid that the little girl was too weak to cling on to life so she was anxious to baptise her, then find a priest to grant her absolution before she met her Maker. Dimly aware of a faint mewling cry, Catherine smiled without opening her eyes as the child was put into her arms.

'Your little daughter, Your Highness. She is beautiful. What is she to be called?'

Catherine opened her parched lips to speak but her voice was barely audible. 'Owen's little girl …'

'Yes, but what is her name, Ma'am? A name. I need to know.'

'… his mother's name.'

'Yes?'

'Marged.'

'I'm sorry, Ma'am?'

'Marged.'

'I will see to it that she is baptised,' said the nun. 'Try to sleep now, my Lady.'

Margery Wagstaff was washing her arms, high up over the elbows. It had been another difficult birth and there was a bluish tinge to the baby's skin that Margery didn't like the look of at all. She didn't hold out much hope that the little one would pull through.

'What's the baby to be called?' she asked.

'I'm not quite sure what Her Highness said. Her voice was very weak. It sounded like Margaret.'

'Margaret it is then,' said Margery Wagstaff. 'Probably doesn't make much difference anyway. As long as the poor little mite has a name to give Saint Peter when she reaches the Gates of Heaven.'

'I don't think she'll be long before she makes that journey,' said the nun, dipping her fingers into the Holy Water.

'And I don't think her poor mother will be far behind her,' said Marjory Wagstaff, drying her hands before crossing herself.

Catherine was dimly aware of someone sitting at the end of the bed and tried to speak. Joanna Troutbeck rose from her seat and dipped a cloth into a little wine to moisten Catherine's lips. She would wait for Catherine to ask her about the baby before telling her that the child had died. Better to distract the Queen rather than upset her.

'Your Highness,' she said. 'A gift has arrived for you from your son the King.' Catherine opened her eyes but said nothing. 'Yes, Your Highness, a most generous gift. Look, a tablet of gold with a crucifix set with pearls and sapphires. It is one of the most beautiful things I have ever seen.' She took the ornament out of its box. 'See, my Lady, it was bought of John Pattesby, the goldsmith, and he works with only the very finest gold. It must have cost His Highness the King a very great deal of money.'

Catherine closed her eyes again as Troutbeck prattled on. Money! What was the use of money? No amount of money could buy her the pleasure of seeing the look of wonder on Owen's face when he held little Marged in his arms. But God only knew where Owen was and the baby was dead. She knew that without being told.

Her eyes remained closed but her mind took flight. How different, she wondered, would her life have been if she had made sure of being in Westminster for the birth of her first child, the heir to the throne? Would her husband the King have lived? And if he had lived, would he still be ruling over England and France with not only one heir but a palace full of healthy children? After all, that was the only thing required of a royal wife. It was no life, really, even though it was seen as the romantic ideal in every fairy tale she had ever been told; the pretty princess marries the handsome prince and they live happily ever after. But if that had happened and Henry had enjoyed a long and successful reign, she would never have known the absolute joy of loving and being loved by Owen Tudor. And there would have been no Tacinda and Thomas, no Edmund and Jasper ... and Marged. Poor little Marged; no sooner had the Lord opened her eyes than He'd closed them again. Catherine hadn't been allowed to keep her, either.

Sister Annunciata took the small body of the dead child and wrapped it tenderly in a winding sheet. She looked down at the little, untroubled face and thought how easy it was to imagine the child asleep. This tiny baby, unsullied and without sin, would be certain of a place in the Kingdom of Heaven. 'Suffer the little children to come unto me, and forbid them not: for of such is the Kingdom of God ...' Nevertheless, she dropped a warm kiss onto the baby's cold forehead before covering its face.

Margery Wagstaff took over from Joanna Troutbeck while Catherine was sleeping and soon found herself dozing in the warm room. The silence was deep and profound as monarch and midwife slept, their job done, their energies spent.

The Queen slept fitfully throughout the night and well into the next day. She would have occasional lucid moments and at other times the three women who attended her would struggle to make sense of what she was saying. Now and then her thin frame would be racked by a spasm of coughing and there was blood on the cloth that Margery Wagstaff used to clean her mouth.

Now, as midnight approached, it was Sister Annunciata's turn to sit with Catherine. She wasn't sure how much the Queen was aware of or, indeed, whether she was able to hear her at all, but she read to her from her own Book of Hours. These were Catherine's favourite prayers, her most personal thoughts. Towards dawn, the candle was guttering unsteadily and the nun's plump chin had dropped on to her chest. She woke with a start as she heard Catherine's voice and found the Queen smiling at her with a strange look in her eyes.

'Sister Supplice,' she murmured. 'I knew you'd come for me. Take my hand. I'm ready to go now.'

The nun reached out and covered Catherine's hand with her own.

Appendix I – Historical Footnote

After Catherine died, Gloucester had Owen summoned before the Council which found him innocent of his alleged offences and he was released. He set out for Wales but he wasn't to escape Gloucester's vindictive persecution that easily. Again he was arrested and consigned to Newgate a second time but, having wounded his guard, he managed to escape. Recaptured yet again, the prisoner was then transferred to Windsor Castle where, in November 1439, he was eventually granted a complete pardon, thereafter becoming a respected member of the royal household.

Henry VI did not inherit his father's talents for strong kingship; rather he was over-pious, weak, and indecisive. He was also given to bouts of mental collapse, like his French grandfather. His reign was dominated by the sporadic civil war known as the Wars of the Roses, in which claims to the throne were fought over by the rival houses of Lancaster and York whose emblems were the red rose and the white rose respectively. Henry's only son, Edward, was the sole Lancastrian heir but he lost his life at the age of seventeen, fighting his father's cause in the Battle of Tewkesbury in 1471. Henry, who had been imprisoned in the Tower of London since 1465, was himself put to death shortly after the death of his son.

Owen and Catherine's children, Edmund (known as Edmund of Hadham) and Jasper (Jasper of Hatfield), remained in the care of Katherine de la Pole, the Abbess of Barking, until 1442 when they were eventually brought to court. After that, the King developed a great fondness for his half-brothers and, in November 1452, he ennobled them as earls, Edmund becoming Earl of Richmond and Jasper Earl of Pembroke.

Edmund married Margaret Beaufort (the great-niece of Cardinal Henry Beaufort) and she was six months pregnant when her husband died of the plague at Carmarthen in

November 1456. The thirteen-year-old Margaret turned to Edmund's brother for protection and it was in Jasper's castle at Pembroke that she gave birth on the twenty-eighth of January 1457 to Edmund's son Henry, who was destined to become King Henry VII.

Throughout his life, Jasper championed the Lancastrian cause, always loyal to his half-brother the King. Owen, too, remained loyal to the Lancastrian dynasty and, as an elderly man, he fought alongside his son Jasper at the Battle of Mortimer's Cross in 1461. Owen was captured in that battle and taken to the nearby town of Hereford where he was executed. Legend has it that as he knelt before the block, he said that the head which would shortly lie in the executioner's basket was once wont to lie in Queen Catherine's lap.

Catherine was buried with due ceremony in the small Lady Chapel at Westminster but her bones were not allowed to rest for long. Wanting to build a suitable tomb for himself, Henry VII had the Lady Chapel demolished, probably with every intention of re-burying his grandmother's remains elsewhere in the abbey. But he never got around to it, neither did his arrogant son Henry VIII. In fact, no one quite got around to burying poor Catherine and she lay above ground in a loose-lidded coffin, becoming quite a tourist attraction. Visitors to the abbey, who were prepared to pay twopence for the privilege, were allowed to look at her embalmed body, even to handle it. Bizarrely, the famous diarist Samuel Pepys wrote that he had kissed Queen Catherine on his thirty-sixth birthday in 1669.

It was an ignominious fate for a woman who had changed the course of history. The daughter, wife, mother, and grandmother of kings, she also had an involvement in the realisation of three major prophecies, namely that Henry of Monmouth would achieve great success in a short life but that his son, Henry of Windsor, would lose all his father had fought for. France, too, lost by an old woman would be saved by a young one, and it was Catherine's own brother who was crowned King of France by Joan of Arc.

Then there was the ancient prophecy which claimed that, one day, a Welshman would sit on the throne of England and indeed Catherine and Owen's grandson, Henry VII, the first of the great Tudor monarchs, was descended through Owen from the royal house of Gwynedd. With Henry's accession to the English throne, the people of Wales slowly reacquired the privileges of an equal race, something which had been denied them since the English parliament of 1402 had passed penal laws designed to ensure English dominance and deprive the Welsh of some of the most basic human rights.

Llanilltud Fawr
2014

Appendix II – Living History

The people who shaped our history are often commemorated in the buildings with which they are associated. London's **Westminster Abbey** is a must-see living pageant of British history and will reward the visitor with a tangible feeling of having touched Catherine's life.

It was not until 1878 that Catherine's remains were finally given a permanent place of burial under the altar in Henry V's chantry. The Latin inscription for her on the altar can be translated: *Under this slab (once the altar of this chapel) ... rest at last, after various vicissitudes, finally deposited here by command of Queen Victoria, the bones of Catherine de Valois, daughter of Charles VI, King of France, wife of Henry V, mother of Henry VI, grandmother of Henry VII, born 1400, crowned 1421, died 1438.*

In fact, the dates given here are incorrect, since she is known to have been born in 1401 and died in 1437. Her painted wooden funeral effigy is on display in the Abbey Museum. She is shown to have blue-grey eyes and, unusually, her head is tilted to the left. Her slight body is about 5 feet 4 inches tall and slim-waisted. It is still possible to see the heads of the nails which, nearly 600 years ago, were used to attach Catherine's own clothes to the effigy.

King Henry V's tomb lies beneath the arch of the chantry. Above him is the Altar of the Annunciation, where prayers were said for his soul. The ceremonial saddle, helm, and shield which were used at his funeral, are displayed in the Abbey Museum. The saddle was originally covered with blue velvet and the limewood shield still has a small section of crimson velvet remaining on the inner side. The domed helm, about sixteen inches high, is a tilting helm so would not have been worn in battle. A fifteenth-century sword, found in the Abbey triforium in 1869, is thought to be part of the king's funeral armour.

King Henry VII: Alongside Catherine's funeral effigy in the Abbey museum is the incredibly life-like effigy head of Henry VII, the first of the Tudor kings and grandson of Catherine and Owen Tudor. He himself commissioned the magnificent Lady Chapel at the east end of the Abbey which bears his name. His tomb is situated behind the altar, and on it lie gilt bronze effigies of the king and his queen, Elizabeth of York.

The Monk of Westminster: Near Shakespeare's memorial in Poets' Corner there is a small stone which bears the inscription *Owen Tudor, Monk of Westminster, uncle of King Henry VII.* This was Catherine and Owen's son who became a member of the Benedictine order. Little else is known about him.
(www.westminster-abbey.org)

Owen Tudor's family home, at Penmynydd on the island of Anglesey off the North Wales coast, is now little more than a group of houses strung out along the B5420 which links the county town of Llangefni with the Menai Strait and the house which stands on the site of Owen's home is privately owned. However, in the local church of St Gredifael, Owen's great-grandparents, Goronwy Fychan and his wife, Myfanwy, lie buried under alabaster effigies. Goronwy's sons, including Tudur who was Owen's grandfather, strongly supported their kinsman Owain Glyndŵr in his rebellion against English rule in the early 1400s, losing their land in Penmynydd as a result. Some of their descendants regained the estate later in the century, but they never achieved the same level of local influence. A fine Tudor stained glass window in the church was mindlessly vandalised some years ago but has since been restored.
(www.anglesey-history.co.uk)

Edmund Tudor, Catherine and Owen's son, was almost certainly born in the manor of Much Hadham, Hertfordshire. Nothing of that building now remains but there is great local pride in the town's early association with the Tudor dynasty.
(www.hertfordshire-genealogy.co.uk)

Jasper Tudor is easier to trace. Born at the Bishop of Ely's manor at Hatfield in Hertfordshire around 1431 he led a fairly well-documented life. Today, though Hatfield House is one of Britain's most interesting historic houses, its Tudor connections are almost entirely with Queen Elizabeth I, as it was her childhood home. *(www.hatfield-house.co.uk)*. Jasper is more in evidence at Pembroke Castle on the tip of the Pembrokeshire peninsula in South Wales. The castle's outstanding feature is its late twelfth-century keep, a massive cylindrical tower rising some eighty feet into the air, with an unusual stone dome. Views from the top are breathtaking and the castle's natural defensive position on a rocky promontory overlooking Milford Haven is immediately apparent. In Jasper's time, it was a comfortable home rather than a fortress and he embellished the domestic buildings with fireplaces and a fine oriel window. His sister-in-law, Edward's thirteen-year-old widow Margaret Beaufort, took refuge in the castle after her husband's death. Her son, Henry, spent much of his childhood here in the care of his uncle, Jasper. Today the castle is owned and run by a private charitable trust and is open to the public.
(www.pembroke-castle.co.uk)

One of the author's few flights of fancy in the book you have been reading is that Owen and Catherine's daughter, **Tacinda**, was born in the medieval castle of St Donat's in the Vale of Glamorgan, overlooking the Bristol Channel. It is known that Henry Beaufort's illegitimate daughter, Jane, was married to Sir Edward Stradling who owned St Donat's at the time but there is absolutely no evidence that Catherine and Owen ever visited them. However, a splendid castle still stands on the site and it has strong American connections. John Quincy Adams, who served as the sixth President of the United States from 1825 to 1829, was descended directly from Jane and Edward Stradling. In 1925, the castle was bought by the American newspaper magnate William Randolph Hearst as gift for his mistress, the film star Marion Davies and Hearst contributed much of his vast wealth to the sympathetic restoration of the castle. The building now houses the international sixth-form Atlantic

College and also boasts a thriving Arts Centre.
(www.castlewales.com/donats)

Neither is there any evidence that Catherine ever lived in
Baynard's Castle, which was destroyed in the Great Fire of
London in 1666. Today, an office block owned by the BT
Group and called 'Baynard House' stands where it once stood.
But the little church of St Andrew-by-the-Wardrobe still exists
though it too was badly damaged by the Great Fire. It was
rebuilt by Sir Christopher Wren, only to be blitzed in World
War II. Subsequently reconstructed within the shell of Wren's
building, this charming church now offers a quiet haven in one
of the busiest parts of London and there is always a warm
welcome for visitors to join the congregation.
(www.standrewbythewardrobe.net)

The following web addresses are for other sites which have
strong associations with the story and all would amply repay the
reader's further investigation:

Windsor Castle (it's wise to check opening times)
www.royalcollection.org.uk

Wallingford Castle
http://berkshirehistory.com/castles/wallingford_cast.html

Hertford Castle (grounds only)
http://www.hertford.net/history/castle.php

Kenilworth Castle (ruins)
http://www.kenilworthweb.co.uk/what-to-see-do/kenilworth-castle/

Dover Castle
http://dover-kent.co.uk/defence/castle_index.htm

Lancaster Castle (check website for access)
http://www.lancastercastle.com/

Author's Note, Bibliography
& Acknowledgements

I don't recall being taught very much at school about the history of my native Wales. The names that echo in the memory of my early education include a few Georges, Jameses, and Williams (including both Pitts), along with Magna Carta, the Corn Laws, and the Boston Tea Party, but it's also fair to say that history was never my strong suit. So it has been a great pleasure to come to the subject later in life, particularly to realise how important a part Wales and the Welsh played in the history of fifteenth-century Britain.

It was a moment of pure serendipity in a second-hand bookshop when I came across a slightly dog-eared volume entitled *Without My Wig*, which turned out to be a collection of essays by Judge Sir Thomas Artemus Jones, published in 1944 by the Brython Press of Liverpool. Clearly the learned judge took great delight in what he described as *'peeps into the back pages of legal history'*. One of those 'peeps' appeared as the third essay in the collection: 'Owen Tudor's Marriage – a Missing Statute'. This was what set me on a path of joyful discovery which revealed fascinating facts at every turn.

I rummaged, searched, and explored many avenues in my quest to discover more about the sensational love story which lay at the root of the Tudor dynasty, and I pored over a plethora of books on medieval history, far too many to list individually. However, I found the following particularly helpful:

- **Lives of the Queens of England Vol. II** by Agnes Strickland (1840/1849)
- **Humphrey, Duke of Gloucester – A Biography** by Kenneth Hotham Vickers (1907)
- **Henry Beaufort, Bishop, Chancellor, Cardinal** by Lewis Bostock Radford (1908)

- *The Reign of King Henry VI* by R.A. Griffiths (Sutton Publishing, 2004)
- *Lancaster and York: The Wars of the Roses* by Alison Weir (Random House, 2011)
- *Hanes Cymru/A History of Wales* by John Davies (Penguin Books, published in Welsh in 1990 and in English in 1993)
- *When Was Wales?: a history of the Welsh* by Gwyn A. Williams (Penguin, 1991)
- *The Making of the Tudor Dynasty* by Ralph A. Griffiths and Roger S. Thomas. (Sutton Publishing, 1985)
- *Owain Glyndŵr: The story of the last Prince of Wales* by Terry Breverton (Amberley Publishing, 2009)
- *The Story of Wales* by Jon Gower (BBC Books, 2012)
- *The Matter of Wales: Epic views of a small country* by Jan Morris (Penguin Books, 1986)
- *A Short History of Wales* by A.H. Dodd (John Jones Publishing Ltd., 1998)
- *The Revolt of Owain Glyndŵr* by R.R. Davies (Oxford University Press, 1995)
- *Owain Glyndŵr* (Pocket Guide) by Glanmor Williams (2005)
- *Medieval Wales* by A.D. Carr (Macmillan Press Ltd, 1995)
- *Owain Glyndŵr Prince of Wales* by R.R. Davies (Y Lolfa, 2009)

Perhaps I owe my greatest debt to the online *Oxford Dictionary of National Biography*, an indispensable source of information on the lives of the men and women who shaped Britain. Its riches are freely available to members of subscribing local libraries and I am grateful to the **Vale of Glamorgan Libraries** service for facilitating my research.

There are some people whom I must also thank. In London I was given a fascinating tour of Westminster Abbey by retired architect Barbara Potter, one of the Abbey's knowledgeable volunteer visitor guides. Members of the Abbey staff were also most helpful.

The same was true of the Rev. Dr Alan Griffin who not only welcomed me warmly to the delightful church of St Andrew-by-the-Wardrobe but provided me with the information which enabled me to feature his fifteenth-century predecessor, Marmaduke de Kyrkeby, in the story.

I am indebted to several writers, including the eminent historian and novelist Alison Weir whom I was privileged to meet at Manchester Central Library's imaginatively entitled 'Pages Ago' conference. Alison has been very supportive, as has Bernard Knight, CBE, the distinguished Home Office pathologist who is also a prolific historical novelist – a true polymath. Under the auspices of the Writers' Workshop, Emma Darwin, Debi Alper, and Andrew Wille provided invaluable guidance. They were all most generous in sharing their extensive understanding of the craft of writing and I learned a great deal from them. (**www.writersworkshop.co.uk**)

Many friends read the manuscript at various stages in its evolution and did me the great favour of honest criticism. I'm grateful to them all for their suggestions.

Lastly, many thanks to Jonah for making graphic sense of the genealogy.

For those who would like to know a little more about the background and family history of Owen Tudor, an occasional journal appears on my web site. It is a purely imaginary record of the journey which took the handsome young Owain ap Maredydd ap Tudur from his home in Anglesey to the royal court in London and set him on course to give his patronymic Welsh name to the best-known and most colourful dynasty in English history. (**www.marigriffith.co.uk/owen-tudor**)

Historical Titles

The Handfasted Wife
Carol McGrath

The Tsar's Dragons
Catrin Collier

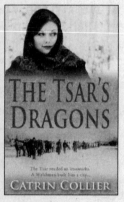

For more information about **Mari Griffith**
and other **Accent Press** titles

please visit

www.accentpress.co.uk